MORE *than* FOREVER

MORE *than* FOREVER

MORE THAN SERIES | BOOK FOUR

JAY McLEAN

Dedication

To my readers, and believers.
Always.

Note to Readers

Please note than More Than Forever (More Than #4) is part #4 in the More Than Series and should not be read prior to reading More Than This (More Than #1), More Than Her (More Than #2) and More Than Him (More Than #3).

MORE *than* THIS

Mikayla

In one night my fairy-tale ended. Or it may have begun. This is my story of friendship and love, heartbreak and desire, and the strength to show weakness.

Jake

One night I met a girl. A sad and broken girl, but one more beautiful than any other. She laughed through her sadness, while I loved through her heartbreak.

This is our story of a maybe ever after.

He was right. It made no difference whether it was 6 months or 6 years.

I couldn't undo what had been done. I couldn't change the future.

I couldn't even predict it.

It was one night.

One night when everything changed.

It was so much more than just the betrayal.

It was the Tragedy.

The Deaths.

The Murders.

But it was also that feeling.

The feeling of falling.

MORE *than* HER

"For every action there is an equal or opposite reaction."
For every choice you make there are rewards, or there are consequences.
It was my choice to walk away the first time.
And my choice to chase her the second.
But sometimes you don't get a choice, and all you get are the consequences.
"Being deeply loved by someone gives you strength, while loving someone deeply gives you courage."

Unless that someone is Logan Matthews.

Because loving him didn't give me the strength to walk away.
It didn't give me the courage to fight for him.
And when it was over, all it gave me was a broken heart.

MORE *than* HIM

"Our deepest fear is not that we are inadequate. Our deepest fear is that we are powerful beyond measure. It is our light, not our darkness, that most frightens us."
–Marianne Williamson

We live in a world of darkness and shadows,
where monsters hide and aim to ruin.
And they did.
They ruined us and turned our dreams into nightmares.
But now we're back.
And we're fighting.
Not just for us, or for each other, but for our light.

Prologue
Cameron

MOM SAYS THERE'S absolutely no pain worse than labor. For sixteen hours, so she says, she went through absolute hell. She jokes that sometimes she wonders if it was worth it. I call bullshit. I say that nothing, absolutely nothing, can feel worse than being hit in the junk with a baseball bat.

Lincoln's eyes are huge as he grimaces. "I'm so sorry, Cam."

I'm folded over myself, too preoccupied with the ache below my stomach. Sometimes, there's a delay with the pain. But not this time. This time it was instant. I try to speak, but nothing comes out. He looks like he wants to cry and I want to assure him that it's all good—but I can't. Liam, Lincoln's twin brother, is laughing. The little punk. I'll be sure to make him do extra shit next practice. "Cam, are you okay?"

I try to straighten, but it just makes the pain worse. "Yeah, bud. I just gotta let it settle."

"I swear I didn't see you behind me." There's panic clear in his voice, and for a second I want to tell myself to suck it up and quit being a little bitch, but I can't do that either. The pain's too overwhelming.

Liam's still laughing his ass off.

My eyes narrow at him, and Lincoln must notice because he turns to his brother and pushes him hard enough that he falls to the ground. That makes Liam stop. He gets up and dusts the dirt off his uniform. "We should go, Linc. We're the last ones here."

Lincoln looks around. So do I. Liam's right, everyone's gone.

"I'm just gonna help Cam pack up," Lincoln replies, picking up the team equipment bag and chucking in the helmets and bats sitting by my feet. He looks up at me again, and I can see how truly sorry he is.

Standing to full height, I do my best to ignore the pain. "It's okay,

Linc. Seriously, it's passed now." It hasn't, but he doesn't need to know that. He finishes packing anyway, and hands me the bag; it's bigger than he is.

I take it from his hands and look around again. "Your mom or dad late to pick you up?"

"Nah," Liam says, the laughter and amusement now gone. "Lucy's here."

"Lucy?"

"Our sister," Lincoln explains.

They both turn to the bleachers. I follow their gaze.

A lone girl sits on the bottom bench. Something flat, black and rectangular is in her hand, kind of like a tablet I guess. Her eyes are focused on it while her foot rocks a stroller back and forth.

It strikes me as strange because the girl looks familiar. She's in my class. She's a sophomore and she has a baby? Stuff like that doesn't happen in our town and if it did, I'd know.

Everyone would know.

"Lucy!" Liam shouts.

She doesn't look up.

"Lucy!" Lincoln this time.

Still, her eyes don't lift, but her foot continues to rock the stroller.

"Luce!" Liam yells again.

Nothing.

My eyes narrow before looking down at the boys. "Is your sister… uh… hearing impaired?"

They both let out simultaneous snorts. "No," Lincoln answers, pulling his cap further down his head and looking up at me. His eyes roll as he says, "She's just reading."

✧   ✧   ✧

SHE SHOWS UP to every game for the next six weeks. Every week she looks sadder, like the life is slowly being sucked out of her.

And you know how I know all this? Because while she's so pre-occupied reading… I'm so pre-occupied reading her.

Lucy

LACHLAN CRIED THE entire walk home, which meant I had to carry him with one hand and push the stroller with the other, all while trying to make sure that Lincoln and Liam didn't run out onto the road. Which would be fine, but I accidentally packed red Kool-Aid instead of their sports drinks so they went a little crazy. I'll remember for next time to keep them separated in the fridge.

Lachlan's still crying when Dad comes downstairs and walks into the kitchen. He offers to take him from my hands but I can see in his eyes how tired he is. I tell him that I'm fine, and motion for him to take a seat.

He hasn't been out of their bedroom much lately, which is a sign that things are getting worse. The doctors said that it was normal—that things would get worse before they got better. I wonder for a moment if doctors have a book of cliché sayings they use to try to justify one's health.

A bitter laugh tries to escape but I keep it down while I watch Dad take a seat at the dining table, his hands already covering his face before he's fully seated.

The microwave beeps and I pull out Lachlan's bottle and feed it to him. Silence fills my ears. I try to remember the last time I heard nothing. In a house full of nine people, silence is rare. My mind wonders on that thought for a short moment before Dad's sigh breaks through. "It's gettin' worse, Luce." His deep voice has lost the fight to fake it. "The doctor came for a house call. It's not lookin' good." He uncovers his face and looks up at me now, his eyes red rimmed from either lack of sleep or held back tears, but most likely both.

"How long?" It's two words. Two words that affect my entire life.

"Three months."

Three months.

I stop breathing.

Lachlan cries and starts spurting his formula through his coughs.

Dad stands and takes him from me.

I walk out of the room, and to the bathroom.

And I throw up.

Three months.

When I'm done, I run the tap and wash my mouth out, then stare at myself in the mirror. Gripping the edge of the sink, I suck in a huge breath and let it out. I do it a few more times until color comes back into my face. "Suck it up, Lucy," I whisper. "You're fifteen. Quit acting like a child."

A few minutes pass and I finally find the strength to open the door and walk out.

Dad's waiting with his arms folded over his chest. No Lachlan. "He fell asleep in my arms. I put him down for his nap," he answers my unasked question. "You okay, kid?"

That same bitter laugh from earlier tries to escape. And again, I keep it down. Because even though he referred to me as one, I'm not a kid. Far from it.

"I'm fine," I lie. "The heat from being out at the field just got to me. I'm fine," I repeat.

His head tilts to the side and his eyes narrow, assessing me.

"I'm fine," I lie for the third time. I walk past him and take the stairs to the only room I can stand to be in right now. She's awake, but she's so out of it, she may as well not be. I curse myself for hoping she would die already. For hoping that it would take the pain away. Not just for her, but for all of us.

Waiting for someone to die has to be the world's cruellest joke.

"Lucy," she croaks out. "How are you?"

I fake a smile. "Fine."

Four fines. Four lies.

She matches my fake smile with her own and pats the bed next to her. I kick off my shoes, lie down and pull my spare e-reader from under the pillow.

She lets out a shaky breath at the same time I switch it on. I don't even know why I bothered picking it up. I know the story she wants me to read to her. I know it word for word. I've read it to her every day since the day the doctors told her she had cancer. I inhale deeply. "The four March sisters sat in the living room…"

MY MOM FELL in love with reading after she read *Little Women*. I fell in love with reading after she read it to me. She said she wanted me to grow up with a house full of sisters. I ended up with six little brothers.

When Mom and Dad tell us their story it's short, but it's sweet. They met college graduation day, somehow never meeting before that. Two weeks later, they were official. Two months later, they were married.

Fate. *It's all about fate, Lucy.* That's what she always told me.

And I believe that.

They gave us all names beginning with *L*. Because *L*—it stands for *love*. And love is something we should be reminded of every day.

I swallow the knot already formed in my throat and turn my head to face her. She's fallen asleep. She's probably been like that for over an hour and I hadn't realized. I kiss her on the forehead and say what I normally say right before I leave her room. "I love you. Goodbye." *Always the goodbye.* Because I never know if it'll be the last words I'll say to her.

Quietly, not wanting to be noticed, I walk to my room and into my bathroom, shutting the door behind me. I lean against it and slide down until my bottom hits the floor.

I cry so hard that I throw up again.

And I don't even care that I do.

Because while Mom is two doors down from me dying, throwing up is the only thing that makes me feel alive.

One
Lucy

A T LEAST THE *wait is over.*

That's the thought that runs through my head during the entire funeral. She's gone, and all I can think about is the relief I feel from not having to wake up every day and wonder *when.*

Dad's family is here and they help me take care of the boys. We wipe their tears, hold them when they cry, assure them all that it'll be okay—even when we have no idea that it will be.

No one takes care of me.

No one.

Not even Dad. He can't even take care of himself.

Cameron

IF HEARTBREAK HAD a face, hers would be it.

I watched her during the funeral, just like I watch her now, walking around her house greeting everyone with a fake smile. I know it's fake because her mom's gone, her dad's a mess, and she has six brothers to take care of. Right now, there is no silver lining. No light at the end of the tunnel. No joy in the face of tragedy. Which is why I find it strange that she hasn't shed a single tear. Not one.

Her baby brother throws up all over her and she doesn't even flinch. She simply hands over the baby to a woman and leaves the room. Minutes go by while I wait for her to return, but she doesn't. And a rush of panic washes through me. I don't know why it affects me so much. Why *she* affects me so much. But I have to find her. I have to make sure she's okay.

7

Her back is turned as she stands in the laundry room, her shoulders shaking up and down. Then she suddenly straightens as if she knows someone's watching. Her hands rise to her face before she slowly turns around.

There's a calmness in her eyes that doesn't seem justified… like a calm before the storm. And then it happens—the storm.

Her face changes and I know the dam is about to break. My heart picks up speed, my palms sweat, and my ears ring—all because I can't stand to watch this happening to her. And even though I can see how hard she tries to hold it in—a single sob escapes her.

I take the steps to get to her. "Lucy," I whisper.

She throws her arms around my neck and pulls me down to her, crying into my chest. She cries so hard that it feels like it's the first time she's ever done it. Maybe it is.

I silently hold her until she's done. There's something about the way she feels in my arms. Like maybe that calmness in her eyes from earlier could be justified.

Maybe I could be her calm.

I *want* to be her calm.

When she's done she takes a step back, wiping her face as she does. Then she smiles, that same fake smile she's given to everyone else. She nods once and brushes past me.

"Lucy," I whisper again, this time to myself.

I try my hardest to read her as she walks away.

✧   ✧   ✧

I WISH I had spoken to her. I wish I had the right words. Even now as I stand at her front door, sweating like a pig from the bike ride after school—I still can't think of anything to say. It's been a few days since the funeral. Today was the first day she was back at school. Not that I was paying attention or wondering where she was because I wasn't.

I knock three times, but no one answers. I can hear kids yelling and screaming. One might even be crying. I knock again and the door opens. One of the younger kids looks up at me, his eyebrows bunched, but he doesn't say a word. "Where's Lucy?" I ask him. He opens the door wider and points to the kitchen, then runs away.

If I were a murderer, they'd all be dead.

SHE'S STANDING AT the island counter with food everywhere, but that's not what I notice. It's the endless tears falling freely.

She looks up when I walk in, the same expression on her face which her little brother had when he opened the door. "Who are you?"

I ignore the irritation at her not remembering me. Or recognizing me. Or the fact that she barely acknowledges me before wiping her face and continuing whatever she's doing.

The kids come into the kitchen, running circles around the island. They're loud. And annoying. She drops what's in her hands and lays her palms flat on the counter. Her eyes shut tight while she inhales a huge breath.

And I can sense it—*The storm is coming.*

I grab one of the kids by the arm. "Where's your dad?" It's the same kid from the front door. He points upstairs and pulls out of my hold and then runs away.

"Who are you?" she says again.

"Cameron."

She looks up and I swear it; time stands still while our eyes lock.

Then a kid screams and it breaks whatever the hell just happened between us.

"I just want it to stop," she whispers. I don't know if it's for me or her, but whatever the reason, I want to make it stop.

Bringing my fingers to my mouth, I whistle. Loudly. My gaze never leaving her.

Silence.

Her eyes go wide. "Who are you?" she says for the third time.

"Cameron," I repeat. This time slower, louder. Maybe my first instincts were right, maybe she is hearing impaired.

She shakes her head, the corner of her lips turning down. "No, I mean I know your name's Cameron. But *who* are you? What are you doing in my house?"

Lincoln speaks for me, "He's our coach."

The boys are standing in the kitchen now. I hadn't even noticed when they came in.

I turn back to Lucy and roll up my sleeves. "What do you need help with?"

Her eyes narrow and her lips thin to a line. "I don't know who you are or what you're doing here, but we're *fine*. We don't need your help."

I don't know what reaction I was expecting from her, but that wasn't it. Before I get a chance to respond, a baby's cry interrupts us. She lets out a frustrated grunt before washing her hands and walking away.

"Hi Cam!" Lincoln says, his smile the same as I'd always seen. It's never faltered. I wonder if he fully comprehends the fact that his mom's dead. Gone. *Forever.*

"Hey bud." I try to keep my voice level so he doesn't see how much I pity him right now. "What do you think we can do to help out your sister a little?"

"Just stay out of her way," the oldest kid says. "She doesn't want our help."

I nod. It makes sense now—her reaction to me. I take a look at each of them and try to justify what I'm doing here. But there is no reason—and right now, I don't think it really matters.

I look out the kitchen window and into their endless yard. "You guys got anything we can use for bases? We could go out, hit a few balls, catch a few—"

The boys are out the back door and setting up before I can finish my sentence.

I follow them, not wanting to wait around and have her ask me to leave again. Minutes pass before the back door swings open and she sticks her head out. "You guys have homework," she yells, holding her youngest brother in her arms. The older ones moan but don't argue; they just file back into the house one by one.

"I'm sorry," I tell her. "I didn't know."

"You don't know a lot," she says, slamming the door shut after her.

"She's sad." I look down at Liam, now standing only a few feet in front of me. "We all are."

"It's okay," I try to console, "you guys are allowed to be sad."

"But she's *really* sad. She gets so sad that it makes her sick."

Two
Lucy

"T HAT GUY'S STARING at you."

I tune Claudia out and hope that she doesn't bring it up again. I don't even know what guy she's referring to but I don't care.

She sighs before asking, "What are you reading?"

Only now do I notice that my e-reader's in my hand, switched on, words displayed... but I'm not reading them. My mind's too occupied by other things. Like the fact that I packed Lincoln a cookie for lunch and not Liam, which ultimately means that when I go to pick them up, one of them will have a black eye. *Great.*

She sighs again, and it pulls me from my thoughts. "I have something to tell you," she says, and the tone in her voice has changed. She's not talking boys anymore. It's something more.

My eyes lift to hers as she ties her hair up in a ponytail. She picks up a fallen leaf from the branch above us, examines both sides before scrunching it up in her hand. "We're moving."

"Where?" I hope she doesn't mean far because Claudia's my best friend—my *only* friend.

"New Jersey."

My heart drops.

I do a quick calculation in my head of how far that is in driving distance. Eight hours, give or take. "You can't drive eight hours to school and back."

She smiles sadly. "We leave this weekend, Lucy. I'm sorry. I've known for a month. I should have told you, but you had so much going on with your mom, and your family, I didn't know how to break it to you."

Tears instantly well in my eyes. I pick up my sandwich, just for something else to do, but the sight of it makes my stomach churn.

11

"It's okay," I tell her. "I'm fine." *What's one more lie, right?* "I have to use the bathroom. I'll see you after class."

"Oh," she says surprised. "Okay."

I stand quickly. Too quickly. My head spins and I feel faint.

And then I do.

Faint, that is.

Cameron

I SEE HER wobble on her feet before she slowly tumbles to the ground. Her knees give out first, then the rest of her. It feels like I should've gotten to her earlier, but seconds of panic took place before my mind kicked into gear. And the rest is a blur.

Her friend's standing over us while I rest her head on my lap.

"What happened?" Logan asks her friend.

"I don't know." She's as panicked as I am, if not worse.

"Is she dehydrated?" Logan picks up what looks like an uneaten sandwich. "Is this hers? Has she eaten?" I don't know why it annoys me that Logan is asking all the right questions and all I can do is stare down at her.

She's breathing, so I guess that's something.

He drops down on his knees on the other side of her and pours water from his bottle into his hand, then he runs it across her forehead and into her hairline.

"Is she alright, mate?" Jake asks. He's new in town and has a weird accent but Logan seems to think he's cool so we keep him around.

Logan does the water thing again, and this time her eyes slowly flutter open.

And I release the breath I was holding.

"It's okay," Logan says to her. "You just passed out." He's in her face now, and I want to punch him for being the first thing she sees when she comes to. I was here first; I was the one watching her when she fell. It should have been me.

She sits up quickly and holds a hand to her head, her eyes slowly moving to everyone around her.

The bell rings but no one makes a move to leave.

"I'm fine," she says quietly.

"I've got a test," her friend says with a grimace. "Are you sure you're okay?"

She nods, but looks down at the ground.

Everyone leaves.

Everyone but me.

"You should get to class," she says.

And then she walks away.

✧   ✧   ✧

I WAIT NEAR her locker after school. I know where her locker is because the day after her brothers told me who she was, I started to notice her a lot more. I admit that day wasn't the first time I'd noticed her. I'd seen her around school but we ran in different circles, had different interests. I always thought she was cute, a little thin, but still cute.

She shows up right after the bell, rushes to get her shit, and then hastily leaves.

And then I do something that turns my creep factor up full notch; I follow her. I don't follow her because I'm stalking her. I follow her because I want to make sure she gets home safe.

You know something that's really hard to do? Ride your bike and creepily follow someone who's walking. I give it to her, she walks fast, but it's hard to pedal slowly behind someone and not attract attention.

She ends up at the elementary school and picks up her brothers. They wait at a bus stop for a few minutes before the bus arrives and they all hop on. I watch them leave. And then I pedal like crazy, taking a shortcut through the woods toward her house.

By the time I get to her driveway, my legs are burning.

And then it dawns on me that I'm standing in the middle of their driveway, which is at least two acres away from anyone else's... and I have absolutely no reason to be here.

Lincoln sees me first. "Hey Cam!" he yells casually.

I panic.

"We know it's a bye this week... if that's why you're here."

Saved.

"Yeah... that's why I'm here."

He smiles huge before waving. "Bye Cam!"

They all head down her driveway. She sees me, but doesn't even bother to fake a smile. That doesn't bother me, what bothers me is that she has absolutely no hint of recognition in her eyes. I've been to her house. I was at her mom's funeral. I held her when she'd passed out no more than four hours ago and she doesn't even recognize me. I bet she's thinking about Logan. *That asshole.* I should've punched him like I wanted to. "Wait!"

She flinches. *Why does she flinch?*

"Get in the house," she orders the boys.

She watches them all get in before turning to me. "What's your name again?"

I swear to God I want to punch Logan and I don't even know why, but I feel like he's the reason she doesn't remember me. I try to keep my voice level, even though on the inside I want to shake her for not remembering me. "Cameron."

"Right." She nods once. "Cameron." She crosses her arms over her chest. "What do you want?"

"I told you yesterday. I want to help."

Her eyes narrow. Her teeth clench shut. But somehow she manages to get out, "And I told you yesterday that I didn't need your help."

I shrug. I have no clue what the hell else to do. I'm nervous. And she terrifies me.

"Why?" she clips.

"Why?" I ask incredulously.

"Yeah. Why?" She takes a step forward, dropping her arms to her sides. "Are you one of those church people… or are you trying to redeem yourself to make up for some sin you can't shake? What is it, Cameron? Do we look like we need help? Do you think *I* need help?"

"Yes," I say before I can stop myself.

Her shoulders sag, and for the first time I see something in her beyond strength, or sadness. Vulnerability. And *fear.* She's afraid.

"Honestly, yes," I repeat, testing the waters. I open my mouth to continue but she cuts in.

"Okay," she sighs. Then turns and walks toward the house. I slowly follow her, knowing too damn well that I have no fucking clue what the hell I'm doing.

✧　✧　✧

THE NEXT THREE days she completely ignores me. She doesn't greet me. Doesn't talk to me. Never says my name. Never acknowledges me. I should be pissed, but I'm not. Because in those three days, I've realized something. I wasn't just there for her anymore; I was there for her brothers too. And regardless of whether she shows it, or whether she wants to admit it, she needs the help.

They all do.

On the fourth day, she does something I never expected. "You're welcome to stay for dinner, I made too much." That's it. That's all she says. And even though she says it in passing, I know the effort it takes for her to offer it.

We sit at her giant dining table while the boys talk among themselves. She reads, and I read her.

And that's how I spend the next few weeks. Each day, she speaks a few more words to me, and each day I find myself caring more than I should.

✧   ✧   ✧

I DRY THE last pot from the sink before she takes it from my hands and places it on the stovetop.

Clearing my throat, I say, "So, I wanted to run something by you."

She nods, her gaze never lifting.

"I was wondering if I could bring my Xbox tomorrow… see if it might entertain the boys for a little bit." I curse myself for my nerves coming out in my voice. "It's just that I'm falling behind on my homework and I thought—"

Her eyes dart to me. "You don't have to come every day. No one makes you."

Frustrated, I let out a breath with a grunt and tilt my head back, looking to somewhere else for a patience that I'm lacking. "I don't mind coming here. It was just an idea. I'll just stay up later and do it when I get home." I sigh, too tired to contain the hurt in my voice. "I'll see you tomorrow, Lucy."

I start to walk away but her hand on my forearm stops me. "I'm sorry," she says so quietly I almost don't hear her. "I just don't want you to feel like you have to be here." She tries to smile but fails. "Bring the Xbox. They'll love it."

15

"Okay." I turn to leave but she stops me again.

"I really am sorry, Cameron." And hearing her say my name without anger or aggravation makes my breath catch. She chews her lip, her eyes wandering back down to the floor. "I don't know why you're here but I don't want to question it. I just want to appreciate it." Her gaze lifts. "Thank you."

✧ ✧ ✧

"THE PRODIGAL SON returns," Mom giggles. She's sitting on the couch in the living room with her boyfriend, Mark. He looks away from the TV when I enter the room.

"Hey Mom." I walk over and kiss her on the cheek. It's been a few days since I've seen her. She spends most nights at Mark's house or he's here.

I reach out to shake his hand but he slaps it away. "What? No kiss for me?" He puckers his lips and waits. I try not to laugh, but I can't help it.

"Maybe you're just not pretty enough," Mom mocks.

He wraps an arm around her shoulders. "Lucky you're pretty enough for the both of us," he says, kissing the side of her head.

"That was lame, Marky Mark," I joke.

His eyes narrow at me. Then he smirks. "You know what else is lame?"

"What?" I lift my chin toward him in challenge.

"Your season's batting average." He tries to kick the back of my knee so it gives out but I step back too quickly. He comes to a stand, the smirk still in place. "My grandma hits balls better than you do."

I laugh. "Oh yeah, I bet she loves hitting them balls."

His features drop. "What are you saying about Nanny Tallulah?"

"TALLULAH?" I break out in a fit of laughter.

"You can talk," he shouts over my cackle. "ALADDIN."

Now my face drops. I look over at Mom, so does Mark. "Who names their kid Aladdin?"

Mom sits up and throws a leg out, kicking Mark in the back of his knee. He falls to the ground before he can save himself. Then she quickly turns to me. "Get him, baby."

So I do.

Within seconds we're on the ground wrestling. Neither of us knows shit about wrestling so we're just rolling on the floor play punching each other. "When the hell did you get muscles, kid?"

"I've been working out." I try to kick him in the nuts but he pulls back.

"Too busy lifting weights to work on your batting skills?"

"Screw you," I laugh out.

The doorbell rings and we stop for a second, but only a second before he takes advantage of the distraction and rolls me onto my back. He starts swatting at my head, pinning down my arms at the same time.

"Cameron?"

My heart beats out of my chest. "Shit."

Lucy stands above us with an unsure look on her face. She looks from me to Mark, to me, to Mark, to me…

"Shit," I say again, trying to push Mark off me.

He lets me stand without a fight.

I straighten my clothes and wipe my palms down my shorts.

What is she doing in my living room?

I run a hand through my hair. My ratty hair. My cap must've come off while we were rolling on the floor. "Shit," I whisper, looking around for it.

Mark places it on my head and then stands next to Mom, behind Lucy, with a huge shit-eating grin on his face. I swallow, adjust my cap and finally get the courage to face her. "Hi."

She smiles, that same fake sad smile as always. "Hi."

And then I panic. *Why is she here?* "What happened? Is everything okay with the boys? I'll ride over—" I start for the front door to put on my shoes but she stops me.

"Everything's fine. You just…" She reaches into her pocket and pulls out my phone. "You left this at the house. I thought you might need it."

My shoulders instantly relax. "So everyone's okay?"

She nods and then looks at the front door. "I better go." Her hand's out, holding my phone.

I take it and lead her to the door, ignoring the look of concern on Mark and Mom's faces. "How did you get here?" I open the door and wait for her to walk through. "Who's watching the boys?"

"I called my aunt. She's at the house but she can't stay long. I just wanted to make sure you had your phone, in case you needed it… for whatever…"

"I didn't need it," I tell her. "You could have waited."

"Oh." Her gaze drops. "I'm sorry."

"It's fine," I say quickly.

She pulls keys out of her pocket and motions to a minivan in the driveway. "I'll see you later, Cameron."

My eyes move from her keys to the minivan. "You have your license?" It doesn't make sense. *If she drove then why was she catching the bus every day?*

Her head moves slowly from side to side while she looks over my shoulder, probably at my mom. "Just my permit. But my dad taught me to drive when I was twelve. I'm okay."

"Honey," Mom says, standing behind me now. "You drove here without a licensed driver?"

"Yes Ma'am. But I'm a good driver. I promise." Tears start forming in her eyes and I don't know why.

Mom stands next to me. "I don't think I'd feel right letting you drive home alone, hon. I'll come with you. Mark!" she shouts over her shoulder, "You follow with Cameron, okay?"

"Oh no." Lucy shakes her head quickly. "You don't need to do that. I'm fine." Her voice breaks. "I didn't mean to put you out. I'm so sorry."

"Just do what she says," Mark hollers from behind us. "It's quicker this way. Trust me."

Lucy nods once, but refuses to look at either of us. She walks to her car, her head down the entire time. Once she gets to her car, she unlocks it, and gets in the driver's seat.

"We're going to talk about this," Mom says with a tone of finality.

✧   ✧   ✧

"SIT." MOM POINTS to the couch.

"It's not a big deal."

She sits on the couch opposite and tucks her legs underneath her. "I don't really know what's happening so I can't justify what's a big deal and what isn't." Her face has lost all color. "Wine!" she yells at Mark, "Now! I have a feeling I'm gonna need it." Mark walks in from the kitchen and hands her the bottle. She swigs from it without hesitation. "Out with it, Cameron. Just give it to me straight."

"What?" My eyes narrow. "What the heck is wrong with you?"

Her shoulders stiffen and her eyes thin to a glare. "Just tell me."

"Tell you what? Why are you so pissed?"

She grips the bottle of wine tighter as Mark takes a seat next to her, rubbing her shoulders to keep her calm. "Why am I pissed?" she seethes. "Maybe because my fifteen-year-old son is about to tell me that he knocked up a girl and has his own sons with her... *and* he's kept it a secret! When did this happen, Cameron?"

I laugh.

All out laugh.

"This isn't funny!" she yells.

I can't stop laughing.

"Stop laughing!"

I hear her. I do. But I just can't. I can't stop laughing.

She throws a cushion at my head while laughing. And crying.

Women are dumb.

"CAMERON!"

I hold up my finger to tell to her to wait a minute while I try to control myself.

"Is that where you've been every night? Seeing to your kids. Oh my God," she moans, "I'm a grandmother."

And my laughter just gets heavier.

"I'm done!" She stands with the bottle of wine clenched to her chest. "I'm going to go knit, or play bingo, or do whatever it is grandmas do... and you can just sit there and laugh at me."

"I'm sorry," I manage to get out. "But it's absurd."

"What is?"

"I haven't gotten anyone pregnant."

I hear Mark release a breath.

"But yes, she is where I've been every night." I take a few calming breaths until I know my words will come out even. "I'm just helping her out."

She sits down again and places the wine on the coffee table. "What do you mean helping her out? She goes to your school? What boys are you talking about? Where are her parents?"

I suck in a huge breath and try to answer her questions as straight as possible. "Yes, she goes to my school. The boys are her brothers—six of them." Her eyes go huge but she doesn't speak. "Her mom passed away a few weeks ago. Her dad is… unstable. So she just needs some help."

She lets out all the air in her lungs and leans back into the couch. "Okay," she says, then shakes her head slowly. "So you've been going over there and what?"

I shrug. "I entertain the boys while she cooks dinner… or whatever. I just help her clean up a bit… get things done. There's a baby, Mom. She's in my class, she's fifteen and she carries the weight of the world. She wakes up, gets them ready for school and her aunt comes during the day to watch the baby while she's in class. But then she goes home, and she does it all over again. She doesn't sleep well. And her brother—he told me she gets so sad that it makes her sick. I don't know what it means but I can't not do anything to help. She's alone. She has no one."

Mom wipes at the fallen tears on her cheeks. "I don't know what to say, Cam. I mean… you've always cared too much. Even as a kid you were bringing home strays… but this… this might be too far, even for you. This is someone's life. Someone's family. You take away some of that burden from her and it becomes yours. That's a huge responsibility for a kid your age. Are you sure no one else can help her?"

Her words instantly piss me off. She doesn't need anyone else. She has *me*. "I just want to help."

She nods slowly, picking up the wine and taking another sip. "We have to talk about this some more. Let me think about—"

"Think about what? I'm not stopping." My tone's defensive. Because even though she's trying to help, I know she's trying to find a way to take Lucy away from me. "You can't stop me from seeing her."

There's shock clear on her face, and I get it. I really do. But she has no idea how much Lucy means to me. And until right now, neither did I.

"Honey, I'm not going to."

"Good." I stand up with a huff. "Because I'm a good kid. You can't deny that. I always do what you ask. I never break the rules and I'm not doing anything wrong."

"I know that, Cameron." She stares up at me with pity in her eyes and I glare down at her. My heart pounds hard against my chest. I'm angry. I'm annoyed. And I'm frustrated because she doesn't understand it. But then again, neither do I.

Then Mark clears his throat. "She's kinda cute, right?"

I can't help the hint of a smile that forms on my face. "I'm going to bed."

"Good night," they both say, but I'm already half way up the stairs.

"At some point, you're going to have to start acting like his dad, Mark, not his cool big brother," Mom says quietly.

"Heather, I'll adopt him right now and start acting like a dad if you finally say yes to marrying me."

I chuckle under my breath.

Mom responds, "That's not gonna happen."

"You're breaking my heart, you know that?"

I close my bedroom door and throw myself onto my bed. I'm exhausted. But then I think about Lucy, and how tired she must be, and it doesn't even compare. Shoving my hand in my pocket, I pull out my phone and bring up her number. I don't even think, I just dial.

"Hello?"

"Lucy?"

"Yeah…"

"Thank you for bringing me my phone. I don't think I said it when you were here."

Silence.

I clear my throat. "It's Cameron."

More silence.

I hang up.

Shit, that was awkward.

My phone vibrates in my hand. Her name flashes on the screen. I stand up and start pacing. The ringing stops. "Shit." I dial her number—busy tone. I try again—same thing. Then mine rings. I answer. "Hello?" I'm so anxious, I smash the phone to the side of my face. And then I drop it…

"Hello? Cam?" The sound of her voice through the speakers fills all my senses.

"Hang on!" I yell. "I dropped the phone." I turn in circles rubbing the side of my face and looking for my phone. *Where the hell did it go?*

"Hello?" she says again.

"Shit."

"Hello?"

I drop to the floor and search for it. It's under my bed. *Of course it is.*

I move the stack of porn hidden there and reach for it. "I dropped my phone. Just wait. Please don't hang up," I yell.

"Okay."

When the phone's in my hand, I start to panic.

A knock on the door has me jumping out of my skin. Covering the phone with my palm, I open the door.

Mark's eyes narrow when he sees my face... then widen when he sees the phone in my hand. A slow smirk develops. "Lucy?" he whispers.

I nod frantically.

He places his hands on my shoulders and shakes me gently. "You got this, kid. Just be yourself." I keep nodding. His eyes wander to somewhere behind me. "Your porn's on display." I turn around to see the last year's worth of magazines spread out on the floor. I must've knocked them over. I kick them back under the bed. By the time I turn back to the door, he's gone.

I blow out a huge breath and bring the phone to my ear. "Hello?"

"Hey."

My fist clenches at my side as an attempt to reign in my nerves. "What are you doing?"

"Uh... not much, just packing the boys' lunch for tomorrow."

"Cool." *Cool?* Loser! I'm a fucking loser!

"What are you doing?" she asks. I can hear her own nerves in her voice and for some stupid reason it's reassuring. Like I'm not the only one who feels like the future lies in this one conversation.

"I'm just laying in bed. I'm exhausted."

She chuckles—it's the first time I've heard it. "I know what you mean."

"Yeah? You can't do the boys' lunches tomorrow morning?"

She yawns, loudly, for so long it makes me laugh.

"I'm sorry," she says. And I can almost picture her smiling. "No. If I do it tomorrow, I'd have to wake up at four. It's just easier this way."

I try to think of a way to help her out. "I'd come over in the morning, but I have early practice."

"Oh no, I don't expect you to do that. You do so much already."

It hits me as strange now—how open she is on the phone, compared to how shut down she is in person.

"Crud bucket," she whispers.

I laugh. "Crud bucket?"

"Lachlan's up. I gotta settle him."

"Oh." My heart sinks. I was hoping to spend some time talking, getting to know her a little.

"It should only take a few minutes. I could call you right back?"

"Yes!" My eyes snap shut. I'm eager. Way too eager.

"Okay. I'll call you soon. Don't drop your phone this time."

"Okay," I say through my stupidly huge grin.

I take the time to settle my nerves so that I don't sound like a dick on the phone. A few minutes later, she calls back. "So your mom and dad seem nice."

"Oh, that's not my dad. He's my mom's boyfriend."

"Really? Well... he seems nice."

"Yeah, they're good people."

"How did they meet?"

"You really wanna know?"

"Yes. I love a good romance. Please, will you tell me?"

So I do—because I don't think I could ever say no to her.

I tell her everything, and she listens and asks questions. And even though none of it really matters to her, the fact that we're actually talking matters to me.

"So you read a lot?" I ask.

"Yeah. Well, I used to. It's hard to find the time now. By the time everyone's in bed, I study. I normally fall asleep with my e-reader on my face." She laughs quietly. "I'm such a dork."

Lucy

HE SIGHS INTO the phone, and I try not to imagine him lying in bed, with his messy, dirty blond hair smeared all over the place, and his huge dark eyes staring up at the ceiling, blinking away the tiredness the way he does. Then I try not to wonder what he's wearing, or not wearing. "You're not a dork," he says. "You're cute."

My breath catches, and he must hear it because he apologizes before I can speak. I push back the hurt of him taking it back. I *want* to be cute for him.

I don't know what we talk about for so long, but by the time we hang up, it's nearly two in the morning. I rest my head on my pillow with a smile on my face. And then I remember everything. I remember what my life is. And what I can't have. And I remember that she's gone. And that I have no right to be happy. To be smiling. I get out of bed and silently move to the bathroom, where I punish myself for even thinking about the possibilities of a happy future.

Three
Cameron

I THOUGHT AFTER what happened last night that things would change. She ignores me at school and goes back to ignoring me at her house. I hoped for a moment that maybe some of the sadness in her would be gone, but she seems worse today. There's an uneasiness in the pit of my stomach telling me that maybe *I* caused it. Maybe I should have said or done something differently. "Are you okay?"

She starts the dishwasher and glances around the kitchen, but there's no one around—the boys are occupied or down for the night. Her frown deepens and her gaze drops. She doesn't answer. She just walks away.

One of these days, I'm going to stop her from walking away from me.

I stay as late as possible without breaking curfew. Just as I'm about to head out the front door, I hear her voice. "Okay Dad," she says quietly, then a door shuts and quiet footsteps come down the stairs. "You're still here?"

I ignore the question, and the annoyance of her mood switch since talking last night. "I wanted to talk to you."

Her eyes narrow in question.

"My dad's coming into town tomorrow for a meeting. I'm spending the day with him, so I won't be at the twins' game… and then I promised my boys I'd hang out with them tomorrow night. Logan's giving me shit that I never do stuff with them anymore…"

"Okay," she murmurs, her eyes darting to mine. And I swear it, I see disappointment in them. "No one forces you to come here, remember? You don't need to inform me, or ask for permission, or whatever."

I swallow my nerves, or anger, or both. I release it all in a giant sigh. "Bye Lucy." And then I leave. I get on my dumb bike, put my feet on the stupid pedals and ride home. The second I'm under my covers, all I want to do is call her. So when my phone rings and her name flashes on the screen, I almost piss my pants. *Almost.* I'm so pre-occupied wondering whether I actually did pee a little that I don't realize I've answered until she says hello for the third time. I bring the phone to my ear but all the words are trapped my throat.

"It's Lucy," she says.

"I know," I clip. Because I've suddenly turned into a dick.

She lets out a heavy breath. "I'm sorry for calling. I didn't mean to disturb you." She sniffs once. *Is she crying?* Fuck. I've made her cry.

Then the phone cuts out, or at least that's what I tell myself, because I *really* don't want to believe that she hung up on me.

I try calling back.

Six times.

She never answers.

✧　✧　✧

SPENDING THE DAY with Dad meant sitting around his hotel room while his phone was glued to his ear. He's a hot-shot sports agent from New Jersey and came here to see a sophomore who has so much potential pitching talent, the MLB was already chasing him. I didn't tell him that I was friends with the kid he was meeting with. If my dad knew we went to the same school, he never mentioned it. And if Jake was interested in my dad representing him then he'd make that choice without any influence from me. He did ask me what my season's batting average was, but his phone rang before I got a chance to answer. And that was that.

I tried calling Lucy.

Three times.

She never answered.

"What's with you, Cam? You've been so out of it lately." Logan's gaze follows some blonde across the room. When his eyes finally leave her, he takes a swig of his beer, then points it at me. "Where the hell have you been lately?"

I shrug and play dumb just as two girls walk up to us. And that's when I know that whatever 'boys night' Logan had planned for us is no longer in play. He and Jake will have their hands full in two seconds. And me—all I can think about is the sad, broken girl I've been spending way too much time dreaming about.

So it's no surprise at all I leave the party and end up where I am... walking down her stupidly long driveway. It's past ten, and the inside of the house is dark. I take the steps to get to their lit-up closed in porch, where she currently stands with her back turned. She's in her pajamas; yellow with blue books on them. "Lucy?"

She slowly spins around—her hair a curtain around her face. And then she looks up...

If heartbreak had a sound, it would be her sob.

She lifts the watering can in her hand and waves it slowly around her. "These were hers," she whispers, pointing the can to the pots of roses around her. Her eyes bore into mine when she continues. "I keep thinking that if I keep them alive, then maybe she'll come back." Her tears fall, but she doesn't wipe them away. I cover the distance to get to her. I don't touch her. I don't speak. I don't know what the hell to do. "Do you think it'll work, Cameron? Do you think she'll come back? If I take care of things like she did... maybe it won't be so bad for her to come back. I don't even care if she lays in her bed dying. She could just do that." She sucks in a shaky breath. *Shit. What the fuck do I do?* "It's my fault," she says through a cry. "I wanted her to die. *I wished for it.* And now she's gone..." Water spills on the floor as she drops the watering can, and then herself—crashing to her knees and burying her head in her hands. And I'm right there with her, holding on to her. "She's gone and all I want is to have her back. I miss her so much." She cries hard into my chest. "I miss holding her hand. I miss her voice. I miss the smell of her." She pulls back slightly and searches my face. Her hand reaches up to my cheek, wiping away tears I didn't know were there. Then she releases a breath, her shoulders dropping with the force of it. Her gaze moves toward the house, then back to me. "Please don't tell anyone," she whispers. And I have no damn clue what the hell just happened. I nod anyway. Slowly, she comes to a stand, bringing me with her. And now we're face-to-face, closer than we've ever been. "Are you hungry?" she asks.

I'm not, but I nod regardless.

She takes my hand and leads me into her house. I don't like being far from her. And right now, I have a feeling she needs someone close.

✧　✧　✧

"YOU'RE NOT EATING?"

She sits opposite me with nothing but a glass of water and slowly shakes her head.

"I kind of feel weird sitting here eating your food alone."

She shakes her head again. "It's yours. I made it for you."

My eyes narrow as I take in her words. "I told you I wouldn't be over today. Did you forget?"

"No." Her fingers pick at a worn spot on the table. "Just in case you decided to show…" she says quietly.

My heart picks up. "Did you want me to show?"

Her head lifts and her eyes lock with mine. She nods slightly. It's a small movement, but one that's enough to flip my entire world off its axis.

I hide my smile with a mouthful of food.

We sit in silence until I'm done.

"You're out past curfew?" She takes my dishes and places them in the sink.

I get up and shake my head. "Curfew's not until one on weekends."

"Oh." She looks from the clock to me—a small smile plays on her lips. It's as confusing as it is gratifying. I force myself to believe that I'm the reason.

I'm the reason she's smiling.

"So…" she starts, looking uncomfortable. "You wanna watch some TV? The boys say we have Netflix. I don't really know how to use it, but I'm—"

"Sure," I interrupt. "I don't really care what we do. I'm just glad you're not asking me to leave."

And there it is; that smile again.

Lucy

WE'RE SUPPOSED TO be watching a movie, but I keep catching him watching me. It makes me uncomfortable, but not in the way that it probably should. It makes me feel like I should change from my pajamas into something nicer. Something prettier. For the first time in my life, I wish I were prettier. I want to be prettier *for him.*

"I have to go," he says quickly, standing up and walking to the kitchen.

I try to calm my breathing before walking in after him. He's washing his dishes from earlier.

"You don't have to do that."

He shrugs, handing me the plate to dry. Normally, he dries, and I wash. He's a good dryer. I rush things, leave wet spots. He does things thoroughly. Slowly. Until it's perfect. I glare at the plate in my hand and make a mental note to dry it until it's perfect.

So that's what I'm doing, drying and inspecting the plate in front of me when he whispers my name.

My eyes snap to his. And then…

Lips.

On me.

On my lips.

Mouth.

Lips.

Mouth.

I whimper. Legit, whimper.

But I don't know what's happening and what I should be doing so I stand frozen like a statue with the plate still in my hand and my eyes closed. And all too quickly—no more lips. *Where did his mouth go?* By the time I open my eyes, he's turned away, looking down into the sink, his hands gripping the edge of it. "Sorry," he says.

I try to ask why, but all that comes out is a continuous, "Wwww." I clear my throat and try to stop the world from spinning. *When did I get dizzy?* I try again. "More mouth." *Shit.* That wasn't what I meant to say.

He chuckles lightly, and it makes me feel dumb, but only for a second before he turns to face me. Taking the plate from my grip and setting it on the counter, he holds both of my hands in his and slowly moves in.

I prepare myself this time. A montage of words from the books I've read about kissing fly through my mind. *It can't be that hard. I can totally do this.* I ignore the pounding in my ears. And then…

Mouth.

Lips.

More mouth.

Lips.

Soft lips.

Is that tongue?

Oh my God.

He pulls away and my eyes snap open. His eyes are wide as he searches my face. "Luce?"

And I die. I love the way my name falls from his lips. His lips...

"Are you okay?" He waits, his eyebrows bunching more with each passing second.

Answer him.

He releases my hands and I think he's about to back away from crazy, but he moves them to my hips.

I die. Again.

"Is this... I mean... have you ever been kissed before?"

My head shakes frantically. I can't control it.

His face lights up.

I don't know why he's happy that he's trying to make out with a pajama wearing, frozen, virgin kisser. That doesn't sound like happy times at all.

"So I'm your first?"

I nod again. The same speed as before. That's it—I've lost control of all bodily function.

"I like that," he says, his mouth slowly descending. He presses his lips softly against mine. I squeeze my eyes shut and pray that I can actually do something this time. "Relax," he whispers against my lips. "I got you."

I feel the moment the tension leaves my body.

And then...

LIPS. Oh. My. God. Lips.

So different this time. Soft. Guiding. He's *guiding* me on my first kiss.

I match my lips to his movements.

And then something happens.

Like a clicking of pieces.

A perfect harmony.

A double rainbow.

My arms are around him now, gripping the back of his shirt. He pulls me closer to him, until I'm on my toes, reaching for him. Not wanting the moment to end. Then...

Tongue.

And everything snaps shut.

My eyes.

My lips.

He pulls back, releasing me slowly onto the floor. Or maybe I just imagined that I was floating on air. When I open my eyes he's right there, his face only inches from me. A slight smirk graces his lips. "You just tell me when you're ready for more, Luce."

By now, I've lost the need to breathe. I yank on his shirt and pull him back to me. "Now," I tell him.

He lets out a soft chuckle, but my mouth on his cuts it off. I'm a mess. My mind is reeling and my body tingles everywhere. I open my mouth slightly, encouraging him to continue where he left off. When his tongue brushes against mine, we moan into each other. He takes control, showing me what to do—making my first kiss *perfect*. He pulls away before I'm ready to stop. I pull him back to me by his shirt. He chuckles again, and this time I don't feel dumb. I just feel *him*—his lips, his tongue, and his hands on my waist, gripping tightly.

We kiss for nowhere near long enough before his phone rings and we reluctantly break apart. His eyes never leave me when he lifts the phone to his ear. "Hey Mom... I know... I'm sorry, I'll be home soon."

I look at the clock with a grimace. It's twenty minutes past his curfew.

"I know," he continues. "No, I left the party... I'm with Lucy. Yes... No... Yes... Okay."

He hangs up and gazes down at me, and almost shyly, a smile spreads across his face. "You're so short."

I laugh at that. But his features flatten at the sound of it. Then heavy footsteps thud down the stairs. My eyes widen and my breath catches. I pull on his shirt until we're in the pantry, and I close the door to hide Cameron from my dad. Or maybe the other way around.

It's dark, the only light coming from under the door. "What's going on?" he whispers. I reach up and cover his mouth with my hand. His fingers circle my wrist and pull it away. Then his arms wrap tightly around me as I slowly crumble to the floor.

I hate these nights.

I hate that he gets like this.

I hate that he's allowed and I'm not.

I hate it.

I hate it so much I let it out in angry tears.

Cameron's hold gets tighter as he brings me closer. So close I'm curled into a ball on his lap.

And the tears won't go away.

I hate everyone.

I hate everything.

Cameron

FOOTSTEPS THUMP INTO the kitchen. I can hear the clanking of glass and the overwhelming smell of whiskey. She's curled into herself, her face pressed against my chest with her silent tears soaking through my shirt. I stroke her hair, wanting to comfort her. I don't know if it helps—but I don't know what else to do. The sound of shattering glass makes her flinch. "Fuck!" The deep tenor of his voice has my heart racing. "Dammit!"

The sound of footsteps thud nearer. She sits up and moves in front of me—like she's ready to protect me. She doesn't need to protect me. *I'm here to protect her.*

"KATHY!" her dad yells. "Kathy!" Quieter this time. And then a loud thump, like a body crashing to the floor. She flinches again. I hold her face and get her to look at me. "It's okay," I whisper. And then I kiss her. Because I don't know what else to do, and I don't know how to make things better. So I distract her from what's happening outside that door. I distract her from what's happening in her life. I distract her from her reality.

When minutes pass with no further sounds, I pull back. "Ready?"

She kisses me once more and nods.

We stand up and I make sure she's behind me when I open the door and peek out.

He's laying on his side, passed out on the kitchen floor, a smashed bottle of whiskey near his feet. She moves around, walks over to him and gets on her knees in front of him. "Daddy," she whispers, shaking him roughly. "Daddy!"

He rolls onto his back and grunts in response. Her gaze quickly flicks to me before she lifts his arm and settles it around her shoulders.

That small look was all I needed to know that whatever fleeting moment we shared before he came down is over, and that the walls that surrounded her have slammed right back down.

"Come on, Daddy. Let's get you to bed." Her tone's flat. Not sincere. Not sympathetic. She struggles to help him stand. Only now do I realize how huge he is. At least six-five. Built like a Mack truck. I don't know how she's holding him up. She's barely five feet tall, weighs the equivalent of his right leg. I step forward, an offer to help, but she shakes her head to stop me.

"Where's Kathy?" he says groggily. She doesn't answer; just keeps struggling to lead him out of the kitchen and up the stairs.

I sweep up the broken glass off the floor and bag at least ten bottles of alcohol. When I come back in through the back door after throwing them out, she's walking into the kitchen. She smiles sadly when she sees me—that wall still in place. "I think your mom's here."

I'd completely forgotten that she was picking me up. "Are you gonna be okay?"

She leads me to her front door, never once looking at me. "I'm fine."

I step to her and take her hands—my eyes searching hers. "Are you though?"

"You can't say anything to anyone, Cameron. I mean it," she snaps.

"I wouldn't, Luce."

"I'm serious." She yanks her hands away. "People will start to worry. They'll send people to check on us and they'll separate us. I'll lose my brothers. And you—you were never supposed to see any of that." She opens the front door for me.

Mom's headlights blind me for a moment. She must see my reaction because she switches them off.

"I'll come by early tomorrow, okay?"

She shakes her head. "No, Cameron. Not tomorrow."

I rear back in surprise, my brows bunching as I search her face for a reason. "Why?"

"I just need time with my family. *Alone.*"

I don't know what to say, so I stay silent.

She flinches when I touch her hand, but it doesn't stop me from gripping it and pulling her into me. "I wish I could help. I wish I could fix things." I kiss the top of her head.

"LUCY!" her dad shouts, his voice causing my blood to boil.

She looks up at me now, her eyes stone cold. "I hate him," she whispers before breaking away and going back into her house.

Four
Cameron

YESTERDAY WAS THE first day since I started going to her house that I didn't see her. It took everything I had to not call her, or to not just get on my bike and ride to her house. I got to school early, hoping I'd catch her before class, but I never saw her at her locker. My eyes kept wandering, looking for her everywhere. By the time lunch rolled around, I began to panic. But when I saw her sitting alone, against a wall of the building opposite the cafeteria, where I currently stood, the panic was replaced with something else. Nerves. Excitement. Anticipation. "I'm out." I pat Jake on the shoulder and squeeze past the people waiting in the food line.

My palms are already sweaty by the time I get to her. I stand over her, but she doesn't see me, her eyes too fixed on the e-reader in her hand. It makes me chuckle, remembering the first time I truly noticed her. "Hey," I say, trying to get her attention.

She doesn't budge.

I softly kick her shoe with mine.

She finally lifts her head. Her eyes widen when she sees that it's me, and slowly, but *surely*, her lips begin to spread into a smile.

"Can I sit?"

She nods, her smile getting wider.

"Am I interrupting your reading?"

She leans forward, looks back down at her e-reader and shakes her head.

I sit next to her and stretch my arm behind her, wanting to be closer... remembering how she felt in my arms. I've thought about it a lot, but I've also thought about what happened afterwards—the shit with her dad and how she acted because of it. "Are you okay?"

35

"I'm fine."

And something tells me that *I'm fine* is her go-to line. Her go-to *lie*.

I raise my hand and tilt her chin with my finger so I can actually see her face.

Her cheeks burn red and I fake a confidence that doesn't exist. Leaning in slowly, I place my lips on hers. She smiles against them, but pulls away quickly, eyeing our surroundings.

I push back the slight feeling of rejection and move on. "What are you reading?"

"Nothing."

"You can't be reading nothing. What is it?"

"It's just about a boy and girl falling in love."

"Yeah? Is the guy a stud? Is his name Cameron?"

She laughs, the sound so powerful it drowns out all other sounds. "No."

"Read me some."

"No."

"Come on. I wanna know what this kid does that makes you so drawn to the story."

"No," she says again. "I'm not reading to you. That's weird."

"Fine." I lean in so I can read over her shoulder.

We're close. Too close. My nose grazes her cheek, and my lips follow. I kiss her cheek; the warmth from her blush heats my lips. She's frozen, like she was on Saturday night, and I love that I have that effect on her. My lips brush down her cheek and into the crook of her neck where I kiss her again.

She jerks back quickly.

And I can't ignore the rejection the second time. "You not into public kissing?"

"No," she says. "It's not that…" Her nose scrunches. "I mean, I don't know if I am. It's just that I don't really know what this is yet… you and me. I think I just need some time to figure it out. And you know me… you know my life… you see how things are for me. I don't know if I can—"

"Okay," I cut in. "Take your time. Decide what you want. But just so you know—none of that means anything to me—your life, I mean. It doesn't change the fact that I want you." I pause, replaying the words in my head. *I just told her I wanted her.* I should feel embarrassed, or at least awkward, but I don't. "I'll wait for you, Luce, until you're ready. Just tell me now, so I don't sit around getting my hopes up… do you think that maybe someday you'll want me, too?"

She bites her bottom lip and looks around again. Then she lifts her e-reader and reaches up to my face, her e-reader blocking us from the rest of the world. She kisses me softly, and longer than I expected. "Yes," she says, pulling away.

I can't help grinning like an idiot. "Good."

She leans in closer so our sides are flush against each other. It's a sign—her way of showing me that she wants me without having to say a word.

I hear Logan and Jake talking loudly as they walk past. Logan stops in his tracks at the sight of us. I want to hide her from him. I don't want him to know who or what she is to me. He smirks, right before he starts humping the air. I shake my head at him.

"Your friends are idiots." She giggles, but her eyes are cast downwards, focused on her e-reader again.

"Yeah, they kind of are." I watch as her eyes move from side to side.

"So I have practice after school, I'll come by right after."

She switches it off and shoves it in her bag. "Baseball practice?"

"Yeah."

"Okay… so you'll be hungry after, right?"

I laugh. "Most likely."

She gets on her knees and throws her backpack over her shoulders. "Good. I'll make extra for you." Her eyes search the area around us, and when she's satisfied no one can see, she places both hands on my shoulders and pushes me against the wall.

My eyes widen in surprise.

"Just a quick goodbye kiss," she says, before moving in and giving it to me.

✧   ✧   ✧

"I HATE THAT guy," Logan jerks his head toward Jake and a new kid.

"The new kid? Dylan?"

He nods. "He thinks he owns the school."

"Really?" I glare over at them. "Apparently he kills it on the basketball court, but I dunno." I shrug. "He hasn't said two words to me. He seems quiet."

"Those are the ones you have to worry about, Cam. The quiet broody assholes get all the girls. Better watch him around that new girl of yours."

I play dumb. "What new girl?"

"Shut up, asshole. You don't think I notice you watching her all the fucking time?"

I lift my chin. "I think if there's an asshole in this entire school to watch out for, it's you."

He laughs and adjusts his cap. "You don't need to worry about me. I'm not into stealing my friends' girls." He shoves his hand in his catcher's glove and smacks my arm with it. "Say the word. Claim her. I promise to stay away and I'll make sure she's untouchable to everyone else."

"I'm not an asshole and she isn't property. I can't own her."

"If that's what you want." He raises an eyebrow. "She's cute. In a couple years she'll be hot. Guys will be all over her. I'm just trying to help out."

I think about what he's saying, and he makes a good point. Only he's wrong—she's hot now. "Fine. I claim her. She's mine."

His smirk is instant. "You can't own someone, you pig. She isn't property."

I laugh. "Fuck you."

Jake struts over to us. "Ya reckon that new kid Dylan can hang out with us this arvo? He seems like a top bloke."

Logan's gaze moves to me, confusion clear on his face. I shrug. He lets out a chuckle before gripping both of Jake's shoulders and shaking him gently. He looks him right in the eye, speaking slowly and clearly. "I have no idea what the fuck you just said."

✧　✧　✧

I DON'T BOTHER knocking when I get to her house, and I'm glad I don't because no one would have heard me over her screaming. "What's wrong with him?" she shouts. I drop my backpack and run to the kitchen. The boys are standing above her, the younger ones are crying… and so is she. Hysterically. She's holding the baby in her arm, with one hand touching his forehead.

I drop to my knees next to her. "What's wrong?"

"I don't know," she sobs, trying to level her breathing. "He won't stop crying and he's burning up. I got home from school and my aunt had to rush out. He was fine, and then he wasn't. He hasn't stopped crying."

"Have you called your aunt?" My voice is strained. I'm scared. I want to help her but I don't know how.

"Get me the phone," she yells at the boys.

Where is her dad?

Leo hands her the phone. Her fingers make quick work of pushing the right buttons. She holds it to her ear while her eyes move to mine. "What did I do to him?" she whispers.

My heart breaks. "It's not your fault," I tell her, but she's already speaking hysterically into the phone. "Aunt Leslee, something's wrong with Lachlan." She can barely speak through her cries. She glances up, taking a look at each of the boys, and then me. "Help," she says. And I know it takes everything in her to ask for it.

I take the phone from her when she's done and dial 911. I try to stay calm as I tell them as much as I know—which is fuck all. Then I hang up and call my mom. "I need you to come to Lucy's. Now." She doesn't waste time asking questions—just tells me she's on her way.

Lucy hasn't stopped crying, and neither has the baby. The older boys are comforting the younger ones as much as possible, but I can see in their faces that they're just as afraid as we all are.

Where the fuck is her dad? And now I'm pissed. Because it's not on Lucy to have to carry all this on her own. "Stay with her," I tell Lucas, the oldest at twelve. He nods, his eyes already filled with tears.

I march up the stairs. With each step, my anger builds. By the time I'm at his bedroom door, rage so strong fills me that I can't even think. I just kick the door and watch it forcefully smack into the wall behind it. "Get up, you asshole." I lean over his passed out form, ignoring the stench of booze. "Your family needs you." I shake him as hard as possible, but all he does is moan in response.

My gaze darts around the room, looking for something to *make him* get up. There's nothing here, just half empty bottles of whiskey. I take the nearest one and run to his bathroom. Then I empty it and fill it with water. I walk back and stand over his pathetic state and proceed to empty it all over his head. He jerks up. "Kathy," he moans. And for a split second I actually feel sorry for him.

"Get downstairs," I grind out. "Your baby's sick and Lucy needs you."

"Lucy?"

"Lucy. You know… your only daughter. The one that's been keeping this family together since *you* checked out."

He sits on the edge of the bed and rubs his palm down the side of his face.

"NOW!" I yell. And it seems like he finally comprehends the seriousness of what's happening.

He rushes down the stairs, tripping on the last step. I help him up and push him toward the kitchen. Nothing's changed in the time I was gone.

The front door bursts open. A moment later it feels like a million people fill the kitchen—the paramedics, my mom, and her aunt.

"Lucy." Her dad sways on his feet, watching her crying on the floor. He hasn't even gone to her yet. My fists ball—it's the only way I can keep my rage in check. A tear falls from his eye. "What did you do, Lucy?"

His words alone release the rage and I punch him.

I can tell that it hurts me more than it hurts him because he barely flinches.

I hate him.

Mom yells my name and the boys start shouting.

Lucy screams.

"She didn't do shit," I yell up at his surprised face. "She's done nothing but almost kill herself looking after YOUR kids. She's fifteen! She doesn't need this shit."

"STOP IT!" she shouts. "Please, Cameron! Stop!"

I stop.

We all do.

Even the baby—who's now in the hands of the paramedic. "Sweetheart," she says to Lucy, throwing a hand out to help her on her feet. "He's just teething. It's painful for them. It's normal for them to get a fever… for them to cry. It's all normal." She glares up at Lucy's dad, but her words are meant for Lucy. "You didn't do anything wrong."

Lucy's breath catches before she shoves past everyone and runs upstairs. I go after her but Mom holds me back. "She might just need some time, honey."

I get out of her grasp and ignore her words. Lucy doesn't need time. *She needs me.* My heart thumps as I take the steps to her room. She's not there, but I can hear her loud cries through her bathroom door. My hands cover the doorknob, but then Mom's words repeat in my head. *She might just need some time.* I press my ear against the door and listen for any sign that she's okay. And then I hear the one sound that changes everything.

She's vomiting.

I turn the knob and slowly push open the door. She's standing over the toilet with her finger in her mouth.

She's *making* herself vomit.

"Lucy," I breathe out. "Stop."

Her eyes stay on me while I watch them turn to stone. Face wet from her tears, she slowly pushes her finger further into her mouth.

I move.

Faster than I thought possible.

I shove her hand out of her mouth and wrap my arms around her, pinning her arms to her body. "No," she cries, but I can feel the strength leaving her. I tighten my hold and bring us both down to the floor. "What are you doing, Luce?" I'm crying. And I don't care. I don't care for anything but her. I grab a towel of the rack and wipe her mouth.

"I just want it stop."

She cries, and I let her.

Her fingers grip my arms so tight I know they'll bruise. But it's nothing compared to the pain I feel *for* her. She wipes her face on my shirt and looks up at me with an emptiness in her eyes I never want to see again. "I want it to stop, Cameron. Please make it stop."

My eyes drift shut. "Okay, Luce. I'll make it stop. I'll make it better. I promise." And I do. I promise her, and I promise myself, right there and then; *I'll make it right.*

I carry her to her bed, thankful that I'd spent the last few months hitting the weights. We lay together on top of the covers, with her head on my chest and my arms around her. At some point, she falls asleep. And just like the light inside of her, I watch the daylight outside her window turn to darkness.

MOM STANDS AT the doorway of Lucy's bedroom with a frown on her face. We've been in here for hours. I forgot that she was here. I bring my finger to my lips and point to Lucy. She nods and quietly walks over to the bed. "How's she doing?"

"Not good." I try to keep my voice low but Lucy wakes anyway. She sees my mom standing over us and buries her head on my chest.

Mom smiles, but it's sad. "Lucy, honey?"

She starts to cry again. I stroke her hair, hoping it comforts her just a little.

Mom sighs. "Pack a bag, sweetheart. You're going to stay with us for a few days."

She doesn't argue. She doesn't put up a fight. She packs her bags, walks downstairs, out of the house and into Mom's car.

She never once looks back at her family.

✧ ✧ ✧

SHE DOESN'T SPEAK on the drive home so neither do I.

We sit at the dining table while Mom makes us food. I haven't eaten anything since breakfast and she puked the contents of her stomach.

Mom places the plate in front of me and I take continuous mouthfuls until I hear her clear her throat. I look up at her, she jerks her head toward Lucy.

Lucy's looking down at her plate with a frown on her face. I set my fork on the table and turn to her. "You need to eat something, Luce."

Her head moves slowly from side to side. "I'm not hungry."

Sighing, I reach for her hand under the table and lean in close to her ear, my words meant only for her. "Please, babe. You need to eat. I'm worried."

She slowly turns to face me, the same emptiness in her eyes from earlier.

"Please," I beg. "For me."

She nods and picks up her fork. I watch her take a mouthful, slowly, almost painfully. Like what she's doing is a form of punishment. She has two more bites before pushing the plate away, her mind lost in a world of her own thoughts.

I wish I could read her better.

Her gaze lifts, first to Mom, then to me, and back down to the empty spot in front of her. "He hates me because I look like my mom."

✧   ✧   ✧

SHE'S LYING IN my bed next to me—her head on my chest with my fingers stroking her hair. My mind is on overdrive, much like the churning in my stomach. She hasn't brought it up so I try hard to forget what I saw in her bathroom—but I'm worried. And I can't ignore that worry anymore. "Lucy?"

She whimpers in response.

"Liam—he told me that sometimes you get so sad it makes you sick?"

She lifts her head, her gaze searching my eyes.

"Is that what he meant… that you get so sad you make yourself throw up?"

Her eyes drift shut, and she releases a breath, along with her fight to keep being *fine*. She nods slowly, almost as if she's sorry for admitting it.

"Never again, okay?" My tone is firm. Final. "I'm not letting it happen again, Lucy."

Tears start to well in her eyes. "Okay, Cameron. I promise."

Mom opens the door without knocking. The concern on her face is overwhelming. "I made your bed on the couch, Cameron."

"Okay," I answer without surprise. I knew I wouldn't be able to stay with Lucy.

I start to get up but she holds on to my arm, gripping it tightly to her chest. "Please," she whispers, her eyes pleading.

I look at Mom, still standing in the doorway. "Please," I mouth.

She nods once and lifts a finger. "One night," she mouths back, pushing the door wide open and flattening her palm against it to keep it in place.

Lucy

I WAKE UP with Cameron's arms wrapped around me, along with a pounding headache. Picking up his phone from the nightstand, I look at the time. Two a.m. Slowly, I lift his arm off me and make my way downstairs in search of aspirin. His dad—no… his mom's boyfriend is at the dining table. Papers and a box of envelopes in front of him.

"Hey." He leans back in his chair and raises his hand in a wave.

"Everything okay?"

I hold a hand to my head, hoping to ease the pain. "Aspirin."

He smiles and motions to the chair opposite him. "Take a seat. I'll be right back."

And he is, with two aspirins and a bottle of water. He waits until I've swallowed both before sitting back down. "Rough night?" he asks. Even though his tone is casual, I can sense the concern in his words.

I nod. "What are you doing up so late?"

He laughs once, understanding my need to change the subject. "Working. Always working."

I eye the mess of papers in front of me. "Need help?"

"You don't want to go back to sleep?"

I shake my head. "I've slept enough. I'm not used to more than a few hours."

"Okay." He perks up. "I need all the help I can get." He pushes the box of envelopes to my side of the table and hands me a list of names and addresses. "I hope you have neat handwriting."

We spend the next few minutes in silence, but I can feel his eyes on me. I keep my head down and write out the addresses like he asked. Then he drops a stack of papers next to my hand—flyers for a sale at a car dealership. Cameron told me that that's how his mom and Mark met. She went in to buy a car, he wouldn't sell her the one she wanted... told her to come back next week when the right model was available. He told her that for a whole two months. For two months she showed up every weekend, wanting to see this new model. Finally, he told her there was no new model, he just wanted to see her.

I examine the flyer again. It's hand drawn, like a comic strip. The general gist is that the buyer leaves as a superhero. *'Let your next purchase empower you'* the headline says. "This is great," I tell him.

"It's pretty awesome, huh?"

"Who drew it?"

He's silent for so long I don't think he heard me. I finally pull my gaze away from the artwork and look up at him. He smirks before he answers, "Cam."

My eyes go wide. "Cameron did this?"

He nods, a sense of pride taking over him.

"He can draw?" My voice comes out louder than expected.

He chuckles. "Yeah, Lucy. He can draw. He's kind of amazing, right?"

I lift the flyer so I can inspect it closer. "Amazing is an understatement."

"I can't believe you didn't know," he muses, shaking his head. And then it dawns on me; all these days he's been at my house, all the hours I've spent with him, he's never told me anything about him. It was always about me. *He* was always about *me.*

Mark must read my thoughts because he asks, "You don't know much about him do you?"

I shake my head, my mind still reeling from my realization. "Tell me about him?"

He laughs. "I'll tell you as much as I think he'll let me."

"Okay."

"Where do you want me to start?"

"How long have you known him?"

"Since he was six."

And that's how we spend the next few hours; with Mark telling me as much as he can about Cameron.

Cameron is an artist. He's an athlete. He's an unbelievably respectful son. Above all that, Cameron has a heart the size of the ocean. But he didn't need to tell me that part. If anyone knew the size of Cam's heart, it was me.

I get up and stretch my back when we're done. "You know you can enter those names and addresses into a spreadsheet and print directly onto the envelopes."

Mark's eyes go wide. "You're a liar."

His seriousness makes me smile.

When I get back to Cameron's room, he's sitting up in his bed with his phone in his hand. "Lucy," he sighs. "Where have you been? I thought you left." The panic in his voice creates an ache in my chest.

"I just needed aspirin. I'm sorry."

He sucks in a huge breath and lies back down, patting the spot next to him. "Come here."

I climb back into bed with him and rest my head on his chest, the same way I fell asleep earlier. His heart's racing, thudding hard against my ear. "I can feel your heartbeat."

"I know," he replies. "I got worried. I don't like not knowing if you're okay."

Five
Lucy

H E'S NOT IN bed when I get up the next morning. I shower in his bathroom, dress for school and head downstairs. "He's in the garage," his mom tells me. "Lucy?"

"Yeah?"

"You're going to be staying with us for a few days… and I know that it's hard—what you're going through at the moment—but I can't let Cameron stay with you every night." She grimaces slightly. "I'm sorry."

"It's okay." I fail at my attempt to smile. "I'll try to be stronger."

She places a hand on my forearm as I try to walk past her and shakes her head slowly. "It's not about—" she cuts herself off with a sigh. "I just can't have teenagers sleeping in the same bed under my roof. You get that, right?"

Only now do I understand what she's saying. It never even occurred to me. Being with Cameron—in his bed—it's not physical, or sexual. "I understand," I tell her. "But you don't have to worry, it's not like that. Cameron—he's my strength. And right now, I don't know that I have any left."

✧   ✧   ✧

"HEY," HE DROPS the wrench onto the workbench and walks over to me. "Did you sleep all right?" I nod, feeling a little shy. He leans his face in closer, his lips already puckered. And my mind kicks into over drive. Mouth kiss? Cheek kiss? *What is this kiss?* I panic, duck my head and swiftly move around him.

Changing the subject to hide my embarrassment, I ask, "What are you doing in here?"

47

He turns to me with hurt clear in his eyes and my heart drops. I step forward and grab his hand—it's as much as I can offer right now.

Seconds pass while we stare down at our joined hands, then he squeezes it once, causing me to lift my gaze and look up at him. A perfect smile spreads on his face, and I've never wanted to kiss him more. So I do, I get up on my toes and I kiss him. It's quick, because I'm not sure I'm ready for more. But when I pull away, I know it's enough. Not just for me, but for him too.

"I was putting pegs on my bike," he says, his smile getting wider.

"Pegs?"

He leads me—with our hands still linked—over to his bike and sets his foot on a piece of round metal sticking out of the center of the back wheel. "Pegs; you stand on them while I ride, so you don't have to walk." He releases my hand, pulls my backpack off my shoulder, and hangs it off the handlebar. "I figure it's the best way we can get around for the next few days. Unless you feel like doing some grand theft auto and driving illegally again?" He jerks his head toward his mom's car.

After the night I had last night, I didn't think it was possible, but somehow, he makes me laugh—the sound surprising to my own ears.

✧ ✧ ✧

I SPEND THE entire day worrying about the boys. By the time the day's over, I'm a mess. "I looked for you at lunch," he states with a grin. He pulls his bike off the rack where I've been waiting for him.

"I had to study," I lie. I wasn't studying; I was in the library reading—getting lost in another world that's not my reality. "I think I should go home, Cam."

His smile fades. "Why?"

"It just doesn't seem right that I'm with you when they need me."

"But—" He lets out a sigh and nods his head. "If that's what you want, Luce. Okay. But can I at least take you somewhere first?"

"Where?"

He takes the backpack off my shoulder and hangs it off the handlebar again. "It's a surprise."

My eyes narrow. "Surprise?"

He sits on his bike and throws a hand out to me. "You trust me, right?"

"Yes," I reply without hesitation.

✧   ✧   ✧

HE TAKES ME to the river which runs behind the townhouses where he lives and starts taking off his shoes.

I look from him, to the water and back again. "No."

"No?" His eyebrows rise. "You said you trusted me."

"I know, and I do trust you, but when you said it was a surprise I thought you meant *'Here, Luce. I got you a unicorn.'* not *'Here, Luce, jump in the river.'*"

His head throws back in laughter. "It's not that bad." He takes my hand with one of his, the other flipping his cap backwards. "Believe me. You need this."

"I *need* this?"

He drops my hand and lets out a frustrated breath. Tilting his head to the side, he eyes me with a bored expression.

"Fine," I mutter, kicking off my shoes.

WE WADE OUT until the water reaches our shoulders—or mine at least. He bends his knees so that we're level.

"What now?"

"Now… you scream."

"What?" I laugh. *He's still doing it—making me laugh.*

He steps forward until we're face-to-face, as close as we can be without kissing. I let out a gurgle sound from deep in my throat when I see his hand begin to rise.

He's trying to cop a feel!

He pauses mid-movement and eyes me warily. "You trust me, remember?"

I nod, but stay frozen.

His palm flattens against my chest, where I'm sure he can feel the hammering of my heart. "Lucy," he whispers, his eyes boring into mine. "I want you to take everything you feel in here…" His hand moves lower, past my breasts and onto my stomach, where it settles. "And everything in here…" He reaches up and holds the side of my head. "And everything in here." My eyes drift shut from his touch. Then I feel his soft lips on mine, kissing me once before pulling back. "I want you to take all those feelings, the build up of all the stress, the worry… take it all… dip your head under the water… and *scream*." My eyes snap open. I search his face for an answer to a question that doesn't exist.

Inhaling a shaky breath, I let his words sink in. Along with every single emotion I've been trying to push down. The worry. The guilt. The stress. The pressure. And most of all, the *grief*. My eyes fill with tears and I try to breathe through the giant knot in my throat. He places both his hands on the side of my face and kisses me again. "Let it go, Luce. All of it."

I feel the water fill my nose first, then my ears, and then my mouth when I open it to *scream*. When I come up for air, my chest heaves with the exertion of my much-needed breaths. I open my eyes to see him watching me with his lips pressed so tight they've lost color. I suck in another shaky breath, dip my head under the water… and I do it all over again. And again. And again.

He stands in front of me. Never speaking. Never interrupting. Never telling me to stop or that I've had enough. He silently waits until I feel *it* leave me. Until all of those feelings are gone and are replaced with one that I thought I'd never feel again.

When I'm done, I silently walk to the embankment and lie down on the grass.

Minutes pass before he's there, lying next to me and linking our fingers together.

Not a single word is spoken.

No justification for what happened.

No explanation for my current tears.

When the cries finally subside and my breaths are level, I turn to him. "You're an artist?"

His shoulders tense. "No."

I release his hand and lean up on my elbow so I can see his face. "That's funny. I saw the flyer for Mark's sale. Whoever drew it is definitely an artist and he said it was you, so that makes you an artist. No?"

He sighs and mirrors my position so we're facing each other. "I wish I was an artist, Luce. But I'm not. Artists—they can picture things in their mind and let it flow out of them. I'm not like that. Yes, I can draw some things, but not all. I can't free hand." He laughs to himself. "Everything I do is lines, angles, symmetrical objects. What I do isn't hard. It's not creative. It's definitely not art. So no, I'm not an artist."

He looks away, his mind wandering to another place. His lips turn down to a frown, and I hate it. I hate that he knows how to fix me when I'm broken and I don't know how to do the same for him. "I tried to write a book once," I say.

He smiles now, his gaze returning to me. "Yeah?" he replies, moving a strand of hair to behind my ear.

I nod. "I got on my computer and typed four words. You wanna know what those four words were?"

"Please."

"Untitled. By Lucy Lovesalot."

He quirks an eyebrow. "Lovesalot?"

I shrug. "It was a pen name, but that's not the point. The point is, I *tried*. I *tried* and I got nothing. One day, I might try again. But you—you put pen to paper, and you produced something. For me, and especially for Mark—who appreciates it so much that he wants to show the world—it's art. That makes you an artist, Cameron, regardless of how you want to see it."

His eyes widen slightly in surprise. And then he smiles; that same perfect smile which still makes me nervous. He leans in and kisses my forehead. "You make me want to try, Lovesalot." He pulls back and looks in my eyes. "You want me to take you home now?"

I shake my head. "Not just yet. Let's stay here for a while."

"I was hoping you'd say that."

✧   ✧   ✧

HE DOESN'T ASK, and I don't tell him, but we end up where we both wanted to be. *His* home.

We spent the rest of the afternoon at the river talking. And kissing. We did a lot of kissing.

I lie in his bed while my body fights a losing battle against sleep.

Touching my lips with the tip of my fingers, I smile against them. I can still feel his mouth on mine.

AND THERE'S THAT same feeling I had after my emotional release. The one that I thought I could never feel again.

Hope.

Six

Cameron

THE NEXT COUPLE of days are a repeat of the last. We go to school, and then we go to the river. We hang out, talk, laugh, and learn more about each other. Each day gets better than the last.

Until today.

I rack my bike and face her. "Have lunch with me today?"

She shakes her head quickly. "I have to study."

"Where do you study?"

"Nowhere, really. Everywhere, kind of."

My eyes narrow. "That's not a real place." I step forward and take her hand. "Why won't you have lunch with me?"

She shrugs just as Logan walks up to us. "Hey, assface," he says, his eyes fixed on our joined hands.

She yanks her hand out of my hold. "See ya," she says, and then walks away.

"What's with her?" Logan asks, his gaze fixed on her ass.

I shove him. Hard. "Quit looking at her."

His eyes bug out. "Holy shit, dude. You got it bad."

"You were staring at her ass."

"I wasn't—"

"I claimed her! I said she was mine! You promised you'd leave her alone!"

His brows pinch, and he shoves me back. "I wasn't checking her out." Then a smirk develops. "Okay, maybe I was." He shrugs and starts to leave.

My fists ball at my sides. "Cocky little fuck," I shout after him.

He freezes and slowly turns around. "What did you say?"

I step forward. "You heard me."

"Fuck you, Cam. This bitch is making you crazy."

I snap. "Don't fucking call her that!" I lunge forward and tackle him to the ground. He's bigger than I am, but I'm angrier. And emotion always wins.

We don't get far before we're being pulled apart. Jake's annoying accent grinds on my nerves. "Leave it alone, mate," he says.

But I can't.

I can't let it go.

✧   ✧   ✧

"I'M SORRY." LOGAN sits opposite me in the cafeteria. "If I was looking at her like that, it wasn't intentional. I meant what I said. I'd never take my friend's girl. Ever."

I watch his face for a sign that he's fucking around, but there is none. "I can't find her."

"She left school?"

"I doubt it." I shake my head. "Yo, if I liked reading, where would I go?"

He laughs. "Um. The library?"

And that's where I find her, in between racks of books. Sitting on the floor and reading. "Lucy?"

Her eyes lift from between the pages and a smile appears—like she has absolutely no idea what she caused this morning. "You found me." She scoots over so I can sit next to her. I take the spot, but I keep my distance. I haven't stopped thinking about the way she was when Logan showed. The dropping of my hand, the refusal to look at me, the way she just walked away.

I think of the right words to use... to spare her feelings. But then I realize, fuck it—I'm the one who's hurt. "So you like Logan?"

She snorts. But her cheeks redden and she looks away. My heart hammers loudly in my ears. There's a burning in the pit of my stomach and I don't know what it is. "Just say it, Lucy. Say you're into him."

She turns to me now, her nose scrunched. "I mean, he's cute, but it's not like I have feelings for him or whatever."

"And what about me? Do you have feelings for me?"

She rears back and looks around us. "What's this about?"

Her non-answer is all I can take. I stand up—just so I can glare down at her. "That's why you won't hang out with me? That's why you don't want me kissing you and shit? It's all fine and good when we're alone, but not in public? Because you'd rather be with him?"

I watch her face change, like she's about to cry, but then a different emotion takes over. She throws her books in her backpack, swings it over her shoulder and stands up. She shoves past me just as I grab her arm to stop her. She can't walk away from this. Not anymore. "Say it, Lucy. Admit it. Tell me you're into him."

She flattens her palms against my chest. The movement's slow and gentle—almost intimate. But then her eyes narrow and her lips purse.

And then she pushes me.

Hard enough that it causes me to fall back and crash into the book-shelf behind me.

Her eyes widen in surprise, but she doesn't look sorry. She looks pissed. "I don't do that shit at school because people talk, Cameron. You haven't heard the rumors because you run in your perfect little upper-circle with all your jock buddies and no one dares talk shit about you. But me—I'm a nobody. Or at least I was. Now though? Now I'm the girl with the dead mom and the alcoholic crazy dad, and you were the one to save me. I'm staying at your house, sleeping in your bed. And *no*—you can't just be doing it out of the kindness of your heart. *Of course not.* Of course I'm *putting out.* Spreading my legs. Whoring myself to you for your generosity. I'm a whore, Cam. Didn't you know?"

I suck in a shaky breath, struggling to let her words sink in. My mouth opens, but nothing comes out.

"So no, Cameron. I'm not hiding from you because I have feelings for your jackass friend. I'm doing it because I have enough shit to deal with as it is. My mom, my dad, my brothers, my entire fucking life! I don't need the petty dramas of high school to make it worse. And if anyone should understand that..." Her shoulders slump with her sigh. She stands there, her head tilted back, looking up at me. A frown pulls on her lips, but its impact has nothing compared to the disappointment in her eyes. Seconds feel like hours as I watch her eyes fill with tears. "I thought we were friends," she whispers. "Maybe someday, we could have been *more.*"

I don't call her name. I don't stop her from walking away. I just drop to the floor and bury my head in my hands and wonder what the hell I'm going to do to keep my promise to make it stop. To make it better. To make it *right*.

I should have been her *right*.

✧   ✧   ✧

HER HANDS BARELY touch me. Normally when we ride her arms wrap around my shoulders, and she leans in so close I can feel her breath on my cheek. Sometimes we talk. Most of the time it's just me talking, trying to make her laugh. Trying to gift my ears with the sound that makes my world stop.

She runs upstairs and into my room. She hasn't spoken a word since school let out. I throw myself onto the couch, cover my eyes with my arm, and drown in an abundance of shame and self-pity. "I'm an asshole," I whisper to myself.

"What did you do?" Mom stands over me with her arms crossed and a concerned look on her face. Before I get to answer her, the front door opens.

Lucy.

And her bags.

I stand up and get to her so fast my head spins. "What are you doing?"

She stares down at the floor. "Going home."

"No, you're not." I try to pull the bags from her hands. My voice comes out desperate and needy. Because I am. I'm a desperate, needy brat and she's my toy. And I don't want to let her go.

"What's going on?" Mom says from behind me.

Lucy's gaze lifts now. "Thank you for allowing me to stay in your home," she says, her voice breaking. "I left some money on the counter for the food and stuff. It's not much—"

"Honey." Mom steps around me. "You don't need to do that. It was a pleasure having you here." She lifts her keys off the hook next to the door. "I'll drive you home."

"MOM!" My name's Cameron and I'm four years old.

"I'll wait out front," Lucy says.

Mom waits until Lucy's out of earshot. "She needs to go home, Cam. It's time."

Lucy

THERE'S A RANDOM woman standing in my kitchen and I want to punch her. "Who are you?"

"You must be Lucy."

My arms fold over my chest. "And you must be dumb because I asked you a question."

"Lucy," Dad's voice booms from behind me. He walks up to the woman and stands next to her. At least he's upright, that's something. He smiles. I want to punch them both. *Who is this woman with my dad, cooking in our kitchen and why is he smiling?* He's moved on. This woman is replacing my mom.

"We're poor," I tell her.

Her brows bunch in confusion.

"You're trying to get my dad for his money. He doesn't have any. We're poor." It's a lie. We're not poor. My Dad has his own construction company. We live on a trillion acres and have the biggest house in town. But she probably already knows all that.

"Lucy." Dad shakes his head. "This is Virginia. She's our live-in nanny."

"Live-in?" I scoff. "Where does she live, on Mom's side of the bed? She died in there you know?"

After the crappy day with Cameron, I don't have the strength to filter my thoughts. He was my strength, and now he's gone.

"Give us a minute," Dad says to Virginia. *More like Vagina.*

When she's left the room, Dad approaches me. He smells fresh. Not like the disgusting smell of booze I'd gotten accustomed to. He eyes me up and down. And even though his beard covers most of his face, like it has for years, I can see the frown. I can see the sadness. "Baby girl," he whispers, wrapping me in his arms. "I've missed you so much."

And I'm no longer mad or pissed off at the world. All of a sudden I'm four years old and my daddy's arms are the safest place in the entire world.

He kisses the top of my head and pulls back. "One day I'll make it up to you. I'll be a better man."

"I don't want a better man," I tell him. I hold on to him tighter and wipe my tears on his shirt. "I just want my daddy back."

✧ ✧ ✧

WHEN I APOLOGIZE to Virginia, she chuckles. "It's fine, Lucy," she says. "At least you didn't call me *Vagina.*"

We both laugh just as the doorbell rings. I look from the door, to her. "I'm a nanny, not a maid." But she opens the door anyway.

Mark stands on the other side. He looks panicked. Or afraid. Maybe both.

"If you're here about Cameron, you can save it."

"Cameron? That little turd?" He shakes his head and loosens his tie. "No. Remember how you told me about the spreadsheet and the envelopes and the printing of said spreadsheet on the envelopes?"

I nod.

"I can't work out how to do it and I have another mail out that I need to do by Monday. I need your help." He links his hands together in front of him. "I'm here to offer you a job. No—I'm begging you to *please* take the job." He shakes his joined hands, begging. "Please."

"When?"

"Saturday."

"That's tomorrow."

He nods.

I shrug. "Okay. I'll see you tomorrow."

Seven
Lucy

MARK DROPS A box of envelopes on his desk. "You got everything you need?"

"Yeah."

It takes longer to do what he wanted because the files on his computer are a disorganized mess. I don't know how long he planned on hiring me for, but I end up writing a list of other things that need to be done.

"Yo," I hear, and then a bang.

A piece of paper is being held up against the window of Mark's office with black and white comic strip gracing the page.

Cameron.

For a split second, I actually consider hiding under the desk, but I'm too late. He's already looking into the office, his hand still pressed up against the glass. His eyes go wide. "What—" His voice cracks.

Clearing it, he removes the sheet off the window and steps into the room. "What are you doing here?"

"Mark—" That's all I can get out. *Holy crud bucket he looks good.* He removes his cap and runs a hand through his hair. His stupidly, perfect, messy hair. And then it hits me—what it is that's making all the words catch in my throat. He's in his baseball uniform. I knew he played, I'd seen photos at his house, but I'd never seen it up close, in real life. *Stupid baseball uniform.*

"So?" he says, a smirk developing on his face. He knows I've been checking him out.

"Mark asked me for some help with some stuff, so that he could get some stuff done and he said he needed help with the stuff." I bow my head in shame of the non-sentence I just dribbled.

I hear his footsteps approaching, but I don't look up. Then I smell him, the same smell I'd gotten familiar with from sleeping in his bed the last few nights.

His arm brushes against my chest, causing me to flinch. I push back from the desk. The wheels of the chair catch on the carpet and then I'm falling backwards…

He catches the chair just in time—his stupid smirk getting wider. *Smirk face.* That's what I should call him. Or *smirk-the-jerk.* I laugh to myself.

He looks at me like I'm crazy.

I am. Him and his stupid hair, and his stupid uniform, and his stupid *smirk-the-jerk* face have made me crazy.

His head tilts to the side as he leans over me, his eyes never leaving mine. Then I do something that's legit crazy.

I sniff him.

"Did you just—"

"No."

"I thought I just heard you—"

"No." I square my shoulders. "What do you want?"

He reaches over me, lifts the phone off the base and presses a few buttons. His eyebrows bunch as he takes me in, eyeing me up and down. He clears his throat, the sound repeating through the speakers of the building. "Marky Mark and the Funky Bunch, please return yourself, and all your 'Good Vibrations,' back to your office. There's a beautiful girl sitting at your desk. No need for alarm. Apparently she's just here to sniff around."

A moment later, Mark walks in. He tries to contain his smile, but it's evident he found it just as funny as I did. I don't laugh though, or even smile, because if I did… *smirk-the-jerk* wins.

He smacks Cam on the back of the head. "What did I tell you about using the PA system as your own personal microphone?" He winks down at me. "You want me to tell the beautiful girl at my desk about that time when you were ten, and you thought you could beat-box? And how I had to upgrade the entire phone and PA system because you spit so much saliva into the receiver, there was a permanent crackle in all the speakers?"

Cam's smirk disappears.

And I laugh.

All out laugh.

It completely takes over me.

I've laughed a few times since Mom died, but not like this. Not so hard that I can't control it. I hold my sides, trying to ease the pain. When I finally settle and open my eyes, Mark's gone. Cam is leaning back against the desk watching me with an emotion on his face I can't decipher. He pushes off the desk and blows out a long, heavy breath. "You make my world stop, Lucy."

✧   ✧   ✧

HE'S CHANGED OUT of his baseball uniform and into workout shorts and a loose tank. Apparently, he works at the dealership sometimes—washing cars and whatnot.

I don't watch him just outside the office window. I don't note that boys like him shouldn't look like that at fifteen. I don't constantly zone out thinking about the way he kisses me. I don't stare at him at all. Nope. Not for a second.

I'm not even watching him as a girl comes up and starts talking to him. He stops what he's doing, drops the hose, and walks up to her. I don't notice that he glances into the office quickly. He won't see me watching, because I'm not.

She cocks her hip to the side and crosses her arms just under her breasts, pushing them higher. I recognize the girl—she goes to our school. A junior.

She laughs at something he says and rubs his arm up and down. I'm on my feet, intensely *not* watching them. Then she steps closer, so close they're almost touching. I don't even realize I've left the building until the sun hits my skin—the heat of it matching the heat of my blood that's pulsating in my ears. Before I know it, my eyes are shut, the hose is in my hand, and I'm pulling the trigger.

Her squeal causes me to snap my eyes open.

Cam's back is to me. His shoulders are lifted and his body's rigid.

"What the hell is wrong with you?" she shrieks.

Cam turns around with a glare already in place. When he sees that it's me, the glare fades. He crosses his arms to match hers. "I think you owe Gabby an apology."

"Oh my God," Gabby cries, before turning on her heels and stomping away.

I do the same.

"Where do you think you're going?" Cam yells after me.

"Calling Logan," I shout over my shoulder. I snicker to myself—proud that I was able to come up with a retort so quickly.

It doesn't last long before a cold burst of water hits my back. I freeze. My hands form fists at my sides as I turn to face him. "You're a jerk!"

"Yeah?" he says, dropping the hose. "I know someone who might disagree with you." He flips his cap backwards, and I know what it means. It's *the* sign. The thing he used to do right before he'd kiss me. I play it out in my head—him stepping toward me, grabbing me around the waist and pulling me to him. And then he'd kiss me.

But that's not what happens.

He turns his back to me and marches off. "Yo, Gabby!" he shouts.

And I lose it.

He was right. He makes me crazy.

I run after him and jump onto his back, wrapping my arms around his neck and my legs around his waist.

He bends over himself, and I think he's going to try to shake me off, but somehow, he swings me around so we're face to face with my legs still around him.

He smirks. "What are you doing?"

Stupid smirk. "I'm going to wipe that stupid smirk off your face."

He chuckles. "How?"

"With my fist."

"Do it with your mouth," he challenges.

My body tenses, and I look around. The reason I didn't do this stuff at school still stands. Nothing's changed. Nothing but Gabby—who's now standing only feet away. "Did you call me?" she asks Cam.

And a fire burns in the pit of my stomach. I know what the fire is now. It's jealousy. "Yeah." I glare at her. "He called you a whore."

Cam chuckles. I don't know why, it's not funny.

"Who the hell are you?" she clips.

I roll my eyes and watch Cam's smirk widen. It pisses me off so much that I wipe it off... with my mouth. I kiss him, harder than I've ever kissed him before. Because it's not just a kiss, it's a message.

When I pull back, he quirks an eyebrow in question. With my legs still around him and his arms holding me in place, I shrug. "I don't like sharing."

"Good," he says before moving in for another kiss. My eyes shut, my lips anticipating the feel of his. But it gets cut short when a burst of cold water sprays us both.

I scream.

He grunts.

Mark stands with the hose in his hand and shakes his head at us. "Cool it," he says, squirting us again. "Shit. You're both drenched. You're useless to me now. Get out of here."

We run, hand in hand, to his bike. I jump on the pegs, soaking wet clothes and all. Leaning in as close as I can, I envelop him in my arms.

He tilts his head to look up at me. "I'm sorry about what I said yesterday, but I don't like the thought of sharing you either. No more games. You're my girl now, Luce."

And I swoon.

Just a little.

✧　✧　✧

WE END UP at the river, sitting on the grass and looking out at the water. "So things are good at home—with your dad I mean. He's okay now?"

"I think so. He hired a full-time, live-in nanny."

"I know."

"How do you know?"

"Mom told me last night." He comes closer and throws a lazy arm around my shoulders. "She organized it. Helped him interview for the right one. She's been there every day watching over things."

My eyes go wide. "What? Why would—"

He shrugs, like what he's saying isn't a big deal. "Because she cares about me, and I care about you, so it's important to her."

I press my cheek against his chest to hide my blush. "She lives in the garage apartment. Her name's Virginia."

He scoffs. "Sounds like *vagina*."

✧　✧　✧

WE'RE BOTH LAUGHING when he rides up my driveway. But it stops when we see Dad sitting on the porch playing cars with the kids.

Cameron's shoulders tense beneath my hands, but he doesn't say anything. They stay that way until we come to a stop at the bottom of the porch steps. I hop off the pegs and brush down my clothes, nervous at the situation about to play out. Cameron stares down at the ground, the muscles in his jaw working back and forth. Then Lincoln shouts his name, causing him to look up.

The grin on Cam's face is instant.

Liam follows behind Linc, the same time the front door opens and Logan and Lucas walk out. Not Jackass Logan, my brother Logan.

Lincoln barrels into Cam, his arms wrapped tightly around his waist. "Are you back now? Are you gonna start playing with us again?"

"I can have the bases set up in two minutes," Lucas says, and even though he's only three years younger than us, I can see he's just as excited to see Cam as the rest of them.

"Yeah yeah," Logan joins in.

Dad clears his throat. "It's getting late," he drawls.

"I'll see you guys at the game tomorrow," Cam says to Lincoln and Liam. To me he asks, "You'll be there, too, right?"

I start to answer but Dad cuts in. "She won't be at the game."

"Oh." Any signs of excitement leave him. "I guess I'll see you at school then."

Dad's heavy feet thud against the porch steps as he makes his way down to us.

I don't know if Cam realizes, but he steps in front of me, becoming a shield between my dad and I. My dad's eyes narrow, but the corner of his lips lift. Dad's a big guy, intimidating to most. Cameron just hasn't read him right.

I hold his hand and squeeze once, so he understands that it's okay—that things are settled and that I'm not afraid of him. Not anymore.

"Lucy," Dad says, his voice softening. "Tomorrow's the first Sunday of the month."

MY BREATH CATCHES. "But..."

Cam steps to the side now, allowing Dad and I to speak.

"I know we've never done it—you and me." Dad rubs his hand across his beard. "And I know that it was a day for you and your mom. But she's not here anymore, Lucy. It's just me now. So I'd like to take you out tomorrow. Just the two of us. If you'll have me."

Eight
Lucy

"**Y**OU LOOK EXHAUSTED." I giggle, watching Dad rub his eyes.

"I'm fine, sweetheart." He takes a sip of his coffee. "So this is what you and Mom did? Shop for two hours?"

I nod. "That's just clothes. We haven't hit the bookstore yet."

His eyes widen in shock, but he reins it in quickly. "And how long does that normally take? A half hour?"

My head throws back in laughter. "No, that's the best part of our day. Normally around four—"

He chokes on his coffee.

"But I can be quick. I have a list. Two—tops."

He shakes his head, his grin getting wider. "It's your day, you take as long as you need."

✧ ✧ ✧

DAD FALLS ASLEEP in a chair at the bookstore. He snores so loud that people start complaining. I make quick work of the books I need and chuckle while I shake him awake. "Kathy?" he mumbles. And it's no longer funny.

"No, Dad, it's Lucy. I got what I need. We can go now."

He looks at his watch. "We've only been here an hour."

"It's okay." I smile sadly. "There's one more place I want to take you."

✧ ✧ ✧

I TAKE HIM to the river—the one that runs behind Cameron's house.

"You trust me, right?"

He eyes me warily. "Yes."

I take my shoes off and motion for him to do the same. He hesitates for a moment before agreeing. We walk into the water as far as I can go. I hold both his hands and get him to face me. "I used to hold it all in, like you do. I kept it inside for so long that I felt like I was going to burst. It was constant—this ache in my heart because I missed her so much."

"I'm sorry—" he starts, but I interrupt him.

"No, Dad. I'm not telling you because I want you to be sorry. I'm telling you because I know a way to fix it. To make it stop. To make it *right*. But you have to trust me."

He sucks in a shaky breath, his shoulders lifting with the strength of it. "Okay," he sighs. "Show me."

Eight times.

Eight times he dips his head, and he *screams*.

And he *cries*.

I've never seen my dad cry.

When he's done, he silently walks out of the water and sits on the grass, just like I did.

I sit next to him and wait. Because I know what it's like to be so lost. And so found. All at the same time.

"You've done this before?"

"Yes."

He turns to me. "That boy... Cameron? He helped you with this?"

I nod slowly, unsure of his reaction.

"Tell me about him?"

"What?"

"You mean a lot to him, it's not hard to see that. So tell me about him."

"He's um, in my class. He's fifteen. He plays baseball. And he lives in those houses." I point to the general area of his house.

"No, Luce," he says. "I want you to tell me about *him*. What kind of person he is. *Who* he is."

And without knowing, my smile is back. "He makes me happy."

Dad chuckles. "That's obvious, but tell me why? How?"

I turn to him now, confused by his words.

He rolls his eyes and folds his hands under his chin. Then, with a high-pitched tone to match that of a pre-teen girl, he mocks, "Oh but Daddy, he's just sooo dreamy."

I laugh and punch him on the arm. He nudges my side in response. And that's when I feel a calmness take over—the kind of calmness that can't be obtained from hiding away, or living your life through the pages of a book.

It's the kind of calmness that *fights* the storm.

I let my mind wander to Cameron. My head racing with so many thoughts, I don't know what to say first.

"So?" Dad encourages.

"He's *fierce.*"

His brows rise. "Fierce?"

"Yeah. The way he cares for me—the way he protects me. It's fierce. *He's* fierce." I take a moment to gather my words. "He's a kid, Dad. We both are. But he doesn't act like it, not with me, and not with the boys. The boys—it's like they're his brothers. And I know that even if I weren't in the picture, he would've still been there—showing up every day. He would have done it for them. Because his heart is huge, bigger than anyone I've ever met. And he makes me smile. He makes me laugh. After everything that's happened, I didn't think I'd be able to get back there. Laughing, I mean. I thought it was impossible to be able to laugh again. But he did it; he made my impossible, possible. And he had absolutely no idea he was doing it."

"He sounds like a good man."

"He is, Dad. Really. You'd like him."

He smiles at me. The same proud smile he's always had. Sometimes, like now, I think he saves that look just for me.

"So when can I meet him?"

Cameron

Luce: I have a field trip all day today, but I don't want you to think I'm ignoring you or 'studying.' Just thought you should know so you don't worry. Or whatever.

I READ OVER the text I received from her this morning. I don't know why I keep doing it. I've memorized it. It's seared into my brain. Because it's not just a text, it's a confirmation of what she is to me.

When I look up, I see Logan watching me. He shakes his head. "I give it two weeks before she owns your balls."

I chuckle and finish dressing for practice. "Quit being jealous." I pat him on the head as I walk past. "One day you'll meet a girl that's gonna knock you off that high horse of yours and you'll gladly hand her your balls."

He scoffs. "Not me, asshole. Never." He shivers. "Ever." The look of disgust on his face makes me laugh.

We all head out of the locker room and toward the field. Just as I'm about to pass the gates, I hear her call my name. I turn around to see her running to me. "Wait!" she yells, and it makes me laugh. Of course I'd wait. I'd wait *forever* for her. She stops only a few feet away from me and bends over, trying to catch her breath.

"Where did you run from?"

"The bus," she pants.

"That's like six yards away."

She flattens her palm on my stomach and attempts to push me, but she's too damn weak and it has absolutely no effect. "I'm sorry Mr. Jockface, I don't run laps for fun."

I smile, watching, and waiting for her breathing to settle. When it does, she straightens to full height. She tries to contain her smile when she says, "I was hoping to catch you before practice."

"Well, you got me."

She chews her lip, her eyes scanning the area around us. All of my excitement from seeing her is instantly drained. Her words come back to me, the ones that tell me she's afraid of being seen with me. Afraid of what people think of her. I make a mental note to find out who the hell said what, and punch them. I've never really been the physical type, but apparently she makes me punchy.

I step forward and hesitate, only for a moment, before bravely taking her hands.

She gasps, her gaze slowly lifting to mine.

My brows rise in question. I need her to know that she's mine now, and all the petty dramas of high school, the whispers and the rumors—they can go to hell. I'll make it right.

She yanks her hands out of my hold. The feeling of rejection almost kills me. But then she rests one on my chest, the other moving my cap backwards. She settles her hand on the back of neck and pulls my face down to hers.

And then she does it again—wipes the stupid smirk off my face with her mouth.

I don't realize I've lifted her in the air until Logan shouts at us to break it up.

I set her on the ground, my eyes never leaving hers.

She laughs quietly before wrapping her arms around my waist. Her head tilts all the way back to look up at me. "So are you coming over after practice?"

"Of course."

"Good, my dad wants to meet you."

My face falls.

She laughs.

"COME ON!" Logan yells.

"See you soon," she says, walking backwards and away from me. Then I grab my hat to cover my junk and sit on a bench. "I need a minute," I shout to Logan.

Stupid boner.

✧   ✧   ✧

MY PALMS ARE already sweating when I knock on her door.

She opens it with a smile already in place. It should calm me, but it doesn't.

"Are you okay?"

I nod.

She eyes me warily before taking my hand and leading me to the kitchen. Her dad's already there—sitting at the counter. He gazes up when I walk into the room.

And then he grunts.

I swear it—even if I'd walked up to the house and seen him cleaning a shotgun on the porch—that single grunt is a shit ton more intimidating.

Lucy walks me to the other side of the counter and motions for me to sit.

I do.

He grunts again.

I flinch.

"Stop it, Daddy," she hisses from next to me.

And then he chuckles, his entire body shaking with the force of it.

I don't dare laugh. Or even smile. I'm too scared to do anything.

She holds my hand under the counter. "He's joking," she says, but it makes no difference.

He comes to a stand, his huge frame shadowing us. He opens his mouth, and for a split second I envision *Godzilla* eating all the people of Tokyo. This is bad. This is really, really bad.

"Breathe, son," he says. And I do. I'd do anything he asks—shotgun or not. "So…" He leans his elbows on the counter and looks between Lucy and I. He let's out a sigh and scratches his beard. "I'm out of my element here. I don't really know what I should be saying." He shakes his head slowly and then looks right at me. But it's not the same look. This one isn't made for intimidation.

We stare at each other for such a long time that I wonder if he's ever going to speak. "She's my little girl, Cameron." His voice breaks. Lucy holds my hand tighter. "She's my little girl and I don't know what to say right now. Kathy—Lucy's mother, she would have been great at this. This whole meeting you… setting rules thing." He smiles, but it's sad. "I just…" his words die in the air. He looks at Lucy with a cloud of failure and disappointment on his face.

I clear my throat. He focuses his gaze on me. I take a deep breath and let it out in a whoosh. "I've been seeing Lucy almost every day since your wife passed, sir. I enjoy spending time with her and the boys. The boys have become like brothers to me. I intend—no—I *hope* to still be able to do that. I have a ten o'clock curfew on weekdays, and a one a.m. curfew on weekends. But I can change that to whatever Lucy wants, or whatever you set for her. I'm not sure if you know that I help coach the twins at the little league games on the weekend. I'd like to be able to take Lucy out afterwards. I don't really know what we'd be doing; she's my first girlfriend so I guess I'd need to think of some stuff. But I can be sure to run things by you first, sir, if that's what you want. We're only fifteen. My mode of transportation is a bike, so I don't think we'd be doing much of anything. I turn sixteen in a few months and plan to get my license. When that happens, I'll come to you and we can set new ground rules. If that suits you, sir."

Silence.

Then his sharp intake of breath fills my ears. He raises a hand, and I flinch and shut my eyes tight, waiting for the impact of his fist on my face.

It never comes.

When I open my eyes, his smile is tight.

"Shake his hand," Lucy whispers.

My gaze moves to his outstretched, waiting, hand. I stand and shake it.

"I'm Tom," he says, and then turns to Lucy. "Could you give us a minute?"

"Dad!" Lucy whines.

"It's okay, Luce," I assure, releasing his hand.

He waits until she's out of the room before speaking. "Lucy describes you as fierce."

I grimace. "Because I punched you? I'm sorry about that."

"No," he says shaking his head. "She says you're fierce in the way you care about her. And the way you protect her."

"I guess." I shrug.

He lets out a heavy breath. "She's right. It's not hard to see that. It's also not hard to see that the boys like having you around. To be honest, Cameron, I'm not really happy that she has a boyfriend. And I'm not happy that said boyfriend has such a big presence in her life. But I'm not going to stop it. It's not to say that I don't like you, I just don't like *it*. But I'll tolerate it. That's all I can offer for now."

I jerk my head in a nod. "And that's all I can ask for, sir."

✧　✧　✧

SHE WALKS AHEAD of me, through the woods behind her house, laughing the entire time. "You should have seen your face!"

"Dude, your dad's huge. A hurricane couldn't move him. I got scared. I'm allowed."

She stops in her tracks and faces me. "Did you have that speech prepared?"

"What speech?"

"Everything you just said back there."

I shrug. "It wasn't a speech, I was just talking."

Taking my hand, she walks us past the woods and to a clearing which opens up to a lake. My eyes soak in the scenery. "Holy shit, this is on your property?"

"Yup." She tugs on my hands to get my attention. "Thank you, Cam."

"What for?"

"For saying what you did. For knowing that he needed help and giving him that piece of mind. He has enough to worry about at the moment, and you, saying what you said, it gives him one less thing to worry about. He appreciates that... even if he never tells you."

I move in to kiss her but she steps back, then slowly starts to lift her dress.

My eyes go wide.

I'm about to have sex.

She's wearing a bikini.

Holy shit.

She shoves my chest. Hard. "Quit staring!"

But I can't. My mouth's dry. I try to swallow. I fail.

She laughs.

My breathing stops.

My dick—I have no idea what the hell it's doing.

She walks to the end of the dock and dives in. "Coming?"

Yeah. *In my shorts.* Right now.

I'm ruined.

Ruined.

Nine

Cameron

IT TOOK ME two weeks to convince Lucy to sit with us at lunch, and another week for her to be comfortable with it.

Her dad came up with a few more rules after he had some time to think about it. He asked for my phone number, which I was more than happy to supply. Schoolwork came first, which was fine, because she ended up helping me study anyway. And the main ones; doors to remain open if we were in a room together, and never, under any circumstance, ever, am I allowed to step foot on the stairs leading to the bedrooms. Ever. For that last one, he made a point of showing me his shotgun. It was meant to be a threat, but when I asked him if he could teach me how to use it, his eyes lit up.

A scrunched up napkin smacks my forehead, pulling me out of my thoughts. My gaze lifts to Logan sitting opposite me. His brows are furrowed as he jerks his head toward Lucy sitting next to me. I turn my attention to her; she's focused on her e-reader, her eyes wildly moving from side to side. She uses a fork to pick at her fruit salad, but she doesn't eat it. Actually, she hasn't eaten anything on her tray.

I switch back to Logan. "What's with her?" he mouths.

I shake my head, telling him to leave it alone. Then her cackle of laughter interrupts us. She laughs so hard her eyes start watering.

The sound of it is so infectious I find myself smiling down at her. "What happened?"

"The guy…" She stops to take a breath. "In this book…" We all wait for her to calm down. "Came in his pants while they were dry humping!"

"How awkward," Jake states.

Logan watches her with amusement in his eyes. "What the hell do you read, girl?"

She shakes her head and wipes her eyes. "Oh man, that was good."

Lucy

"I HAVE TO talk to you about something," he says.

My body immediately tenses. I try to hide my reaction and finish watering the plants on the porch.

He takes a seat on the steps and motions for me to sit next to him. "I don't know how to bring it up and I'm scared that it's going to upset you."

I turn to him now, trying to mask my emotions.

I knew it was coming.

Setting the watering can down by my feet, I take the few steps toward him. I hesitate a moment, not sure that I'm physically capable of taking the blow he's about to deliver. I find the strength I need before sitting down and taking his hand. "It's okay, Cameron. I understand." I turn my body toward him. "I mean I was expecting it to happen, I just didn't want it to happen so soon."

He looks down at me, his frown consuming his entire face. "So, you know what I want to talk about?"

I nod slowly, knowing things were too good to be true. I had to be grateful it lasted as long as it did. "Yes," I answer. "And it's fine. You don't need to spare my feelings. I'm just thankful you came into my life."

He opens his mouth to speak but I interrupt him. "You don't have to tell me, but do you think I could have done anything different? Could I have been better somehow?"

He rears back, his brows bunching. "What are you talking about, Luce?"

"Maybe I kiss wrong or something. Is that it? Or, is it because you wanna kiss other girls? Please don't tell me you've *already* kissed other girls." I feel the bile rise to my throat, but I push it down.

"Lucy—"

"I know that your friends are like that. I hear the stories, you know— that they go out and make out with random girls, or whatever. Was she just a random girl? I don't know what would hurt more. No—don't tell me. Ple—"

"Lucy—"

"Oh man. I was prepared to be hurt." I suck in a breath and press a hand to my heart. "I didn't think it would hurt this much."

"LUCY, stop!" His voice is loud. Commanding. His hand rises and wipes at my cheeks. Tears. I was crying. I was so overwhelmed with the pain of heartbreak that I didn't realize I was crying. "Baby." His eyes roam my face. "What are you talking about?"

"You." I push his hand away and ignore the look of hurt that washes over him. "You kissing other girls."

He shakes his head slowly. "Lucy, I'm not kissing other girls."

"But you want to, right?"

He fights to contain his smirk. "What the hell is going on in that head of yours?"

"You! You're in my head," I whine. "You used to make out with girls all the time. I know I wasn't your first kiss. And you told my dad that you've never had a girlfriend before, so I know they didn't mean anything to you and now you're sitting on my porch steps and you want to break up—"

"Whoa." He covers my mouth with his hand. All signs of his previous smirk completely gone. "Stop." His breaths are heavier now, matching mine. He slowly removes his hand, cautious of whether I plan to keep talking. "Babe," he sighs. And I start crying again. He wraps an arm around my shoulders and pulls me into him. Then he starts laughing.

He's laughing at me crying.

I try to stand so I can kick him in the head and run inside, but he holds on to me tighter. "You're crazy," he states.

I pull away, using strength I didn't know existed. "I hate you!"

He laughs harder, wrapping both arms around me this time.

I should have stood up when I had the chance and kicked him twice. "Stop it, Luce. How the hell could you possibly think I'd be with anyone else but you?" He grasps my shoulders and holds me away from him so he can look me in the eyes. "I'm crazy about you. How can you not see that? How can anybody that sees me with you not see that? Yes, there have been other girls. And yes, they didn't mean anything to me. But you do, Luce. You mean the world to me."

Breathe.

He leans in carefully as if hesitating. And then he kisses me. Slowly.

Softly. And with each second his mouth is on mine, he repairs my broken heart. When he pulls back, his eyes penetrate mine. "Better?" he whispers.

"Yes."

"Good." He smiles and kisses me again, quicker this time. "Are you going to let me speak now?"

I can't help the laugh that escapes. "Yes."

"Okay." He pauses a moment, preparing his next words. "That night you thought Lachlan was sick… and I walked in—"

"No," I interrupt. I look away from him, too embarrassed by what he saw. "If you're asking if I'm still doing it, the answer is no."

"Good. That's good."

Moments of silence pass, neither knowing what to say next.

"Can I ask you something else?"

I can hear the wariness in his voice and it makes me nervous, but I suck it up because he's earned the right to all the answers. "You can ask me anything."

"Why did you do it?"

"Do what?" I say, even though I know exactly what he's asking.

"Make yourself throw up like that? Is it because you think you're fat—because I can tell you now—"

"No." I turn to him so we're face to face. He likes that—likes to be able to see my face. He says it's because he likes to *read* me. "When Mom started to get sick, things got hard for me."

"It's okay," he says quickly, "you don't need to talk about it. I'm sorry for asking."

Inhaling a shaky breath, I move closer and let him hold me. "Things got hard. It's like every day passed and I was barely living through it. The sun rose and all I felt was emptiness. It was the same. Every single day she was dying. And every day I was watching. Waiting. And it never seemed to end. I felt like it was happening to me. Her death felt like it was mine. And sometimes I'd cry for hours. Sometimes it would be silent, and other times I cried so hard it made me throw up. The first time I did it, it wasn't intentional. And then it started to happen more, and I started to feel something. Looking back, I don't even know what it was. But it made me feel… alive? And I needed that. At that time, I needed to feel something different. Something that didn't make me feel like I was living in an eternal loop surrounded by death."

"I'm so sorry, Luce." His voice breaks, and I know without having to look at him that he's holding back tears. I know because regardless of what I thought was happening only minutes ago, I know how he feels about me. I know the *fierce* protectiveness he has for me. "What changed?"

I look up at him now, his eyes are glazed, watching me with an intensity that makes my heart hammer against my chest. The ache is still there, but it's not heartbreak. It's something else. Something that kids at fifteen shouldn't be feeling. "What made you stop?" he asks.

I don't hesitate. I don't skip a beat. "*You*, Cameron. *You* changed. *You* came into my life and *you* healed me. *You* made me feel alive again."

I tell him the truth, and with that, I give him my heart. *Forever.*

Ten
Cameron

SHE STANDS IN front of her locker and chews the last of her apple, making sure that I see it. She's been doing that a lot since the conversation we had on her porch a few weeks ago. It's kind of cute—the way she wants to assure me that I have nothing to worry about. She could be two hundred and fifty pounds and I'd still worry about her.

She hands me the core to put in the trash, then reaches into her locker and picks up a note. She unfolds it and reads it slowly, about as slow as the smile that pulls on her lips.

"What is it?" I ask, trying to keep my curiosity in check. There's a note in her locker… and whatever it says is making her smile. *Someone else* is making her smile.

She puts the note back and shrugs. "Nothing."

"I call bullshit, Luce. What is it?"

Her eyes roll as she reaches back in, grabbing the piece of paper and slapping it against my chest.

> **Thanks for being an awesome lab partner.**
> **You make learning fun.**
>
> > **–Adam.**

I scrunch up the note and toss it in the trash. "You make learning fun?" I scoff. "What a douche thing to say."

"It's nice," she says, her voice laced with sympathy. "Leave it alone."

"You think it's nice?" I laugh once. "You're being naïve, Luce. He wants in your pants."

Her jaw drops.

I roll my eyes.

JAY McLEAN

She narrows hers.

"Whatever. Some other guy's leaving notes in your locker and making you smile. I'm supposed to be okay with that?" I slam my palm against a locker and walk away. She shouts my name, but I ignore it. Maybe she thinks I'm being a dick but I don't. I have every right to be pissed.

"Cameron!" She pulls on my arm, stopping me from going any further.

"What!" I turn around, prepared for an argument, but she's smiling. *I'm pissed and she's smiling at me.*

She yanks on my hand and leads me out of the hallway and through the exit so we're alone. Throwing her hand out, palm up, she says, "Phone."

"What?"

"Give me your phone."

I do what she says. Logan was right, in the couple of months we've been dating, she's made quick work of owning my balls.

She taps the phone a couple times and then hands it back to me. "That's my locker combination," she says. "You can go in there and check it whenever you want. I have nothing to hide from you, Cameron."

My shoulders slump. I hadn't realized how tense I was until now. "Which Adam is it, Lucy? Masters or Deluca?"

Her lips thin to a line.

I try to get past her but she rests her palms flat on my chest and pushes until I'm against the wall—her tiny frame presses into my front, blocking me from going anywhere. "Stop it," she says, her eyes dancing with amusement.

"This shit's not funny. Tell me or I'll punch them both."

She laughs at that, and for a split second I want to, too. I sound like an asshole. I *am* an asshole. I put a hand on her waist, the other in her hair, pulling her closer to me. "I don't like it," I say, forcing myself to calm down. "You're mine, and assholes here need to know that."

"Okay." She nods, reaching up and kissing me quickly. "Um…" She chews her lip and looks away, her cheeks redder than they were only moments ago.

"What, Luce? What were you going to say?" I duck my head and block her vision, making sure she has no choice but to look at me.

"The older girls, I see them wearing their boyfriend's jerseys… with their names on the back… you—I mean me—we… we could do that?"

My eyes widen, and so does my pathetic grin. "You'd want to do that? You're not an object. I don't want you to think that I own you."

She shrugs. "Why not? I'm yours."

I NEVER DID find out which Adam it was so I threaten to punch them both. Logan laughs, but I don't care. Lucy makes me punchy.

Lucy

I LOOK DOWN at the jerseys on top of my feet. They've just fallen out of my locker. There has to be over twenty of them. All with the name Gordon printed on the back.

"I didn't know which one would go best with these short frilly skirts and cowboy boots you always wear, so I gave you choices." He kisses me once, tugging on my top, before leaning his shoulder on the locker next to mine. "Good morning."

I try to contain my smile. "Morning." I pick a random one and shrug it on. "How do I look?"

He stands frozen. Eyes wide, mouth open, frozen.

"Cam?"

He snaps out of his daze and looks around—the halls are empty. He knows I like to come to school early, so now he does, too. Apparently spending every second of our free time together isn't enough. Not for us. We need the extra half hour.

Taking my hand, he leads me to an empty classroom. He closes the door behind me and slowly maneuvers me against it. He leans in close, his breath brushing my cheek when he whispers in my ear, "You look…" He pulls back, unable to finish his sentence. His eyes roam me from head to toe. I can feel the heat take over my body. He moves in, placing his lips on mine, but he doesn't move them. It's like he's hesitating and I have no idea why. Finally, he opens his mouth, letting out a moan at the same time.

And then he kisses me.

Holy shit, does he kiss me.

We've kissed before, more than a few times. Each kiss is better than the last. But they've always been just that. Kisses. This—this is driven by pure need. Pure want.

He pauses, takes a breath, and whispers, "Shit." Then continues where he left off. I pull on his shirt, wanting him as close as possible. There's resistance. *Why is he resisting?* I release his shirt, grip his hips, and roughly pull him to me.

He immediately stops kissing and lets his head fall on my shoulder. And I'm glad he does because my jaw's on the floor and I've lost the ability to move.

"Luce," he whispers, stepping back.

I try to swallow, but my eyes won't leave the huge bulge in his shorts.

"It's not like I can help..." His words die in the air when he sees my hand rise.

The rest of my body is frozen, but my hand won't stop reaching for him. My eyes are fixed. They can't look away.

"Luce," he says again, almost like a warning.

My hand flattens on his stomach as I take a step forward.

I lift my head to see him watching me. Not my hand, but my face. His eyes bore into mine. His mouth's clamped shut and his jaw's tense.

I move my hand lower.

His eyes drift shut.

Lower.

He lets out a groan.

And then I touch it.

"Shit," he breathes.

"Penis," I squeak.

✧   ✧   ✧

PENIS.

Penis Penis.

Penis Penis Penis.

THAT'S ALL I'VE thought about since touching him this morning. I had to draw a diagram of test tubes in science lab. You know what I drew? Penis.

Penis Penis.

"I HAVE A lot of homework tonight, so maybe skip coming over?"

He pulls his bike out of the rack but refuses to look at me. "Okay, see ya!"

Cameron

FOR TWENTY MINUTES I try to catch Mark's gaze while him and Mom sit on the couch watching TV. When he finally realizes, I inconspicuously jerk my head toward the stairs. "My room," I mouth.

His eyes narrow in confusion.

I widen my eyes, and do it again, as if doing so will make him understand.

He shakes his head slowly.

"Now," I mouth, and then run up the stairs and into my room.

He makes me wait another ten minutes before knocking on my door. He must be able to see the panic on my face because his confusion turns to concern. "What's with you?"

"Something's wrong with my dick."

"WHAT!"

I shut the door and tell him to keep it down.

"I'm panicking here, kid. What the hell?"

"You should be panicking! I'm panicking. Something's wrong with my dick."

His voice rises. "What the hell does that mean? What happened to it?"

"Lucy touched it and she—"

"Lucy touched your thing?" he shouts.

I pick up the nearest thing I can reach and throw it at his head; a piece of paper. "Keep your voice down, jerk. Mom doesn't need to hear about my broken dick!"

"It's broken!?" he shouts again.

I sigh and flop down on my bed.

"Okay." He starts pacing the room. "Rewind and tell me what happened from the beginning."

"Okay." I blow out a breath and try to calm down. "So she touched my dick."

"Where?"

"MY DICK! Are you not listening?"

"Settle down, asshole. Where were you when she touched…" His face contorts to a grimace. "You know… your…"

"My dick? At school."

"HOLY SHIT! What the hell are they letting happen in schools these days?"

"What?" I yell, frustrated. "No! It's not like she pulled my pants down in the cafeteria while we were all eating lunch and decided to tug me."

"Gross."

"Shut up!" I stand up and start pacing with him. "It was like… a little brush."

"A little brush?"

"Her hand! It kind of just… brushed me."

"And then?"

"And she hasn't spoken to me since. She didn't want me at her house. She thinks it's broken or something."

"What the hell?" He stops pacing and rests his hands on his hips, shaking his head and looking down at the floor. "So what do you want me to do?"

"I don't know!" I throw my hands in the air. Then drop my pants. "Check it!"

"Jesus Christ!" He turns swiftly—one hand covering his eyes, the other waving me off. "Put your pants back on!"

I sigh and pull them up. "I don't know what's wrong with it!"

"I'm not a doctor, I can't tell. Do you even have pubes yet?" He turns slowly, opening one eye first, scoping me out, then opening the other.

"Yes, I have pubes. I'm not eight."

He rolls his eyes. "So she brushed a hand on your… you know… and then she didn't want to see you?"

"Yeah. Me, or my broken dick."

He laughs, but then stops when he sees that I'm not even close to joking. "She's probably just nervous, or embarrassed. I'm sure it's nothing. You guys are young, probably too young to be touching each other like that. Maybe it just surprised her and she feels awkward. You just need to talk to her. Like adults… and go from there."

I nod, my breath finally resembling something like normal.

He walks to the door and places his hand on the handle. "You okay, Cam?"

"Yeah," I rush out. "I think so."

"Okay." He turns the doorknob, but doesn't open the door. All signs of amusement and panic have left him. "Thank you for coming to me with this. It means a lot."

I shrug, confused by his words. "Why wouldn't I?"

✧   ✧   ✧

"SO WE NEED to talk about what happened yesterday." We're at the dock on her lake, sitting opposite each other. We're trying to study but I can see her eyes keep wandering to my junk.

"About what?" she says, her eyes forced to focus on her textbook.

"About what happened in the classroom."

She looks up at me now. "Penis?"

I throw my pen in the water and lie down on the wooden planks. "Oh my God," I groan. "I can't believe we're having this conversation. I want to die." *Stupid Marky Mark and his stupid advice can get funked.*

"What's wrong?" she says, her voice dripping with innocence. She has no idea I spent all night examining my broken dick. And not in the good way, either.

"I don't think we should do it again," I say, the same time she says, "I want to touch it again."

"What?" we both huff.

I sit up, bend my knees and rest my elbows on them. "Lucy..." I shake my head, not believing what I'm about to say. "I think maybe we need to cool it with that. Look at how we reacted. I just think maybe we're not mature enough to deal with that kind of stuff. The sex stuff."

"But penis," she whispers.

I eye her curiously, but continue anyway. "I know that I may have gotten a little… full on yesterday, and I apologize. But I think we should keep these hormones in check, just for a little bit."

"So, no penis?"

"No penis." I laugh. "And I think you should stop calling it a penis."

She throws her head back in laughter and lies down next to me. Taking my hand, she says quietly, "But I can't stop thinking about penis."

A slow chuckle builds in the back of my throat. "You better shut that shit down. Get rid of it now."

She sucks in a loud, long breath. "PEEEEENNNNIIIIIIIIIISSSS!" she shouts. "Wow, I feel so much better now."

Eleven
Cameron

"**W**HAT THE HELL are we doing here? And what's that smell?" She sniffs the air with a look of disgust on her face.

"I want to show you something." I lead her through the junkyard until I find what we came for. "So, what do you think?"

We stand in front of an old bus, and I mean *old*. Late-sixties-VW-hippie-bus, kind of old.

She looks at me like I'm crazy. "What do I think about what?"

I shake my head and stand in front of the bus, tapping it a few times. "I think I'm going to name her Filmore, like in that movie *Cars*."

"Yeah." She rolls her eyes. "Six little brothers, remember? I know the movie."

"So?" I ask again.

Her eyes narrow. "Why a bus like this though? I mean, why not just get a normal car?"

"I don't know." I shrug. "I figure I'm a few months older than you, so I've got a few months of driving you and your brothers around."

Her eyes widen. "What?" she almost yells. Then tears instantly well in her eyes.

I step closer and make her look up at me, just to be sure I wasn't imagining it. "Why are you crying? What happened?"

"You can't buy a bus to drive me and my brothers around, Cam. That's just stupid."

"What?" I cross my arms over my chest. "Who says I can't?"

"Me!" She points to herself. "You're fifteen years old, Cameron. You don't need to do this. You don't need to take care of me, or my brothers. They're not your responsibility!"

"Lucy, I've already bought it, and you need to calm down. It's not like—"

"No, I will not calm down." Great, now she's pissed. "You can't choose a car based on me *or* my life."

"Why?" I yell. And now I'm pissed.

She takes a deep breath, her fists balled at her sides. "Fine, Cameron," she snaps through clenched teeth. "I'm breaking up with you!"

My heart drops. What? "What?" I say out loud.

She turns in her spot and starts walking away. I chase after her, pulling on her arm to stop her.

She turns to me, her eyes narrowed.

"You can't break up with me, Luce. Come on." My voice breaks. I'm on the edge of crying. I'm a pussy. I admit it. But she's threatening to walk and I can't let it happen. She's my world.

She must realize what she's done because her glare turns to sympathy and her mouth turns to a frown. "I'm sorry," she says, wrapping her arms around my waist and looking up at me. "I didn't mean that."

I hold her head close to my chest, waiting for the beating of my heart to settle.

"Okay," she agrees, "I'll let you buy it on one condition."

I pull back and laugh a little. *Fine, I'll entertain her.* Raising my eyebrows, I say, "What? What's your condition?"

Getting out of my hold, she walks back to the bus. She sticks her head inside and looks around before turning to me. "The day you get your license…" She takes two steps to cover the distance between us. "You pick me up and take me somewhere secluded, and we make out in the back. For *hours.*"

My eyes go huge and I slowly nod. "That can be arranged."

She smiles. "And I'm talking full on making out, Cameron. I mean, I want you shirtless and horizontal." I try not to look down at my shorts, positive I'm sporting a semi. She continues, "And *I* want to be shirtless and you better be touching boob."

I choke on air.

She giggles and then crosses her arms over her breasts. "Deal?"

I think I agree, but I can't be sure, because now all I can think about is boob. I place my hands on her waist and gently push her until she's against the bus.

And then I kiss her.

Her hands go to my hair, tugging a little, and bringing me closer to her.

And we kiss.

When she finally loosens her hold, I pull back.

She kisses me once, and then sighs. "You really bought this bus, huh?"

I nod.

"So that you can help me out with my brothers?"

I nod again. "Of course, Luce, you're my girl. It's my job to take care of you."

Her eyes glaze over with tears again.

I wanted to kick myself for making her cry. But before I can say anything, she wraps her arm around my neck and brings me down for another quick kiss. She pulls away and says, "I *really* like you, Cameron."

I grin. "Yeah?"

"Yeah," she says dreamily.

And then my heart begins to race.

My palms begin to sweat.

And all I can hear is the blood pumping in my ears.

"Good," I respond, and then inhale a huge breath. "Because I'm kind of in love with you, Lucy."

Her eyes bug out. Her jaw drops to the floor. "What?" she breathes out.

I lift my chin and fake a confidence that doesn't exist. "You heard me."

Silence.

It's the longest three seconds of my life.

Then finally, "Cameron, I love you so much."

And then she kisses me.

FIVE WEEKS, THREE days and eight hours later, I touch boob.

✧ ✧ ✧

"I'VE BEEN THINKING," she says, snapping her bra back on. I've parked the bus near her dock on her lake. It seems fitting—considering it's become our spot.

I crack a few windows in the bus and then sit back down next to her. She lays her head on my lap and looks up at me. And I can't help but smile. "What have you been thinking?"

She lifts her head to kiss my bare chest and then starts tracing hearts over it. "I think I want to wait. For sex, I mean. I was thinking about what you said, you know... after Penisgate."

I laugh. "Penisgate?"

"Yeah, you know... all scandalous things end in 'gate.'"

I suppress my smile. "Yeah."

"Okay, so after Penisgate... I got to thinking... and I think you're right—about being ready... emotionally. I don't think I am yet."

"Okay, so we wait." I shrug.

"If that's okay?"

I roll my eyes. "Of course it's okay, Luce. I'd never make you do something you weren't ready for. You know that."

"I know," she says, kissing my chest again. "The thing is, I don't want to promise you a time or date or anything, because I can't tell, and I don't want you—"

"Stop," I cut her off. "You don't need to promise anything. When it happens, it happens." And as the words leave my lips, there isn't an ounce of doubt in my mind that I'd wait forever for her.

"What?" She must see that my head's somewhere else because she asks, "What are you thinking?"

My mind's racing with so many thoughts, so many emotions—that I struggle to find the words. I struggle to speak. "It's dumb."

She reaches up and runs a finger across my jaw. "Tell me anyway."

I lift my knees, causing her head to rise. I kiss her softly, knowing that our lips are raw from making out for so long. "Luce..." I blow out a breath and ignore the ache in my chest. I don't know what it is, or why it's there. "Sometimes I think that this—you and me—this could be as good as it gets for the rest of my life and that would be perfect. I feel like I've loved you for eternity, and it's not even close to long enough. Even now, when it's summer and there's no school and we can spend every second of every day together, it doesn't seem like enough. Do you think it's normal? To feel that? To be sixteen and feel like your life begins and ends with one person?"

She shakes her head slowly. "It's not dumb," she says. "And I don't know what's normal. I know that I love you, and I know that I feel sorry for all the people that never get to experience the kind of love we have. Even if it's short lived."

My brows bunch. "You think ours will be short lived?"

She shakes her head slowly. "I don't think anything can ever get in the way of our love. Ever."

Lucy

THERE'S A BANGING on my bedroom door—or so I think. When I open my eyes I'm not in my room. But the banging is incessant.

"What's going on?" Cam blinks rapidly, trying to wake himself. The banging won't stop.

"LUCY!" Dad's voice jerks us both awake. "LUCY!" he shouts again. He's slamming his palm on the back window of Cam's bus.

"Oh my God, Cam. We must've fallen asleep!"

He doesn't speak, his focus solely on my breasts. I look down. "Shit," I whisper. I'm not wearing a shirt, just my bra.

"LUCY!"

I find my shirt and rush to put it on, even though I know it's too late. Dad's face is pressed against the window. I'm sure he's already seen us. And Cam—he's shirtless, too.

"Nothing happened," he rushes out. "We didn't do anything wrong." And even as he says it, I can see the panic in his eyes. "We just need to explain it to him, okay? It'll be fine."

He puts on his shirt and opens the door. "Mr. Preston," he starts, his hands going up in surrender. "We fell asleep. I'm sorry. It's my fault. I should—"

"Shut up!" Dad growls. "Just shut up, Cameron."

"DAD!" I try to get off the bus but he grips my arm tight and roughly pulls me down. He uses so much force I fall to the ground. "Dad, stop! You're hurting me!" I pull out of his hold and try to straighten.

Cameron's arms are around my waist, helping me to stand upright. But I can't. Dad's pulling me away again.

Away from Cameron.

"Mr. Preston." Cam's in front of us now, walking backwards and trying to talk sense into him. "I swear to you, nothing happened."

But Dad doesn't care.

And now I'm crying.

I use all of my strength, shrug out of his hold, and run to Cameron. He stops walking and moves me behind him, becoming a shield between us, like he's done before. "We fell asleep—" Cam starts.

"Shut up!" Dad shouts. "I told you to shut up!" He shoves Cam out of the way so forcefully that he hits the ground hard.

I try to say his name but I can't. I can't because my cries won't let me. I can't breathe. I can't see through the tears.

Then Dad looks at me—right into my eyes. And even through his anger I can see the truth; *shame.*

He sucks in a breath, as if trying to calm himself, but it doesn't work, because his eyes narrow and a look of pure hatred washes over him. If he says what he says next to *ruin* me, it works. "What would your mother think if she were alive? What do you think she'd say if she knew her daughter was a *whore?*"

Empty. Darkness.

That's all I feel. That's all I see.

Somewhere in the distance, I hear Cameron's voice. "Don't you dare talk to her like that."

His hand on mine is pure fire.

It burns.

It hurts.

I hurt.

Everywhere.

I open my eyes, and I let the numbness from the hurt drive me. "Go home, Cameron."

✧　✧　✧

EVERY DAY FOR the next two weeks he knocks on our door. Vagina tells him I'm not allowed visitors; Dad's orders. But she knows. She sees me. She understands. It's not just Dad that won't allow it. I won't either. Every day I watch him from the window in my room as he gets in his shitty bus, the one he bought for *us.* He sits in the driver's seat and looks up at my window—for minutes that feel like hours. I know because I watch him. I watch him watch me, and I do nothing to make the pain go away. Not for him, or for me.

Dad doesn't speak to me. He won't even look at me. I'm his only daughter. His daughter—the *whore*.

I don't leave the house. I barely leave my room. The place is always full of people, full of laughter, full of joy. Me? I'm empty. I feel nothing. Absolutely nothing but the constant churning in my stomach. Sometimes, I let that churning feeling control me. And sometimes, I empty that feeling.

Cameron

FOR TWO WEEKS I try to see her. I need to make sure that she's okay. If she feels half of what I feel, I know she's hurting. And the kind of hurt she feels shouldn't exist. Which is why I find myself in the last place any sane person would be. "Is Mr. Preston here?"

The middle-aged man removes his hard hat and looks up from the blueprints in front of him. He eyes me up and down quickly before asking, "You here for a job?"

"No, sir." I take a look around the construction site. "I'm here to speak to Mr. Preston."

He nods and walks away.

And I wait.

With sweaty palms and a hammering heart, I wait.

"What do you want?" His voice makes me jump, but I hide the reaction.

"I need to talk to you."

"I have nothing to say to you."

He starts to leave, and for a split second I almost give up. I know men like him; my dad is just like him. His pride comes first and his sense comes second. He wants to be right, even when he's wrong, and he likes to have power over me. But this is bigger than his pride. And it's bigger than him and I. "I think Lucy's sick."

He freezes, his shoulders rigid, and his breath heavy. He slowly turns to me, his mask faltering. "What do you mean she's sick?"

I ask him to talk somewhere more private. No one needs to know his business, and I'm not one to air it publicly.

He takes me to his portable office and sits behind his desk. I stay standing. I don't want to get comfortable, and he shouldn't have that luxury either. "While your wife was dying, Lucy was making herself sick. She'd make herself throw up." I sniff back my stupid tears and speak through the lump that's formed in my throat. "She said she did it to feel alive. That when things got really bad, she wanted to feel *alive*. That night when Lachlan was sick and you came to your senses... I walked in on her doing it. She says she hasn't done it since, but I haven't been around for the past two weeks, and I'm guessing you haven't either."

He doesn't respond. He just looks out the window, too ashamed to face me... to face up to what he didn't know.

"I'm telling you because I care about her."

He turns to me now, his tough-guy persona completely wiped.

"I'm telling you because I love her. I love her more than absolutely anything in this entire world. I'm hurting not being able to see her, so I can't imagine how she's feeling. I have my mom, I have her boyfriend, and they help me get through every day. She probably has no one."

He leans his elbows on his desk and drops his head between his shoulders.

"If she's doing it again... if she's chasing that high of feeling alive... if she's so far gone that she's making herself sick again... I'll never forgive you. And one day, when she somehow gets through all of this, neither will she."

Twelve
Lucy

I DON'T BOTHER answering the knock on my door. If it's one of the boys, they'd just walk in. But I know it's not them because they haven't been around for days. They must know. They must be able to read me. Just like Cameron can.

Dad enters without explanation. I sit at the edge of my bed, facing the bathroom. That's where he goes; drill in one hand and a wrench in the other. His footsteps are heavy as he walks to the toilet and drops the lid. Then he proceeds to screw the lid onto the base.

I should care—but I just don't.

When he's done, he gets his wrench and removes the faucet and handles from the sink. He opens the cupboard underneath and works on something there. Finally, he gets up and walks out of the bathroom. I think he's going to leave, but he doesn't. Instead, he sits on my bed next to me and drops his tools. And then he cries. Hard and loud, into his hands.

I should care—but I just can't.

"Help me," he says quietly. "I don't know what I'm doing."

And then it finally dawns on me—what he just did. He must know. Cameron must have told him.

"I hate you," I whisper, my gaze unfocused.

"I know."

"You made me hate myself."

"I know, Luce. I'm sorry."

Tears fall. I let them. "You know what the worst part is?"

"Tell me. Talk to me, please."

"The worst part is that you made me feel ashamed—when I have nothing to be ashamed of. And you used Mom's memory to make me feel like that. You took something beautiful from me and you made me ashamed of it. I love Cameron. And I know Mom would have loved him too. You know how I know? Because she would have seen him for what he is. She would have seen the boy that was there for me every day when *you* couldn't be. When I needed you the most, you turned your back on me. But Cam—he didn't. He wouldn't. Even now, after everything we've put him through, he's still here. He still shows up every day. He still cares enough to tell you that I need saving. But I don't need you to save me, Dad. I need Cameron. And I don't care what you say. I don't care how you feel because you don't understand. You don't understand because you didn't care enough to ask. All you did was call me a whore—and you used Mom to fuel your fire. I hate you for that."

I hear his sob get louder, but I don't care.

"You might think that we're young, or that we're naïve, but you married Mom after two months. You think if you guys met when you were fifteen that your feelings for each other would have been different? You think your lives would be different? You think this home—this family you both built together would be different?"

I stay silent and wait for his answer.

It never comes, and it pisses me off, because I deserve answers. I face him now, no longer afraid of him. "Do you?"

He shakes his head slowly. "No, Lucy. I don't think so."

"That's what I thought." I turn away, returning my focus to nowhere ahead of me. "Now imagine someone took that away from you. Imagine if you couldn't have the one thing that gave you *hope*. That's right... it did get taken away. Mom's been taken away. But the difference is that you got your life, you got your kids, you got your home. You got to share all of that with your love, your *hope*." I turn back to him now, making him look me in the eyes. "Mom would've fallen in love with him, just like I did. And I hate you because you took my *hope* away from me."

✧   ✧   ✧

"LUCY." I WAKE up to Dad shaking me gently. When I open my eyes, I see that it's daylight. It's the first time I've slept through the night since the last time I saw Cameron.

My head's pounding from all the crying.

"Lucy," he says again. "Get up. We need to go. Meet me downstairs in ten minutes."

I don't even question him. There's nothing left to question. After our talk, he cried some more, and apologized until I told him to leave. By the end of it, I was physically and emotionally exhausted.

He drives to a familiar neighborhood, one that I haven't been to in two weeks. He stops at the front of Cameron's townhouse and jerks his head to the front door. "Go get your boyfriend."

I don't think twice. I'm already smiling when I get to his door. It opens before I get a chance to knock. His eyes go wide, and then he laughs—the relieved kind of laugh. I throw my arms around him and kiss him a thousand times. But I feel his body tense, and I know that he can see Dad waiting. "What's going on, Luce?"

And it's then I realize how much I missed him. His voice. His dark eyes. His dirty blond hair. His perfect face. His smell. Everything.

"I don't know." I shrug. "He just brought me here and told me to get you. Are you coming?"

His gaze moves from Dad's car to me. "Babe, I have to work at the dealership."

"No you don't." Mark's voice sounds from somewhere in the house. A second later he's behind Cam, rubbing his shoulders. "Go be with your girl." He smiles over Cam's shoulder. "Lucy." He nods once. "It's good to see you. We've missed you around here."

WE DRIVE INTO town in complete silence. I sit in the front and he sits in the back chewing his nails. They never even greet each other.

✧   ✧   ✧

"WHAT'S GOING ON?" he whispers from next to me.

I watch Dad pacing the floor of the doctor's waiting room. "I don't know," I whisper back.

The receptionist calls my name and I stand up, so does Cam. We still don't know what we're doing here. "Let's go," Dad deadpans.

An older man—the doctor I presume—holds the door open for all three of us.

"Dr. Matthews," Cam says, shaking the doctor's hand. He holds the back of a chair and waits for me to sit before taking the seat next to me.

"How are you, Cameron?" the doctor asks.

My brows pinch in confusion.

"I'm okay, sir." He holds my hand and settles it on the desk in front of us. "This is my girlfriend, Lucy."

The doctor smiles at me—the kind of warm, genuine smile that I find rare. "I see you're batting above your average," he says to Cam.

Cam chuckles. "Yes, sir. And I know it, too." He faces me and motions his head to the doctor. "This is Logan's dad."

My eyes go wide. "Oh."

Dr. Matthews lets out a laugh. "I promise I don't have my son's asshole tendencies." He winks, and I find myself relaxing.

"He's not so bad," I tell him. "He saved me from bullies once."

His smile is instant.

"You never told me that," Cam states.

I shrug. "It wasn't important. It's not like I'm into him," I joke.

Cam scoffs. "Nice. I'll remember that."

Everyone laughs. Everyone but Dad. Instead, he clears his throat, causing us to stop and pay attention. He steps behind me and places his hands on my chair. "I would—I mean, it's up to them—but I think it would be a good idea to discuss birth control."

I choke on air.

Cam lets out an indescribable sound.

Dr. Matthews' eyes dart between us. "Is this something you two would like to consider, or at least discuss?"

Silence.

Dead. Frickin'. Silence.

Then Cam clears his throat, similar to Dad only seconds ago. "We've spoken about it, sir. We want to wait until we're both mature enough to handle it emotionally. Lucy hasn't given me a time frame and I'm happy with that. I told her I'd wait, and I meant it. I'd wait forever. I don't know that it's something we have to think about right now, but if it would help her father—for his peace of mind, then I think it's a good idea." He turns to face me, squeezing my hand at the same time. "If you're comfortable with it, babe, I think it might be something we should do."

I nod. Not for me or my Dad, but for Cameron. Because he said *we*. It's something *we* should do.

Cam and I decide on Implanon—a tiny rod that gets implanted just under the skin on my arm and lasts for three years. Cam hates it. He thinks it should be him doing something, not me. He cringes as he watches it get inserted. "I'm sorry," he whispers, but he has absolutely nothing to be sorry for.

✧ ✧ ✧

I THOUGHT THAT Dad would drive Cameron back to his house, but he doesn't. He drives us home and asks us to wait at the dining table. "I'm scared," I tell Cameron.

He puts his arm around my shoulders and kisses my temple. "You don't need to be scared, Luce. You never have to be scared when I'm here."

The scraping of a chair has us pulling apart. Dad sits opposite us, his gaze moving from me to Cam, and back again. Then slowly, he pushes a piece of paper toward me. A brochure. *Family counseling.* I look up at him. "I don't need counseling."

Cam settles his hand on my leg under the table.

"I know," Dad says. "But I do, Luce. I need help. Not just with raising you kids on my own but *coping* with having to." He leans his elbows on the table and speaks only to me. "You were absolutely right with what you said yesterday. You don't need me to save you, you have Cameron. But I need saving. And I have no one. The counseling is for me."

I open my mouth to speak but he raises his hand to stop me.

"You can't forgive my actions based on my words. Forgive me when my actions have proven that I deserve it."

✧ ✧ ✧

"I STILL HATE him." I bury my face further into his chest and throw my arm over his stomach. We're lying on my dock, waiting for the sun to set.

"I know. He said some pretty harsh things."

"Do you think your mom would let me live with you until college?"

He laughs softly. "I think I'd find a way to sneak you in and out even if she said no, but I don't think that would solve anything. It wouldn't make things right."

"I know," I sigh.

"I get where he's coming from. It has to be hard for him. And you're his little girl. He's struggling with losing your mom, and now he thinks he's losing you too."

I sit up and lean on my outstretched arm so I can look at his face.

He reaches up and moves my hair away from my eye. "I don't know, Luce. It's hard for me to understand. My dad—" His sigh cuts him off. "It's like he knows I exist, he just doesn't care that I do. He doesn't even pretend to. He doesn't even try. So it's hard for me to see things from your perspective when all I can see is a man trying to heal and make things right with you." He tries to smile, but it doesn't work. "All I'm saying is that I think he means well. He doesn't know how to deal with it. We just need to support him and give him time."

And even though I don't agree with him, I nod anyway, because he did it again. He said *we*. *We* need to give him some time.

He smiles and pulls me back into him. "I love this time of day."

"Sunset?"

"Yeah. You wanna know why?"

I nod against his chest.

"Because it reminds me of us."

"How?"

"Because it's eternal, the rise and fall of the sun. It's *forever*. Just like us."

Thirteen
Cameron

"**H**EY, YOU WANNA hear something really lame?"

She smiles and shuts her locker door. "What?"

"Mom, Mark and I do this thing a couple of nights a year. It's called Movie Madness."

"What do you do in said Movie Madness?"

"We have a movie marathon." She hands me her books so she can tie up her hair. It used to be a dark brown, but the summer sun has made it lighter than I've ever seen. She asked me if she should dye it—make it lighter again. I told her she didn't need to. The darker it was the more her blue eyes stood out. She laughed and asked if I'd been reading her books. I didn't really know what that meant, but obviously it was a good thing because it started a make-out session that lasted two hours.

"That sounds cool." She starts to walk away, and I follow, her books still in my hands.

Logan walks past and makes a whipping motion with his hand.

"Fuck you," I mouth.

His head throws back in silent laughter. Then he stops walking and his eyes glisten with amusement. "Hey, Luce," he says, walking up to us.

She turns to him. "Yeah?"

"Did you have a growth spurt or something over the summer?" His eyes wander up and down her body.

"No."

"Oh." He eyes me quickly before returning his gaze to her. "Just seems like these little skirts of yours are getting shorter. Or maybe it's just been a while since I've seen you." He steps forward. "I didn't realize how much I missed you until now." He stretches his arms out, an invitation to hug him.

I wait for her reaction, my fists already balled. Her eyebrows pinch as she looks from him to me and back again. She shakes her head quickly and ducks under his arm and into mine.

I laugh. "Get your own girlfriend to hug you."

He shakes his head and chuckles. "Jake!" he shouts. "Come hug me!"

Jake walks over with his eyes already narrowed. "Nah, mate, I'm good."

Dylan and his girlfriend Heidi join us and Logan quickly comes up with an excuse to leave. He does it a lot when those two are together. The bell rings and everyone bails. "So what about your movie madness?" Lucy asks, taking her books back.

"Oh, yeah. It's tonight. You wanna come?"

"It's not a family thing?"

I roll my eyes. "You are family."

Ducking her head, she tries to hide her smile. "Okay." She looks back up, her smile still in place, and kisses me longer than she's ever done at school. "I'll see you after school. I love you." And then she's gone.

I stand in the middle of the empty hallway, smiling like an idiot.

"Get to class!" she yells over her shoulder.

I don't even have my books.

✦ ✦ ✦

ONCE SHE'S CLIMBED into Filmore and clipped her seatbelt on, she turns to me. "What movies are we watching?"

"We watch all of our favorites, mine first, then Mom's and then Marky Mark's."

"What are they?"

"*Back to the Future, Aladdin,* and *Lethal Weapon.* And after that, they said we can try to watch your favorite."

She smiles again, that same shy smile from earlier. I move in, kiss her cheek, and start to reverse out of the spot.

We make it a mile home before my car breaks down.

"Stupid Filmore." I kick the tire.

She comes up and wraps her arms around me, trying to calm me. "I feel bad that you spent your money on this. I know you were doing it for me, but you could have got something more reliable."

I sigh. "It doesn't matter. It's done now."

"You don't think it's fixable?"

I shake my head, my smile tight. "It's going to cost more to fix than it's worth. I'm just pissed. It's not your fault. I'm sorry."

She pulls her phone out of her bra. Her skirts and tanks rarely have pockets. "Dad?" she says, holding the phone to her ear.

My eyes narrow in confusion.

"Filmore's broken. Can you organize a tow?" She gives him our location.

Ten minutes later he arrives. Another five minutes and the tow truck shows up. Half an hour after that, I'm told that Filmore needs a new home in car heaven. Basically where I found him.

Tom stands in front of us shaking his head. "I'm sorry," he says sincerely. "I know you got Filmore to help out with Luce and the boys and I appreciate it." His words don't surprise me. Luce says he's been doing therapy twice a week over the last few months since he started. She's gone to a few sessions with him and they've been working through his issues. She tells me that it helps, and I'm glad it does. She says I gave her a new perspective, that even though he messed up, he's *trying*. Which is more than I can say for my dad.

He rubs his hand across his beard and looks between Lucy and I. "You guys heading to our house or what?"

Lucy answers for both of us. "We were gonna go to Cam's." And even though we can walk to my house, we accept his offer for a ride. Because it's not just about the ride, it's the message behind it. He's making an effort. Not just for Luce, but for me, too.

✧　✧　✧

"WHERE'S FILMORE?" MARK asks, walking into the kitchen.

Lucy exaggerates a pout. "Car heaven."

Mark's eyes move from Lucy, to Mom, then finally to me. "That sucks, bud. I'm sorry."

Shrugging, I state, "It was inevitable." I let out a bitter laugh. "Just means Lucy's back to riding shotgun on the back of my bike."

She snorts. "I don't mind, babe. Worst comes to worst, I'll just get my license. I only held off because I like you driving me around."

We gather our snacks and move to the living room, where she positions herself lengthways on the couch and lifts her legs for me to take a seat. Once we're settled, she pulls her e-reader out of her backpack and switches it on.

Mark shrugs on his *Lethal Weapon* shirt; one that says *'I'm too old for this shit.'* Mom used to hate it. She thought it was a bad influence on me. We still haven't told her about the time I hit him in the face with my baseball bat and he dropped the *C* bomb. I was nine.

Mark chuckles and shakes his head at Lucy just as Mom throws a fake Persian blanket over them. "It's Movie Madness, Luce. No books," he jokes.

"It's okay," I cut in, "she can read. I'm used to it."

"I have two chapters left, and then I'm all in."

"Shit," I clip. "My Delorean." I quickly run up to my room and grab the model car Mark got me because he knew it was my favorite movie. Actually, come to think of it, that was the day after he dropped the *C* bomb. Maybe he had ulterior motives. *Asshole.* I'm still laughing to myself when I get back downstairs.

"What's funny?" Mom asks.

I lift Lucy's legs and reposition myself. "Remember that time I gave Marky Mark a fat lip with a bat?"

Mom chuckles.

I hold up the Delorean and quirk an eyebrow at Mark.

His eyes go huge as he shakes his head in warning.

✧   ✧   ✧

I'M TRYING TO watch the movie but her feet on my lap keep rubbing each other. It would be fine, only they're *on my lap.* I glance at her quickly but she's too consumed in her book, her eyes darting from side to side. She smiles softly. I've learned that it means the characters have done something overly cheesy. I want to smile with her, but all I can think about are her feet rubbing against my dick... and the hard-on that's building faster than it should.

Containing a groan, I pick up a cushion and do my best to not disturb her while I lift her feet, placing the cushion on my lap to hide myself.

I hear Mark chuckle and look up at him. His hand is raised in a fist, motioning it up and down; the universal sign for rubbing one out. I glare at him. He laughs harder. I bring my hand up to my face and give him the finger right as Mom's eyes shift to me. "Did you just give me the finger?"

I shake my head quickly. "No."

"I saw it," Mark says. "He totally did, darling."

Mom rolls her eyes just as Lucy squeals. She sits up and holds her e-reader to her chest. "Cameron, they just had their first kiss!" She sighs dreamily.

"Yeah?"

She nods quickly, her smile mimicking the excitement she feels. And it hits me—how different she is now compared to when we met. I wonder how much I have to do with that… if me being in her life has made that significant of an impact.

"Ohhh," she coos, gripping her e-reader tighter. "I loved my first kiss so much."

I laugh and put my arm around her, bringing her to my side. "Yeah?" I ask, my eyes never leaving hers.

She nods again, and my heart tightens. I used to feel it a lot—that tightening in my chest. It took me a while to work out what it was; *love*—the kind of love that shouldn't exist for two sixteen-year-olds. It's almost too much. Too heavy. Too soon. I used to worry about what could be left. What is there to look forward to when you fall in *this* kind of love when you're so young? And then I worked it out. *Forever.* I have forever to look forward to.

"These books are wrong, Cam. The way they describe first kisses…" She leans up and kisses me, not caring that Mom and Mark are in the room. "It's not even close to how I felt." Her smile begins to fade, and a seriousness takes over. "I love you. You know that, right?"

I look away from her. I have to. "I know, babe," I respond, faking a casualness to my voice. "I love you too."

She throws the e-reader on the coffee table and wraps her arm around my stomach, moving in as close as possible.

"Your book finished with a first kiss?"

"No," she says, "I just don't see the point of reading and living in someone else's world when my reality is so perfect."

✧　✧　✧

MARK STANDS AND stretches his arms, singing *Johnny Be Good*. When he's done belting out the chorus, he announces, "Time for Cam's movie!"

"I thought we were watching *Aladdin* now?" Lucy says.

Mark laughs. "She doesn't know, does she?" he asks me.

I sigh, knowing what's coming next. "No."

"Know what?" She sits up higher and faces me.

Mom speaks up, her words meant for Lucy. "Your boyfriend's middle name is Aladdin. He hates it."

Lucy lets out a snort before clamping her lips between her teeth. Her face turns red.

I shake my head. "You can laugh," I tell her. "Everyone else does."

So she does.

And even now, when she's laughing so hard *at* me, the sound of it still makes my world stop.

"Actually," Mark says, waiting for Lucy to quit laughing. "I want to show you something. Just us." He turns his attention to Lucy, who's now wiping tears from her eyes. "I promise to have your boy back soon."

She nods, still trying to compose herself. "Take his magic carpet, it'll be faster."

✧　✧　✧

"ARE YOU TAKING me somewhere to kill me?"

He rests his forearm on the steering wheel and glances over at me. "Yes."

"That's a shame. If you've been with Mom all this time thinking that you can replace me and take my place in her will—you've chosen the wrong girl. You've seen where we live, right? All that's left for me when she's gone is that Persian rug."

"Dammit," he mocks. "All that sex for nothing."

I gag. "That's gross, Mark. Don't bring that shit up again."

His head throws back in laughter just as he pulls into his street. He parks in front of his house and kills the engine.

"What are we doing here?" I ask, confused. I've only been here a handful of times since they started dating. I heard them once, arguing because he wanted us to move in with him. His house was a lot bigger. Not Lucy's house big, but much bigger than our old, tiny townhouse. Mom told him she didn't want me to have the instability. He lived further out of town, so I'd have to catch a bus to school. But it wasn't just that. She also said that she worked hard to build a home for us since Dad left, and she didn't want it to all be for nothing. He understood, but I have a feeling it wasn't the last time he asked her.

"One," Mark says, facing me. "Don't talk shit about your mom. I'm with her because I love the shit out of her. You should know what that feels like. You have Lucy, and to be honest, I'm kind of jealous that you found her so young. I wish I'd found your mom first. I wish I was the one you'd call Da—" he cuts himself off.

I blow out a nervous breath. It's rare that we have serious a conversation. Squirming in my seat, I wait for him to speak. All the words I wish I could say are stuck in my throat.

"Second," he sighs, then shakes his head. "Never mind. Let me just show you."

He presses the remote for the garage door and steps out of the car.

I follow him into the garage and wait while he turns on the lights. The only thing here is a car, but it's covered. He glimpses at me quickly before slowly lifting the cover.

My eyes bug out of my head. "Holy shit! Is this a—"

"Delorean? Yup."

"Holy shit!" I walk a full circle around the car. "Holy shit!" I'm so giddy I can't even contain it. "What?" I look up at him. "I'm so confused right now. Did you rent it?"

He laughs quietly. "No." Scratching the back of his head, he continues, "I actually bought it a year ago." He pulls a set of keys off a hook on the wall. "I've been building it slowly, making some modifications. The last part came in a few days ago." He presses a button on the keyless remote.

I watch in awe as the two doors rise. "Hydraulic doors!" I shout.

He laughs again. "Pretty cool, huh?"

I nod, too excited to speak.

"Take a seat."

I hesitate a moment, not sure that I want to touch and ruin anything, but then sense kicks in. "It's a fucking Delorean!"

I sit in the driver's seat and hold the steering wheel, sure that my mouth is hanging open in shock. I wait for him to sit in the passenger's seat before turning to him. "How come you've never driven it over?"

"Because," he starts, his voice shaky.

I take in the interior of the car and fiddle with the buttons on the dash.

"Cameron."

I look up to see him watching me.

"I haven't driven it yet."

"What? Why?"

"Because it's not mine, Cam." He holds up the keys between us. "It's yours."

My breath catches on a gasp. I don't speak. I don't move. I don't blink.

He scratches his head again. "I got it and wanted to give it to you for your sixteenth birthday, but you got Filmore, which is fine, because it wasn't a hundred percent ready. Then I was going to wait and give it to you as a graduation present, but it's kind of perfect timing. Filmore's in heaven now and it's finally ready for you."

I release the breath, still not fully understanding what's happening. "Does Mom know?"

"Of course. I made sure to run it by her. She thinks I'm crazy, but even still, I think if she didn't approve I still would've done it."

"Why?"

He shrugs and looks away. "I don't know. I mean, I don't want you to take this the wrong way, but you deserve something like this. I think your dad's kind of an ass for not seeing that, and not appreciating you. If I were your dad, I'd be so proud of the way you turned out. Your mom always says how she wishes she could give you more—"

I open my mouth to interrupt but he speaks before I can get a word in.

"That's the thing, Cam. You never ask for more than what's given. You understand and appreciate everything you have. Your mom—she never has to worry about you. You could have turned out a lot worse. Hell, you could have turned out like me." He laughs to himself, but I'm drowning in too many emotions to have a reaction. "I mean... I'd like to think that I had something to do with that—the way you turned out. Whether it's legal or not—to me, you're my son. And this is something I wanted to do." He blows out a heavy breath and stares out the windshield.

I look down at the keys in my hand.

We sit in comfortable silence as I let his words replay in my head. Then I say something that I've been too ashamed to admit to anyone but myself. "I wish you were my dad, too."

He clears his throat.

I keep my eyes cast downward, not wanting to let him see the tears building in them. "You've always been a better dad than him, and I don't ever see that changing."

He clears his throat again, a little rougher this time. "Let's go home. You can pick up Lucy and cruise around a bit. I know this great, secluded parking lot. I used to take all the girls there when I was your age. We'd steam up the windows, if you know what I mean."

I look up at him now, his smirk in full force.

"I'm telling Mom," I state. Then I put the keys in the ignition, squeal like a girl when it turns over, and drive off... in my fucking *Delorean*. Bitches.

✧   ✧   ✧

SHE MOANS INTO my mouth and pushes herself closer into me. She's straddling my lap while I sit in the driver's seat. It's the closest we've ever been, but the space in this car doesn't give us much choice. I have to thank Marky Mark for that. I remove my hand from her breast and move it down her stomach, feeling bolder than I ever have. I run a finger between her waist and the band of her skirt, a sign of what my intentions are. She whimpers and circles her fingers around my wrist, stopping me from going further. She pulls back. I drop my head on her shoulder.

"I'm sorry," she whispers.

I try not to show my true feelings. I'm frustrated. Sexually. Mark was right, I'm gonna have to take care of myself tonight. "It's fine, I'm sorry for pushing it."

"You're not pushing it." She sighs and pulls as far back as possible. "I just have a thing about... you know?"

My brows pinch. "No, Luce. I don't know. What?"

She looks around the abandoned parking lot Mark told me about. "Vaginas," she whispers.

"What?" I laugh.

She slaps my chest. "It's not funny, Cam. Vaginas are weird."

I laugh harder. "What the hell are you talking about?"

"They're weird. They're like the ugliest things in the entire world. Floppy skin and flaps and holes."

"Oh my God." I'm holding my stomach now, unable to keep my

laughter in check.

"Cameron!" she shouts. "I'm serious. I've seen the pornos under your bed!"

I should be ashamed, but I'm too busy laughing.

"Those vaginas aren't real! They can't be. And even if they are, they're still not something nice to look at. I can't even imagine what it would be like for you to see it, let alone touch it! TOUCH IT!" she scoffs. "I don't even want to touch my own. And believe me, I've thought about it." Her eyes are wide as she nods frantically. "Every night after these make out sessions we have... I want to touch myself. I really do. But all I can think about is floppy folds and random holes!"

My face falls. "Wait. What?" Shit's no longer funny. "You want to touch yourself?"

"Yes! All the time!"

I push her off me, shove my hands down my pants, adjust myself and take her home.

"It's not even curfew," she whisper yells as I push her out the door.

I drive home, faster than what's legal, run upstairs, lock my door, and... well... you can guess. The mental image of Lucy touching herself brings me to the point of explosion...yes, *explosion*, in less than a minute.

I call her as soon as I've cleaned up and don't bother lying about my actions. I tell her that I'm sorry for being vague, but not sorry for kicking her out, because if I didn't, something really, really bad could have happened. Or, something really, really fucking good.

IN MY GODDAMN *Delorean*.

Dammit.

Fourteen
Cameron

"**I** NEED TO pee," Lucy whispers. She wanted to get out of the house and spend some alone time together, so I took her to the movies.

I peel my eyes off the screen and focus on her. "Babe, it's like the fifth time since the movie started."

"I know." She kisses me quickly. "I'll be quick."

She's gone less that a minute before her seat is taken by someone *not* her.

"Tess." I nod, my eyes never leaving the screen. "What's up?"

"Was that Lucy?" she says quietly.

I roll my eyes. Before Lucy came along, Tess was my go-to. When we were at parties, we'd always end up together. It never went further than kissing, although one time we got close. I've heard she tells everyone about me. Logan told me she still wants something to happen, even though she knows I'm with Lucy. I'm thankful word hasn't gotten to Lucy yet. She's made it clear more than once that she doesn't like sharing. "You know it is. What do you want?"

She leans in closer, her cheap perfume invading my nostrils. "You've been together a while now, just thought you'd be done with her already. Honestly, I don't know what you see—"

"Shut up," I bite out and face her. "Don't talk shit about Lucy. Ever. And you better go before she gets back. She's gonna be pissed if she sees you in her seat."

She smiles. Like she's suddenly won a game I didn't know we were playing. "So she knows about me?"

"No," I huff out.

"She has no idea about our past?"

I sigh. "We have no past. We made out a couple times. That's all."

Her smile gets wider. "Then she has nothing to worry about, right?"

"Cameron?" Lucy's voice pulls my glare away from Tess.

I try to act cool, even though I'm already afraid of how the rest of the night will play out. "Hey babe."

Tess giggles. "I was just keeping your boyfriend company while you were gone. You know? Reminiscing on old times." Her eyes shut and she starts humming.

Lucy clears her throat.

I swallow my fear.

"Quit moaning like a dick deprived whore and get out of my seat." She crosses her arms and takes an intimidating step forward.

Tess leaves without a word.

Lucy reclaims her seat.

I fail at stifling my laugh.

"Shut it, Cam."

Lucy

"YOU DON'T THINK I know the shit she says about you two?"

"I don't know what you want me to say!"

We're both yelling on the drive home. It's our first shouting match, and to be honest, it's kind of liberating.

"You should have told me! I shouldn't have heard it from people at school!"

"There's nothing to tell!"

"She was your girl before me! I think that's something!"

"She wasn't my girl, Luce! I told you! There was no one before you!"

"Oh, I'm sorry!" I exaggerate. "What I meant to say was she was your *whore* before me!"

"That's not fair! I told you I'd been with other girls. That wasn't a secret!"

"Screw you, Cam!"

His face falls.

And then he begins to laugh.

"What the hell is funny?"

He pulls the car over on the side of the road and faces me, his face contorted with his held in laughter.

And I lose it. "Screw you twice! In your ass! With a chainsaw!"

He all out laughs now—not even bothering to contain it.

I try to get out of the car but the stupid door takes forever to lift.

"Stop," he says, leaning over and closing the door before I can get out.

"I'm sorry," he begins, but another laugh bubbles out. He tries to stop it before he loses control. This happens a few more times while I sit with my arms crossed and wait for him to settle. "You're just so damn cute when you're angry. It's kind of one of the reasons I'm so in love with you."

I feel the tension leave my shoulders.

Sighing, he eyes our surroundings. "Come here." He pulls on my arm and helps me across so I'm seated on his lap. Moving the hair out of my eyes, he kisses my forehead once. "Luce, if I could erase my past and wipe out all the girls I've been with, I would, instantly. But even if I could, it wouldn't make a difference. You're the only girl that's ever mattered to me. The only girl that *will* ever matter. If you want, I can write a list so you can walk through town and call them all whores. I'll hold your hand and we can do it together. But it won't change the fact that you and I— we're above all that. What we have is bigger than all of it. Forever, remember?"

✧   ✧   ✧

HE TAKES MY hand as we climb my porch steps. "Are we good?" he asks.

"Yeah babe." His speech and the drive home helped calm me down.

We stop at the top of the stairs when we see Dad sitting on the porch, an abundance of papers on the table in front of him. Some of them are scrunched up on the floor.

"Dad?"

His gaze lifts. "Hey kids, how was the movie?"

I pull on Cam's hand until we're standing next to him. Shrugging, I answer, "The book was better."

"What's this?" Cam says, his eyes frantically scanning the papers on the table.

"It's the cause of all my problems, Cameron," Dad sighs.

Cam pulls out a chair and takes a seat, his eyes never leaving the spread of papers. He picks one and brings it closer to him. I've been around Dad's work enough to know that they're development plans.

"Coffee?" I ask them.

"Yes, please," they both answer.

When I come back out with their coffees, they haven't moved. I doubt they've even spoken.

I take a seat next to Cam and watch him. His brows are drawn in concentration. His lips are pressed tight but his eyes—his eyes are everywhere, taking everything in. I turn my attention to Dad, who's doing the exact same thing. "What's the problem?"

He sips his coffee and sighs. "I was so close to finalizing this contract with these developers. The draftsman I hired had it all planned out, and it looked great. Last minute, the developers changed their minds."

"Why?" Cam asks, his gaze never lifting. He pulls another sheet off the pile and inspects it.

"They say they want more yard space." Dad leans forward on his elbows. "The draftsman got pissed and quit. I have until Monday to submit a new plan and I got nothing." He rubs his eyes. "I can't lose this contract, but I have absolutely no idea how the hell I can change it."

I smile and pat his forearm. "I'm sure you'll work it out, Dad."

I get up and walk to the front door. "Cam?"

"Huh?"

"You coming inside?"

"Yeah," he says, taking one final look before standing up and joining me.

I LIE ON the couch with my feet on his lap trying to read. The TV's on but he's not watching. Instead, he's tapping away on his phone, his features bunched in concentration. "What are you doing?"

"Nothing," he says quickly.

I leave him alone. Clearly, I'm interrupting.

"Shit," he huffs, roughly shoving my feet off him and onto the floor. "Sorry," he says, but he's half way out the front door.

I get up and run a hand down my skirt. I should be angry, but I'm too damn confused.

Cam is standing next to Dad at the table, his finger pointing to the plans in front of them. "Flip it!"

"What?" Dad says.

"Flip it. You want more yard space? Flip it. No one uses the front yard anyway, especially when it's not fenced. It's just wasted space so a car can fit in front of the garage. Flip it. Enter from the back. Single blocks between lanes right?" He's talking way too fast, and it's clear my dad can't keep up. "Just enter from the back and move the kitchen to the other side, that way they're looking into the yard instead of the street. You can move the top floor forward this way, and the master can have a balcony if you want and the... what are these?" He points to the plans.

"The support posts?"

"Yeah... them. You can extend them, right? If the buyers want to pay a premium you can build a patio there." He taps his finger twice. "You can raise it, have a spa or something. There's nothing blocking it... what? What's that?" He looks closer. "The laundry room window. You can get rid of the window. No one needs that shit."

Dad blows out a slow breath. "I'm trying to understand what you're saying, Cam, but I can't picture it."

Cam groans. "Just flip some of the elements."

Dad grimaces. "I don't get it."

"Just flip it!" His words come out frustrated, and he knows it because he apologizes right away.

I stand next to him and settle my hand on his back to calm him.

He looks down at me with his lips pursed, but it's obvious his thoughts are elsewhere. Wrapping his arms around my shoulders, he brings me flush against him and kisses the top of my head. And that's how we stay, with him silently holding me, and me having no idea what the hell is happening. Dad watches, but he doesn't speak. And slowly, I feel Cam's body relax. He pulls back and smiles, genuinely this time. "Okay," he breathes out. He turns to dad. "Have you got a blank sheet of paper and a pen?"

He sits on the seat with the pen in his hand, but then he freezes. "Go on," Dad tells him.

He swallows loudly and looks up at me. The look of hesitation and self-doubt in his eyes almost kills me. I rest my hand on his shoulder. "You don't have to if you feel like you can't."

He blinks once and rushes out all the air in his lungs. Then he snakes his arm around my waist and pulls me onto his lap. "You make me want to try," he whispers in my ear.

And then he does it.

He puts pen to paper.

With one hand on my waist and the other working frantically, he begins to create something amazing.

"Holy shit," Dad repeats over and over, but I don't think Cam hears him.

Dad's eyes keep moving from Cam's hand to me, his head shaking slowly the entire time.

When Cam's done, he throws the pen on the table and pushes his sketch under Dad's nose. His gaze lifts to mine, the same uncertainty from before fills them. "You did good, babe," I assure.

"Good?" Dad's voice booms.

We both turn to him.

"Holy shit, kid. How did you—I mean—I've been sitting here for hours and you, you sit down with a pen and a piece of paper and you make something. You get it. You have an image in your head and you make it happen." He shakes his head again and lets out a disbelieving laugh. "Did you know he could do this?" he asks me.

I nod proudly.

He looks at Cameron. "What you have is absolute raw talent." He starts to pack the papers in the briefcase but pauses mid movement. "You could be an architect."

Fifteen
Cameron

"**Y**OUR GIRLFRIEND'S LOOKING hot these days."

I turn to Matt, whose eyes are fixed on Lucy sitting in the bleachers. Her dad and a few of her brothers are with her. They've been coming to all my games recently. I asked her why; she just said it was because they wanted to support me.

"She's always been hot," I tell him, trying to keep my jealousy in check.

"You guys have been together what? A year now?"

"A year and a half."

He lets out a long, low whistle. "That's a long time. The sex doesn't bore you already?"

I quickly drop my gear bag and shove him hard. He falls to the ground with a stupid smirk on his face. "Shut the fuck up."

He laughs while he gets up and dusts himself off. "Dude, we're just talking. What's your problem?"

I shove him again, but this time, he's ready for it. Lucky for him, Jake and Logan get between us.

"Quit talking shit or you'll really see what my problem is."

I feel Lucy's presence before I hear her. "What made Punchy Cam come out?" she asks Logan.

Matt laughs again. *I fucking hate this kid.* "Nothing baby," he croons, winking at her.

My fist begins to fly but Logan's arms hold me back.

Matt continues anyway, "Just talking about how boring your sex life must be."

"Come on, babe," she says, holding my bag up for me. She pulls on my arm until I've turned and we're walking away.

"What? You can go around throwing insults but you have nothing for him?"

She's silent all the way to her car—her mom's old one. She got her license a few weeks ago. I guess the novelty of me driving her everywhere had finally worn off.

I sulk in the passenger's seat while she starts the car. "Is he right?"

"What?"

"Are you bored? Of our sex life, or lack of?"

My eyes roll so high I see stars. "No. And I don't care that he said that. I care that he thinks he can talk shit about you. And now you're letting him get away with it."

She turns to me now, with an emotion on her face I can't decipher. "Are you, though? I mean, is that why you're really pissed? Not because you think he might be right?"

I throw my head back against the seat. "This is dumb, Luce. I'm not having this conversation."

"Fine," she murmurs, pulling out of the spot.

✧   ✧   ✧

"MATT'S BEEN TALKING shit about your virgin ass."

I freeze with the burger halfway to my mouth. Glaring at Logan first, and then the entire cafeteria, I answer, "Matt can lick a shit stained ball sack."

Jake laughs, Logan—he just smirks. "You guys haven't…?"

I sigh, dropping the burger on my tray and crossing my arms. "It's no one's business but ours. We don't have a problem with it so no one else should."

He nods slowly. "That's a long time."

"I thought I had it bad," Jake murmurs.

Logan scoffs. "Shut up with your self appointed vow of celibacy. No one gives a shit." He turns to me. "Cam though—"

"Shut up." I throw my burger at his head, but he ducks too fast, and it hits the chick behind him.

The girl turns, her eyes narrowed. "Hey babe, you do something different with your face?" Logan says to her.

Her cheeks redden before she turns back around, giggling with all her little friends.

"You're fucked," I tell him.

He stretches his arms out. "At least one of us is."

Jake backhands Logan's chest before jerking his head to get my attention. "Are you guys waiting—for marriage I mean—because if so, that's cool. No judgement."

I shake my head. "No. It's not like that…" I lean forward on my elbows and move in so no one else can hear. They do the same. "She has this thing with vaginas."

Logan's eyes go huge. "You mean she *likes* them?"

I rear back. "What? No! What? No! Oh my God, no! She thinks they're *weird*."

Logan pulls away, his face a mixture of confusion and disappointment. "What the hell does that mean?"

Shrugging, I answer, "I have no idea. She doesn't want me to see it or touch it."

"You can't even look at it?" Dylan asks. I hadn't even realized he'd joined us.

I shake my head. "It's like she thinks it's the Bermuda Triangle or something. She's too afraid to let anyone venture in or out."

We all laugh, but I cut mine off when I see her approaching. "Shut up, she's coming."

They do their best to stifle their laughs.

"Oh my God, babe, I'm so hungry." She sits on my lap and starts to pick at my food.

"So am I," Logan says. "You know what I'd love right now?" He looks around the table. "*Tacos.*"

Jake covers his mouth to stop from spitting his drink. Once he's settled, he leans back in his chair. "You know what they have at Subway now? *Ham Wallets.*"

Dylan pipes up. "I had to return this shirt at the store yesterday. It had *wizard sleeves.*"

"What?" Lucy asks.

And then it hits me—what they're doing. "Shit."

"I know that store," Logan muses. "They have costumes right? I wanted to get this one of an *axe wound.*"

They all crack up, unable to keep it in any longer.

"I hate that store." Jake this time. "It smells like *clams.*"

I feel Lucy tense. "What the hell?" she whispers.

"*Whispering eye,*" Logan sings, just as Heidi takes a seat.

"*Meat curtains,*" Dylan deadpans.

"*Coin purse.*" Jake again.

"*Pink sink.*" Logan laughs.

Then Heidi speaks up. "Why are you all talking about vaginas?"

Lucy gasps loudly before turning to me. "You told them?" she squeals.

I shake my head, but my lips are clamped between my teeth and my face is red. I want to laugh. *Oh my God, I need to laugh.*

"*Punaani,*" Logan shouts.

"Stop it!" Lucy deadpans. "It's not funny you guys! They're weird. And ugly. *Really* ugly!"

The others shake their heads at her. "No, they're not," Dylan says.

"I don't know." She eyes us all one by one, before leaning in and whispering, "What if I have a clitorusaurus-rex?"

✧   ✧   ✧

SHE'S LEANING AGAINST my car waiting for me after school. "I'm going to the mall with Heidi."

"What?" I was smiling a second ago, and now I'm pissed. Not at her, but because Logan's right. About the being whipped thing. Not the sex. Maybe a little about the sex. "You never hang out with Heidi."

"I know." She shrugs.

I drop my bag and step forward, pushing her into my car. Holding her hand, I lift it and place it around my waist, then I drop my head on her shoulder and hope that no one else can hear me. "I feel like I haven't seen you in forever. I miss you."

She chuckles quietly. "We spent all of yesterday together."

"It's not enough."

She twists her finger through the hair below my cap. "Are you being needy?"

"Yes." I kiss her neck.

"I'll come by afterward."

"I can come with you."

She pulls back, her cheeks already red from her blush. "You can't, it's a girl thing."

My eyes narrow. "A girl thing?"

"She's taking me to clean up my *wizard sleeve.*"

✧　✧　✧

I DON'T KNOW what the hell she means by *cleaning up her wizard sleeve* so I do what any normal teenage boy would do; I go home, run to my room, open my laptop and Google it. I'm on the third page of Google Images when I feel a hand on my shoulder. "Your mom has that landing strip thing."

I shut my laptop and dry heave. No joke. I run to the bathroom and bend over the toilet, trying to mentally remove my mom's landing strip from all the vaginas I've just seen.

Mark leans against the doorframe with his arms crossed and a smirk on his face.

"You're an asshole."

"I try." He shrugs. "Let me guess, you're going to call it research?"

I stand up and wipe the spit off my chin. "Lucy—" I cut myself off. "Never mind."

"You sure? All jokes aside, if you need to talk about it, I'm here."

I eye him as I pass, looking for any hint of mockery. *Mockery?* Is that even a word?

Throwing myself on the bed, I cover my eyes with my arm, and then I tell him.

Everything.

Even about the now infamous clitorusaurus-rex.

He listens the entire time, never interrupting. When I'm done, he lets out a breath with a whoosh. "You're on your own, buddy."

And then he leaves.

I just told him about my girlfriend's vagina-lock and all he does is *leave.*

"I'm never getting laid."

✧　✧　✧

"I HAVE A solution to your problems, Luce," Logan says.

It's been three days since Vaginagate and it's been the major topic of conversation during lunch. Everyone's talking about my girlfriend's vagina, and I haven't even seen it yet.

"What's that?" she asks.

"Liquid courage."

I should tell him to shut up, but he kind of has a point, and I'm not the only one who thinks so. Lucy slowly swivels on my lap, her eyebrow raised in question.

I shrug. We've never gone to parties together. I just assumed it wasn't her thing. Occasionally I'd go out with the boys and have a beer, then leave and find myself on her doorstep. After the fifth time, her dad stopped questioning it.

"What do you think?" she asks.

"I think you should do whatever you want, babe."

Lucy

"RUN BACK UPSTAIRS and change, girly," Dad says, but he's smiling.

"You're lucky," I tell him. "I'm seventeen and going to my first high school party."

His eyebrows rise. "Are you gonna drink?"

I grab my keys off the counter. "Do you want me to lie?"

"Yes."

"Then no. I'm not drinking."

"That's my girl."

✧   ✧   ✧

CAM'S FRONT DOOR opens before I can knock. His mom stands at the entryway with her eyes wide. "You look…"

I grimace. "Whoreish?"

She laughs. "No, hon, you look beautiful."

I look down at myself. I'm not wearing anything too different from what I wear every day. My skirt's a little shorter and my top's a little tighter. Heidi helped me pick them out. I don't know if that's a good thing or not. "Hon," she says again. "I'm just—" She laughs and shakes her head slowly. "You're like a daughter to me, and I just feel like I've watched you grow up, you know? You look like a woman, and I'm just used to my little girl."

Her words cause an ache in my chest, and instantly I'm crying.

She raises her hand to pat my cheek, or so I think, but she's wiping away my tears. "You thinking about your mom?"

I nod, because I don't want to speak. I don't want my words to replace the echo of hers in my mind.

She moves forward and wraps me in her arms. "I couldn't have wished for a better girl for my Cameron."

"What did that asshole do?" Mark's voice booms from behind her. We pull apart laughing.

"Nothing," Heather says, patting him on the chest. "Let's go." She winks at me. "Cameron's in his room getting ready, and *we* are going on a date night."

"I hope I get laid," Mark jokes, as they both brush past me.

I run upstairs and open Cam's door without knocking.

And then I freeze.

He's walking out of his bathroom in nothing but boxer shorts—both hands holding the towel, roughly drying his hair. His body is wet, not all over, just on his shoulders. My eyes transfix on a bead of water as it falls slowly down his collarbone, down his chest, past each ridge of his abs. *When the hell did he get those?*

I try to swallow, but my mouth's too dry. And now, so are my eyes, because I can't blink. I don't want to. I don't want to miss it when the bead of water gets caught in the hair just above the waist of his boxers and disappears into…

Holy shit.

A gasp catches in my throat.

"Hey," he says, his eyes focused on mine. But only for a moment before they trail down, and down, and then back up. They stop at my breasts, widening as they do. He licks his bottom lip, then slowly runs his teeth across it. The movement so slow, so mesmerizing.

I can't take my eyes off his mouth.

His hand lifts the towel as he wipes his chest. And now my eyes are there, watching him—waiting for his next move. He moves it lower, down to his perfect stomach.

I lick my lips.

He lets out a moan. "Fuck," he says, covering himself with the towel, but it's too late. I've already seen it.

"Lucy," he whispers, and I slowly peel my eyes away from his covered hard-on and look at him.

His eyes are dark—darker than I've ever seen them. He steps forward, the hunger in his gaze so evident. He licks his lips again as he grips the edge of his door.

"Where's Mom?" he asks.

"Date night," I whimper.

He nods once, his eyes never leaving mine. He drops his towel and places his hand on my waist as he slowly pushes the door closed with the other. The motion of our bodies causes me to back up against it. He rests his hands on the door on either side of my head and leans in. His lips barely touch mine when he whispers, "So we're alone?"

I suppress my moan and nod slowly.

His tongue darts out to lick my lips. Slowly. From one side to the other. "I bet you taste as good as you look."

And that's when I lose it.

My head flings back, hitting the door behind me. My eyes drift closed, waiting for more.

And he gives it.

He gives me more.

His mouth covers mine; soft, wet, just like his tongue when he swipes it against mine. "Babe," he moans into my mouth.

My hands reach up, gripping his shoulders and pulling him down. His hands move to my waist, his fingers curling and his thumb slowly rubbing my bare stomach. And then they move. Lower. Down my skirt—his fingers bunching the material. For a split second, I wish he were wearing a shirt, one I could grip and then rip off him.

Fuck.

My legs rub together, trying to ease an ache building in the pit of my stomach. He releases my skirt and runs his hands down to my bare thighs. One hand lifts my leg, and places it around him. He pushes into my center. Just once. But it's all I need.

His other hand moves higher on my thigh, the touch so light it makes me shiver. He doesn't notice. His movements don't falter. Not for a second. Not until his hand is covering my ass. "Fuck," he spits, right before he grips it tight. So tight it hurts. And turns me on. He lifts me off the ground, my legs automatically going around him. I can feel him between my legs, his hardness pressing into me. He pulls back from my mouth, his eyes burning with lust. Both his hands grip my ass now, as he stares down at my breasts. "Take your shirt off." It's not a question. It's a demand—one that I don't argue with.

He swallows loudly. His eyes are everywhere, all at once. He pushes into me again, his hands squeezing me tighter. I can feel the wetness building. I should be ashamed, but I'm not. I want him to know how badly I need him—how much he turns me on.

He grunts, lifting me higher against the door and placing his mouth on my breasts, just above my bra. His gaze lifts, but his mouth stays. "Are you okay?" His words comes out rough, fueled by his desire. His voice vibrates my skin, and now it's my turn to push into him. That's all the answer he needs. His teeth clamp around my bra, pulling it down and freeing a breast.

And then he does something he's never done before.

My back arches when I feel the warmth of his mouth on my nipple. First one, then the other. He moves one hand off my ass and snakes it around my back. And then we're moving. He walks me with my legs still around him to his bed. He lays me down slowly and stands to full height. My eyes shut tight. I can feel his gaze on me, taking me in from head to toe. He lifts my legs and removes my boots. Slowly. Taking his time. "Fuck, Luce, you're beautiful."

I open my eyes, no longer self-conscious. No longer afraid.

He shakes his head from side to side before placing a knee on the bed, between my legs. He uses it to push them further apart. I know what he wants. I nod slowly, so he knows that I want it too. He leans down, his hands slowly moving up the inside of my thighs. The material of my skirt lifts with the movement of his hands.

And then I panic.

I try squeezing my legs together but his strong hands stop me. His palms flatten on the top of my thighs—making it impossible. "If you want me to stop, *say it*." He licks his lips again, waiting for me to respond. But I can't speak. I can't lie. I don't want him to stop. So I answer him the only way I can, I let my muscles relax and spread my legs wider for him. He doesn't go slowly this time. His fingers curl around my panties and he pulls them down my legs. The cold air hitting my wetness makes me gasp.

"Come here," I manage to get out.

He doesn't hesitate; he gets on the bed next to me and kisses me. First my mouth, then my jaw, and then down my neck. He kisses my chest, moving lower with each kiss. His tongue leaves a trail of wetness on my breasts. He takes one in his mouth again, using his tongue, his lips, his teeth, all of it driving me insane beyond the point of anything I've ever felt before. "Cameron," I whisper.

His gaze lifts.

I remove his hand from my breast and push it lower where we both want him to be.

"Are you sure?"

I don't reply with words, I just push his hand further down.

The first touch has my head lifting off the pillow.

He sucks my nipple harder.

"Holy fuck," he moans, running a finger slowly up, and back down again. He moves his mouth to my other breast, right before I feel him inside me. He lifts his mouth. "Baby," he pants.

My back arches.

My eyes shut.

My breath catches.

My world *stops.*

A door opens.

"Cameron?"

"Mom!"

Screams.

That's all I can hear.

Screaming and yelling.

I'm screaming.

Cam's yelling. "Get out!"

I reposition my bra and try to hide. But we're both on top of the blankets and I can't pull enough off to cover myself.

I'm crying.

I'm crying tears of embarrassment and shame.

Cam covers himself with one hand and tries to cover *me* with the other.

"Get out!" he yells again.

But his mom's frozen in the doorway, her eyes fixed on something on the floor. *My panties.* "Oh my God," I cry, jumping off the bed and picking up my clothes.

I run to the bathroom and lock the door, trying hard to stay silent.

It doesn't work.

"Get out!" he says again, "Can't you hear her crying? We'll talk about this later. Not now."

"Cameron," I hear her say, and then heated whispers.

I quickly dress and grip the door handle. I want to hide out, but it's not fair to him. He shouldn't be dealing with this on his own.

I silently open the door.

"Just tell me," she whispers loudly. "Are you guys having sex?"

"No," I answer for him, wiping the tears off my cheeks. "But I think I want to."

"What?" Cam clips. "*Right now?*"

I shake my head. "No. Not now, but soon, I think."

His eyes widen, but he doesn't speak.

"What's going on?" Mark says, now standing behind Heather. His gaze moves from Cam, to me, and then to the bed. "Oh…" He nods in understanding.

"Mom," Cam pleads. "I can't talk about this—"

"Actually," I cut in. "Cameron, do you mind leaving? I'd like to talk to your mom for a moment."

He turns to me quickly. "What? No, babe. If you want to do this now, we do it together."

"No." I shake my head. "That's not it. Can you just go please?" I beg, letting out another sob.

His shoulders drop. "Babe…"

"Please?"

"Come on," Mark says. "Let the girls talk."

✧ ✧ ✧

"WE HAVEN'T HAD sex," I tell her.

She sits on the edge of the bed next to me looking down at the floor.

"Actually, this is the first time anything like this has happened, and I'm sorry. I'm sorry if you think that it was a breach of your trust because we did it under your roof, but it wasn't planned. I don't want you to stop trusting me. Or Cam." My words end in a sob. "I don't want you to hate me."

She sighs loudly and takes my hand. "I don't, honey. It's just a lot to take in. I could never hate you."

I mirror her position and look down at the floor.

Moments of uncomfortable silence pass.

The ache in my chest gets tighter. "Mom told me once that I'd know... when it was time, I mean. She said that I'd feel it in my heart." I face her now, my eyes filled with tears. "And I do. I feel it for Cameron. I'm so in love with him," I cry. "And I'm scared."

She grips my hand tighter. "What are you scared of?"

"Sharing something like that with someone. It's not just physical. Not for us. That's why we waited so long. But it's not just that. I mean... I have so many questions and I don't know—"

"You have questions?" she interrupts, her voice laced with sympathy.

I nod.

"You can ask me," she says. "Ask me anything."

I look up at her and let the tears fall. "Does it hurt?"

She lets out a small laugh, but not in the mocking sense. More like understanding. "Yes," she states. "I'm not going to lie to you. It does. And to be honest, it probably will the first few times. Don't expect it to feel amazing like they make it out to be. It takes time. Because you're right, it's not just a physical connection you're making. It's emotional. Extremely emotional." She stops to take a breath and then squeezes my hand again. "Lucy."

I look up at her.

"I know that your mom's not around. I know that she would have been a lot more prepared for these types of conversations than I am, but I want you to be comfortable coming to me. Cameron's not the only one in this family who loves you."

Cameron

"So..." MARK SAYS, taking a sip of his beer.

"So..." I answer, kicking my feet onto the coffee table and doing the same.

We've never had beers together, but he says that this *occasion* calls for it.

"So…" he says again.

"So…"

He leans forward, resting his elbows on his knees. "I have to ask."

I look up at him.

He raises an eyebrow. "Clitorusaurus-rex?"

I laugh and throw a cushion at his head.

"Ready to go?" Lucy says from the bottom of the stairs.

Mom's eyes narrow at the beer in my hand. "Mark made me," I tell her.

I quickly grab Lucy and haul ass out of there.

Sixteen
Cameron

"I'M NOT DRINKING anymore tonight so I can drive home." I pick up a pink colored drink from the cooler that's set on the kitchen counter. I have no idea whose house we're at. "We call these bitch drinks." I uncap it and hand it to her. "They taste like punch, but they're still alcoholic so just—"

She cuts me off by handing me back the empty bottle. "Or you could just chug it. Either way works."

She smiles. "That was nice. Give me another one."

I uncap another one but hold it behind my back.

She pouts.

"Lucy, listen to me. You keep going like that, you're gonna puke or pass out, and none of those are good times, especially for me."

She steps forward and wraps her arms around my waist, tilting her head all the way back to look up at me.

"So just chill, otherwise you're going to miss the fun of the actual buzz."

"I understand," she coos.

TEN MINUTES LATER she's buzzed.

"I told you to cool it," I laugh.

We're out in the yard, taking up a seat on the recently abandoned patio furniture. She's sitting sideways on my lap with one arm around my neck. "Quiet, Cam."

"I said that you—"

"Shh!" She covers my mouth with her hand. "Quiet! I don't want to hear it."

Logan comes and takes a seat opposite us. "How's that liquid courage going, Luce?"

"Fuck you and your liquid courage," she tells him.

His eyes widen.

"You and your liquid courage can suck it."

Logan laughs now. We all do.

Then a random girl approaches him. "I found us a room, you coming?" He doesn't even look surprised; he just stands up and follows behind her.

Lucy's jaw drops to the floor. "Is he? And she? Are they?"

I shrug. "Probably."

She gets off my lap and stands between my legs, resting her forearms on my shoulders. "We should do that," she muses.

"What?" I chuckle. "Have meaningless sex?"

"No." She leans in closer. My hands settle on the back of her thighs, under her skirt, just beneath her ass. Truthfully, I haven't stopped thinking about finishing what we started.

She kisses my cheek, then my neck, and then lightly bites my earlobe. "I want to finish what we started," she whispers.

Instantly, I'm up.

Not just standing, but *up.*

For a split second, I fight a war against myself. "I don't want to take advantage of you in your state."

"Pssh," she scoffs. "If anyone's going to be taking advantage, it's me... of you..." She reaches up and pulls me down to her; her mouth's already open, waiting for me.

I HOLD HER hand tightly while we walk through the party. The house is filled, and the music's loud. I take her upstairs where I know it'll be quieter. "Are you sure?" I ask, stepping foot on the landing.

She rolls her eyes and starts knocking on the doors on either side of the hallway. After the fifth one, there's no cussing, no bang of something being thrown against the door. Grinning from ear to ear, she slowly opens it, making sure we're not disturbing anyone. She switches on the light, but it's not a bedroom, it's a bathroom.

I gently rub her shoulders. "We can keep—"

"This will do." She pulls me by my shirt and closes the door behind me.

And all of a sudden I'm nervous. Because I let my dick think for me, and I have absolutely no idea how far she plans on pleasing it.

"I don't want to have sex," she says casually.

The tension leaves my shoulders.

I'm about to ask her what she wants, but some asshole decides to bang on the door. She huffs out a frustrated breath, opens the door slightly and peeks out. Then a roar of laughter escapes her. I open the door wider so I can see what the hell's so funny. Matt and Tess are holding hands on the other side.

"What's funny, bitch?" Tess clips.

Lucy just laughs harder.

Tess steps forward, but Matt holds her back.

"The whore and the pindick," Lucy snorts. "Isn't that like throwing a hotdog down a hallway?"

I stifle my laugh.

"Yeah?" Tess says, her eyes narrowing and her neck snapping when she adds, "I blew your boyfriend's hotdog two weeks ago."

Okay. So, this one time Logan made me watch a video of these two hot chicks rolling on the ground throwing punches. He asked if I thought it was hot. I told him yes, but I lied. I didn't see the appeal in it at all.

I guess I just needed one of those chicks to be Lucy.

Picking her up from her sitting position on Tess's stomach, I throw her over my shoulder and go back in the bathroom. Slowly, I set her on her feet and wait for her heaving breaths to settle. When they finally do she looks up at me, her eyes already narrowed. "It's true isn't it?"

"What?" I can't help but laugh. It's just as absurd as that time Mom thought I got Lucy pregnant.

"She blew you!"

I laugh harder.

And you know why?

Because.

WOMEN. ARE. DUMB.

A snarl forms on her lips, and her eyes fill with rage. I sense it before I see it. Her palm raised, ready for an attack. I grip her wrist roughly.

Her eyes thin to slits.

She tries it again with her other hand.

I do the same thing.

"I hate you," she says. She bites her lip. The rage in her eyes is long gone and replaced with something else completely. *Lust.*

I use my body to pin her to the wall, my hands still holding her firmly in place.

Bending my knees, I place an open mouth kiss on her neck. "You love me."

Lucy

HE'S PINNING ME against the wall with his body, one of his legs between mine, pushing into my center while his hard-on presses against my stomach. I want to touch him. Everywhere. But his grip on my hands tightens every time I try to move.

"I hate you," I say again.

He smiles, that same cocky smile he gets when he knows he's turning me on.

He raises my arms above my head and holds them in place with one hand, the other moving to my chin, lifting it so he can look into my eyes. Whatever he sees makes his eyes widen slightly. He blinks once, long and hard—like he's trying to refocus. He leans down, licking his lips as he does, then runs his tongue lightly between my lips. "You don't hate me," he whispers.

But my mind is a fog and I have no clue what the hell we're even talking about anymore. "Yes I do," I say anyway.

He pulls back, that same cocky smile still in place. He moves his hand from my chin, down my neck and onto my chest. The backs of his fingers brush down my strained nipples. My hips jerk forward, grinding into his leg. His hand flattens on my stomach, moving higher and lifting my shirt. I feel the cold air hit my breasts before I realize what's happening. He pulls his leg back; the same time I feel the warmth of his breath between my breasts. I arch my back, inviting him for more.

Dammit, I need more. I reach for him, but his grip on my hands tightens, again. "I want to touch you."

"I thought you hated me."

I'm too far gone. Not from the buzz of the alcohol, but from letting him have me like this. "I do hate you," I breathe out.

He moves his hand to my back, his fingers deftly unzipping my skirt. It falls silently and bunches at my feet.

"I bet you don't," he murmurs, his teeth brushing against my nipple. He runs a finger between my legs, over my panties. "Yup," he says, popping the *P*. "You definitely don't hate me."

His hand moves under my panties and onto my ass. Moaning, he starts to move in again.

I turn my head to the side, avoiding his kiss. "I want to touch you. Please, Cameron." I feel his fingers relax on my wrists, and I try to move. This time he lets me.

I flatten my palms under his shirt and finger the dips of his abs.

He pushes my panties past my hips, past my ass, and watches them fall to the floor. Then he dips his finger inside me, slowly moving in and out.

I unbutton and unzip his jeans and roughly tug them down. I sense his body go rigid, but I don't stop, not until he's freed and my fingers are curled around him. I moan when I feel the warmth of his dick in my hands. "Show me what to do?"

He removes his mouth from my breast and kisses me softly, using his spare hand to guide mine to his pleasure.

It only takes minutes for that ache in my stomach to reach its peak. "Something's happening," I whimper while my eyes shut tight and my body tenses.

"You want me to stop?" He sounds panicked.

I *am* panicked. "Fuck no."

"Good," he says, our eyes locking. His fingers work while my hand moves up and down.

"Oh my God."

His fingers...

"Oh my God."

In. Out.

"Oh my God," I repeat.

"Lucy, I'm so close."

In. Out.

"Cameron!"

"Kiss me."

So I do.

My eyes roll to the back of my head.

My hips jerk forward. And if possible, he gets even harder in my hands.

His mouth.

His fingers.

"FUCK!" I moan.

And then it happens. Over and over. And over. And over. It builds. Slow. But fast.

I roar. *ROAR*. My head thrashes, smashing against the wall behind it.

He comes at the same time—on my hand, his jeans, my shirt, everywhere.

My body goes limp.

He pulls back, his eyes closed and his jaw tense.

His breathing is heavy, matching mine. His eyes open but they seem distant.

"Oh my God."

A hint of a smile forms on his perfect face. "Was that okay?"

I nod.

"We should probably clean up."

I chuckle as he walks to the sink. He runs the tap and leads my hands under the running water. When I'm done, he uses a hand towel to clean my shirt, his jeans, and then finally his hands. I sit up on the counter and wait for him to finish. When he is, he looks at me with eyebrows raised and a smirk on his face.

"That was amazing," I tell him, wrapping my legs around his knees and bringing him between me.

He finishes buttoning his jeans and rests his forehead on my shoulder. "You were amazing." He kisses my neck, up my jaw and to my mouth. "We should probably get out of here before we do something stupid."

I laugh. "I think I need a drink."

HE GIVES ME a drink.

I ask for more.

And now I'm puking into the bushes while he holds my hair out of the way. "I'm sorry, babe. I should've stopped you."

It's not his fault. I wanted to drink so that I could stop myself from raping him in public.

"Oh my God," I mumble, thinking about the way his fingers felt inside me.

"I'm sorry," he repeats.

I puke again.

When I'm done, he helps me to sit down on the sidewalk. He was halfway to helping me get to the car when my stomach decided it didn't want whatever was in there.

"Are you okay?"

I nod, but my head is heavy and I'm ridiculously tired all of a sudden.

"Will you be alright here while I get the car?"

I nod again.

"Just don't talk to anyone, okay? I'll be quick."

I see him stand, his phone halfway to his ear before I drop my head and take a nap.

Naps are good.

"HEY." I HEAR a girl's voice from above me. I don't recognize it but I know it's not Tess and her clapping vagina. "Are you okay?"

I lift my head—too quickly.

She's with others, but she tells them to get the car and meet her back here. "You not feeling great?" She sits next to me and crosses her legs.

I don't know who she is, but she seems nice enough. "I puked."

She giggles quietly. "Yeah, I can smell that."

Grimacing, I face her. "I'm sorry."

She shakes her head, her smile warm. "It's fine. We've all been there."

"You don't go to my school," I tell her.

"No. I don't think so." She nudges me lightly. "What are you doing out here by yourself?"

"My boyfriend's getting my car. He's gonna come to me and save me. He saves me a lot."

She chuckles at that. "That's a good boyfriend. How long have you been together?"

I don't even find it odd that a stranger is talking to me while the smell of my puke surrounds us. Maybe I'm drunk, or maybe she just seems so genuine that it doesn't matter. "Since sophomore year," I answer.

"Me too!" she perks up. "Well, not your boyfriend obviously, but mine."

I can't help but smile. "Better not be my boyfriend. I'd have to cut you, and I don't want to do that. I like you."

She laughs quietly again. "No, my boyfriend's in college. We do the whole long distance thing."

I raise my knees and rest the side of my head on them, knowing that the girl I'm facing is just talking to keep my mind off puking. And it's nice. She's nice. "That must suck. Cameron and I are... what's that word? Unseperatable?"

"Inseparable?"

I snort. "Yes, that's it! And I want to be a writer."

"Hey," she says, her eyebrows raised. "Not every writer needs to know all the words, they just need to know how to use them."

"That's true."

I hear footsteps begin to approach and try to lift my head, but it's too damn heavy. "Lucy?" Logan says, but then sniffs the air.

"I puked," I announce loudly.

He squats in front of me, next to stranger girl. "I know. Cameron called and said to come out and take care of you. Here," he says and hands me a bottle of water, "have this."

I take it and chug it all down. I burp when I'm done, but he doesn't seem to care. Neither does stranger girl. "Did I interrupt your... you know..." My eyes dart from side to side, making sure that no one can hear me. When I know it's safe, I continue with a whisper, "Sexy times?"

He chuckles and shakes his head. "No, Luce. And even if you did, you know you're my number one girl."

"Careful," stranger girl tells him. "If her boyfriend's anything like her, he might cut you."

Logan laughs, louder this time. "Oh, he's tried," he responds. I don't know what he means but I don't ask.

"I'm Logan," he says. He must be talking to stranger girl because I know his name's Logan. I'm not a dumbshit. I drop my head on my knees again.

"It's nice to meet you, Logan. I'm Amanda." A car pulls up to the curb. "And that's my ride."

I lift my head and wave goodbye.

She gets in, not another word spoken.

Seventeen
Cameron

S HE'S FALLEN ASLEEP in the passenger's seat while I replay the night in my head. I never really wanted it to happen like this, the first time we were… I dunno… intimate? I wanted it to be something she'd remember. Something that she'd be excited to call Claudia—her friend in New Jersey—and tell her about. I didn't want it to be in a bathroom at a party while she was buzzed. I don't regret it, though. Not for a second. Which I guess is the reason why I'm wearing a shit-eating grin as I pull into her driveway.

The porch light is on and her dad's sitting at the table—his usual spot when he's working late.

I crack a window and get out of the car, making sure to close the door quietly so I don't wake her.

"Hey Cam," he says, as I climb the steps. His eyes are red, and he looks tired. I notice the half empty bottle of whiskey in front of him. "She passed out?"

"Just fell asleep." My gaze moves from the bottle to him. "Everything okay?"

His eyes drift shut, but he nods. "Just having a night cap." He leans back in his chair and looks toward Lucy, whose head is resting on the window of the car.

"I was just going to carry her to her room if that's okay with you?"

"She drink tonight?"

"You want me to lie to you?"

He chuckles. "Yes."

"Then no, she didn't drink. She didn't puke either."

His face turns to a grimace. "At least she's experienced it once, right? I'm glad you were there with her."

139

"Of course."

He inhales deeply and looks at his watch. "Curfew at one?"

"Yes, sir."

Rubbing his hand across his beards, he asks, "You think you can call your mom? Ask her if you can stay with Luce tonight? She might need someone in case she gets sick again."

My eyebrows bunch in confusion. We've never spent the night together, but I guess we've never asked. We just assumed it wouldn't be allowed. "Are you sure?"

His eyes close again, like he almost can't control it. "Just don't take advantage of it, okay?"

"I'll just text her, she's probably at Mark's anyway." I hit send, and not a second later her name flashes on my screen. She speaks to Tom quickly before agreeing.

He tells me to leave Lucy in the car and sit with him for a bit. "Are you sure you're okay?" I ask him.

He doesn't respond to my question. "You ever had whiskey?"

I shake my head.

He pulls a glass off the tray and starts pouring.

It's the second time today an adult has given a minor alcohol.

The liquid burns in my throat. Tom laughs.

"That's…"

"An acquired taste," he finishes for me. "It's for grown men."

I try it again. Same reaction.

"How's school?"

"Good. Lucy keeps me in check."

"College plans?"

"Still the same."

He leans back in his chair, his arms folded over his chest. "Tell me again?"

And even though I have a feeling he already knows it all, I tell him anyway. Because I don't think it's about the college plans. I think he's just lonely.

I NEVER REALLY thought about college until Lucy came along. At first, it was just because I knew she wanted to go to UNC. She said that's where her parents met on graduation day. It wasn't until Tom saw my sketch and said that I could be an architect that I started taking it seriously. Lucy helped me to switch classes and start a plan. For now, UNC's a dream. I doubt I'd get accepted, and even if I did, we wouldn't be able to afford it. Mom and Luce have been going crazy looking into the grants and scholarships. They said it would be unlikely I'd get financial aid because of Dad's income, not that we ever see any of it.

I try to stay out of it. They may think it's possible, but I don't want to get my hopes up.

The original plan was for me to follow her there, get a full-time job and maybe a little apartment for us. Now, it's most likely community college and, somehow, scrape together enough change for a tiny studio apartment. I don't think she'd want to live with me in a place like that, but I don't want to be too far from her that I wouldn't be able to see her every day. Everyone knows my plans, and the only one that has questioned me following my *high school sweetheart like a sick puppy* is my dad. I would argue with him, but I can see his point. On paper, it seems crazy. In real life, crazy would be *me* if I didn't get to see her every day.

Tom nods while I explain all of this to him, but I doubt he's really listening. "Are you sure you're okay, Tom?"

"Yeah," he sighs. "I'm having a rough day is all."

I rub the back of my neck nervously. "You want to talk about it?"

He eyes me now, his gaze so intense I almost forget to breathe. "Lachlan called Virginia Mom." He rubs his eyes with the heel of his palm. "Actually he's been calling any woman he sees Mom. Virginia said it was because he gets confused at the playgroups she takes him to." He sighs and sips his drink. "I just miss her, Cam." He sniffs and wipes his eyes again, trying to hide his tears. "Some days are good, some days are bad. Today's a bad day. But two days ago, I had the worst kind of day. I forgot her." He sniffs again, clearing his throat roughly. "I went an entire day when I didn't think about her, and I went to bed thinking it was a good day, and then I realized why. I don't want to forget her, but it hurts too much to always remember her, you know?"

"No." My voice breaks, I clear it quickly. "I don't know," I answer truthfully. "And to be honest with you, I don't ever want to know. I can't spend a day without seeing Lucy. I don't even want to begin to understand the world of hurt if that were forever."

He nods, his tears falling faster than before. "Hey, remember that time you and Lucy were here, and she was telling you how she pictured your first house? You know, after college."

I laugh once. "Yeah, she was so detailed she asked me to sketch it."

He reaches over the table to his briefcase and clicks it open. He pulls out a few sheets of paper and goes through them. "This is your sketch, right?" He pushes my sketch across the table.

"Yeah, that's it." I smile. "How did you get this?"

"You left it on the coffee table."

"Oh."

He opens his mouth to speak, but nothing comes out. Then he sighs heavily and drops the rest of the papers in front of me. "I built it," he states.

Before I can wrap my head around what he's just said, he continues, "About a mile from here, still on our property. I'm going to show Luce tomorrow. She needs somewhere quieter, she's always complaining she can't study with all the noise. Just don't abuse my trust, okay Cam?"

I shake my head. "No, sir. I wouldn't."

"I know." He nods slowly. "I know that." He sighs again. "Can I be honest with you?"

"Always."

"I don't know... maybe when you guys go off to college, you can come visit me every now and then. That cabin will always be there for you two. Maybe summers you can come home? I know the boys will miss you." He wipes at his eyes again, unable to hold it in any longer. "You coming into Lucy's life the way you did—I don't know what would've happened if you weren't there—if you weren't there to see her suffering. Sometimes I wonder what she'd be like now if you..." He clears his throat. "I'm just grateful you're around for my little girl."

I watch as he stares down at the table, his eyes red raw from all the tears he's been crying, probably well before I showed up. And I've never felt what I feel now—this intense ache for a man who's lost half of himself. A man who's so hurt and so confused by his wife's memory that he's stuck. Not wanting to move forward but afraid to go back. "My wife would've loved you, kid," he mumbles, his eyes never lifting.

And even now, when he's so emotionally drained, he's still thinking of her. He still calls her his wife. I wonder if he'll always think of her as that, even when she's long gone. His *forever* wife.

I suck in a breath and swallow nervously. Squaring my shoulders and lifting my chin, I inform, "I'm going to make Lucy my wife one day."

"I know," he says without hesitation. "And when that day comes, you come see me, okay?"

◇　◇　◇

"MY MOUTH TASTES pukey," she says, stumbling to her bathroom. I don't think she's drunk anymore, just tired. She pauses with the toothbrush in her mouth and glances at me quickly before opening the cupboard under the sink and handing me a new one. When she's done, she flops onto her bed, her legs dangling off the edge with one arm covering her eyes. "Good night."

Chuckling, I stand over her and take her in. All of her. My heart does that thing. That tightening thing, the one that randomly reminds me of how in love with her I am. "Let's get your clothes off."

"Seriously, Cam?" she whines. "My brothers are in the next room."

"Yeah, Luce," I mock. "I was planning on having my way with you. Why do you think I'm here?"

She leans up on her elbows, her eyes unfocused. She glares at me curiously, questioning if I'm serious.

I roll my eyes and ask, "Where are yourPJs?"

"Bottom drawer," she says, pointing to her dresser.

I pull out the drawer and find the ones I bought her for Christmas last year. The pair that says *Boys in books are better.* She laughed when she opened it, but pounced on me and kissed all over my face. "It's a lie, you know?" she said. "No fictional boy has ever compared to you."

I pull them out of the drawer, but stop halfway when I see a book underneath. It's leather bound and old looking. "Is this your diary?" I tease, turning to her.

"What?"

I lift it and show her.

"Oh, no. That's my mom's. She gave it to me before she died."

"Oh." I feel like an asshole.

"It's okay," she says. "Actually, bring it here."

I pick it up carefully and take it to her, along with her PJs. I undress and re-dress her slowly. Taking in every curve of her body. When I'm done, she gets into her bed and pats the spot next to her. I shrug out of my jeans and get in. "This is nice," she says. "Having you here. Spending the night with you."

We get comfortable, side by side with her head in the crook of my arm. She places her mom's diary on my chest. "I used to read it when she started to get really sick and she could barely talk. I'd take it into my closet and read with a flashlight." She yawns loudly. "Sometimes I'd take my covers and throw them over me. She used to do that with us kids. She'd create a makeshift tent in the living room and sit us in a circle while she read us stories. I always sat next to her." She laughs once, but it's the sad kind. "She used to pretend that she didn't know words and get me to read them to her. She'd make me feel so smart, you know?" She wipes her eyes across my arm. The warmth of her tears soaks my skin. "I miss her."

"I know, baby."

"Will you read some to me?"

"Are you sure?"

She nods through a yawn. "Just a little, until I fall asleep."

I pick up the diary and flip it to the first page. Then I start to read to her.

When I was a kid, we had a dog. A car hit it when I was ten. I cried and cried. I screamed and yelled and Mom would hold me in her arms and tell me that it was okay. "But I love Mimi," I'd tell her. "I love her so much! More than anything in the entire world!"

Mom laughed at me. "Wait until you have kids," she'd said.

And I never believed her, not until now, not until I write this entry with Lucy in my arms. She's an entire day old. And she's more perfect than the greatest harmony, or the brightest double rainbow.

She's more than I ever let myself dream.

Tom's sitting in the chair in the corner of the room with a blanket thrown over him, snoring lightly. I don't know who had a worse time during labor: him or me. He cried. He's never cried. Not that I know of, anyway. But he did. He cried like a big old goofball. He said he was jealous because now he'd have to share my love. But he was wrong.

Love has no limits. No boundaries. No time. It's eternal. Forever.

And as I look down at my little baby girl, I've never felt such truth before.

So Mom, if you can somehow read this—from where you sit in your fluffy clouds in heaven—I want you to know that you were right. There's absolutely no love greater than the one you have for your children. Nothing.

I stop reading and glance down at her; she's fallen asleep. Her eyes are closed and her breaths are even. Her mouth's partially open, drooling onto my arm. I should be grossed out, but it's kind of cute.

I get more comfortable and read more of the pages. More of the life of a woman I wish I got the chance to know. A lot of the entries are about Lucy, and I wonder if each of the boys have something similar—a piece of her to keep forever.

I don't even realize how heavy my eyelids are until I get to the last page, but it's in different writing. It's Lucy's. I look down at her again. She hasn't moved since getting in this position. I question whether to read it or not, but she let me read it. She *wanted* me to.

Dear Mom,

I've never wished for you to be alive more than I wish now. I wish that you were here so you could sit in the closet with me while you pretend to be engrossed in all my girly secrets, like you used to when I was a kid. We'd giggle together and you'd ask me questions that were so insignificant to you, but you'd make them feel so significant to me. You always did that. In a house full of seven children, you always managed to make us all feel like individuals. Each of us was our own selves. But each of us was a piece of you, and Dad, and each other.

But you're not here. And every day I miss you more and more. Even though some days, especially lately, I think about the hurt of missing you less and less. I hurt less and less, Mom. And do you want to know why? It's a secret, but I'll share it with you.

It's because of a boy.

His name is Cameron.

And I think I'm in love with him.

I know you'd giggle now, and think to yourself, 'You don't know true love, you're only fifteen.'

But you'd keep asking questions anyway, and you'd make me feel less dumb for thinking that if this isn't true love, then I don't want to know what true love is. I just want to feel this—whatever I feel for him—forever.

Because in a time of nothing but pain, and anger, and empti-ness, and hurt… he healed me.

He made it stop.

He made it better.

He made me fall in love.

Love.

I love him.

And he shows up every day, thinking that I don't see him. That I don't want to speak to him. That I don't pay attention to him. But I do.

Some day I'll get the nerve to kiss him.

And someday after that, I'll get the courage to tell him that I love him.

Or… I could just sit here and keep dreaming about how hot he is. Maybe I'll just do that.

I blow out a breath and give my heart time to settle. The thumping weakens. The pace slows. The ache is still there. I rub my hand against it, hoping that it'll ease it somehow. But it's not a pain causing it. It's *love*.

I close the diary, set it on the nightstand, and switch off the lamp. I wrap both arms around her, bringing her as close as possible, but not close enough.

"I love you, Cameron," she whispers.

"Forever, Luce. I love you, forever."

Eighteen
Lucy

"I CAN'T BELIEVE Dad built that cabin for me!"

Cam yawns loudly and shakes off his sleepiness. "I know. How cool is it?" He yawns again.

"Are you okay, babe?"

He throws his head back against the car seat. "I'm so tired, Lucy. I don't know how you sleep as little as you do and still function."

I pull over in front of his house and turn to him. "I'm used to it."

He yawns again. "Come hang out for a bit?"

"You don't wanna sleep?"

"Later. I'll always choose you over sleep."

We sit on his couch for five minutes before he pulls me down to a laying position and lies in front of me. He wraps his arms around my waist and throws a leg over mine, pulling me flush against him. "I should go—"

"Shh! Be quiet."

I laugh as he settles his head comfortably on my breasts. "Maybe just—"

"Shh!" he says again, squeezing me tight.

A minute later he's out. And not long after that, so am I. I don't know how long it is after we both fall asleep that I hear the front door open. I lift my head to see Mark and Heather walking in. Our positions haven't changed so I lift my finger to my mouth to let them know he's asleep.

She smiles warmly and walks to him. Shaking him gently, she whispers his name.

He moans in response.

She does it again.

One of his eyes opens and a hint of a smile forms. "Boobies," he says, before rubbing his face on my breasts.

"Cameron!" Heather and I yell at the same time.

He must hear his mom's voice over mine because he lazily tilts his head back to face her. "Mother," he deadpans, then resumes his position.

Mark jokes, "Heather, you should get cock blocker of the year award."

"I hear that!" Cam says, raising his hand for a high five which never comes.

I giggle.

He positions his leg further around me and brings me closer to him.

His mom sighs, but there's amusement in her eyes. The same kind my mom had when she'd see us doing something stupid. "Maybe you should—"

"No." Cam squeezes me tighter, his head never lifting, his eyes never opening. "She's mine. Don't take her away."

He rubs his head against my chest again, trying to get comfortable. I run my fingers through his hair. It's rare that I get a chance to do it when he isn't wearing a cap. It's gotten shaggier, and darker, since we'd started dating. He's changed a lot since then.

Heather laughs quietly. "I was going to say why don't you take Lucy up to your room and sleep there?"

"Oh." He lifts his head to look at me. I'm already watching him, smiling, wondering how I got so damn lucky. His eyes drift shut again. "Will you carry me, babe?"

"Ooh," Mark whispers. "He's doing that fake drunk-from-fatigue thing he used to do when he was a kid so I'd carry him in from the car."

Cam groans in response, and then dramatically pulls away. First one leg, then one arm, then somehow he spins completely around and onto all fours on the floor. We all watch in amazement as he makes something like standing look like the hardest physical thing in the world. Once he's on all fours, he drops to the floor and curls into a ball. I have to nudge him with my foot to get him to wake up again. "Fine," he sighs, but he doesn't move.

"Fine, I'll be in your bed waiting for you."

"She has boobies," Mark chides.

Cam grunts, before standing up and taking my hand to lead me to his room.

He closes and locks the door, then leans against it. "I was told there'd be boobies," he says, his voice hoarse from sleep.

I laugh as I get into his bed. "Come back and hold me like you did. That was nice."

"So no boobies?"

I shake my head.

"Why does everyone lie to me?" He shrugs out of his jeans and peels off his shirt from the back, like guys do. I watch him the entire time.

"I know you want me," he says, smiling as he joins me in bed.

Five minutes later, he's quietly snoring next to me.

Cameron

"IT WAS AMAZING," I hear her whispering. "It's like nothing I've ever felt before. Even when I've dreamed about it, it never felt like that." I throw my hand out searching for her, but she's not there.

"I can't do that!" she whispers loudly.

I sit up and try to get my bearings.

"What am I supposed to say?" she giggles.

I look around my room like a dumbass trying to find her. The thing is—I'm one of those assholes who needs to sleep when I'm tired. And there's a reason for it; it's because I turn into a dumbass if I don't. Proof: I'm looking under my bed for her.

"Oh my God, Claudia. I can't do that." She laughs.

The bathroom door's open and I can see her reflection in the mirror, leaning back on the counter with the phone to her ear.

I fling my body back and try to get comfortable again.

"So I just say, 'Hey Cameron, thanks for letting me have the best mind-blowing orgasm and letting me come on and around your fingers. Wanna do it again?'"

"I'm up!" I shout. Fuck, I'm *up*.

She laughs loudly. "I'll call you back, Claud."

She struts out of the bathroom, gets on the bed and settles her legs on either side of me, straddling me. "You heard what I said?"

"Yup."

JAY McLEAN

"So?"

I try to hide my smile, grip her ass and pull her into me. "So?"

Her cheeks redden.

I raise an eyebrow. "Are you going to ask me?"

"No!" She drops her head on my shoulder, too embarrassed to face me. I lace my fingers in her hair and curl them, pulling lightly so her head tilts back and I can see her face.

She licks her lips, her eyes burning with lust. Then she thrusts forward, pressing her heat onto my dick and pushing her tits closer to my mouth. Her eyes seem to narrow and widen at the same time. A resolve washes over her features. She leans forward, kissing me once, softly. My fingers tighten; one in her hair, and the other on her ass. She pulls back, her eyes never leaving mine. "Please fuck me soon, Cam."

And at her words, I lose control. I throw her off me with so much force, she rolls over twice on the bed before landing on the floor with a thud. "Cam!" she screams, but I'm too busy slamming the bathroom door, getting in the shower, and turning the cold water on. I get in, boxer shorts and all, and start to... well... you know.

She bangs on the door. "Cam!"

"Fuck, yeah. Say my name," I whisper. My eyes are shut as I imagine her under me. Me between her legs and inside her.

"Cam!"

"One more time, babe," I say a little louder. *Fuck. I'm a creep.*

"Cam!"

I laugh. And come. At the same time.

✧   ✧   ✧

I SPEAK TO Mom, ask her if I can spend the night with Lucy in her cabin. Apparently Tom had already spoken to her. In fact, he asked for her approval before he went ahead and built it. She made a dramatic show of losing her son forever. Lucy felt bad and said that I should stay home. That was a week ago. We've spent every night in here since. Actually, we've spent every spare second together since.

I try to respect her dad's wishes and not take advantage, so I keep my hands off her until we go to bed. But I can't do anything about my hard-on once we get in there.

She usually stays up reading. I fall asleep pretty fast, waking only when she's done and she scoots down with me. We fall asleep with our arms around each other and her head on my chest. And we stay that way until we wake for school.

✧　✧　✧

FUCK.

I'm having a wet dream, and I'm in Lucy's bed. I'm gonna come in my shorts. This is bad. This is really fucking bad.

Body: No man, it's happening. Just accept it.

Brain: You can wake up before it happens. It's fine.

Body: Goddamn, it feels good. It's so warm. Did you know it would be this warm?

Brain: I don't know. I just think things.

"Fuck, baby, you feel so good," I mumble out loud. *Shit.*

I feel her giggle.

Body: What the hell do you mean 'feel' her giggle?

Brain: Dude, wake the fuck up!

"Huh?"

My eyes snap open. I look down at my dick… in her mouth!

"Holy fuck!"

I try to pull back but she holds my hips in place.

Brain: Dude, let it happen.

Body: Fuck yeah, dude. *Please* let it happen.

"Oh my God."

She pulls back, causing the cold air to hit my dick. "Does it feel okay?"

"Yeah babe. It feels so good."

She smiles, her mouth descending again. "So I should keep going?"

Body: Is she stupid? Of course she should keep going!

Brain: Wait. Did you even shower today?

Body: Who the fuck cares. Shut up, brain.

"Uh huh!" I lay my head back on the pillow, close my eyes. And I take it. "Oh my God," I moan again, feeling the pleasure of her mouth around me.

I do my best to hold back. Not wanting to come. Not wanting to thrust up and force it into her. "Oh my God."

She pulls back again.

I look down at her.

Her e-reader's next to my thigh and she's swiping across the screen.

"Are you seriously reading right now?"

"No." She shakes her head. "I'm researching."

I lean up, just enough to fling her e-reader off the bed. It flies across the room and bounces off the wall. "Fuck the research babe, you're doing amazing."

I grab the back of her head and push it back down.

She laughs, before taking me in her mouth again.

Body: Fuck yeahhhhhhhh!

"Tell me how you like it, baby," she says, my dick still touching her lips.

"Uh huh, just keep going."

Brain: That wasn't very nice, Cam.

Body: Shut the fuck up, brain.

"Cup my balls." *What the fuck? What did I just say?*

She sits up.

Body: Noooooo!

Her brows pinch. "What do you mean *cup?*"

I try to show her with my hands. "You know, like... hold them."

"Hold them?"

"Not hard... like don't grab them. Just *cup* them."

She shrugs. And then she cups them.

Body: Holy shit, dude!

Brain: I know, right?

"Please don't stop, Luce."

"Oh." She looks surprised. "You want me to do both at the same time?"

"Uh huh."

"Okay." She shrugs before getting back to work.

Body: Ho. Lee. Shit.

Brain: You don't deserve this, asshole.

Body: Seriously, shut the fuck up, brain.

"Give me your other hand," I tell her, leaning up so I can reach it. She gives me her hand. I take it and wrap it around the base of my cock, and show her how to move it.

She gets it right away.

"Fuck," I moan.

Body: Yeaaaahhhhh buddy!

My hips start moving on their own, matching her movements. "Babe," I warn.

Body: Not yet, man.

Brain: He can't help it.

"Babe, I'm gonna come."

She works faster, more determined.

Brain: She's not going to…

Body: Not yet! Not yet! Oh. Fuck…

I let out a grunt when I come. I pant, trying to level my breathing. She takes it all.

Her head lifts. Then her hands cover her mouth.

"Are you okay?" I pant.

She raises a finger, asking me to wait, and then she runs to the bathroom.

I hear the tap running, and her spitting. Then she brushes her teeth. Spits. Brushes. Spits. This happens four more times.

I lean back on my pillow, my fingers linked behind my head.

Body: Fuck yeah! You're a boss!

Brain: You, Cameron Aladdin Gordon, are a goddamn stud.

My cheeks hurt from grinning so wide.

She walks out of the bathroom with a bottle of mouthwash in her hand. Her mouth moves as she sloshes and gargles it. She looks at me with eyes narrowed, but she doesn't speak. She just walks back into the bathroom and spits it out. When she's done, she comes back out and glares at me. She picks up her e-reader off the floor and starts swiping the screen.

"What's wrong, babe?"

"Shh," she snaps.

I lay back down and get comfortable, my hands still behind my head, marveling in the glory of receiving my first blow job.

"This is bullshit!" she clips. "Either this book is fucked up or the woman who wrote it is one crazy-ass bitch."

I chuckle.

She glares.

I stop.

153

She goes back to the e-reader, her eyes scanning the lines. "Here," she points to it. "It actually says, 'Oh my God you stallion,'" she reads. "'I love your throbbing member in and around my mouth. I love the taste of your load. It's my favorite taste in the entire world. Come for me again.'" She looks up at me. "No, Cam. Just. Fucking. No."

She walks to the window, and before I can ask her what the hell she's doing, she's opening it and throwing the e-reader outside.

"It's bullshit, Cam. No one wants that shit in their mouth."

I all out laugh now. "What did you expect it to taste like?"

She shrugs, her face contorted in disgust. "I don't know. Not that. Like... maybe what you had for dinner."

"Hot dogs?"

She mock shivers and gets into bed.

"So, no more blow jobs?"

She throws an arm and a leg over me. "I'm not saying never, I'm just saying not for a while."

Chuckling, I kiss the top of her head and bring her closer. "Thank you, baby."

She tilts her head back to look at me. "So it was okay?"

"It was amazing."

She smiles. "I did good?"

"You did better than good, Luce."

She grins from ear to ear and kisses my chest. "It's kind of hot. I actually enjoyed it. Until you know... the whole funky spunk in my mouth thing."

Nineteen
Lucy

FOR THE LAST two weeks he's spent every night at my cabin. Some nights we have dinner at his mom's house and I tell him that he should stay there. His mom jokes that he may as well move out. I'm not sure if Cameron knew that she was joking, because now he has a drawer in my dresser, half my closet space, and the bathroom is filled with shaving products and manly cologne. Not that I'm complaining. I love having him close all the time. What I don't love is the fact that he barely touches me.

Two weeks we've slept in the same bed. Him in nothing but boxers, and me, in my tank and panties trying to look cute. Still, he won't touch me.

And I have no idea why.

And I'm frustrated.

So much so that watching him chew the end of his pen while he sits opposite me at our dining table is turning me on. That, and the fact that he's shirtless. And hot. When did he get so goddamn hot? I mean, he was always cute... but now... holy shit *I'm wet.*

And now he's licking his lips. God, I love his lips.

I squeeze my legs together, trying to ease the ache.

My eyes drop, focusing on the words in the textbook in front of me. We're supposed to be studying, but all I can think about is his mouth. I glance up. He's doing it again. The licking lip thing. Oh fuck, now he's biting it.

I wonder if I ever turn him on just by looking at me.

I gaze down at myself. I'm wearing a shirt that Logan bought me after Vaginagate. It says '*I hate tacos, said no Juan ever.*'

Nope. I highly doubt I turn him on.

I sigh loudly.

His eyes lift and his lips curve into a smile. Oh my God, his smile. His *lips*.

He slowly comes to a stand, his palms flat on the table. "Luce," he says.

"Mm?" I murmur, even though inside, I'm saying, *Take me! Take me now!*

"You got pizza sauce on your face."

I die.

He walks into the tiny kitchen and brings back a napkin for me.

"Thanks."

"You're welcome." He settles back in his seat, his eyes already concentrating on his homework on the table.

I sink down in my chair, feeling frumpy and stupid. And horny. *I'm so horny.*

Maybe I can make him want me. My lips curl at the corners when a plan comes to mind. I've read it in books, seen it in movies, surely it'll work.

Slowly, I raise my foot; maybe I can make him hard by rubbing him the right way. The instant my foot makes contact with his leg, he jerks back. "Holy shit!" he shouts. "Is that your foot? It's fucking freezing."

I drop chin to my chest. "Sorry," I mumble, my face burning with embarrassment.

"Are you cold?"

I glance up at him. He's on his feet, running a hand down his bare chest. *LICK.*

"What?" he asks.

Crap, I said lick out loud.

His look of confusion is so fucking hot I think I want to rape him. Yup. Going to stand up and just start humping his leg.

"Are you sick?" he asks.

"Huh?"

"Your feet are cold, but your face is red, like you're burning up, and you keep moaning and squirming in your seat." His eyes narrow even more. "I'll get you socks and an aspirin. Sit down, babe. Take it easy."

I grumble in my seat while I wait for him to come back. When he does, he kneels on the floor between my legs, and picks up my foot. My eyes drift shut, imagining his beautiful mouth kissing, licking, sucking its way up to my center. *I need him.*

"All done," he informs, causing me to open my eyes. He's covered my feet with socks, but he hasn't kissed me. My eyes glare at my legs. Maybe they're hairy. Maybe he just thinks I'm ugly. That could be it.

He leaves and comes back with a glass of water and an aspirin. "I wonder what's wrong with you. You shouldn't be getting your period for another week, right?"

I want to love him for being so in tune with me that he knows my cycle, but I can't think about that. Not when I want to lick him all over.

He takes his seat again, all relaxed and hot like he has no idea what I'm going through. He picks up his pen and lifts it to his already open mouth. He licks his lips once, so fucking slowly, then he runs the end of the pen across the bottom one, spreading the moisture.

I whimper.

Legit, whimper.

I sit up straighter and try to level my breathing. Round two, I think to myself. I raise my foot again, more determined this time.

And then...

"FUCK, LUCY!"

I wince at his words and shrink into my seat.

"You just kicked me in the balls, what the fuck?" He's shouting, on his feet, bent over at the waist.

"I'm sorry!" I shout back, standing and going to him.

"What just happened?"

I panic. "I had an itch."

"ON MY DICK?"

I'm trying to hug him, hoping it will make it better, but he pushes me away.

"I'm sorry!" I say again.

"It's okay," he says, a little calmer this time. He slowly straightens and places a hand to the side of my face. "It's okay," he repeats. "I'm sorry." He leans in and places his wet mouth on my dry one. "It just fucking hurts."

He tries to pull back but I grip his hips and refuse to let him go. I kiss him again, longer than he did. "You want me to kiss it better?" I ask.

His eyes go wide. "Huh?"

I smile, trying to be sexy, and then drop to my knees. I stare up at him while he chews his lip again. Curling my fingers around his shorts, I make a show of pulling them down and freeing him. Then my eyes widen. "Oh."

"What?"

"It's just—"

"Well, it's not hard, Luce. What did you expect?"

"I know. I just didn't expect it to be so small."

"Fuck you," he says, but he's laughing. He pushes his hand against my forehead until I fall back. I save myself with my outstretched arm.

He pulls his shorts back up and walks to the kitchen. "I hate you," he shouts over his shoulder.

I latch onto his back, wrapping my legs and arms around him. "I'm sorry!" I tell him.

"No. You're not forgiven." He bends over and swings me around until I'm in front of him with my arms around his neck and my legs around his waist. He sits me on the counter and peels me off him. "You have man hands," he clips.

I frown and raise my hands to look at them.

"And you drool in your sleep, it's fucking disgusting."

I wipe my mouth with the back of my man hands.

"And you—" He cuts himself off with a sigh. "Nothing. I got nothing. You're perfect." He links our fingers together and kisses the back of each of my hands. "And you don't have man hands. That was mean. I'm sorry."

I pull on his hands until his arms are around me and I scoot forward, trying to get as close to him as possible. I run my fingers down his bare chest. "I want to lick you," I tell him, unashamed now. "All over. Your lips first. I love your lips." I kiss him slowly, feeling his fingers dig into my waist.

He pulls back before I'm ready. "I have homework."

"Oh."

He sighs as his hands pull at his hair. "I just need to learn self-control with you. I can't just… I promised your dad… we can't always…"

I kiss him again, deeper this time. "But I'm so horny, Cam. I need a release."

He grunts, before picking me up and throwing me over his shoulder. He walks to the bedroom and throws me roughly on our bed. "I'll get you off, Luce," he says as a warning. "And that's as far as we go, okay?"

I nod.

He pulls on my ankles until my legs are off the bed. "Take your shirt and bra off. I want to see your tits."

I sit up. "Bossy Cam." I smile. "I love bossy Cam."

He folds his arms over his chest and quirks an eyebrow. He's hard now, made evident by the huge bulge in his shorts. I reach out to touch him there, but he pulls away.

"Luce, you get off and you only. I'm not playing."

Five minutes later, my shorts and panties are off and his mouth is exactly where I want him. My fingers curl on the bedspread under me. "Holy fuck, Cam."

He doesn't falter, not for a second. His fingers slide in and out, his mouth kisses, and his tongue licks. He started faster, more rushed. I asked him to slow down, so he did. And now—now he's perfect, bringing me to the edge twice, only to pull away smiling.

"Cam!"

And he starts again.

"You have to let me…" I breathe out.

The vibration of his response against my wetness has me squirming. He uses his forearm to hold down my stomach, keeping me in place.

My hips thrust forward, wanting more of him. And he gives it. Fuck, does he give it.

My back arches off the bed. I'm panting his name, over and over. He never stops. Not until the last wave hits me and my body collapses.

"I can't feel my legs," I moan. "Or my face."

I gaze down at him through heavy eyelids. He stands at the end of the bed, his hard-on tenting his pants. He picks up my discarded shirt and wipes his mouth. Then he looks at me. From my head, all the way down to my toes. He's never seen me fully naked before. His eyes trail back up as he licks his lips. "You're so fucking sexy, Lucy. I was so close to coming just from tasting you like that."

I sit up and pull his shorts down, freeing him completely. "I want to have sex, Cam. Please?"

I scoot up on the bed until my head hits the pillow, and then spread my legs for him. "I'm ready," I tell him, my voice coming out a whisper. And a ton of emotions hit me full force. *I love him.* I don't want to share this with anyone else, and I lie here, prepared for him. Waiting for him. While he stands at the end of the bed looking at me, fighting a war in his head.

I don't know why I waited so long, not when I've always been so sure of him. Of us.

"Please, Cameron."

He kicks off his shorts and climbs onto the bed and between my legs. "Lucy, I don't—"

"Do you love me?" I ask him.

He rests his forearms on either side of my head as his eyes scan mine. "You know I do."

"Then why are you hesitating?"

He shakes his head, then rests it on my shoulder, slowly dropping his hips so I can feel his hardness against me. "I didn't want it to be like this... in the heat of the moment. I wanted to make it romantic. You know, hotel room, candlelit dinner, open fireplace, rose petals and shit."

I take his head in my hands and lift it so he'll look at me. "I don't care about that stuff. I just want you."

He nods. "I'm nervous."

"I'm scared."

"Maybe we shouldn't."

"No, I want to."

He looks down my body, to where we're about to join. Leaning on one arm, he uses the other to position himself. I feel it where I think it should be, and I wait.

"Are you sure?" His voice breaks. "I don't want you to feel forced—"

I nod. "I love you."

"I love you, too." He kisses me, the taste of myself on his lips turning me on more. I push down a little, welcoming him.

"I love you so much, Luce," he says, pushing into me.

My eyes squeeze shut, trying to stop from groaning in pain when he fills me.

"Are you okay?" he whispers in my ears.

"Mm hmm," I answer—my eyes still closed to avoid the tears from falling. "Is that it?"

"No, babe, I'm not even half way."

I whimper. "Okay, just go. Do it. Get it over with."

"Lucy." His voice is shaky. "Maybe we're not ready. Maybe we—"

I let out a sob. It hurts so much and he's not even in yet.

"I can't do this, Luce, not when you're crying."

"No!" I press my hands firmly on his ass so he can't move.

He lifts his head, sniffing once. "Okay."

Then a pain so unbearable takes over my entire body. I scream so loud that it's surprising to my own ears.

"I'm so sorry," he says, his body shaking. "Shit shit shit."

He tries to pull out but I hold him in place. "I just need to get used to it," I cry out. "Just hold still for a moment."

"I can't, Lucy. You're fucking crying. I made you cry. This is not how I wanted this to go. This should've been perfect for you and I ruined it."

"Stop it," I whimper. "It is perfect, Cam. You're perfect. I just—"

"I hate this," he cuts in, wiping his eyes on my shoulder and refusing to look at me. "I can't keep going, Luce. Not like this."

I sniff back my tears, and I suck it up. Because this isn't just about me, it's about him, and I'm ruining it for both of us. "It doesn't hurt anymore," I lie. "Start moving."

He lifts his head, his eyes searching mine. "Are you sure?"

"Yeah, babe." I nod. "Just go slow, okay?"

"It won't take long, I—I promise." And then he moves. It hurts like hell, but I keep it in. I do my best to stay silent, to not wince in pain, to not beg him to stop.

"I love you, Lucy," he whispers, raising his eyes to mine—with so much emotion, so much heart—and for seconds that feel like hours, we stare at each other.

And then he kisses me, and we *make love*.

And it's perfect.

Just the way he wanted it.

Cameron

AFTER I CAME, she practically ran to the shower, and that's where she stayed for a good half hour. I didn't know what to do. I didn't know what to say. And now—she's crying in my arms and I'm lost. I'm *so* lost.

"I'm not crying because it hurts," she says, somehow reading my mind.

"Then why?" I whisper, scooting down on the bed and under the covers so we're face to face. "Tell me."

"Because I'm emotional." She sounds almost embarrassed. "I felt so much just now, with you inside me like that, and it was more than just physical. I don't..." She blows out a heavy breath. "I don't want you to share that with anyone else."

"What?" I ask, confused.

"I just don't want to think about the future, and if anything happens... it hurts so much to think that you could share something like that with someone else, something so pure, and intimate. I hate—"

"Stop." I cut in. I have no idea where any of this is coming from, but I don't question it, because if there's one thing I know from living with Mom, and being with Lucy, it's that women are dumb. "Do you think that I want that? That I'd want to be with other people?"

"I think eventually you—"

"You're wrong, Luce. So wrong it's not funny." I roll onto my back and contemplate what I'm about to tell her—because I know it's wrong for kids at seventeen to think about what I think. But I look at her now, with tears in her eyes, and I don't care. I tell her anyway, "I think about our future a lot. More than you want to know."

"Yeah?" she asks, a hint of a smile forming. "What do you think about?"

She sits up in front of me, removing the covers from both of us, and crosses her legs. I do the same, and lace our fingers together. "I think about marrying you, Lucy, and having a lot of kids."

She laughs quietly, her tears almost gone. "How many kids?"

"Well, at least four," I tell her honestly. "Four girls. Meg, Jo, Beth and Amy."

She gasps quietly. "Like in *Little Women*?" she says, her voice coming out high, like a little girl.

I nod. "Uh huh."

"You read the book?"

Shaking my head with a grimace, I reply, "I watched the movie."

She laughs, before shuffling closer to me. So close, she's straddling me. "What else?"

"I'd want a couple boys at least. You know, so I'm not surrounded by crazy."

I watch as her head throws back in laughter. "You're lying," she says.

"I'm not. I've even designed the house we live in. I figure your dad can build it for us. It won't be for a while but—"

"Cam," she whispers, tears falling again. But I know her cries now. I've learned to read them. These are the good kind. The happy ones.

"My favorite room in the house," I start, pulling her closer to me. "Is gonna have these huge double doors, like the ones on the town library."

She smiles.

I continue, "I'm gonna design a sign for the door, it's going to say 'Mom's Manor.'"

Her eyebrows bunch. "Your mom's gonna live with us?"

I laugh. "No, not *my* mom. It's going to be your room. You'll be *Mom* by then."

"Will you sketch the room for me?" she asks hesitantly. She knows I'm still a little uncomfortable with showing her my stuff. But the way she's looking at me now, I'd find a way to fly to the moon if she asked me.

"Yeah, babe."

She squeals, jumps off me, and the bed, and goes to her backpack to pull out a pen and notepad. I sit against the headboard with my legs spread and wait for her to sit between them. When she's comfortable, I set the notepad in front of her and wrap my arms around her waist and settle my chin on her shoulder. I touch the pen to paper…

And then I draw.

Her room in our future house.

And I explain to her what everything is, and what I envision. Wall to wall shelves of nothing but books. Her own fireplace. Her huge, comfortable armchair, and then the smaller ones in front of it. So her and our kids can sit in there and read, or she can read to them. She cries the entire time. But it's nothing compared to how she reacts when I tell her the best part—the half room hidden behind one of the bookcases. It opens up when you pull a certain book, the book being *Little Women*. "We can hang linen from the low ceiling," I tell her. "That way you and our kids can have your own makeshift tent, like your mom did for you. And you can read them stories, have them help you with the words, you know?" I pause and wait for her sobs to stop. "You can tell each other secrets. You can build memories, Luce. And you can remember them, too. You can remember your mom every day."

Twenty
Cameron

LUCY GOT INTO early admission, we all expected she would, but that didn't stop us from celebrating like crazy—a small one with family, then a big one with friends. For now, her and Jake were going to be at UNC. The rest of us were still waiting. Our friends never really planned on going to the same college together, it kind of just happened.

She cried that night, though. She said it was bittersweet; that she didn't know what she'd do if I didn't get in. She told me she wouldn't go without me. I told her she was being dumb, and that I'd go with her regardless, even if it meant full-time work and night classes. Even if it took me ten years to get a degree, there was no way I'd let us be apart.

Now, she's crying for a different reason. "Cameron," she squeals. And I laugh. She waves my acceptance letter in the air before lunging at me, kissing me a thousand times. "I'm so proud of you!"

"Thanks, babe." Truth is, I'm proud of myself too. I've worked really hard over the last year to get that one letter. The only problem is that I don't know if I can afford to go, but I don't let that ruin the moment.

"Does your mom know?"

I shake my head. "No. I just went there quickly to check the mail but she wasn't home. I came straight here."

"We need to celebrate!" she says.

My grin is instant. "How?"

✧ ✧ ✧

IT TURNS OUT that Lucy is a lady in the street and a freak in the bed. We didn't have sex for a few weeks after the first time because she was still physically healing. After the fourth time, she kind of got obsessed.

165

Honestly, we both did. For a few months though, she was bleeding on and off. We went to see Dr. Matthews about it; he said it might be the effect of the Implonen. He took it out and we chose the IUD instead. Since then, she's been fine. Better than fine.

"PULL MY HAIR!"

I'd laugh but I'm so fucking close to coming that if I moved wrong, I would.

"PULL IT!"

"Okay!" I yell. I reach up and tug her hair.

"FUCK YEAH, BABY!" She's on all fours, on the floor of the living room. "GRAB MY TITS!"

I reach around and do what she asks, trying to not lose the rhythm of my pumps. Fuck, I love her like this.

"RUB MY CLIT!"

"I DON'T HAVE ANY MORE HANDS!"

She grunts and starts slamming her ass into me. I feel her tighten and I know she's close. I try to hold off until I know she's done. When she starts, she growls and falls on her forearms, her ass in the air, ready for the taking. And I take it. Oh fuck, do I take it.

✧   ✧   ✧

"IF YOU WON'T take my money, you should at least ask his dad!" Mark whispers loud enough that we can hear them in the kitchen from the living room of Mom's house.

Luce and I look at each other while we sit on the couch. She smiles sadly and takes my hand.

For two weeks since we got the acceptance letter, this is what it's been like. After the first few days of searching for grants and looking into financial aid, we gave up. Mom's savings were only enough to cover a semester, if we were lucky. And that didn't include housing. That meant a two and half hour drive each way.

"His dad hasn't paid a cent to you guys ever," Mark continues.

"That's because I never asked him to. And what's wrong with you? You think that the life I've built for us isn't good enough? Huh? Do you think we need that money?"

"I hate this," I whisper.

"I'm sorry."

Mark responds, his voice getting louder, "I just don't understand why you won't let me pay! Why are you so stubborn that you won't accept help?"

Lucy squeezes my hand. "Maybe you can speak to Mark? Maybe he can lend you the money."

I shake my head.

Mark adds, "He's my son, Heather! Whether it's on paper or not! You don't want to move in with me, that's fine. I let it slide. But I don't understand why you won't let me take care of my family!"

Mom cries.

So does Lucy.

Mark apologizes.

I reach for my backpack and pull out the community college catalogs I've collected and start going through them.

Lucy kisses my cheek. "I'm so proud of you," she whispers, her breath shaky.

"Thanks," I tell her. "But it was all for nothing."

✧　✧　✧

IT'S BEEN THREE weeks since I got the letter, and a week since I sent off the applications for community college. I plan on going there this weekend to look around for any job opportunities.

"Dad invited us for dinner tonight," Lucy says with a grimace. "I guess to celebrate me getting into UNC. He said he's been waiting for you to get your letter. I guess he's just been hesitant because you can't go, but he still wants to take us, and your parents too… I mean your mom and Mark."

"Of course," I tell her. "Did he not want to do it earlier because he was afraid I'd be upset or something?"

She shrugs. "I guess."

✧　✧　✧

WE MEET TOM and the rest of the boys at one of the few family restaurants that can accommodate a family their size. Mom and Mark have worked out their issues about him paying. He doesn't understand why we're both so stubborn, but he's accepted it and moved on. I think we've all moved on from the high of me being accepted in the first place.

"I have eleventy-three sticks hidden in Filmore," Lachlan, Lucy's youngest brother, the baby of the family, tells me from his position on my lap. After Filmore died, Tom got it towed to his house and Lachlan's been using it as his own little clubhouse since.

"Eleventy-three?" I ask him. "That's a lot of sticks."

He raises a finger, and then curls it, asking me to bend down to his level. Once my ear is to his mouth he whispers, "I have to hide them from the others. Don't tell."

I chuckle. "Okay, dude. I swear it. I won't tell a soul."

He grins from ear to ear.

"Cameron's an amazing secret keeper," Mom tells him.

"It's true," Mark agrees.

Lachlan's eyes narrow from me to Mom then back again. "Your mamma's pretty," he says. "I'm gonna marry her."

I laugh.

Mark chimes in, "Sorry, Lachlan, she's all mine."

"Did you call dibs?" he shouts.

Mark rears back in surprise.

"DIBS!" Lachlan yells. "I WIN!"

The table erupts with laughter, just as a tray of champagne is set on the table.

Tom hands them to Mom, Mark, Lucy and I, and then takes a seat. "Before we do a toast to my little girl," he says. "I wanted to mention something real quick."

"Daddy," Lucy whines.

"Daaaaddy," Little Logan mocks, rolling his eyes.

That gets laughs.

"It's okay, Luce, it's not about you, or how you used to eat your boogers until you were seven."

She gasps.

We laugh again.

"Actually," Tom continues, looking right at me. "Remember that sketch you made one night? The night when I was panicking and thought I'd lost the deal?"

I nod. "The development ones?"

"Yeah. You remember how I told you that I took it to the developers and they loved it? After that I had to find an architecture firm to do the proper blueprints. I went to Bradman. Have you heard of them?"

I nod. "Yes sir, they're one of the biggest architecture firms in the state."

He smiles. "They didn't change much with your plan. They actually thought it was amazing—what you managed to do from just your eye alone."

Lucy holds my hand under the table, smiling as she does.

Tom adds, "Anyway, we're working together again on a new development so I had a meeting with them today. I was there for two hours while I waited for all these kids who were in and out of Mr. Bradman's office. When I finally got to meet with him, I asked him what it was about. He said they were experimenting with a scholarship program—"

"You got him an interview?" Mom cuts in, her eyes wide with anticipation.

Tom huffs out a breath. "No," he says, and I can see the instant disappointment in Mom's eyes. "See that's the thing," Tom continues. "I mentioned you, asked if he remembered that sketch. He didn't realize that you were still in high school. He thought you were in college, already on your way…"

He sips his champagne while we all wait for him to continue.

"And?" Lucy says, sitting on the edge of her seat.

"And they don't want an interview," he deadpans.

My shoulders slump in disappointment.

"They said they don't need it. Your work is miles above the other kids. They want to offer you the scholarship, Cameron. But just for the first year, until they decide if it's beneficial to the firm. It includes housing, and they—"

"The whole first year?" Mom whispers.

I can't breathe.

Tom nods.

Mom drops her head in her hands. "I'm sorry," she sobs, getting up from her seat. "Excuse me."

And then she's gone.

"Babe." Lucy gets my attention.

"Did you know?" I ask her, still unable to breathe.

She shakes her head. "I swear it. This is the first I'm hearing about it."

I pass Lachlan to her and leave the restaurant. I need fresh air. I need to think. I need to clear my head.

"Cameron," Mom says. I didn't even know she was out here. She throws her arms around my neck and pulls me down to her.

She cries.

And I let her.

Twenty-One
Cameron

"**D**AMMIT, LUCY, I'VE wanted to get you out of this stupid prom dress ever since I saw you in it."

"You think it's stupid?" she asks, unlocking the door to the cabin.

It only takes a second before I have her up against the wall and I'm inside her.

"I like this dress," she moans, her head throwing back against the wall.

I grab her ass and lift her so I can slide in better.

We're both buzzed. No. Beyond buzzed. We're drunk, and having sloppy sex. It's one of my favorite types of sex, because with her, there are *types* of sex.

Some nights, she wakes me after reading something and wants to try it.

I swear to God I'm the luckiest asshole in the world.

"I think there's too much of this dress," I tell her, my mouth sucking hard on her neck.

She rips my shirt open, and buttons fly everywhere. One hits her in the eye. "Ow!" she winces, holding her hand to it.

"You're too rough, Lucy. You need to learn to control yourself."

She scoffs. "I'm rough? What about that time you tried to shove it in the wrong hole?"

I laugh onto her nipple, now in my mouth. "You were begging for it!"

"Not in my ass."

"One day."

"Why did you tell everyone I take it there?" she moans. I don't know how she can talk with me slamming into her like this.

"Because I'm drunk."

"Valid. I read about it though, you have to start with your pinky finger or something. And then two, and then you can probably do it. Wait. For your sized cock, maybe three or four fingers."

I stop and straighten up so I can look at her. "Are you trying to make me come early?"

She laughs and nods.

"I'll do it right now, Luce," I warn.

She laughs harder. "We gotta be quick, they're all out there waiting. They're gonna know what we're doing."

I carry her to the bed and throw her down, then remove the rest of my clothes.

"I'm sure they already know what we're doing, babe."

She struggles to slip her dress off. I wait impatiently. When she's done, she lies on her back, her legs already spread.

I climb on top of her and enter her with ease. "You're getting loose," I joke.

"Maybe your dick's getting smaller."

We laugh. "We must be wasted," she adds.

"Speak for yourself, I can go all night with this shit."

"Cameron?"

I look down at her face, her eyelids heavy from the alcohol. "Yeah, babe?"

"I know I'm drunk, but thank you for never cheating on me. That Mikayla girl must be a mess. And Jake's good people for taking her in like that. I'm just glad I've never experienced that."

"Um..." I pause mid thrust. "You're welcome?"

"She's cute... Mikayla... if we ever have a threesome with another girl, I'd want her to look like that."

I start thrusting again. "Keep talking shit like that and I won't be able to take care of you, Luce."

Her hands run slowly down my back. "I'm your girl, Cameron. It's your job to take care of me. Always."

Lucy

CAM AND I make everyone breakfast the next morning, everyone but Jake. He wanted to make sure that Mikayla got home safe.

We sit in the living room and eat, talking shit about the night before. Logan looks around the cabin. We've spent a few nights here the last year, drinking and being stupid. Out of all the things I'm thankful for about

Cameron, his friends are one of them. When Claudia left, just after my mom passed away, I struggled with the idea of having no friends. But his friends took me in, made me part of the group. Now, I don't remember a time where they weren't part of my life. Even Logan, who I thought was a dick, has become one of my best friends. "What are you guys going to do when we get to UNC?" he asks.

"What do you mean?" Cam says.

"I mean you won't be rooming together. You guys basically lived with each other the last year or so. What happens there?"

Cam and I glance at each other quickly. We've spoken about it, but try not to think too much. We know we'll miss each other, but we also know that we'll do absolutely everything we can to spend every spare second together. "We'll make it work," Cam says, kissing my temple.

Logan's phone rings, breaking the tension. "Waddup?" he answers. Then his eyebrows bunch. "Yeah, bro. Hang on..." He places his phone on the coffee table and sets it to speakerphone. "Okay," Logan says.

"Umm..." Jake's deep voice comes through the speakers. He sighs heavily into the phone. "It's about Mikayla..."

✧　✧　✧

I EXCUSE MYSELF and go to our room. I hear the others say goodbye and then the front door closing. I cover my head under the sheets and continue to cry.

The bed dips, cold air hits my back, and then Cameron's warm arms are around me. "Lucy?" he whispers, his voice hesitant.

I sit up and face him. He leans back against the headboard and pats his lap twice. I climb on him, knowing my face is a mess from all the uncontrolled tears.

"You're hurting?" he asks.

I nod.

"Talk to me."

I try to settle my sobs, my voice coming out strained when I say, "I think I should reach out to her. I think that I should be a friend. Maybe she doesn't have any left after what happened. I don't know. I just feel like I should do something."

My breaths are broken with each inhale. I cry hard and loud into his neck.

"I know, babe," he says. "It's because you care so much. You feel everything so intensely. You hate seeing devastation around people, and you want to be their rock. You've always been like that."

I pull back and look in his eyes as they scan mine.

"Even before your mom died you took care of your family. And when she passed, you took care of your brothers, your dad, everyone but yourself. You wanted to be the glue that held them together, but you're allowed to break, Lucy. If you want to be her friend, I'll support you, but you have to let her break."

I nod and cry again. I can't stop crying. "You're my rock," I tell him. I rub my eyes with the back of my hand. "I don't know how I would have gotten through any of it if you didn't show up every day. If you weren't there…"

"Shhh." He pulls me closer and rubs slow circles on my back, the way he always does when I'm upset. "Don't think about it."

"But I have to!" I lean back again so we're face to face, because we need to have this conversation. "I'm not being petty and insecure, Cameron. This is real life, this isn't a fairy tale where everything ends with a happily ever after. What if we go to college and things change? What if something or someone gets between us? What then?"

"Stop," he says, his eyes glazing. "I hate thinking about this."

"I know, but we need to."

"No we don't, Luce. I love you. You love me. That love's forever. Nothing else matters. I promise."

"You can't promise that. You can't predict the future. You can't tell me that we'll be forever when you don't know."

He lets his head fall back onto the headboard and looks up at the ceiling.

"I'm serious, Cam."

"I know, babe," he sighs, then straightens up and holds my head in his hands. Our eyes lock for the longest time. Like we're taking each other in for the first time, or the last. It could have been seconds. It could have been hours. Then he speaks, "I love you, Lucy. I'll always love you, even if you don't know it. So… even if forever isn't eternal, I promise to love you for *our forever*."

I try to sniff back my sobs, but it doesn't work. "And what happens if *our forever* is short? What if something happens?"

He kisses me softly, for so long, that I almost forget why I'm crying. He pulls away, but not enough that his lips leave mine. "Then I will love you, for *our* forever *more*."

Twenty-Two
College, Sophmore Year
Cameron

T HIS GIRL HAS been looking at me strange since class started. I'd seen her before but we've never spoken. I see her get up from the corner of my eye and start walking toward me. She dresses differently than Lucy, not in a bad way. Just different.

The scraping of the chair next to me has me flinching, but I don't look up.

"Hey," she whispers.

"What's up?" I try to keep my tone even. Not unfriendly, but not friendly either. I don't want her getting the wrong idea.

"You're Cameron, right?"

I nod, my eyes staying fixed on the plan I'm working on.

"I'm Roxy."

"Cool."

She laughs quietly. "It's okay," she says, "I'm not trying to hit on you, if that's the reason you're being an asshole right now."

I can't contain the chuckle that escapes. Finally lifting my eyes to hers, I ask, "What's up?"

"You work at Bradman, right?"

"Kind of. It's unpaid. They float me so I can study here."

"Oh." She smiles with excitement. I can't tell if it's genuine or not. "That's kind of a big deal."

I shrug. "Not really. It's more of an '*I know people who know people*' deal."

She continues to smile, her thick long black hair swaying with her nods.

My eyebrows draw in. "Why?"

"Oh," she says, laughing again. She laughs a lot. Not fake, I don't think. More like carefree. "I applied for a job there. It's not much but it's good experience. I was hoping maybe you could..." she trails off.

"Could what?" I ask. I know what she wants but I feel like being a dick.

She smacks my arm with the back of her hand and rolls her eyes. "You're going to make me ask?"

"Yup."

"Fine," she sighs. "Dearest Cameron, if you would be so obliged to perhaps offer a good word in response to myself, that would be more than fabulous. You are also welcome to state the fact that I have fairly large bosoms, if you so wish."

My eyes drop to her tits quickly. And then I curse myself for doing it.

She laughs again. "I was kidding about the tits, but hey, whatever works. Thanks, Cam."

She spins on her heels and walks away.

"What's your name?" I shout after her.

"Roxy!"

"Did you tell me that already?"

"Yes," she says and laughs.

❖   ❖   ❖

I RUSH TO my dorm straight from classes to get dressed for work. Lucy's sitting outside my door with earphones in and her e-reader in her hand. I kick her shoe with mine. She looks up and smiles. "Hey." She packs her shit in her bag and stands while I unlock and open my door. "I've missed you today."

I shrug out of my clothes and look for my work ones. "Me too," I rush out, dropping to the floor to look for my shoes.

"You have to work tonight?"

She's standing in the middle of the room and getting in my way. I pick her up and set her on my bed so I can find my shirt. "Yeah, babe." I find the shirt under a pile of shit on my desk and sniff it. It'll do.

"When do you leave?"

"Ten minutes." I turn full circle in the room, scanning the floor. "Where are my shoes?"

"Cameron."

I stop what I'm doing, take a breath, and turn to her. "What?" I snap.

She smiles sadly. "I'm sorry, I just miss you."

My shoulders drop. *I'm an asshole.* I release the shirt from my hand. "I'm sorry, baby. Since they made part of the scholarship working at the firm, and classes, and actual paid work, I've just been busy. I'm sorry," I repeat. "I shouldn't be taking it out on you."

My workload freshman year was fine. I had classes and I worked part-time at a video game store. This year, they changed the scholarship to include unpaid hours there. I agreed because I didn't feel like I had a choice, but now we're months into the second semester and it's starting to kill me.

Pouting, she gets off the bed to pick up my discarded shirt off the floor. She walks back and stands on the bed, opening the shirt for me to put on. She kisses me, leaning forward as she does. My hands move to her waist, my fingers digging into her skin. It feels like forever since I've touched her. "I miss you," I whisper, pulling back from her lips.

She focuses on buttoning my shirt from the bottom up. I watch her eyes narrow in concentration. My hands move lower on her waist, down to her ass, and squeeze once.

She chuckles and presses her body into mine. "You want me to drive you to work and pick you up? It's an extra ten minutes each way we can spend together?"

"Yeah, babe. I'd love nothing more."

She smiles and kisses me again.

"I'm sorry," I say for the third time. Because she doesn't deserve the way I know I've been treating her lately. Like she comes second. And she doesn't. She'll always come first.

"It's fine, Cam. You're stressed." She shrugs. "Also, you need pants."

✧　✧　✧

I SPEAK TO my bosses about that Roxy girl from my class. I don't have much to say, apart from the fact that she's in my class. They tell me they've already chosen her for the position, which is kind of cool, because everyone else who works here has a giant freezer sized rod stuck up their ass.

I tell Lucy about it on the drive home. She has fifty questions about

Roxy which I can't answer. The only thing I know about her is that her name's Roxy, and I could maybe guess her bra size. I leave that last part out.

"So she just came up to you and asked you to put in a good word? What if she sucks, Cam? That's on you."

I throw my head back against the car seat and settle my hand on her leg. "Don't worry about it, babe."

I close my eyes, too exhausted to keep them open. She wakes me when we get to campus. "Your dorm or mine?"

"Yours, babe." Mitch, my roommate, who everyone calls Minge—which apparently is British slang for pussy—snores like a freight train. Lucy's slept over a couple times while he was there. She kept threatening to get up and punch him in the dick. One time, she actually did. We now have a No Lucy Post Luna policy.

✧ ✧ ✧

MY ALARM GOES off sooner than I'd like. She moans, rubbing her face on my chest. "Turn it off."

I rub my eyes to wake them up. "I can't. I have an early class."

"Skip it."

"Sure," I say, trying to peel her off me.

She holds on to me tighter. "No. It's so warm in here, and so cold out there. Just stay. Five more minutes."

She's right, she is warm. But I need to get to class. I try to get up again but she moves, like a tiny ninja, and covers me, her legs on either side of me. She glances over at Rose's—her roommate—side of the room. The bed's empty. She chews her lip to cover her smile. "Five minutes?" And this is my favorite version of Lucy. Her eyes are still heavy from sleep, her hair's a complete mess, there's no make-up, just Lucy. The Lucy I fell in love with. The Lucy I can't say no to. "Five minutes," I tell her. It comes out a warning. I reach over and set a timer on my phone. When I look back, her shirt's already off.

Five minutes turns to an hour. Because five minutes with Lucy isn't enough. *Forever* with Lucy isn't enough.

She laughs while watching me frantically dress. Her door opens and Rose walks in just as I'm pulling my shirt over my head.

"Good fuck?" Rose asks.

"Always," Lucy answers.

I search around for my phone and wallet while they continue to talk about me.

Rose laughs and kicks my phone from across the room. "*O* count?" she asks Luce.

"I lost count after three."

"I still say you lie about that."

I freeze with my wallet halfway in my pocket. *Why would she lie?*

"That's because you've never been with Cameron."

She giggles while I kiss her goodbye. "Love you, babe."

"Love you, too."

Then Rose pipes up. "I could love you too, Cameron."

I shake my head. "See ya, Rose."

She slaps my ass as I walk past. "Later, stud."

"Don't touch my boyfriend's ass you whore."

Lucy

"I DON'T GET it, Luce." Rose takes a hair tie from my dresser and starts pulling up her short blond hair. "Most girls struggle to reach a climax and you say Cam gives you multiples. How? Please. Tell me. I've been chasing an *O* for the last two months."

"Maybe you should stop whoring around and settle down."

She scoffs and looks at me like she's going to puke. "Un-fucking-likely."

I laugh at her reaction. "I don't know." I shrug. "I think it's different with us. Some people, like you, get off on being with different people. We've been together since we were fifteen. We were each other's firsts. We kind of worked with each other. Does that sound dumb?"

"No," she says seriously, taking a seat on her bed and crossing her legs. "Please, go on."

"I guess we kind of just taught each other what we liked. We know each other inside out—"

"Literally," she cuts in.

I throw a pillow at her. "You know what I mean. We just know each other's bodies. We know what works and what doesn't. We take care of each other."

She quirks an eyebrow. "I bet you do. Hey!" She sits up a little higher. "You know who I wouldn't mind teaching me how to take care of them?"

I eye her suspiciously. "Who?"

"Jake Andrews."

It's my turn to scoff. "Good luck with that."

"No chance, huh?"

"Nope."

Her shoulders sag, then they lift again and her eyes widen. "Logan Matthews? He'll do reaaaal good."

I shake my head. "Nope. Officially off the market."

"What?" she asks incredulously. "I screwed him twice last year, and he said he didn't do relationships."

I shake my head harder. "Trust me, Rose. He's off limits. Amanda owns his balls."

"Your friend Amanda?"

I nod.

"Wow. Didn't see that coming."

"That's what she said."

Twenty-Three
Cameron

I'M TOO BUSY working on my sketch that I don't see who places the cup of coffee next to it. "It's a thank you," a girl says from next to me. I don't need to look up to know it's Roxy. Her voice has a huskiness that makes it unique.

I lean back and glare at my work. Something's off but I can't pinpoint it. "For what?"

"I got the job."

I turn to her after a few more seconds. "You just found out? You spoke to me about it a week ago."

"They called me this morning. Wait. Did you know before that?"

I nod. "I've known since that day."

Her smile is huge. "So you did put in a good word."

Shrugging, I answer, "Yeah, but you already had it before I mentioned anything."

"Oh." Her smile falters and her gaze drops. "Well, in that case, I didn't buy you that coffee. They made the wrong one and gave me two. I didn't want it to go to waste."

I laugh and shake my head. "Well, thank you anyway."

I lift the coffee to take a sip but her hand settles on my arm and a grimace takes over her face. "It's one of those choca mocha vanilla caramel things. I don't think you'd like it."

Laughing again, I set it back on the table.

"Who drinks that shit," she continues, sticking her tongue out and making a gagging sound.

"My girlfriend, Lucy. She loves that stuff. I don't know why—"

"Let me guess," she cuts in, eyeing me up and down. "I bet you're the kind of guy who's going to say 'I don't know why, she's sweet enough.'"

My mouth clamps shut.

She rolls her eyes and taps her finger on my sketch. "You have two light sources and your rendering's off."

I narrow my eyes, focused on my work. She's right. Sighing, I say, "Too bad I want to be an architect, not an artist."

She raises an eyebrow. "Too bad I want to be an artist, not an architect." She pushes off the table and starts to walk to her station.

"Yo, Roxy."

"Yeah?" she says, continuing to walk away.

"Congrats on getting the job."

She turns now, grinning from ear to ear, and makes a show of dusting off her shoulder. "Thanks C-Money."

✧　✧　✧

Logan: *Are you alive?*

Cameron: *Barely.*

Logan: *Want to hit the cages?*

Cameron: *I have class till 2, firm from 2:30 to 5:30 and then store from 6-9.*

Logan: *Fuck man, I don't pity you.*

Cameron: *No shit. If you see Lucy at some point, tell her I love her.*

Logan: *She's shopping with Amanda.*

Cameron: *So you texted me because your girl's busy and you're needy?*

Logan: *Shut up, asshole.*

✧　✧　✧

Cameron: *I love you babe. I finish at the store at 9.*

Lucy: *I love you too.*

Cameron: *I miss you like crazy.*

Lucy: *I miss you too!*

✧　✧　✧

I'VE BEEN LISTENING to Chris, the asshole I work with, talk about porn for the last fifteen minutes. "These two chicks, hot as fuck, are going down on each other…"

I glance around the store and make sure no one's around. I don't want kids to be subjected to the shit he's saying.

"And they're making all these noises. I'm sitting at my desk, rubbing one out. I shut my eyes, so close to exploding… and then this dude's voice comes through." He makes a disgusted sound. "This dude walks into the room, butt naked, gut out…"

I start to laugh.

"The dude's like eighty. 'Hey babies' he grunts… and I'm staring at the screen, wanting to puke, feeling my dick shrivel in my hands."

My head throws back in laughter.

"It's not funny, asshole." He shoves me lightly. "What would you know? When was the last time you even watched porn? When was the last time you were alone so you could do it?"

I'm about to answer, but Lucy does it for me. "We watch it together," she says from behind me.

I spin quickly, surprised by her presence. I don't even try to hide my excitement. "What are you doing here?"

"Dude," Chris says, "your eyes just lit up like a kid on Christmas."

I ignore him and link my fingers with hers.

"Rose wanted to borrow my car so I asked her to drop me off. Is it okay I'm here? I just missed you, but I didn't know if you were going to be busy tonight."

"No." I shake my head and take her in from head to toe. "I'm glad you're here."

She leans up and kisses me quickly.

"It's dead," I tell her. "I'm just going through some pre-orders." I take her hand and pull her behind the counter.

"I don't think non-employees should be in the exclusive zone," Chris says.

I lift Lucy and sit her on the counter. She crosses her stocking covered legs, exposed by the skirt she's wearing. "Is that skirt new?"

She nods, a smile taking over her. "I got it today."

"I like it."

She glances at Chris quickly. "I'll show you the other stuff I got later." Her cheeks redden, but she doesn't explain. I already know what she's talking about. She's starting to have a thing for those garter belt suspender set things. I haven't complained. It's sexy as all fuck.

I bite my lip to stop a moan from escaping and try to focus on the screen in front of me, but all I can think about is her bent over my bed. The last set she got was black and red. She rested on her forearms, with her ass in the air and told me to take them off with my teeth.

My eyes shut tight as I try to adjust myself. I hear her giggle. When I open my eyes, she's watching me. She nods almost imperceptibly.

"Chris," I snap. "There are a few boxes in the store room that you need to unpack."

I hear his footstep fade, then a door open and close. I don't take my eyes off Lucy. Her eyes follow Chris to the store room, and when she knows he's gone, she slowly uncrosses her legs.

I stand in front of her, my hands lightly touching her legs. They move from the outside of her thighs to the inside, where I push them apart. "Not here, Cam."

But I'm too far gone to care.

"There are cameras everywhere."

I lean in and kiss the side of her neck. "Then they can watch."

She snakes her arms around my neck as my hands go further up her thighs. I run my fingers under the suspenders, moving higher as I do, until my hands find where her thighs meet. I run my thumb over her panties. "What color are they?"

She tilts her head back, allowing me to kiss her neck better.

If a customer walked in right now, I'd probably punch them. Kid or not.

She pulls my face away from her neck and looks me in the eyes. My mind's too filled with lust that my gaze is unfocused. She licks her lips before speaking, "Maybe we should tell Chris not to unpack those boxes in the store room and go do it ourselves."

I kiss her once and help her off the counter. Then I take her hand and lead her to the store room where I open the door. "Yo, out."

Chris laughs and shakes his head mid unboxing. "I can't even rub one out to porn." He pats me on the back as he walks past.

Once we're inside I close the door and turn to her. "Show me."

She eyes the room quickly and then points to the camera. I stand so I'm in front of her, blocking its view. "Show me," I say again.

Her hands brush down the side of her skirt and her fingers slowly curl, bunching the fabric. With each second she makes a show of lifting it higher and higher, my dick gets harder and harder. I start bouncing on my toes, waiting for the reveal. She starts to laugh before lifting it up. Up. Up.

Purple.

"Fuck, Luce."

She laughs again and straightens her fingers, dropping the skirt back in position. She starts to make for the door, all the while I'm thinking about bending her over and me peeling them off with my teeth. Hearing the doorknob turn has me coming back to reality. I slam my hand against the door, stopping her from opening it, and pull her back to my chest. She moans when she feels my raging hard-on against her back. "Cam," she whispers, her body tensing. "The cameras can see everything."

I flatten my hand against her bare stomach and flick the light switch next to the door. It's pitch black now, the only light coming from under the door. "I need to feel you, Lucy."

Her body relaxes against mine. I settle my hands on her legs, trying not to rush things, but I want inside her. Bad. She moans again when my hands reach higher and skim her ass. I pull her panties aside and run my finger across her warm center. She's already wet, making it easy to slide my fingers inside her. She's breathing heavy. Almost panting. "Fuck, Cam."

I work my fingers in and out slowly; the way I know she likes it. She drops her head forward, banging it against the door.

"Don't stop," she moans. But I wouldn't dare. She starts to tighten around my fingers, and I know she's close. I shut my eyes and imagine her face, her eyes widening and rolling higher. A bead of sweat across her hairline and her bottom lip between her teeth, the way she does when she's about to come.

"Please don't stop," she says again, a little louder this time. I reach my free hand up and pull her top down to release a breast. I palm her nipple softly.

"Fuck, Cam."

My breaths are short, coming out in spurts, just like hers.

"Make me come, please," she begs. "Please."

I release her breast and unzip my jeans.

"No," she squeaks. "We can't fuck. I don't want to run through the mall to clean up with cum dripping down my leg!"

I let out a frustrated grunt and try to think. "I'll pull out," I tell her. I look around, my eyes more used to the dark space, and reach into a box on the shelf next to me. I grab a promo shirt from the pile and set it aside. "I'll blow into a shirt." I kick a full box of games against the door and tell her to stand on it. She's too short for me to take her this way. It's the reason we have a footstool in her shower back home.

She steps on it, no questions asked.

"Hands against the door, baby."

The entire time, my fingers continue their work inside her.

"Yes, babe," she obliges. I don't know if it's a game for her, but I love taking control. And I know she gets off on it when I do.

She stands with her legs spread, her hands flat on the door and her ass sticking out, waiting for me.

I pull down her top and free both of her breasts, touching and grabbing them rougher than before. And then I pull my fingers out and let out a groan when I'm inside her.

I try to go slow, try to take care of her first, but she's moving herself on me saying, "Harder, Cam, faster. I need it."

So I give it to her. Harder. Faster.

Within minutes she's trembling, panting "I love you" over and over. I can feel her sweat forming on her tits. As soon as I know the last wave has taken her, I pull out and furiously jerk off into the shirt I prepared earlier. I start to feel it building and let out an uncontrolled sound. She turns and pulls my face to hers, knowing that nothing gets me off quicker than her kissing me. I laugh into her mouth as I come, trying to remember the last time I jerked off into an item of clothing.

When we're done, I flick the light on, trash the shirt and start to peel the tape off a box.

"What are you doing?" she says, adjusting her clothes.

"Working," I tell her. "I don't want to get fired."

Lucy

CHRIS SNIFFS US when we walk out of the store room. "I hate you guys."

I settle on a beanbag in front of the consoles they have set up in the corner of the store, and pull out my e-reader.

Cam goes about his business and stocks shelves and reprices things. Every time he walks past, he kisses me—a different spot on my face each time.

I stay in my place and wait for them to close up for the night. "Ready, babe?" His hand's out waiting for me to take.

"For you? Always."

✧   ✧   ✧

"I MADE YOU something," he says, glancing at me from behind the steering wheel.

My eyes light up and I throw my hand out squealing, "Gimme gimme gimme!"

He narrows his eyes and scrunches his nose. "What the hell did you just say?" He laughs. "You know the deal."

My shoulders sag with my sigh. I close my eyes and set my hands, palms up, on my lap. I hear the unfolding of paper, one of my favorite sounds in the world. And then he places it on my hands.

Ever since we got to college he'd been sketching more. Not just lines and floor plans, but actual *drawings*.

"Okay," he says warily. "Open."

I peer down at the sketch. It's of me sitting in the beanbag reading. His work has gotten so much better since he started taking the right classes in college. I've told him that I want to wallpaper my room with them, but he doesn't want anyone seeing them. He says he's uncomfortable with it, and he doesn't think they're good enough to share. But he's wrong. They're beyond amazing. He doesn't do it often, so when he does it's like a major reward for me. But the best part—or maybe the worst—is that he only ever draws me. *I'm* his art, so he says.

"I love it," I tell him, picking it up to examine it closer.

"Yeah?"

"Yeah, babe. It's one of the best so far."

"I need to work on my rendering," he says.

"It looks perfect to me."

"That's because my source is perfect."

I drop my chin to my chest to hide my smile. Five years on and his words still have the ability to make me blush. To make me fall in a new type of love, every single day.

✧   ✧   ✧

I WAKE UP to his face only inches from mine. His eyes are shut, peacefully sleeping.

I rub my nose against his chest and sniff.

His body shakes with his quiet laughter. "Did you just sniff me?"

I lean up and sniff his neck. "Mmm, you smell different when you're awake."

He kisses the top of my head. "That's not creepy at all."

"Hey! You watch me when I sleep."

"Yeah, but that's because I feel like I don't see you enough lately. I have to take as much of you in as I can."

Rose scoffs from her bed. "You guys are sick. Like, legit sick. You make me wanna puke."

I laugh into his chest.

"Don't be jealous," Cam says, his voice crackly from sleep. "We make you want to settle down and fall in love." He smiles down at me, his brown eyes searching mine.

Rose makes a puking sound effect. "I'm gonna shower. You guys have ten minutes to make babies but I'm not sending warning signals before I come back out."

We don't make babies while she's gone. We stay in the exact same position. Holding each other close, and we *talk*. Because it's not just about sex with us. It's about *life*. He's my life.

Twenty-Four
Cameron

"**P**SST."

I glance up to see Roxy looking over my cubical.

"Is it just me or do all the people who work here have a bus sized rod stuck up their ass?" she whispers.

I chuckle and shake my head. "Nope. It's true."

"And you have to work here for free?"

Sighing, I drop my pen on the desk and lean back in my chair, linking my fingers behind my head. "All part of my scholarship, remember?"

"That must suck."

I shrug. "At least I'm here, right?" I dramatically wave my arms in the air. "Living the dream."

She snorts, and then leans in closer. "What are you doing after work? You wanna grab a bite?"

"Can't. Going out for a friend's birthday."

She smiles and nods. "The infamous, and ever elusive, sugary sweet Lucy going with you? Will I get to meet her one day?"

I'm taken aback by her description for a moment, but only for a moment before I decide I don't care. "You should. She's picking me up, five thirty on the dot."

She fake claps with eyes wide and feigned excitement. "I can't wait."

❖   ❖   ❖

LUCY'S LEANING AGAINST her car just outside the office doors when Roxy and I finally make it down. We got held back for a meeting and then the stupid elevator was broken so we hoofed it down the stairwell. Roxy had to take her stupidly high heels off so she didn't break an ankle or some shit.

I see Lucy's eyes widen slightly when she sees us but she recovers quickly. "Hey," she says cautiously, her eyes darting to Roxy.

"Hey babe, sorry I'm late. We got held back and the elevator's broken." I lean down and kiss her quickly.

"So that explains the no shoes?" she says, pointing at Roxy.

Roxy laughs. "Yup, I didn't want your boy here to carry me down eighteen flights of stairs."

Luce smiles, but it's tight.

"I'm Roxy." She sticks her hand out for Lucy. "You must be Lucy. C-money's told me a lot about you."

She glances at me quickly, before shaking Roxy's hand. "C-money?"

Roxy laughs again. "Just a dumb name I gave him." Her eyes move from me to Lucy, and then she purses her lips and rolls on her heels. "Anyway, you kids have a good night. I've got a bus to catch."

"Wait. What?" I pipe up. "You're catching a bus? Where's your car?"

"It's shot. It's at the shop. Blew a flux capacitor."

My head throws back in laughter. "Dude, you totally referenced my favorite movie."

"Yeah? Who the hell doesn't love *Back to the Future*, right?"

"Where do you live? We can give you a ride." I turn to Lucy, but her gaze is cast downwards, staring at the ground. "Right babe?"

She looks up. "Huh?"

"We can give Roxy a ride home?"

She smiles and looks between Roxy and I. "Of course."

✧   ✧   ✧

ROXY DIRECTS US a good twenty minutes out of our way. Lucy stays quiet the entire time while Roxy and I reel off quotes from *Back to the Future*. She leads us to a street with run down single story, semi-detached houses, and points to one on our right. "This is me."

"I always thought you lived on campus," I tell her.

"You've been thinking about me?"

I see Lucy's grip on the steering wheel tighten.

Saving my ass, I choose not to answer.

"No, C-money, I'm local enough." She opens the door and hops out of the car. "Thanks for the ride, Lucy. I appreciate it."

"You're welcome," Lucy says quietly.

I wait for the door to close before settling my hand on her leg. "Are you okay?"

She nods, but never looks at me.

I don't know what to say so I keep my mouth shut.

We're halfway home before she decides to speak. "So, you and Roxy get along well?"

"I guess."

"She seems nice."

"I guess."

"She has a nickname for you."

"I guess."

"She can quote your favorite movie."

"So can a lot of people."

"You spend a lot of time together?"

"We work and have a few classes together, so yeah, I guess."

"Do you guess she's attractive?"

"What?"

Finally, she glances at me. "She's pretty. You never told me she was pretty. Or sexy. Or, like, a version of you but with a vagina. I bet her vagina's pretty, too," her voice breaks, like she's about to cry.

I lean forward so I can see her face. Yup. Tears. "Pull over."

"No."

"Please, Lucy. Pull over."

"Why? So you can tell me she tried to show you her vagina?"

"Oh my God. Lucy, pull over now."

She finally listens, and pulls the car over, but continues to look straight ahead. I unclip my seatbelt first, and then hers. Reaching up, I move her chin with my finger until she's facing me. "Why are you crying?"

She rubs at her eyes and inhales deeply. Then let's it all out in something that sounds similar to this, "Because I miss you so much and we never get to spend time with each other, not like last year and not like in high school when we spent all our time together, and now all that time is being used up and you're spending it with a girl who's hot, at least ten times hotter than me, and she calls you names and can quote your favorite movie, and all I do is read while you watch that movie, and I'm a shit girlfriend because I should pay attention to the movies you like, and I wish I was hotter and curvier like her, oh my God, did you see her curves? Her body is out of this world and I'm frumpy and stupid and you hate me and you're going to leave me when she shows you her vagina, which is probably a lot sooner than when I showed you mine, and I'm crying because I love you and I miss you and I hate that curvy vagina girl is going to take that from me."

I want to laugh, but I know it's wrong so I keep it in. "Lucy," I start. "Since I saw you sitting on the bleachers at the twin's game, I've never looked at another girl. Not because I didn't want you to find out, but because I already knew no other girl would compare to you. I don't care if you can't quote my favorite movie, and you don't care that I don't know what book Will and Layken are from." I do, but I don't tell her because it would just make her feel shittier about herself. "That stuff doesn't matter to us. I haven't done or said anything to ever make you feel the way you're feeling. And I'm sorry if I haven't said or done anything lately to let you know that you shouldn't be feeling what you're feeling. If you're having insecurities, that's my fault, and I'll try to fix it. But you should know that I only ever see you, and only you, and that's the way it's been since we were fifteen."

"Stop it," she whispers, her eyes fixed on mine now.

"Stop what?"

"Stop making me fall in love with you."

I smile now, taking her face in my hands. "I'll never stop that, babe, ever." I kiss her slowly, until I can no longer taste the tears on her lips. Until she knows that she owns every part of me. *Forever.*

✧   ✧   ✧

I DON'T KNOW why chicks take so long to get ready. "Babe! I'm sure you look fine, the limo will be here in ten minutes."

"I'm sorry you offered to drive your friend home and now I have to rush," she shouts.

A minute later her bathroom door opens and she steps out. I let out a low whistle. She looks hot. Hotter than hot. Her black dress is short, and tighter than normal. I don't know what the hell she was talking about Roxy's curves for because Lucy's body shits all over anyone else's. "Or we could just stay right here and I can spend the next ten minutes undressing you." I reach over and pull on her legs until she's standing in between mine. My hands wander under her dress, my thumb flicking the garter suspenders. A smile takes over my face, because I can already sense the shit ton of fun we're going to have tonight, especially if she has a few drinks.

"You don't think it's a little slutty? Or too, I don't know, daring?"

I shake my head. "I like you slutty," I tell her. "But slutty just for me, okay?"

She laughs and nods her head. "You should see what Amanda got for Logan when we went shopping."

"Oh yeah?"

"He's going to have a reallll happy birthday."

Rose walks in while my hand is still on Lucy's ass. "Jesus Christ. Are you two ever not about to, in the middle of, or just finished screwing?"

"Rose," I greet, as Lucy swats my hands and pulls down her dress. "I can't help it, Lucy's an animal. It's in her blood. Six brothers, remember?"

"Oh that's right," Rose agrees with a smile. "You better not sneeze around her, you might knock her up."

"That's what birth control's for," Luce says. "Unfortunately for you, the IUD doesn't protect you from STDs."

I block the pillow that gets thrown at her head.

✧　✧　✧

"THAT WAS GOOD times," she yawns through a shiver.

I take off my jacket and put it around her shoulders. "Yeah, it was. I think Logan had a good night. Pretty sure him and Amanda got it on in the bathroom."

She stops in the middle of the sidewalk with eyes wide. "Shut up!"

I chuckle. "Yeah, I'm not kidding. Pretty sure he finger fucked her at the table too."

"The one we were all sitting at?" she shouts.

I laugh harder. "Yup."

"What the hell are you doing watching them, you creep!"

"I'm the creep? Okay sniffy."

Her eyes narrow, right before her head throws back in laughter.

She walks up the stairs to her dorm on wobbly feet. I walk behind her in case she falls. Also because I like to watch her ass. I reach up and grab two handfuls. She doesn't even flinch. She knew it was coming. And I plan on coming. Soon. All over her face. Fuck, I'm drunk.

✧   ✧   ✧

"WHAT IS THAT noise?" She pushes her head further into my chest but the ringing won't stop.

"What the hell time is it?" Rose moans from her bed.

"Shut up," I tell all of them.

"Babe, it's your phone."

I blindly search for my phone on the nightstand and fling it across the room.

"Ow!" Rose groans.

"Sorry babe."

Lucy pulls back. "Huh?"

"Shut up," I tell her.

Then the ringing starts again.

"Luce, that's your phone now," Rose says.

Lucy sits up slowly. I open one eye to look at her. Her hair's all over the place, her makeup is smeared, she has a line of dried drool on one side of her mouth and her clothes are twisted. And she's never been more beautiful. "Who is calling so early?" She looks so confused it makes me laugh.

I sit up, just so I can pull her down with me. "Forget it, babe, just come back to bed."

Her phone starts to ring again, the same time mine does.

"Dude," Rose says. "You've got eighteen missed calls."

"What?" I sit up now and motion for her to throw my phone over.

Lucy reaches across me for her phone. "Micky?"

I try to focus my tired eyes on the screen and hit answer. "Yo, Jake?"

"You need to come to the hospital. It's Logan and Amanda."

Twenty-Five
Lucy

LOGAN WOULDN'T SEE anyone at the hospital. We stayed for hours hoping he'd change his mind, but he never did. On the second day, we were told that he'd been discharged. Amanda was still there. She said she hadn't seen him either, but that she thought he'd be home waiting for her. He wasn't. No one knew where he was. That was a week ago. When I went to see her at her house, Ethan, her brother, told us she needed time. She didn't want to see anyone who reminded her of Logan, at least for now. I understood, but I worried for both of them.

Now, we're on our way back from Logan's house. His dad answered the door looking worse than I'd ever seen him. He said Logan had been locked up in the pool house since he got out of the hospital. He hasn't left, and he hasn't spoken to anyone. He told us to try, but also pleaded that we leave him alone if he didn't answer. He said it was best if no one pushed him, and that Logan just needed time. Logan didn't answer when we knocked. We didn't expect him to.

Cam squeezes my hand to get my attention. He glances at me quickly from the driver's seat of his Delorean. "You wanna stay at the cabin tonight? We can drive back early tomorrow for work. I think we just need to be away from the rest of the world for a bit."

I nod in agreement. "I think that sounds perfect."

✧   ✧   ✧

HE TAPS HIS finger on the side of my head. "What's going on in that beautiful mind of yours?"

I don't know how long we've been in bed, lying side by side, looking into each other's eyes. We haven't spoken a word, but that doesn't mean we haven't been communicating.

"I'm trying to understand it," I tell him.

"Understand what?"

I sigh and touch my forehead to his. "I don't get why such bad things keep happening to good people. First Micky and her family, and now Logan and Amanda. And I get that he wanted to keep his past a secret, I understand that, but I don't know why he won't talk to anyone now. I thought we were friends."

He runs his hand under my shirt and onto my back, where he rubs slow circles. "I wouldn't take it personal, Luce. I mean we're best friends. We grew up together, and he never told me either. Maybe I should have been a better friend to him, I don't know. I guess the only thing we can take from it is that life's short. Too short to be thinking that forever's always gonna be there."

I pull back slightly and lift my eyes to his, knowing he's already watching me. I reach up and move his scruffy hair away from his eyes, then run the back of my fingers across the rough growth on his face, remembering what it was like when we were fifteen and he never had to worry about shaving.

His eyes drift shut at my touch, and when he opens them, they're filled with so much emotion, so much need, so much of *him*. He clears his throat before speaking, "Sometimes I wish I could be back here, back to this cabin when we were in high school and had no worries in the world. When we spent every second of every day together, and it was just you and me. Before the pressure, before college, before scholarships and work and *life*."

"Just you and me and *our forever?*"

"Yeah, baby." He kisses me once. "I love you, Luce. More than I ever thought possible." His eyes begin to glaze, but he blinks it away. "Let's never let the bad things in our lives outweigh the good."

"Does it ever scare you?" I ask him.

"What?"

"That we live too much for each other. Do you ever wonder what would happen if anything—"

"Shut up," he whispers, cutting me off. "I'm going to make love to you now, and we're going to forget that you just said that."

So that's what he does—makes love to me.

And I do. I forget. I forget everything else in the entire world—because he *is* my entire world.

Cameron

WITH CLASSES, STUDYING, work at the firm and work at the store, I've barely had time to see Lucy. We do our best to sleep in the same bed at night, but even that's becoming a struggle. I'm barely awake through all of it, which is why it's kind of cool Roxy is around to keep me in check. "Are you dying?" she says, pulling up a chair and sitting next to me in class.

I laugh once, drop my pencil and turn to her. "What the hell?"

She shrugs. "You've been missing a few classes lately and you missed a day at work the other day. Also, and please don't be offended, but you look like ass."

"I have a lot going on." I stretch my arms and yawn loudly.

"Yeah?" She rests her forearms on the desk and leans closer. I look away when my eyes catch way too much cleavage. "Anything I can help with?"

Shaking my head, I answer, "No, just stuff with my best friend, and all this other shit is getting on top of me. I don't have time to relax, and I have to keep my grades up or they can withdraw my scholarship, and Lucy—"

"Is she bugging you to always spend time with her? Does she not understand?"

My eyes narrow. "No. That's not it at all. She gets it... I think. It's both of us, really. We both want to be with each other but it's happening less and less, and I think that it's throwing me off balance. She keeps me grounded, but it's harder now..."

She smiles a sympathetic smile. "Is there something you can cut out to free up some time?"

I can't help but laugh. "No, there's nothing. I need to do it all. I need to work at the firm or I have to find a way to pay for this education. I need a job, so that I can eat. I need to eat to live. And I need to live to see Lucy."

She smiles, that same smile from only seconds ago. "Sounds like you do it all for Lucy."

I roll my eyes. "I do everything for Lucy."

"Huh," she says, before getting off her chair and walking away.

I don't know what she means by 'huh,' but I don't care enough to think about it.

✧　✧　✧

I QUICKLY DRESS for work and head back down to my car. "Cameron," I hear, and I already know who it is without turning around. Roxy's running toward me barefoot with her heels in her hand. "Please tell me you're going to work right now."

"Yeah," I shout, waiting for her to catch up.

"Oh my God, I rushed out of class and to the bathroom to change and then I missed my bus and ran all the way here." She drops her shit when she gets to me and bends over, trying to catch her breath—her shirt's so low that her tits nearly fall out.

I turn away.

When she finally settles enough to stand upright, she crosses her arms over her chest and shivers. "Anyway," she says, rubbing her arms. "Can I get a ride?"

I shrug out of my jacket and hand it to her. "Sure," I tell her, jerking my head toward my car. She covers herself in my jacket, but doesn't put her arms through.

"Holy shit," she laughs out. "A Delorean?"

My smile is smug; it always is when people realize what I drive.

I press the button on the remote and stand back while the doors lift for her. "Please," I mock, throwing my hand out for her to take, "step into my time machine."

Her head throws back with laughter, as she gets in ass first, with her legs together so she doesn't show off too much of what's under her short-ass skirt.

"You're an idiot," she says.

"I know." I laugh.

I close her door and lift my head, and then my heart stops.

"Hey," Lucy says, her eyes slowly moving from Roxy to me. But having Roxy sitting in the car isn't what made the beating of my heart falter. It's not even the fact that she looks hurt by it. It's the fact that her eyes are red and puffy like she's been crying for days.

"What's going on?" I stand so I'm in front of her and take both her hands in mine.

She lifts her gaze, but her eyes are unfocused, not looking at me, but past me. "I've been trying to call you."

My eyes narrow in confusion. I pull my phone out of my pocket and see over twenty missed calls. "Fuck, I switched it to silent when I was in the library. Are you okay?"

Her eyes dart to Roxy in the car, before coming back to me. "Yeah, go to work." She fakes a smile. "I'll talk to you later about it."

She starts to turn but I hold her hand tighter. "Lucy."

"It's fine," she clips. "Call me when you're done." She stands on her toes and kisses me quickly, but I swear it—there's a second of hesitation where she almost stops herself. She jerks back, like maybe she's doing something wrong.

She roughly yanks her hand from mine.

And all I can do is watch her walk away.

The honking of my horn gets my attention. Roxy taps at an imaginary watch on her wrist.

✧ ✧ ✧

I CAN'T FOCUS. I can barely stay awake. I look at the clock. Half an hour left. I need to go home. I need to call Lucy, find out where she is, see her, and talk about what happened that made her cry.

I just need Lucy.

Which is why when my boss comes to my cubicle and tells me that Roxy and I need to stay back to digitalize some files from the Wilmington branch, I go to the men's bathroom and punch a hole in a door. It's the worst fucking timing, but I don't argue. I can't. So instead, I lean against the counter and dial Lucy's number.

"Hey," she answers, the same sadness in her voice from earlier.

"Luce," I breathe out, and I can already imagine her face turning from sadness to disappointment. "I have to work late tonight."

Silence.

"I'd get out of it but—"

"It's fine," she cuts in. "What can you do?" She sighs loudly before adding, "Call me when you're done, okay?"

"Yeah, babe, I will."

More silence.

"I love you, Luce," I say, but she's already hung up.

✧　✧　✧

"I CAN'T BELIEVE we have to do this shit," Roxy states. Everyone's left the office but us. We're stuck scanning a bunch of documents and filing them into the server. The job's boring, monotonous, and it doesn't help my mind from wondering about what the hell is wrong with Lucy.

"We're gonna be here a while," she continues. "You wanna order some Chinese or something? I'm starving."

"Sure. Whatever."

Fifteen minutes later we're sitting on the floor with a spread of containers in front of us. My mood has brightened a little; maybe I just needed some food.

I suck on a noodle, letting it splash all over my face just like Lachlan does when he eats spaghetti.

"You're a mess," she says. She lifts a napkin and goes to wipe my face.

I pull back. "I got it," I tell her.

Once I'm clean, I loosen my tie and pull it over my head, then take off my shirt. I only have two shirts suitable for work, and the one I'm wearing can last another shift before I need to wash it.

Ten minutes later we're almost out of food. "I'm so full." She untucks her blouse from her skirt and lies on the floor. "I feel like I need a nap."

"I feel like I want to eat more but won't be able to fit it."

She laughs. "Do the dad thing."

"What dad thing?"

"You know, undo your belt and pants, let your gut hang out."

"Dude, that's an amazing idea."

She laughs as I make a show of undoing my belt, but I stop at my pants. I polish off whatever's left and copy her position on the floor with the empty containers in between us.

Once I'm settled, she faces me. "So I gotta ask you something, but I don't want you to take it the wrong way."

"Okay?"

She leans up on her elbow and turns her body to face me. Her cleavage even more exposed now. "The other day, you said something about how you do everything for Lucy; what did you mean?"

"I don't know. It's just the way we work, I guess. We do everything for each other."

"How long have you guys been dating?"

"Since we were fifteen."

"Holy shit," she says incredulously. "That's a long-ass time."

"I guess." The food, the exhaustion, my life—it's starting to take its toll. If I closed my eyes, I'd be asleep. I wonder if I could nap. Just ten minutes.

"So you guys chose colleges and everything together and you got in the same one. That's pretty cool."

I nod, my eyelids heavy. "Yeah. Kind of. Not really."

"No?"

"No. I mean I'd go wherever she was. I didn't know that I wanted to be an architect or that—I mean, that I had it in me or whatever." I let out an exhausted sigh. "I didn't really plan on college. My mom and I—we're not poor, but we're not really financially able to afford college, you know?"

"Yeah." She laughs. "You've seen where I live, right?"

"Yeah…"

"Cam?"

I open my eyes and face her, trying to avoid her chest.

"If you hadn't met Lucy, what do you think you'd be doing?"

I don't even hesitate to answer. "Probably selling cars at my mom's boyfriend's dealership."

She nods, like she understands. "What do you think would make you happier? This or selling cars?"

I swallow nervously, because I know my answer is wrong. I know it feels wrong. And I know I shouldn't be voicing it, but I do anyway. "Selling cars."

"Huh," she says, lying back down.

I move my gaze from her and back up to the ceiling, but I catch something from the corner of my eye. Not something, *someone*. I sit up, faster than my stomach likes. "Lucy."

"I didn't know," she says, shaking her head.

"What?" I'm on my feet now, walking the few steps to get to her.

Her eyes move down my body and focus on my waist.

I look down at my unfastened belt. "It's not what—"

"It's okay, Cameron." She looks behind me at the pile of my discarded clothes.

My heart's beating out of my chest. "Babe…" I know what this looks like to her—but she's so wrong.

"I didn't know," she says again.

My mind's reeling. My insides are twisted. There's a lump in my throat as big as the ball of anxiety in the pit of my stomach.

Say something.

She blows out a heavy breath, her eyes so full of tears that if she blinked, they'd fall.

And then she does.

She blinks.

They fall.

I break.

"Lucy."

She fakes a smile. "I came to…" She lifts the paper bag in her hand.

"You brought me dinner?" I finally manage to say.

She nods. Her tears fall faster. "But you've already…"

Her eyes finally move from behind me and rise, up, up, up to mine. And my world stops. For a completely different reason. A reason I've never had to feel before. It's like I'm falling. Or *fading*.

"I didn't know that you didn't want this. I didn't know because I never asked. I'm sorry, Cameron," she sobs. She sets the bag on a desk next to her and wipes her eyes. Then she squares her shoulders and lifts her chin, sniffing back her tears as she does. "Call me when you finish, okay?"

"Wait." I pull on her arm to stop her from leaving. "I don't—"

"It's okay," she says. Her teeth are clenched when she adds, "Seriously, Cam. It's fine."

My breaths are short and I can't seem to settle them. I'm afraid of what she's thinking, what she's feeling. I pull on her arm until she's closer to me. I lean down to kiss her but she turns her head, avoiding me.

"Come on, Lucy," I whisper, my desperation for her ears only.

Roxy clears her throat from behind us. "Cameron, you can go. I'll finish up here."

I don't even think. I just gather my shit, mouth a 'thank you' to Roxy and leave.

But she's already ten steps ahead of me.

"Lucy," I shout after her.

She gets in the elevator and waits for me to catch up. "Logan's gone," she deadpans, staring down at the floor.

"What?" I huff, pressing the button to the ground floor.

"He left."

"What do you mean left? Dropped out?"

She looks up at me now. "No. He's gone. Left the country. Nobody knows where he is, or when, or if he's coming back."

I pinch the bridge of nose with my thumb and index finger, trying to weaken the pounding in my head. There's too much to take in and I don't know which thought to run with.

The elevator dings and she steps out, I follow, still not knowing what to say.

She walks out of the building and unlocks her car. "I organized a study group tonight, and I'm already late. I'll call you later, Cam." She gets in her car and drives away.

And I'm left standing on the sidewalk wondering what the fuck just happened, and why I feel like my world is falling apart.

✧   ✧   ✧

EIGHT TIMES I call her.

She never answers.

I stare at my phone and drop down on my bed. And then I dial Jake's number.

"Yo," he answers.

"Hey, what are you doing?"

He laughs once. "Stalking Logan's Facebook, trying to work out where the fuck he is."

"So it's true?"

"Yeah, man. Dr. Matthews called today and told me. He won't give any more information, just that he's left." He lets out another laugh, a bitter one. "I'm watching this video of him when we were at Lucy's cabin. He's drunk and doing—"

"The MC Hammer dance?"

"Yeah. He was so wasted that night."

A quiet moment passes, both of us thinking about that night.

"Anyway," he perks up. "You wanna talk to Luce?"

"What?"

"I figured you're calling to speak to Lucy?"

My heart drops. She lied. I don't think she's ever lied to me. "She said she had study group. She's there?"

"Yeah, dude. She's talking to Kayla."

"What are they saying?"

"I don't know, man. They're in the living room, I'm in the study."

"Well, fuck, go eavesdrop. What are they saying?"

"I can't do that."

"Jake." His name comes out a warning.

"Fine," he clips. "But you owe me." He sighs into the phone and I hear a knob turn.

"Okay," I whisper. I keep my ears pressed to the phone, not wanting to miss a word.

"Kayla's saying that she's sure it's nothing."

"What's nothing?"

"Shut up. Do you want me to listen to them or not?"

I clamp my mouth shut.

"Okay, so Lucy just said that she's never worried before. That it was always kind of a joke, like a show… the jealousy and stuff…"

My hand squeezes the phone so tight I'm scared I'm going to break it.

"She says it's different now, she's actually afraid. She says things have changed, that you've been different lately. She says she has a reason to worry now." After a moment, "Who's Roxy?"

Fuck. I rub by eyes and try not to cry like a bitch into the phone.

I hear a door close, then Jake's deep voice. "Dude…"

"What!"

"She's fucking crying. Like all out sobbing."

"Fuck."

"Cameron, what the hell did you do?"

✧　✧　✧

YOU'D THINK CONSIDERING how tired I was that I'd be able to sleep, but I can't. I tried calling her again, but her phone was busy. *Who the hell is she talking to?*

Throwing my covers off, I get dressed, grab my keys, and drive the few minutes to her dorm. Rose answers, but there's no Lucy. I curse and try to call her again. Still busy. I sit my ass on the floor next to her door and wait. I don't care how long I have to wait. I need to see her. I know I won't be able to relax until shit's resolved and she's in my arms again. I'm about to doze off when my phone rings. Her name flashes on the screen. My heart picks up. "Babe," I answer.

"I've been trying to call you."

"I've been trying to call you."

"Where are you?"

"At your dorm, where are you?"

"At your dorm."

I sigh. "We're a mess tonight."

She laughs.

My world stops.

"Stay there, I'll come to you."

"Wait," she says, and I can hear her feet clicking against the floor. "Is Minge in there?"

"He was when I left."

"Then you stay there—" she cuts herself off and the footsteps stop. Her voice lowers when she adds, "I mean, if you wanted to spend the night together?" She says it like a question, like she's unsure of my answer.

"Luce, I don't want to be anywhere else."

"Good," she perks up. "I'll call Rose to let you in, warm my bed for me, okay?"

"Okay."

"Hey, Cam?"

"Yeah?"

"I love you."

My eyes drift shut and I feel all the muscles in my body slowly relax. "Forever, baby."

✧   ✧   ✧

I REST MY head on her chest, my arms around her waist and my leg over hers. I hold her as tight as I can, afraid that if I let her go she might not come back.

Her fingers run through my hair. Her chest rises and falls, faster than it should. I lift my gaze; she's already watching me. "I didn't mean that I'd be happier without you, Luce," I whisper.

She pulls back and scoots lower on the bed so we're face to face, and pulls the covers over our heads. "So what did you mean? Will you explain it to me? I've been trying to understand, but I can't." She swallows loudly and I know she's trying to hold back a sob.

"I just meant it would be easier. I'd be happier, right now, if I got up every day, did the same routine and got to go home every night and just be with you. I'm so fucking stressed at the moment. There's so much going on and the stuff with Logan—I'm drained, babe. Physically and mentally drained. Once I get over finals, I'll be fine."

"Why didn't you tell me?"

"Because the times I have with you are the only times I look forward to. It's the only time I can drop the ball and just relax and be myself. I want my Lucy time separate from everything else."

"And why were your clothes off?"

I sigh and spend the next hour answering her questions as honestly as I can. I have nothing to hide, nothing to lie about.

"I know she's your friend and you have to study and work with her, and I'm trying to be okay with it. I'm trying so hard not to be the annoying jealous girlfriend but it's hard for me."

"I don't know what you want me to do. I can't drop the classes. I can't quit the—"

"I know," she cuts in. "Just... think about my feelings. That's all."

"Okay, babe. That's fair." I lean in and kiss her quickly. And then I test the waters. "How was your study group?"

She looks away. "It was productive," she lies.

Twenty-Six
Lucy

A S MUCH AS it hurts me to admit, things have changed. I don't know if it's me, or him, or both of us. Ever since the night at his work when I walked in on him and Roxy 'talking,' he's been... *off.*

He's always busy, which is fine, I get that. But he's also been moody. I try my best to match his moods. When he's happy, I'm genuinely happy. When he's down, I try to support him. For five weeks since that night, I've been trying to do everything I can to be there for him. To be what he needs and what he wants. We've spent every night together, because it's the only time we have. And when he tells me he's stressed and needs a release, I give it to him.

The second Minge leaves the room for class he's on me. "I miss you so much," he whispers.

MY HANDS SPLAY across his chest. His hands work on my breasts while I move on him. He licks his lips as his eyes bore into mine. Our breaths are heavy, uncontrolled by the pure lust driving us. He removes his hands and leans on his elbows, taking my nipple into his mouth. His eyes never leave mine. I continue my pace, waiting for the tension to build.

And then it does.

My eyes widen, like it's still a surprise that he can make me come.

"Baby," I pant.

"I know. I got you."

He sits up, grabs my ass roughly and pulls me closer to him.

My head throws back. His hips thrust faster, working me over the edge.

"I wanna see you," he says. He licks his lips again then bites down on his bottom lip when he sees my face. Then he runs his finger along the sweat forming in my hairline.

"Cam!"

"Fuck, Lucy."

His fingers curl in my hair, pulling my face down to his waiting mouth.

We come together.

And then, we fall apart.

HE WALKS INTO the shower and waits for me to get out to hand me a towel. "Thank you," I tell him.

He's gazing down at the floor, chewing his thumb. I watch his throat bob when he swallows. "You didn't say I love you," he mumbles.

"What do you mean?"

He looks at me now, for seconds that feel like hours while I self-consciously dry my naked body. "After we have sex, you always tell me you love me. You didn't this time. You got off me and came straight in here. Why?"

My eyebrows bunch, but I recover quickly. I try not to let his tone hurt me. "I'm sorry," I step forward and kiss him lightly. "I guess I just thought you had an early class so I didn't want to take up too much of your time."

"It's Tuesday," he clips. "You know I don't start for another hour."

My eyes drop to the floor, and I wait for my heart to stop pounding so hard. For the hurt to stop aching so much. I look up and fake a smile. "I'm sorry." My voice breaks, and I look away before he knows exactly how he made me feel. Because he doesn't need to worry about me, not on top of everything else.

I turn around and slowly start dressing.

His arms curl around my waist, before he wipes his eyes on my shoulder. I feel the warmth of his tears against my skin. "I'm an asshole."

I push down my emotions and settle my hand on the back of his neck. "It's okay, you're stressed."

Sighing, he pulls back and turns me to him. "Four more days, Luce. Four more days, and I'll make it up to you." He picks me up by my waist and sits me on the counter, spreading my legs with his hands so he can stand between them. "Just please be patient with me. You deserve so much more than the way I've been treating you lately. You do everything for me, and I don't even appreciate it."

"It's okay—"

"No, it's not Lucy. I feel like you come here and we have sex and that's it. We—"

He must see my gaze drop, because he cuts himself off.

"What?" he whispers. "Is that how you feel? Do you think I use you for sex or something?" His voice cracks. Maybe because he knows he's right.

I keep my eyes down, not wanting him to see my reaction. "I don't think you use me," I tell him. "And it goes both ways, Cam. I mean, I don't have to sleep with you… but I do."

"Why do you?" He lifts my chin so he can see my face. His eyes dart between mine as he takes me in. All of me. "Why?" he repeats.

I hesitate to answer, because I don't want to lie. But I'm scared of how the truth will make him feel.

His brows furrow and his mouth turns down to a frown. "Lucy, why?"

I push down my nerves, and the knot in my throat, and I tell him the truth, even though it kills me. "Because you spend all your time with a girl who I don't trust, and I want you to remember what's waiting for you. I want you to think of *me*, even when you're with her."

His eyes narrow, and I think he's about to lose it. About to yell at me like he's never done before. But then his shoulders sag and his features flatten. "Baby," he sighs. He wraps his arms around me—so tight, for so long, that slowly, he pieces us back together again. "I'm so sorry that you feel that insecure about us. I'm sorry I haven't noticed. I should have." He pulls back slightly. "I don't ever want you to feel like my world doesn't begin and end with you. And *I* need to cut this shit because one day you're going to wake up and realize that there's someone better out there who's going to treat you right, Luce. And when you do…" His eyes narrow to a glare and a snarl pulls on his lips. His nose scrunches, right before he grunts, "I'll find them, and I'll *kill* them."

My head throws back in laughter.

He raises an eyebrow. "You think it's funny?"

I nod through my snorts.

"I don't think it's funny," he says, but he's smiling. "Seriously, Luce. I know the woods behind your house pretty well. I'm sure I could hide a dead body in there. I'll make it so it looks like little Logan did it. If any of your brothers were going to kill someone, it'd be him."

"Stop it." I laugh. "He would not."

"Lucy," he deadpans. "This one time, when I was at your house, even before you attacked me with your virgin kisses—" He stops while I let out a cackle. "I poured him a bowl of cereal. He got out of his chair, picked out a knife from the drawer, sat back down and started stabbing the bowl. I asked what the fuck he was doing—but in nicer terms, *obviously*, because I was still trying to get in your pants… you know what he said?"

I shake my head, my smile in full force.

"He looked up at me and said…" He leans forward so his lips are to my ear and whispers, "Practicing to be a serial killer. Join forces, Cameron."

I push him away, my body shaking with laughter. "He did not."

His eyes are wide as he shakes his head. "Swear it, Luce. This shit's too good to make up."

Cameron

"OH MY GOD," Roxy whines, flopping into the seat next to me. "I just handed in Masterson's project. Talk about cutting it fine. Not like we've had a few weeks to work on it," she scoffs.

"The roof design?"

"No." She laughs. "The *entire* design."

I tense. "What?"

"Yeah," she says, now looking worried. "The entire design's due tomorrow."

Whatever look just took over my face has her eyes widening. "Cameron?"

"The entire design is due tomorrow? When the fuck did this happen?"

"Um. Just over a month ago," she says, like I'm a dumbass for not knowing.

"Fuck."

"You haven't finished?"

"Roxy, I haven't even fucking started. I didn't even know it was due. Was I in class?"

She eyes the ceiling, like she's deep in thought. "Dude..." she says, finally looking back at me. "I think it was that time when your friend got attacked and you missed a couple classes."

"Why the fuck didn't you tell me?" I'm on my feet now, my heart thumping so loud in my ears I can barely see straight. "How much will it affect my grade if I don't hand it in?" I'm panicking, trying to keep down the bile that's risen in my throat.

She grimaces. "Thirty percent."

"Fuck." I get up and start packing my shit. "What time?"

"What?"

I want to yell at her for being stupid and not understanding. Instead, I try to take a calming breath. "What time is it due?"

"Oh. Nine."

I run my hand through my hair and pull. Hard. Closing my eyes, I try to work out if it's even physically possible for me to get it done, or whether to just take the grade and hope it doesn't affect my funding.

"Cam, are you working tonight?"

I shake my head, feeling the adrenaline course through me.

"I have a studio set up in my shed out back. If you have all your sketches, I can help. I don't know that I'd be very good. I'm an artist, not an architect, remember?"

"Please," I beg, because I have no other fucking choice.

✧ ✧ ✧

I TEXT LUCY when we get in my car. I tell her I have a last minute study group on a project I didn't know existed. I tell her it'll be a late night, and that I'll call her when I'm done. And then I tell her I love her.

I fought a war in my head about whether to mention that Roxy was my study partner. I chose not to because I didn't want her to worry when she has absolutely no reason to.

After five minutes, my phone starts blowing up. Not just her, but Jake and Dylan, too. I switch it off, because if I don't I won't be able to focus. And I need to fucking focus.

We walk through her house to get to the yard. It reminds me of Mom's house. The one I grew up in. Last year, she finally bit the bullet and sold it. Now she lives with Mark—and they've never been happier.

Roxy's shed has been converted into an art studio with homemade light boxes and drafting tables. Kind of like the ones Tom made me, only nowhere near as good. She has her art framed and hanging off the walls. She's good, really fucking good, but I don't have time to take them in.

She finishes switching the lights on and turns to me. "I'll call for pizza and then we'll get started, okay?"

I nod as I pull out my folio and spread my sketches on the desk. "Where the fuck do I even start?" I mumble to myself.

I feel the warmth of her hand on my back. "It's okay, C-Money. We'll get it done. Even if it takes us all night."

"What about you?" I ask, stepping out of her reach.

She shrugs. "I have a final in the afternoon. I've studied my ass off, I'm good."

Sighing, I say, "You're saving my ass, Rox. Thank you."

She shrugs again. "I'm sure you'll find a way to pay me back."

She winks.

I ignore it.

✦   ✦   ✦

MY EYES ARE so fucking heavy and my body is so fatigued, that I can't even draw a straight line using a ruler.

She sets a cup of coffee next to me. "You're almost done, Champ. You got this."

I stand up and stretch my legs and then my arms, yawning loudly as I do.

She sips her coffee and looks over my work. "Hey, your rendering's gotten a lot better."

"Thanks." I drink my coffee quickly and get back to work.

Half an hour later, I'm done.

She fake-claps and cheers, not wanting to be loud. I have no idea how long we've been in here, working almost non-stop.

"Thank you so much," I tell her.

She punches my arm. "No problem."

We walk through her house and out to my car.

Or what should be my car.

Only it has no wheels.

She snorts.

I glare at her.

"Sorry." She grimaces.

"Who the fuck would jack my wheels?"

"I'm sorry," she says sympathetically. "I probably should have warned you about parking a Delorean in my neighborhood."

I drop my bags, my folio, and myself onto the sidewalk. Pulling my phone out of my pocket, I lift my knees and rest my arms on them.

"I'd give you a ride," she says, sitting down next to me. "But my car's still not fixed."

I turn on my phone. Ten missed calls from Lucy, Jake and Dylan. Then I curse when I see the time. "It's three?"

"Yup."

"Oh my God." I go through my phone contacts, deciding who the fuck to call. I try Jake first, he doesn't answer. I try Dylan, but his phone's off. And then I do what I should've done first, but was too afraid to do. I call Lucy.

She answers on the first ring. "Hey," her voice is scratchy from sleep. "Did you just finish your study group?"

"Yeah," I sigh, shaking my head and trying to avoid the inevitable.

"We were trying to call you."

"I know. I switched my phone off so I could focus."

"Oh okay. Well, I need to tell you something. Are you coming by now? I'll unlock the door."

"Fuck," I accidentally say out loud.

"Cameron?"

And for some reason Roxy thinks it's a great time to pipe up. "Just tell her, C-Money."

I narrow my eyes and shake my head at her.

Lucy gasps. "Do I need to ask who that is?" she whispers.

"Luce, the fucking wheels on my car got jacked and I'm stranded. I wouldn't ask if I didn't need your help."

Silence.

Finally, she speaks, "Why doesn't someone else in your study group give you a ride?"

I blow out a long, drawn out breath. "Because, Luce, there was no one else."

She hangs up.

I text her the address and put my phone away.

"You want me to make you a bed?" Roxy asks.

"No, she's coming."

"How do you know?"

"Because I know Lucy. And I know she loves me, even when I don't deserve it."

Twenty minutes later, she's here.

✧   ✧   ✧

SHE HASN'T SAID a word. She hasn't even looked at me. Not until she stops the car and nudges me to wake me up. "You're home," she deadpans.

I sit up and look around. We're at my dorm. "Stay with me tonight?"

Her eyes stay fixed on mine.

My breath catches and a slow burn forms in my chest as I watch her eyes fill with tears. She doesn't blink. She doesn't let them fall. Instead, she nods and makes her way out of the car and toward my room. I follow behind her, not speaking, not knowing what to say, so that I can bring us both back to this morning, after we talked shit through and everything felt like normal. Nothing feels like normal lately, and right now, I *need* normal.

I open my door and wait for her to get into bed. She lies on her side, facing the wall. We face each other when we sleep. That's the way it's always been. So this is more than just her lying in my bed. It's a message. A form of punishment—one that I deserve. I get in behind her, push one arm under her pillow and the other around her waist, and I pull her close. "Lucy, can I at least explain?"

Her breathing gets faster and her body tenses. "Dylan enlisted in the Marines. He didn't want anyone knowing so tonight was his last night. He wanted to say goodbye to you. That's why we were calling."

My eyes drift shut when I hear the disappointment in her voice. I get it. I'm disappointed in myself. I should have been there for him. And I shouldn't have kept it from her. I should have been honest from the start. I should have done what she fairly asked and thought about her feelings.

I know she's doing everything she can to keep it together because I can feel her chest heaving, and then stopping. Starting. And then stopping. "Maybe you should try to remember your old friends. The ones who've always been there for you."

And now I'm pissed because I *know* who my friends are. She doesn't need to fucking remind me. "You think I wanted to miss out on saying goodbye to him? He was one of my best friends. Now he's gone, Logan's gone and Jake's always busy. I have no one left."

"You have Roxy."

My voice rises. "You don't even fucking know what happened, Lucy."

She flinches and drops her chin to her chest, like she's physically shrinking in my arms. I roll onto my back, and pinch the bridge of my nose, hoping to God it relieves the pounding in my head and the ache throughout my entire body.

"Your mom called," she says quietly. "They want to come here on Friday after your last final. They want to take us out for dinner. I said you'd call her back."

"Why? You could have just said yes."

"Because," she answers, her voice strained. "I didn't know if you'd be up to faking it."

"Faking what?"

"Faking us."

Twenty-Seven
Lucy

H E SHAKES MY arm gently. "Lucy," he whispers. My eyes drift open, expecting to see his chest, the way I've woken up more times than not in the past. But I don't see him. All I see is the blank wall of his room. I feel the bed dip, and then his hand on my arm again. "Luce."

I flip onto my back and stare up at the ceiling. My emotions from last night flood my mind and I don't want him to see the tears already forming.

"Baby." He clears his throat. "I made you something."

My eyes snap to him, and my heart breaks at the look on his face. His brows are drawn and his jaw's clenched. His eyelids are heavy as he blinks. Once. Twice. His breaths are long, slow, like it takes everything in him to keep it together.

Sitting up, I put my hands on my lap, palms up.

I close my eyes and I wait.

I whimper when I hear the sound of paper unfolding. The sound which reminds me of how much he loves me.

And I let the walls between us crumble.

My heart thumps against my chest, waiting for the moment he tells me to open my eyes.

"Open them," he whispers.

I do.

But I don't look down at his sketch. I look at him. And for once, I try to *read* him. Because he's always been an open book. He's always been so raw, and so sure about what he feels, and what he wants. But now... now, I have no idea. I have no idea what he wants. Or if I'm even part of it.

"Are you gonna look at it?"

My gaze drops to the sketch in my hands. It's not of me. Not *just* me.

217

It's of us, from above, lying in bed. My face to his chest, our arms around each other, holding on. "You're my art, Luce. My *heart*."

A tear falls. I feel the warmth of it slowly trickle down my cheek, onto my chin, and finally land on the sketch.

"What do you think?" His voice is so low, I barely hear him.

I watch as the tear soaks into the paper, the wet stain getting wider and wider.

He sighs, pulling me from my trance. "I have to go," he says, leaning in toward me.

My eyes squeeze shut.

His lips touch mine for what feels like eternity.

And I do nothing.

"Kiss me," he says shakily against my lips. "Please."

"I can't, Cameron."

"Why?"

"Because I love you so much, and it would feel so good, but it would hurt so, *so* bad."

✧   ✧   ✧

IT'S CLOSE TO ten at night by the time we talk. He calls and tells me Minge is at an all-night cram session and asks if I want to come over. I tell him I'm tired and just want to sleep. He doesn't argue. He doesn't even sound disappointed.

"I'm sorry," Rose says. She sits on her bed and fakes a smile.

"For what?"

"For what's happening between you and Cameron. I know it seems like it, but I'm not really that heavy of a sleeper. I hear everything, Luce."

My gaze drops to the floor. I don't respond. I don't know how to.

"He'll make it right."

I eye her now, wondering how she's so sure and I'm not. "What makes you say that?"

"Because he's Cameron. And you're Lucy. You're team *Luca*. You guys are forever. If you two can't make it work, then we're all screwed."

✧   ✧   ✧

FOR THE FIRST time in a long time, I'm smiling. Finals, at least for me, are over. I throw my arms in the air, celebrating. "Freeeeeedom," I mock shout.

"Okay settle down," Micky says. "Some of us aren't done yet." She pulls on my hand until I'm sitting on the floor with her, between two shelves of books. We're in the library where a lot of students are, studying their asses off. "Now be the bestest friend in the whole wide world and help me," she pleads, her eyes wide.

"Okay." I laugh. "Let's see what you got."

After three hours, she finally closes her books. "I'm done," she moans. "My brain can't take anymore."

"I don't know why you're so worried, you got this."

She starts to pack up and I do the same.

"So you and Cam are hanging around for the weekend for his work and then what? You go home for a couple weeks?"

At the mention of his name, any semblance of happiness fades. That *was* the plan. He couldn't get off work at the firm for the weekend so we were both going to hang around. It was only one weekend at the firm, and then he was free from there until next school year. He still needed to work at the store, but he was able to get his shifts covered for two weeks so we could go home and visit with our families, and then we'd have to come back. Jake and Micky were going back to Jake's for the rest of the summer and said we could stay there. The plan was perfect. Until it wasn't.

I do my best to fake a smile and nod, knowing that she'd want to talk about it if she knew something was up. I don't want her to worry, and I don't want to talk about it. She rushes to leave so she can catch Jake before he has an exam. I hang around and read for a bit, knowing that Rose won't be done for another hour. I don't want to talk about what's been going on with Cam, but I don't want to be alone either.

When I know it's time, I start to make my way to the exit.

Cameron

ROXY CALLED AND asked if I needed help with tomorrow's final. I told her I'd need a second brain because my current one was useless. She laughed at that, and said to meet her in the library. I called Lucy before I left. I wanted her to know what I was doing. If she flat out said not to, I wouldn't have, but she didn't answer. And I sure as shit needed the help.

"Sometimes I watch you," Roxy whispers from next to me.

"That's not creepy."

She chuckles, the huskiness in her voice coming out full force. "No. I mean when you're sketching, or planning. It's like you're bored. Like you wish your fingers would do something more exciting than draw straight lines. Do you draw? For fun, I mean?"

I shrug, not knowing what else to do.

"I want to be an artist, Cam," she starts. "I wish there were some form of job security in being an artist, but there isn't. So I design. I don't love it, but I do it. Why do you do it?"

I turn to her now, but she's already looking at me. "Lucy's the only one who's seen my work. She thinks I should show the world. She tries to get me to enter competitions, even if it's anonymously. She thinks I'm good, but I don't know if she's just saying it for the sake of saying it. I don't even know if she knows what good is."

"Show me."

"I don't have anything."

"Bullshit," she clips. "If you're anything like me, you do it whenever something inspires you. Don't be afraid." She draws a cross over her heart with her finger. "I'll be honest. If it's shit, I'll tell you. How else are you going to know?"

I push down my nerves. My palms are already sweaty from the thought of actually showing someone else.

"Come on," she encourages.

I reach down into my backpack and pull out a sheet of paper. I unfold it and place it face down on the table. "Show me," she says, bouncing in her seat.

I suck in a huge breath and forcefully blow it out.

And then I flip it.

She gasps.

I hold my breath.

And then...

"Cameron?"

Lucy.

My eyes lift.

My world ends.

Lucy

SOMETIMES I WONDER what it was like for Mom—to know that every day things went from bad to worse—and she couldn't do anything about it. And then I wonder what it felt like for her when the fight was over and she took her last breath.

For years I wondered.

But right now, I think I know.

My eyes are fixed on the sketch as my tears cause it to blur with each passing second. It's Cameron's work. I know it is—because I live and breathe his art. When he's not around, I stare at the pages—for hours sometimes. Sketch after sketch, pictures of me, and of our life together.

But the one I'm looking at—it's not me.

It's *her*.

He's on his feet moving toward me, but I can't move. I can't tear my eyes away from his drawing of *her*.

"Baby," he says, panic clear in his voice.

My eyes shut tight. More tears than I thought I could hold stream down my face.

I flinch when he touches me.

"Fuck Lucy, it's not—"

I turn away before he can finish. I run outside, where I finally let myself breathe.

"Lucy," he shouts after me, pulling on my arm so I'm facing him. "It's not—"

"Stop it!" I shout through my sob. "Just stop, Cameron! I don't want to hear it."

He pulls at his hair and curses the sky. Then he looks down at me through his lashes. "I love you, Lucy," he sighs.

That's it.

That's all he says.

My fists ball. My heart pounds hard against my chest. I want to yell. I want to scream. But I don't do either. Instead, I clench my jaw and I whisper, "I don't believe you."

He steps forward, reaching for me again. But I pull back, disgusted by his touch.

I try. I try so fucking hard to keep it in. To hold it together. But I can't. I can't fucking do it anymore. "When did you draw her?"

He shakes his head and says my name again. But it's not a fucking answer. And it's not enough.

"When!"

He rubs his eyes along his forearm. He's crying. Good. He fucking deserves to. "When she was in my dorm once."

I feel the bile rise in my throat. I want to puke. I want so badly to feel something else. Something *not* this. My hand presses against my stomach—hoping to ease the ache. "Were you alone?" I let out another sob as I imagine them. Working together. Alone. So alone that he had time to draw her.

He drops his head, but his eyes—they stay on mine. And then he nods, just once, but it's more than enough.

And even though I already knew the answer, it doesn't stop the pain, or the anger.

"Lucy, it doesn't mean anything."

And then I lose it.

I shove his chest so hard it makes him fall back a step. "It doesn't mean anything?" I shout. "Cameron. You said *I* was your art. You said I was your *heart*. And now you're saying that it doesn't mean anything?"

His hand reaches for me again but I push it away. I hate that he can make me feel like this. I hate that he can make me *hate him*.

I drop my shoulders and try to level my breathing. I try to speak, but my voice is strained. "That was mine, Cam. Your art was mine. It was something you shared with me. *Only me.*" My body shakes with each sob. "You gave her a piece of me. A piece of us. You shared something that was so special to me, and you gave it to someone else. You gave her your heart, Cam."

He just stands there watching me, not able to say a word. Because he *knows*—he can't say anything to make it better.

To make it stop.

To make it right.

I turn around, walk to my car, and rush to get in, just so I can cry in peace. So I can let my heart *shatter*.

He follows, getting in the passenger's seat. "Lucy, please."

"Get out!"

"Baby."

"Cam! STOP!"

He flinches at the harshness of my words, but I don't care.

"You need to stop. All of it. Just stop! Please. You can't keep hurting me like this." I'm pleading with him, begging him to leave me the fuck alone. "I can't take anymore of it!" I drop my head on the steering wheel and I cry. And cry. And cry. "It hurts so much," I say to no one.

I hear him sniff, see him wiping his eyes, but I can't force myself to care.

He created this.

He made this happen.

"It hurts so fucking much," I tell him now. "*You* hurt me." I sit up so I can face him. "Just get out, please, Cameron."

He throws his head back against the seat. And that's how we stay. Me watching him. Him crying. Me sobbing. Feeling everything around us slowly fade away.

I'm *fading*.

To blackness.

Just like Mom did.

Then he opens the door and steps out of the car—not a single word spoken.

Twenty-Eight
Lucy

I SPENT ALL night crying so hard that I threw up. Numerous times. I told Rose I got drunk to celebrate the end of finals—she didn't believe me, but she didn't call me out. She held my hair while I did everything I could to not knock on Cameron's door and demand an explanation. She helped me into bed, and held me while I cried—until I was so fucking exhausted from all of it that my cries finally lost their fight to control me.

✧ ✧ ✧

WHEN MINGE OPENS the door to their room the next morning with a smile on his face, I don't question it.

When he sees that it's me and his face falls, and he partially closes the door, alarm bells start ringing.

When I ask him what's up and to open the door, and all he does is shake his head, I *know* something's wrong.

I flatten my palm against the door and shove it forward. He doesn't stop me.

When I see Roxy sitting on Cameron's bed, I die a little.

The bathroom door opens and he steps out, wearing nothing but sweatpants and a towel around his neck. He sees me first, and whatever look I have on my face—he matches. And then his eyes move to the girl on his bed. The one I can't bring myself to look at.

"Fuck," he spits, hurriedly taking the steps to get to me.

I step back, with my hands up so he knows I don't want him near me.

I swallow down the puke that's threatening to make its way out. My hands ball, but there's something in my right hand stopping me from forming a fist. And then reality sets in, and I remember why I'm here. I throw the phone past his head and watch it smash against a wall, shattering to pieces.

Just like my fucking heart.

He doesn't flinch.

He doesn't take his eyes off me.

"Your phone must have fallen out of your pocket when you were in my car. Your mom called—wanted to know about dinner tonight. I said yes, because I didn't have the heart to tell her."

He steps forward, out of his room, and closes the door behind him. "Tell her what?"

I shake my head, trying to settle my heart. Trying to calm myself down. Trying to stop myself from punching him in the fucking face.

"Tell her what, Luce?"

"That her son's an asshole."

If possible, his frown deepens.

And I do my best to act like I don't care—when inside, all I want to do is forgive him. Hold him. *Love him.*

Cameron

"YOU'RE PISSED AT me?" Roxy says, linking arms with mine as we walk out of the final exam.

I yank my arm away from her grip. "I'm not pissed at you. I'm pissed at the entire fucking world, but you're not making shit easier for me. I mean, I'm grateful for your help, but you showing up in my room uninvited—"

"Hey, it's not the first time. Last time I showed up to help you study, you didn't seem to have an issue."

I sigh, defeated. Because she's right. Everyone's right, and I'm fucking wrong.

"Anyway," she perks up. "I made a few phone calls about your car—turns out my cousin jacked your wheels, he apologizes." She lets out a cynical laugh. "He spent today putting them back on, but we need to catch the bus back to my house."

With all the shit going on with Lucy and finals, my car was the last thing on my mind.

I shove my hand in my pocket searching for my phone to text Lucy, but I don't have one because she decided it was a fucking good idea to smash it against a wall. When she did it, I didn't care. Now—I'm a little pissed.

"Let's go," I tell Roxy. "But I need to go straight there and back, I don't have time to fuck around."

✦　✦　✦

"I WAS GONNA hotwire it and take it for a spin," Roxy's cousin, Joe, says. "But Rox said she'd grab my balls and put 'em in a vice. Ain't nobody want that shit."

I laugh.

He continues. "She's got that Latina fire, you know?"

My eyes snap to Roxy. "You're Latina?"

She scoffs.

He snorts. "What? The big titties and fat ass didn't give it away."

She smacks him on the back of the head. He chuckles, but then his eyes narrow. "How long you two been bumpin' uglies?"

I choke.

She speaks for me. "We're not. Cam has a girl."

"Huh," he says in response, then turns to Rox. "Yo, last final today right?"

She nods.

"Good. I got you a case of beers—put it in your studio. Let's drink."

"Sounds like a plan," she says through her own chuckle.

Joe eyes me for a moment. "What about you, rich kid? Up for a beer?"

It's not really a question, because his hand has curled around my neck and he's already leading me through the house.

"I'm not rich," I tell him, feeling the buzz of the beer in my head. It was supposed to be one, but I'm on my third, or fourth. I don't know. The only thing I know is that it's the first time in a long time that I've relaxed and been able to be myself.

"Yeah?" He eyes me up and down. "But you drive a Delorean? Those things ain't cheap."

"My mom's boyfriend got it for me. He's rich. Not us. We're... common folk."

"Common folk meaning poor," Roxy chimes in.

I stand up and stumble to pull another beer from the case, not even caring that it's warm. I raise one to Joe in offering. He shakes his head. They both laugh. I don't know why. Maybe I'm slow on the uptake because of the beers, or maybe I'm just missing something. "No, bro," Joe says. "A stint in rehab and AA means I stick to the soda." He lifts his can to show me. I hadn't even realized he wasn't drinking. I let his words settle, and then howl with laughter.

"What?" he asks, smiling as he does. "What's funny?"

I flop back on the couch and wait for my laughter to die down before I speak. "Just that you go to AA, but you think it's okay to jack wheels and steal shit."

"Hey!" he says, pointing a finger at me. "I'm like a Robin Hood of the hood. Steal from the rich—give to the poor. Besides..." He shrugs. "Jacking wheels never hurt family." He and Rox share a look, but I don't delve deeper.

"What about your girl?" Joe asks out of nowhere.

"Lucy?"

He shrugs. "If that's her name."

"What about her?"

"She common folk, too?"

I snort with laughter. "No, dude. Her family's loaded."

"Huh," he says. "Is she cute?"

Instantly, I smile. I don't realize that I do, but I do. And it feels like a first. "Yeah, man. She's cute. Beautiful. Sexy as hell, really."

"Oh, shit. You're like... in love with her?"

"Of course," I tell him, not skipping a beat. "I've loved her since we were fifteen and I'll love her forever." I search for my phone again, before remembering I don't have one, so I pull out my wallet instead. I open it and show him the picture of us I keep in there.

He lets out a low whistle. "Shit, man, you weren't kidding." He pats my back, as if congratulating me. He should be proud. I *am* proud. I did fucking good with Lucy.

His eyebrows bunch, as if deep in thought. "I screw rich girls some-times. Just for fun, you know? But I'd never date one. It's one thing for sex, but to be in a relationship..." His face turns to a grimace. "That's gotta be tough. I mean, for me—I'd always feel like the relationship was on a timer… until she found something better. I'd feel like I was always trying, always chasing, even though I already had the girl."

His words hit me like a ton of fucking bricks.

I don't respond, because I don't know how to. Instead, I stand up and grab another beer. And then another. And another.

They continue to talk shit about their lives, their families—never once noticing me drowning in a sea of my own insecurities.

"Yo, Cam," Joe says after I don't know how long.

I lift my heavy head and try to push back the effects of booze when I fake a smile at him. "Yo."

"Where's your girl tonight? Shouldn't you two be celebrating?"

My eyes widen at his question. "Shit." And then I laugh, because I have no other fucking choice. "I gotta go."

Lucy

HIS CAR PULLS up outside the restaurant, music blaring and brakes squealing. I eye Heather and Mark for a quick moment, but they're too busy watching the scene play out.

The passenger's door rises; Roxy steps out first, and then Cameron from beneath her.

I look away—too heartbroken to see anymore.

"What the hell?" Heather mumbles. She says my name, but I pretend to not hear her. I stare down at the table, trying to hide my sadness and disappointment that I'm sure is evident.

"Hey," he says, taking his seat next to me.

"Is that your car someone else is driving?" Mark asks.

"Yeah," Cam laughs, "It's all good. The dude's in AA—he's straight as an arrow." He puts his hand on my leg under the table. "Hey babe." He kisses my temple quickly, and then moves away. "Mother."

I don't know what her reaction is because I'm too afraid to look up.

"So," Cam says loudly. "What's everyone ordering?"

Heather sighs. "We've already eaten."

Cam's fingers on my leg dig in. "What do you mean?"

I push his hand off me and finally lift my gaze. Ignoring the stench of beer reeking from him, I face him. My voice comes out a whisper. "You're three hours late, Cameron."

His face drops and he looks around the table. "Huh," he says. "Would have been cool to have a phone so I could actually tell the time." He glances between Mark and Heather. "Did Lucy tell you she threw it at my head and smashed it on a wall?" He laughs a bitter laugh. "Bet Princess didn't tell you that."

And now I'm crying. I frantically wipe my tears and stand up. "I'm gonna go," I squeak out. I shut my eyes and try to regain my composure. "Heather, Mark, it was nice seeing you again. I'll be sure to come by and visit over the summer."

I don't wait for a response. I rush to gather my stuff so no one sees me break down.

His hand curls around my arm, spinning me to face him. He's on his feet now, towering over me. "So what?" he snaps. "Things aren't going your way so you just walk?"

I glance around the restaurant, knowing people are watching.

"What about me, Luce? When the hell do I get to walk away from it? Never! That's when. You think I want to be here... playing happy boyfriend? *All* the fucking time, that's what I am." His voice gets louder with every word.

I flinch, like his words physically hurt me. Because they do. They hurt so damn much.

"I'm so fucking sick of this pressure. All the time—this goddamn pressure."

I want to speak. I want to tell him to shut up. But I can't breathe.

Finally, he releases my arm. "'*You could be an architect, Cam,*'" he mocks, and then he laughs once. "Your dad tells me that I could be an architect and all of a sudden I'm changing my fucking classes and reworking my entire life plan. You wanted to go to UNC, so that's where I went. You never asked me what I wanted, Lucy. Not once."

Silent tears fall and I wipe them. But I don't look away. I want to see his face, so I can remember it clearly—the moment he destroyed me. Destroyed us.

"Your dad '*encourages*' me by making me a draft table and light box and I'm supposed to appreciate it, when really, what he's saying is '*Hey, poor little dumbshit, you're not good enough for my daughter, make something of yourself!*'"

"Cameron!" Heather snaps.

I stay the same, crying, feeling every part of me falling apart.

"He's drunk." Mark tries to calm Heather down. But whether he's drunk or not, it makes no difference.

"I'm sinking under this pressure, Lucy! From you, from my parents, from your dad. You all expect me to be something and I don't even know if I want to be that! The classes, the studying, the scholarship, the work… I never wanted this. I never asked for it! You did! You wanted me to be this!" His words come out clipped, harsh.

"Oh, and the scholarship!" he laughs again—that same bitter laugh. "You don't think I know your dad's floating me? No architect firm wanted to support me. It's his money! I'm not fucking stupid, Lucy." He's in my face now, pointing his finger down at me. His brows are furrowed and his nostrils flare. He's so mad, but he's *so* wrong. "How the fuck do you think that's supposed to make me feel? I can't fail. I can't drop the ball. I'll disappoint everyone. And all you guys do is push push push. I'm on the fucking edge here, Lucy! How much more can you push?"

I suck in a breath, my voice so quiet compared to his shouts. "I didn't know I was pushing you, I just thought I was encourag—"

His eyes roll, cutting me off. "Of course not, Luce!" he yells again, louder than ever.

People gasp.

I flinch.

"You don't get it! You don't understand! Because everything's been handed to you. You've been raised with a silver spoon in your mouth and you've never had to worry about a goddamn thing in your entire fucking life!"

And there it is.

The moment of destruction.

My body shakes. Not from the sob. Or the adrenalin. But from the hurt.

My eyes shut.

I breathe in. Out.

Once.

Twice.

It feels like eternity.

My hands flex, ball.

Flex.

Ball.

"Lucy, honey," Heathers coos. And I don't need to see her to know she's crying.

Breathe.

Shut. It. Out.

Inhale.

Exhale.

Once.

Twice.

My eyes snap open, fixed on Cam.

All blood has drained from his face.

His shoulders sag.

His eyes are sympathetic.

"Lucy?" Mark sighs.

I turn to him and fake the perfected smile I mastered when I was fifteen.

"I'm fine," I tell him.

A single *fine*. A single *lie*.

"I'll see you later."

And then I walk away.

Away from my forever.

Cameron

HER EYES SNAP open, and when they do, I die.

What the fuck did I just do?

It's been years. Five, to be exact—since I saw that look in her eyes.

The same look she had when I saw her in the laundry room at her house after her mom's funeral. It was the calm before the storm—only this time, there was no storm. No breaking of the dam. Back then, I wanted to be the reason for that calm look in her eyes. And now I am— but it was the wrong kind.

I should have been the calm. Not the reason.

I slump back in my chair, wondering how the fuck I'm going to fix this.

"Her dad isn't paying for your scholarship," Mom says quietly. "The first year was genuine, Bradman gave you that scholarship fair and square. The year after, they wanted to pull it. It wasn't beneficial for them. Tom knew—he came to us—offered to pay for it." My gaze lifts, trying to focus on her. "I wouldn't accept it, Cameron. And I knew you wouldn't either. So I sold the house and went to Bradman. I asked him to say it came from them, because I knew you wouldn't accept it from me. They said they would do it if you worked there. I didn't know, Cam. I didn't know that it was going to be too much for you, and that you'd turn into this." She sniffs and wipes her tears, then turns to Mark. "I'm going to try to catch Lucy. She needs a mother right now."

There's a stabbing pain. Right in my heart. I want it to hurt—more than it does. I deserve to feel the pain.

Mark—he just shakes his head, a look of disgust on his face. "When did you become an asshole?"

And then he gets up and leaves.

Everyone leaves.

A familiar figure holding a tray comes into my vision. She starts clearing the table. I slouch in my chair, kick my legs out, and tilt my head back, eyeing the ceiling. "I fucked up, Amanda."

She doesn't respond, just continues clearing the table.

I sit up now, trying to compose myself. "I've lost her and I don't think I'll ever get her back."

She freezes mid movement, and then faces me, her eyes filled with tears. "At least you know *why*, Cameron. I didn't even get that."

Twenty-Nine
Cameron

AFTER EVERYONE LEFT I sat at the bar and drank until I could no longer feel my face. Amanda ignored me the entire time. She hates me too.

I wanted to call Lucy but I had no phone. And I doubt she'd answer.

I *think,* Ethan, Amanda's brother, who was there watching over her, gave me a ride home. I say I think, because I don't really remember.

I ended up at her room, knocking louder than I should. Rose answered, but she told me she hadn't been home all night.

Now, I'm sitting at my cubicle at the firm with my head on the desk and my arms covering it, trying to drown in my own self-pity and sorrow.

"Hey C-Money."

I grunt in response.

"I drove your car back. How you feelin'?"

My head's pounding. My body aches. My heart is *dead.* I try to reply, but all I can do is moan.

"Heads up," she says.

But I'm slow to react, and then Lucy's voice fills my ears. "Cameron."

My head lifts. My eyes snap to her. And all of a sudden I'm alert. I know my heart's alive again because it's hammering so hard, so fast. "Babe," I croak.

She smiles. That same fake fucking smile from last night. And from the days after her mom died.

Roxy shifts from her leaning position on my desk. "I'm gonna go," she says slowly.

"No," Lucy cuts in. It's fast. Too fast. She's afraid to be alone with me. "It's okay, Roxy, stay." Her eyes move to me. "I just came to give you the key to the cabin and bring your stuff from my dorm."

Only now do I see her holding a box. All my shit's in there, including the folio where she kept all my sketches. My sketches of her. My *heart*.

She continues, "I cleared out the room overnight, so I wanted to give it to you."

Fuck.

The burning in my chest is so strong I feel like I'm going to burst.

I stand up and clear my throat. "I thought we were leaving on Sunday?"

She smiles again. I've never hated a smile so much in my entire fucking life. "I know you wanted to stay at the cabin because you felt awkward staying at Mark's house." That was a lie. I didn't care where I stayed. I just wanted to be with her. Alone. I wanted her to myself so I made it up.

"I told my dad you were gonna be there. I haven't told him what happened, so you don't have to be uncomfortable."

Even though I know the worst is happening, still, I ask, "What do you mean what happened?"

Fuck her fake smile. Fuck it all.

She sets the box on my desk, and the key next to it. "I gotta go," she sighs, looking down at the floor. "Micky's in her car waiting." Her gaze lifts. Her eyes bore into mine. "She's taking me to the airport, Cameron."

"What!" I step forward and take her hand. "Where are you going?"

She pulls out of my hold. "I'm just going away for a little bit."

"Away?" My heart pounds faster. Harder. Panic rushes through me. "Away?" I repeat. "Away from me?"

She has that look in her eyes again. That calm which shouldn't exist, not when the world around us is falling apart.

She nods once.

And I lose it.

I pull on her arm and drag her into an empty office. Slamming the door behind me, I turn to her. "What the fuck is happening right now?" I say to anyone that will listen.

She just stands there, her arms at her sides and sadness in her eyes I hoped to never see again.

I link our fingers. She lets me. Then I lean against a desk and pull her between my legs. She pulls a hand out of my hold and raises it, reaching up to wipe the tears on my cheeks. I can't stop crying. Her name leaves my lips. It sounds like a plea.

"I'm sorry, Cameron," she whispers.

Why the fuck is she sorry?

"I'm sorry you felt like I pushed you, or pressured you—"

"Stop."

"No." She rests her forehead against mine. "I need to say this, and you need to hear it." Her voice is strained as she talks through her own cries. "I believed in you, and your art, so much that I thought I was encouraging you. I never thought that—" Her voice breaks, she clears it before continuing, "I never thought that I was pressuring you, or pushing you. And I'm so sorry. I'm sorry you never felt like you were good enough. I'm sorry I never told you that I would love you regardless of what you chose. Regardless of who you wanted to be. I'm sorry our time together has been about me. And that *you* have *always* been about *me*. Cameron…" She stops to take a few calming breaths. We both do. We stand, our foreheads touching, breathing the same air, but there's endless space between us. "I loved you before you told me. I loved you before you kissed me. I loved you every day since we were fifteen. And I've loved you more with each passing day. But last night, you *destroyed* me. You took that love and you *ruined* me."

I drop my head onto her shoulder and sob uncontrollably. I release her hand and wrap my arms around her waist. I don't want to let her go. "I fucked up," I tell her. "I fucked everything up. And I didn't mean any of it."

She can't control her cries. And neither can I. She pulls back, holds my head in both her hands and looks me right in the eyes, wiping my tears as she does. "I would have loved you, every single day. Forever, Cameron."

My head slowly shakes from side to side, because I know what this is. And I don't want it to happen. "Don't say that," I almost shout. "Don't, Lucy. Please. You're talking like we're *done*. Like it's *over*." I stop to take a breath. "We promised each other forever. Don't you remember? Forever, Luce. You promised me."

"We both did," she says, her voice calm now. "We promised each other *our* forever. But maybe *our* forever is over."

My fingers curl into the back of her dress. I don't want to hear any of it. I don't want to believe it. "Don't say that," I beg. I plead. "I don't know how to fix this."

She pulls back, reaching behind her to unclasp my hands. I grip tighter.

"Cam, please," she sobs. "I have to go. This hurts too much."

And at her words, I release her. Because the last thing I ever wanted was to hurt her.

She leans up on her toes, the saltiness from both our tears combine with our kiss.

One kiss.

One final goodbye.

"I loved you so much," she whispers.

And then she's gone.

I drop my head in my hands and sit on the floor, too exhausted to stay standing.

And then I cry. Get angry. Cry. Get angry.

And then I do it all over again.

Because she said *loved*.

She *loved* me.

Thirty
Lucy

L UCAS MEETS ME at the airport in New Jersey. He was the one who answered when I called last night to speak to Dad about Cameron staying at the cabin. He knew instantly something was wrong. I told him what happened, and I told him not to tell anyone. He let me cry for I don't even know how long. And when he knew I was done he said, "Luce, I'm sorry. Shit happens. You don't deserve it. Let's get fucked up." I laughed, and twenty minutes later we had flights booked to New Jersey.

We wait outside the airport for my friend Claudia and her brother Jason to show up. We all grew up together. Jason and Lucas were inseparable when they were kids, and even now, years later, it's like time hasn't passed at all.

"So my parents are away for a few weeks, somewhere in the Bahamas. We have the house to ourselves," Claudia informs, winking at me in the rear view mirror.

I try to smile, but the ache in my heart stops it from showing.

"How small is your fucking car?" Lucas says from next to me. He's crouched over in the tiny space of Claudia's two door. "My nose is itchy but I don't—" He starts to wiggle around, making a show of not being able to move.

I scratch his nose for him as a joke. He sighs when I do. "You're just lucky you got Mom's height," he tells me.

I laugh. A genuine laugh. He smiles when he hears it. And it hits me, how much things have changed. I miss my family. I miss my friend.

"Hey guys," Jason says, turning in his seat to look at us. "Your mom was what? Five-one? Five-two max. And your dad's what? Six-five?"

Lucas and I glance at each other quickly, and then nod at Jason.

His nose scrunches. "How did they have sex? A lot of doggy style I'd

239

think."

"DUDE!" Lucas yells.

"That's sick," I tell him.

Claudia pipes up. "What are you doing thinking about their parents having sex?"

Lucas makes a gagging sound.

I lean back in the seat and look out the window, promising myself to *try*. Try to live without my *forever*.

✧   ✧   ✧

"HE HASN'T CALLED?" Claudia sits on the lounge chair next to mine.

"He has no phone, so no. But I don't know that he would. And I don't know that I'd answer. I think I need time, you know?"

She smiles. "Are you sad?"

I lift my sunglasses on top of my head and face her. "No, Claud. I'm devastated."

✧   ✧   ✧

THE NEXT DAY, Jason and Lucas spend a good three hours reminiscing about their high school days together. They enjoyed it so much that the day after that, five of their friends showed up from home to hang out with them.

Now there are seven boys in the house. The pool is always in use, music is always up and alcohol is always flowing. And that's the way it's been for the last two weeks.

Sometimes Claudia tries to get me to talk about Cameron. I don't really have much to say, so I stay quiet. But that doesn't mean I don't think about him. All the time.

"You think it was about time?" she said once. I asked her what she meant. She just shrugged and said, "He's always been so great, what you've always needed and wanted. You always made him out to be so perfect, and I didn't really ever believe you. Five years you guys have been together and this is the first time you can say anything bad about him? So he has flaws, so what? Maybe that's what makes him perfect."

Cameron

Jake: *Kayla just told me she went by the cabin but Lucy wasn't there.*

I THROW MY phone on Jake and Micky's coffee table and slump back on their couch. I've been staying here since the day after Lucy left. I didn't bother to go home. I didn't want to stay at our—I mean *her*—cabin. And Mom and Mark... I can't even deal with hearing the disappointment in their voices, let alone seeing it in their faces.

Slowly, I stand up and stumble to the fridge for another beer. This has been my life for the past two weeks—sitting around feeling sorry for myself and drinking until I can't think anymore. Thinking hurts way too fucking much. So does feeling.

There's a knock on the door. "Lucy," I whisper. My heart thumps as I try to gather my thoughts—try to remember the last time I showered. I sniff my armpits, and then my shirt. I think I'm good.

Another knock.

"Hang on!"

I take a look around the living room, there's nothing but empty packets of junk food and beer cans.

Knock knock.

Fuck it.

Taking long strides to get to the door faster, I place my hand on the handle and take a few calming breaths. "You got this."

I open the door.

"C-Money."

My shoulders slump—along with my entire fucking body.

"That's not happiness to see me," she coos.

"Roxy." I nod, leaving the door open and sitting back on the couch. She closes the door behind her and follows, sitting down next to me.

"How the hell did you even know where I was?"

"I ran into your roommate at a party last night. He told me."

Fucking Minge.

She adds, "So, I probably don't need to ask how you are... going by the state of your appearance, I take it you and Lucy are done?"

I shuffle further away from her and lean my elbows on my knees. "I don't know."

"Cameron," she says, scooting closer and running a hand down my arm. I try not to flinch at her touch. She sighs. "Do you want to get your mind off her?"

I laugh once. "You give me a way to stop thinking about her, and I'll do it."

"Cameron," she says again. And it's kind of settling—familiar in a way that I can't explain.

"What?"

Then she moves her hand from my arm to my leg, forcing me to look at her for the first time since she got here. She smiles at me and my guard drops a little. She's the first person who's treated me like I actually have feelings. "We're friends, right?" she asks.

I shrug. "I guess."

Her hand moves higher up my leg.

"I could help you forget her," she whispers.

My eyes narrow.

Realization sets in.

Then a thousand fucking emotions run through me. "Can I ask you something?"

"Anything," she says, smiling again.

"Are you into me? Like *into* me. Did you ever want to be more than just friends? The whole helping me study and all that shit—was there more to it?"

She looks away for a moment, as if contemplating her next words. "I kind of thought I made that obvious."

My eyes shut.

Inhale.

Exhale.

Her hand on my leg squeezes once.

She says my name again.

And now I know what Lucy felt all those times I read her—that calmness she felt, the one right before the storm.

I open my eyes, the booze doing nothing at all for my now clear head. "But you knew I loved Lucy, right? I mean, I never said or did anything to make you feel otherwise. There was never a time where I made you actually think that I'd choose *you* over her."

Her eyes search mine when she speaks. "It was just a matter of time," she says with an unjustified confidence. "You and me—we're the same people. She's different than us, Cameron. She's better than us. People like you and me belong together. For her—you were just a phase. A hobby. A moment of slumming."

"Shut up!" I clip.

She laughs in disbelief.

If she were a guy, I'd punch her. "You don't know shit about us—or our relationship. You don't know anything." I shake my head and stand up, and then I release the *storm*. "You took advantage of me, Roxy. You knew I needed help and you became that, but I had no fucking idea you had ulterior motives. Maybe to you, what you were doing was obvious, and maybe I'm naïve, or maybe I'm just so in love with another girl that I never even noticed it. I never thought of you like that. Not once. Not even for a second. But you're right about one thing—she is better than me. And I'm the luckiest asshole in the world for having her and keeping her for as long as I did. So whether or not things work out with us—just remember that it had nothing to do with you. You didn't win. I won't let you."

Her eyes thin to slits. She opens her mouth to speak but I cut her off. "I'm going to my room. You have five minutes to get you and your whore clothes out of here, and if you don't, I have no issue kicking your fat ass out the door."

I walk to my room and slam the door, then lean against it and drop my head between my shoulders.

I try to level my breathing. Try to settle my nerves. Try to find that *calm* again.

Because she worked out the one insecurity I've always had but never let myself voice.

✧   ✧   ✧

A HALF HOUR later, there's another knock. I don't bother getting my hopes up this time.

Minge stands on the other side with a six-pack of beer. Like I need any more beers.

"Yo," I say.

"'Sup." He sniffs the air. "You smell like expired feet."

I open the door and sit on the couch, my favorite place in the entire world.

"I brought beer as an apology," he says.

"Why are you sorry? Because Lucy left me? That's not your fault."

He sets the beer on the table and sits on the recliner. "No, because I was buzzed last night and told that hot chick, Roxy, where you lived."

"She's not hot," I bite out.

243

"Maybe not Lucy standard hot, but for me she's hot."

I don't respond.

"Anyway," he adds. "I just thought I'd come by and say sorry, and warn you that she might show up soon."

"She already has."

"Oh shit. How did that go?"

I ignore his question and drop my head in my hands. "I need to speak to Lucy."

"Have you called her?"

I face him now, sighing loudly as I do. "I'm scared."

"Why?"

"Because what if she doesn't answer? Or hangs up on me? And I'm not there to see her face, to know what she's feeling. I'll spend the rest of my life wondering why she did it... I think I need to see her, like, in person."

"And you don't know where she is?"

I shake my head.

"Well... I mean you've known her forever. You know all her friends and family. She said she was going to the airport, right? So where could she be going that she needs to fly there?"

I pinch the bridge of my nose, trying to stop that thumping in my head. And then it hits me. "Fuck. I need money for a plane ticket."

He doesn't skip a beat. "I have money."

"What?"

"Yeah, I have money. Don't let these shitty clothes and bad hygiene fool you," he laughs. "How much do you need?"

"How the fuck do you have money? You don't even have a car."

His eyes roll. "I'm a free spirit. Save the environment, all that shit. Although, I do need to rent a car for a couple weeks. You have a car. I could just rent yours. It's kind of like fate, huh?"

Even though I suspect he's talking shit—for a moment, I actually consider the possibility. But only for a moment before reality sets in. "I can't," I say, pissed off at the world. "I gotta work on Monday."

"So, today's Saturday... that means you have tomorrow. Where do you plan on flying?"

"New Jersey."

He smiles.

I smile.

And somehow, the world starts spinning again.

Thirty-One
Lucy

I SWITCH MY e-reader off—unable to concentrate on the words—and take a sip of my soda. I don't enjoy chasing a buzz when Cam's not around. "Better get used to that," I mumble to myself.

"What?" Lucas says, sitting on the chair opposite me. We've spent almost every day outside, in or around the pool.

"Nothing," I answer.

He nods, but keeps looking at me strangely.

I watch the mayhem going on in the pool filled with seventeen-year-old boys.

"It's pretty cool here," he says. "Was this what your last high school summer was like? Chilled out with your friends back home?"

Slowly nodding my head, I reply, "I guess."

His brows bunch. "When did Dad build the cabin?"

"End of junior."

"Ohhhh." He nods slowly, then his features change to a look of disgust. "I think I can guess what you got up to then."

I laugh. "It wasn't *just* that. Our friends came around a lot. Replace the pool with the lake, the bar with a bonfire, and the mansion with my cabin, it comes pretty close to this."

He opens his mouth to speak, then shuts it, then opens it, then shuts it again.

"Say it," I tell him.

He smiles, but it's sad. "Have you spoken to Cam since you left?"

My gaze drops and my features straighten. "No."

"Lucy…" he sighs.

"What?"

"When I said that we should come here, I kind of meant for a few days. I thought maybe you needed to get away, clear your head. I didn't think we'd be here for two weeks. I didn't think it was *that* big a deal, you know?"

"Lucas, I've been with Cam for five years, how is it not a big—"

"That's not what I meant," he interrupts. "Just give me a second…"

I wait.

And wait.

"I've known Cameron a long time," he starts, "as long you've known him. He's like a brother to me, Lucy. He's a brother to all of us. You know when people ask Lachlan how many brothers and sisters he has; he tells them he has one sister and six brothers. He always, *always,* says Cam's name first."

I drop the sunglasses that were on my head to cover my eyes; shielding him from the tears I know are coming.

"After Mom died, he was there. Nobody knew why, but nobody asked. When shit got bad with Dad, he stuck up for you. He did what I wanted to do but never could. When you had an eating disorder—"

"You knew?" I tremble.

He nods. "We all knew, Luce. We just didn't know what to do to help you. But Cam—he knew. Somehow, he made it *stop.* He saved you, which meant that he saved all of us, because you were our rock. You became a parent to us when we had no one. And you *needed* saving. You needed someone to help you carry that weight."

I try to breathe through the pain, through the hurt, through the cries that are bursting to escape.

"I just think you should maybe talk to him, Lucy. I think that fifteen-year-old kid who gave up his world and made you *it* deserves that. Don't you?"

I nod, because the giant lump in my throat won't allow me to speak.

"Good," he says, a slight smile on his face. "Because he's here."

"What!"

He jerks his head to the side gate where Cameron stands, looking down at the ground with his hands in his pockets.

"You told him where we were?"

He shakes his head. "No. I was out front when a cab dropped him off."

I look over at Cameron again. My heart beats so fast, so loud, that I feel it everywhere. "Not now!" I plead with Lucas.

"Now Luce," he says, getting up from his seat. "It's time."

I suck in a shaky breath as I watch him get up and spin on his heels. "Hey..." He turns back around. "I love you, Lucy goosey smells like poopsy."

I let out a laugh. And a cry. "I love you too, Lucas mucus smells like pukas."

He shakes his head and walks away... toward Cameron. Toward the one guy I've spent two weeks trying to forget.

Cam's head lifts when he sees Lucas approaching. They shake hands, and then he looks at me.

And my world stops.

Breathe.

In.

Out.

Cameron

"HEY." I HAVEN'T been this nervous since the few seconds before I finally worked up the courage to kiss her.

I sit on the chair that I saw Lucas on, but I'm distracted. *Who the hell are all these guys and why are they here?*

"Hey," she says quietly. My eyes drift shut when I feel her hand on the side of my face. "Stop it," she whispers.

I work up the nerve to open them so I can see her. And when I do, my world stops. She's lifts the sunglasses off her head and her clear blue eyes pierce into mine.

"Stop what?" I croak.

She smiles softly. "This." She rubs her hand on my jaw. "Your jaw's all tense... and this..." Her thumb brushes the space between my eyebrows. "They're Lucas and Jason's friends. Don't worry." And for some stupid reason it means something. Like she knows what I'm thinking and she cares enough to ease my fears.

"Hey," I say again because I don't know what else *to* say. And then I take her in and my jaw tenses and my brows furrow again. She's in a plain white bikini, and nothing else. "Can we talk, somewhere more private?"

"Um." She looks around, like she's afraid to be alone with me. "Okay." She stands up and I follow, walking behind her along the length of the pool. The kids in there all stare at her with their mouths hanging open. I try to glare at them all one by one.

Lucky for me, Lucas is on my side. "Quit perving on my sister, ass-holes. I catch you doing it again, I'll beat the shit out of all of you."

She walks into the house and up the stairs. It takes everything in me to not touch her, but her ass is in my face and...

"Just here," she says, pulling my attention away from her ass. She opens a door and steps into a bedroom. Then she sits on the bed, her almost naked body on full display. "Lucas said you got out of a cab. Did you fly here?"

I nod, trying not to stare at her body.

"Can you afford that? How did you know I was here?"

I glance at her quickly, before looking away. "I rented out the Delore-an to Minge to buy tickets, but no, I didn't know you were here. I just had no—"

"You rented out your car for plane tickets and flew here on a whim?"

I nod again.

"Cameron..."

I don't know what she means by saying my name but I don't ask. I'm too fucking nervous, and anxious, and emotional. I'm *way* too emotional.

"You look nice," I tell her. Then roll my eyes and laugh at myself.

She tries to smile. "I've put on a bit of weight lately, but I'll hit the gym again when I get back on campus."

My eyes narrow and move to her. "So you're coming back?"

"Of course I'm going back. My life's there... well, what's left of it anyway." Her gaze falls to the floor, watching her legs kick back and forth on the edge of the high bed.

"And what do you mean you'll hit the gym again? You went to the gym?"

"Yeah." She nods. "Toward the end of the year... you were always busy and I just—I wanted something to do, so I asked Jake to take me... well not take me, but be there when I was. I knew you wouldn't like me going alone, and I didn't want to ask..."

There's a shooting pain in my heart, the same one that's been there the last two weeks, but it's sharper and hurts a fuckload more.

I lean back on the wall opposite her and shove my hands in my pockets. "I kind of hate that I didn't know what was going on in your life. We still saw each other every night, apart from the last—"

"It was different, Cameron," she says quietly.

I nod slowly.

"I mean the few days before we broke up was…"

My world stops again, but for a different reason this time. My face must show it, because she stops talking. "Are you okay?"

I slide down the wall until my ass hits the floor, unable to stay upright. "It just hurts," I tell her honestly. "I guess when you left you said *maybe*. You said that *maybe* our forever was over. I guess deep down I was keeping hope." I sniff back my emotions and look down at the floor. "It's fine. I'm sorry."

"Me too," she whispers.

Moments of silence pass before I finally speak. "How have you been?"

She shrugs. "I've been… I don't know. Thinking?"

"Yeah? What have you been thinking?"

"I think I have questions I'd like to ask you, but I'm scared."

My eyes snap to hers. "Ask them. Please? Ask anything." I'm desperate—too desperate. But I don't care.

"Have you seen her since?"

My body tenses, and her hands rise to cover her gasp. I don't know what I was expecting her to ask, but that wasn't it.

"When?"

I drop my head between my shoulders and inhale deeply, waiting for the courage to speak. "Yesterday."

Her sob has my eyes lifting to her. She's bent over herself, one had covering her mouth, and the other on her stomach. "Why?" she says, but before I get a chance to respond she's off the bed and walking toward me—or so I think, but she brushes past me and through the door next to me. A bathroom. I stand frozen while I watch her drop to her knees in front of the toilet and lift the lid. Then sense kicks in, and the vision of her at fifteen doing the exact same thing flood my mind.

"Stop!" I try to shout, but it comes out a whisper. I get to her and pin her arms to her sides. "What are you doing?"

She tries to push me away, but I hold on to her tighter. And slowly, I feel the fight leave her.

I let her go, but hold her shoulders so she has no choice but to look at me. "Fuck, Luce, have you been doing it again?"

She shakes her head, but there's a wariness in her eyes telling me she's lying. "I'm fine," she says, and now I know she is.

I exhale all the air in my lungs and release my hold on her, then I eye the ceiling, trying to level my thoughts.

She stands up and walks to the sink to splash water on her face.

"Have you?" I ask again, coming to a stand.

She doesn't answer in words, but her tear filled eyes locking with mine is answer enough.

"Fuck." I spin on my heels and leave the bathroom, and then make my way to the bedroom door.

"Where are you going?" she asks, panic clear in her voice.

"I never wanted this, Luce. I never wanted to be the reason why you're back there, doing something so wrong. *I* created that. *I* made you want to do that again. I can't... I just can't. I need to let you go."

"Tell me what happened," she says, her arms crossed over her chest.

"What?"

"Why did you see her again? Are you guys... are you dating now?"

"What! No. Fuck no, Luce. She came over yesterday because asshole Minge told her where I was."

"And what did she want?"

I sigh, and I let the inevitable happen. I tell her the truth. "She told me she was into me."

"That fucking whore!"

If it were any other time, any other person, I'd be laughing. But this isn't a laughing matter.

"What did you say?"

"I told her to get her and her whore clothes out of the house or I'd kick her fat ass out of there."

And somehow, amongst everything we're going through, her lips pull at the corners and a smile comes through. "Really?"

My eyes drift shut when I hear the hopefulness in her voice. "Yes, really, Luce. I'm sorry that I never picked up on it, or that I didn't do anything to stop it when you felt it was going that way. I just never noticed it, but I should have listened to you."

Her arms drop to her sides and she releases a breath.

"And you?" I ask.

"What about me?"

"You're making yourself throw up again?" I stand so I'm only feet in front of her.

Her head tilts all the way back to look at me, the way she's done so many times before. "No. Not intentionally. It was only once, Cam. Never again."

"When?"

She sits on the edge of the bed and looks down at the floor. "The night I saw your sketch of her."

My heart drops to my stomach.

She lifts her legs onto the bed, raising her knees and wrapping her arms around them. "Why did you draw her?" she struggles to ask.

My heart breaks, but I tell her the truth. "Because I'm an asshole. Because she came to my dorm once and offered to help me study. I needed the help, because I was struggling so much, and I took it. I should have said no." I lean back against the wall opposite her.

"And you were alone?"

I nod, my eyes never leaving hers. "She came in, but I left the door open. I didn't want her getting any ideas. She was working on something of mine at my desk and I sat on my bed while I waited. I started to fall asleep and I knew I shouldn't because I wouldn't be able to wake up, so I picked up a pen and paper and I just did it. It was so dumb. I just—I wasn't thinking. I didn't do the one thing you asked me to do, and that was to think about your feelings. I'm so sorry, Luce. I can't even tell you how sorry I am. I fucking hate myself for what I did." I stop to take a breath, not realizing how badly I was holding it all in until I could no longer speak. "I haven't been able to pick up a pen and paper since. I can't—I fucking hate myself."

"Cameron..." she says again—with so much sympathy I want to punch myself. I don't deserve her sympathy. "You know," she continues, "I've been thinking about it, a lot. About what you said at dinner."

"Oh my God." I moan and cover my head with my arms, too ashamed to face her.

"I've known you a long time, Cameron. I think I know you pretty well, right?"

I look up, not bothering to hide how I truly feel. "You know me better than I know myself, Luce."

"I know, right?" She kicks her legs out and sits on the edge of the bed again. "That's what I mean. So it doesn't make sense to me—why you would say all that stuff that night. I mean… you broke me, Cam. You ruined me, and you ruined what I thought we had. You left me devastated and for what? Because you were drunk? That can't be all. That can't be a valid enough reason. There has to be more. And I just don't get it."

"Because, Luce." I tilt my head up and stare at the ceiling. Then I push down my hurt and my fear, and most of all my pride. "Because sometimes when I'm with you—I feel like people can tell."

"Tell what?"

"That I don't belong. That you're way too damn good for me, and sometimes I wonder if you'd even look twice at me if I weren't the only thing standing in front of you. What if we met under different circumstances? What if you didn't rely on me? What if you still had friends when I started to chase you? What if Claudia was there… would you have even talked to me?"

"Cam," she says skeptically. "Of course—"

"No, you say that, Luce. But you don't know. And I know it sounds horrible, but I always felt like I was less, and I put you on a pedestal, and I shouldn't have. And with Roxy—"

She flinches, but I keep going. I *need* to keep going. "With her, it was the other way around, and there was nothing romantic, or physical with her, but it just felt like I deserved what I had. She just made me feel like it was okay to not be able to afford college, or fancy things, or have to work to support myself. I didn't feel like a dumbass for not being smart. I know that you can't understand that."

She cries now, her hands frantically wiping her tears. "Are you saying that I made you feel like that? Did I not show you how I felt? How much I loved you?"

"No!" I drop to my knees at her feet. "It's not you. You never did anything wrong."

"Then why?"

"It's so hard to explain. It's like every day I woke up with you in my arms and it felt like I was counting down the seconds until you realized what you were doing and you'd be done with me. So you could move on and find someone who would provide you the life you're used to, the one you deserve. I can't do that. I can't even—"

"Stop!" she says harshly. "Just stop." She stands up and walks to her dresser, pulling open the top drawer and holding something in her hand. When she returns, she sits on the floor and faces me, then slowly reveals what she picked up. "Do you know what this is?"

There's a rock in her hand. "A rock?" I say nervously, because I'm pretty sure she's about to throw it at my head.

"Cam, this is a rock from our river."

I suck in a sharp breath.

"I skipped a class the day after you brought me there the first time and I found this, and I've kept it ever since. I keep it because that's where you helped me piece together my broken heart. That's where a boy I barely knew took me and taught me that it was okay to break—that I could hold it in forever, or I could let it go and heal. And every day, since that day, I remind myself I'm *healed*, and that *you* healed me. And money, and material possessions—they didn't heal a broken heart, Cameron. Only you did."

She's crying.

I'm crying.

And then I let out a bitter laugh. "I want to hold you but I don't even know if it's okay to hug an ex."

"What?" she says, her eyes huge. Then she presses a hand to her heart. "Wow," she cries, rubbing her chest. "It hurts so much."

"What hurts?"

"You, calling me an ex," she says quietly. "It's so final."

"Yeah, well you said we broke up earlier. I'm pretty sure you shredded my fucking heart."

She looks up, wiping her tear-streaked face. Her head moves slowly from side to side. "I don't like it."

"I fucking hate it, Lucy." I move closer, wanting to touch her, but I don't know what the hell she wants. "I don't want to be broken up," I say quietly, looking her right in the eyes.

She pouts. "I don't want to be your ex."

I lick my lips as I stare down at hers. "So what do you want?"

She blinks, swallowing loudly when she does. "I don't know." She shuffles back—away from me. "I think I want more time."

"Okay." I nod, feeling a shitload more hopeful than when I got here.

"I'll give you all the time you need. I'll give you forever, Luce."

She inhales a shaky breath, looking from my eyes to my lips. I lick them again. *Please kiss me.*

Before she gets a chance, my phone rings. I silence it, but I can't ignore it. "My dad's assistant is waiting for me. I couldn't afford a cab back to the airport so I asked Dad for help. He wouldn't leave his office, so he sent his assistant."

"Okay, I'll walk you out." We stand at the same time. I wait for her to replace the rock in her dresser, but she pulls out shorts and puts them on. Then she does something that sends a thousand silent messages. She puts on a shirt—my high school gym shirt, the one which has my name on the back. "Ready?" she asks.

"No," I breathe out. "I'm not ready to leave you yet."

"But you have work tomorrow?"

"I know."

"And I still need time, Cam."

I close my eyes and take a few calming breaths. And then I remember why I'm here, and what I expected. And I know that what she's giving is more than I could have ever dreamed. She's giving me *hope.*

Thirty-Two
Cameron

I WAS RIGHT. Minge didn't really need my car, which is evident because he's been sleeping on the couch at Jake and Micky's since I came back from New Jersey a week ago. I've quit drinking myself into a stupor, gone to work, and pretty much done nothing else. Nothing but think about Lucy and check my phone every five minutes.

She said she wanted time and I'm doing everything I can to give her that. Which is hard. Really fucking hard—especially because she didn't give me a hint of how much time that was.

So when my phone beeps and Lucy's name shows up with a text message, I almost piss my pants. Almost.

"It's Lucy," I tell a half sleeping Minge sitting on the recliner.

"Mm?"

I kick his leg. "Lucy. The text. It's from her."

He sits up now, his eyes wide. "What does it say?"

"I don't know," I rush out. I drop the phone on the coffee table and rub my hands against my shorts. My palms are sweating. My heart's thumping.

"Read it!" Minge shouts. He's on the edge of his seat, his hands gripping the armrests tightly.

"I'm scared," I yell back, my voice matching his.

He smacks his hand on the back of my head. "Quit being a pussy and man the fuck up. Read the text, asshole."

I rear back in surprise. Minge—he's always so relaxed, so easy-going. I've never seen him excited or anxious about anything.

"Okay," I huff out, and blow out a breath.

I pick up the phone and open the message. "It's a picture," I tell him. I don't know how I managed to get the words out through the huge fucking grin on my face.

"And?"

I show him the text. It's of her wearing a hoodie with a picture of Marty McFly from *Back to the Future*. Above the picture it says *That was heavy,* and underneath it says, *Do you even lift, bro?*

Her words were the killer though.

Minge smiles as he hands it back. "*Thinking of you?* That's a good thing right? She's thinking of you!"

"I know!" I wipe my forehead with the back of my hand. *Why the hell am I sweating so much?*

"So?" he chides.

"So? So what?"

"What are you gonna write back?"

"Fuck." I release the phone like it's fire in my hands. "I don't know! What should I write?"

"I don't know, dude." He's as panicked as I am. "Something witty? She thought you were funny right?"

"I guess. I don't have anything funny to say!" I pick up the phone again. "I'll just—" I type out a text and hit send without thinking.

"What did you say?" Minge asks, his voice high pitched.

"I miss you."

"I MISS YOU!" he yells in disbelief, then throws his body back into his chair. "What the fuck? You didn't even work your way to that. You just went straight for it. Now she has nowhere to go! What if she doesn't want to say I miss you back? Then what? What will she say?"

"Shut up." I'm on my feet, pacing the floor. "You're making me fucking nervous."

"I'm just saying... you should have eased into the feels. That was a shit move."

"Fuck!" I link my fingers behind my head and stare up at the ceiling. "How long has it been since I texted back?"

He shrugs. "Like, thirty seconds."

"She should have written back by now."

"You need to calm down."

"I was calm!" I shout. "You and your easing into feels bullshit made me nervous. It's your fault!"

✧　✧　✧

"HOW LONG HAS it been?" I ask him.

He looks at his watch. "Three minutes."

I pick up my phone, make sure the ringer's on and it's charged, and then throw it on the couch.

✦   ✦   ✦

"HOW LONG NOW?"

"Seven minutes," he says. "I told you to say something funny. Not *I miss you.*"

"Shut up."

My phone beeps with a text. We both lunge for it. I punch him in the gut when he gets to it first.

"You're fucked," he groans, his arm pressed against his stomach.

"Quit being a pussy and man the fuck up." I close my eyes and breathe deeply, waiting for the adrenaline to settle. When I open them, Minge is back on the recliner, but he's on his feet, squatting at the edge. "What the fuck are you doing?"

He ignores my question. "What the fuck did she say?"

I look down at my phone and open the text. "I miss you too!" I laugh, relieved at her words.

He cheers.

And then we hug, jumping up and down as we do.

It lasts a few seconds before we both realize that we're twenty-one-year-old dudes and not nine-year-old One-Directioners.

He clears his throat and does something that looks like flexing his muscles.

I belch.

Because right now, I think it's important we both remind ourselves that we're manly assholes.

"So what are you going to write back?" he asks, just as I hit send.

I grimace.

"What the fuck did you write?"

"Um…" I hesitate to tell him.

This time he punches me in the gut, swiping my phone out of my hand at the same time.

"I LOVE YOU!" he shouts. The same disbelief as last time. "WHAT THE FUCK IS WRONG WITH YOU?"

I rub the back of my head in annoyance. "I don't know. She should know that I love her, I thought... I just... I just wanted her to know."

He rolls his eyes so high, I'm sure he can see the back of his head. "Now we're going to sit here anxiously and wait for her to write back. What if she doesn't say it back? What are you gonna do then? Do you even fucking listen to me?"

"Shut up!" I know he's right, but I don't want to think about it.

✧   ✧   ✧

"HOW LONG?"

"Two minutes from the last time you asked me." We're both squatting on our seats, staring at the phone in the middle of the coffee table.

"Come on, Luce," I whisper.

"She can't hear you, dickhead."

"Fuck you," I clip, my eyes never leaving the phone.

Finally, after what feels like forever, she writes back. This time, neither of us move. We just stare.

"I'm scared," I tell him.

"You should be, asshole."

"You're supposed to be my friend."

We both keep staring at the phone, not looking at each other when we speak.

"Yeah," he says, "and friends are supposed to listen to friends. I don't see you listening to me."

I squeeze my eyes shut and work up the nerve to pick up the phone. I tap the screen. Open the text. And then read it out loud. "I love you, too. I'm coming home tomorrow. I know it's late notice, but could you pick me up from the airport? I think I'd like you to be the first face I see."

"FUCK YEAH!" he squeals.

I fist pump the air.

And then we hug.

Jump up and down.

Spin in circles.

High five.

Then sit back down and crack open a beer.

"So what did you write back?"

"That I'd move heaven and earth to be there."

"Lame."

"Also, you need to cover my shift tomorrow."

"I don't even work there."

"I don't even care."

Lucy

"SO HE'S MEETING you at the airport?" Claudia asks.

I finish dressing after my shower and look down at myself. "Yeah," I shout so she can hear me from her room on the other side of the bathroom door. "I texted him this morning with the flight details." I open the door so she can see me. "Does this look okay?"

Her brows bunch, but her lips curve at the corners. "You guys have been together how long? Do you think he cares how you look?"

"I know," I say, almost sheepishly. "But I still want to look cute for him. But not over do it, you know? Just cute-casual."

"Lucy," she laughs. "Are you nervous?"

I nod. "So nervous. And to kiss him? I think it would be like kissing him for the first time, you know? We've never gone this long without each other." I shake out my hands, trying to calm myself.

"You look cute," she comforts.

I go back in the bathroom and take one more look. Tank tops and frilly skirts—that's the way he'd always described how I dress, so I make sure I'm wearing my best ones. And cowboy boots. I know he loves those.

A sharp shooting pain goes through my stomach. Like cramps, but worse. Actually, it's been happening a lot lately. I've ignored it, but the last one was the worst yet. I grip the edge of the counter, trying to breathe through the pain. "Shit," I whisper. The tightening in my stomach is unbearable. And then I pee myself. *What the hell?* I start to look down at my legs, wondering what's happening. The pain gets worse. My eyes shut tight. My breathing stops. And then I pee some more. I can't control it. Just like I can't control the cry that escapes me. I hear Claud say my name, but she's far away. Everything seems distant. The pain stops. I open my eyes. My gaze already pointed at my legs. But it's not pee. It's blood. I release my breath, feeling tears flowing down my cheeks. "Claud!" I try to shout, but it comes out a whisper. And then the pain comes back. Like a thousand knives stabbing my stomach. I fold over myself, my arms crossed over my waist.

And then it happens again.

The blood.

"Claud," I cry out.

I collapse to the floor. My pretty white frilly skirt now soaked in blood. I run my hand up my leg, covering it in red. So much red. "Claudia! Help!"

The bathroom doors swings open. "LUCY!"

"I don't know what's happening!" I scream. "What's happening?"

The pain takes over. I can't keep my eyes open…

"LUCAS!" I hear her yell.

I can't stop crying.

I can't breathe.

I can't…

"Cameron…"

Empty.

Darkness.

Cameron

I CHECK MY phone for the third time, making sure that I got her flight details right. The plane landed forty-five minutes ago. I watched everyone get off, everyone but her. I've tried calling. Six times. Her phone rings out. If she were delayed, surely she'd call me.

I ask the woman at the airline desk, but she won't tell me if Lucy even boarded the flight. I'm starting to get worried that maybe she changed her mind. Maybe she doesn't want to come back. Or even if she does, maybe she doesn't want to come back to me.

Then my phone rings, and Lucas's voice fills my ears. "Cameron." His voice is strained. "It's Lucy. She's in the hospital. You have to come. Now."

I tell him to text me the details as I rush back to the airline desk. I try to pay for a ticket to New Jersey, but my card gets declined. I even try the emergency card Mom gave me. Declined. I call Minge—I'll sell him the fucking Delorean if it means getting me to Lucy. He doesn't answer. I sit on the floor in the corner of the airport, shaking from crying so hard. I try my dad. His assistant tells me he's in a meeting. I curse her until she hangs up on me.

Lucas: *Princeton Hospital. I'm scared. Please hurry!*

I drop my head between my shoulders, dial a number, hold the phone to my ear, and I wait.

He answers first ring.

"Cameron? What's up?"

"Mark." My voice breaks. "I need your help."

That's all it takes.

An hour later, Mom and Mark arrive. He pre-purchased tickets on the way and an hour after that, I was in the air. We all were.

"Do they know anything?" Mom asks.

I shake my head, trying to keep everything together. And I do—until she pulls me in her arms and whispers, "It's okay, baby. You'll be with her soon."

Thirty-Three
Cameron

LUCY DOESN'T TALK about her mom's death often, but when she does, she tells me that the wait was the worst part. The not knowing. I always thought it was strange—but now, after sitting in the waiting room of the hospital for twelve hours—I get it. I completely get it.

The nurses at the desk said it was family only beyond that point. I begged, I pleaded, I even tried to bribe them with Mark's money. Nothing worked. And then I got angry, beyond angry, and was asked to leave and cool off.

"I am her family!" I shouted at Mark while I paced back and forth outside the entrance.

"I know."

"We've been together longer than some married people and apparently that's not good enough!"

"I know," he said again.

After five minutes and me kicking the shit out of a trashcan, I was finally calm enough to go back in. Mom tried to be strong, but she was struggling just as much as I was.

I sit on the floor with my head between my knees and I wait. And wait. And wait.

Then I feel someone sit down next to me. I think it's Mark so I don't bother looking up. "Cameron." Tom's deep voice echoes in my ears.

My head lifts and my eyes snap to his. "Is she okay?"

His eyes are red and tired, like the time we sat on his porch and talked for hours. It seems like forever ago. "You can all come back now, but she only wants to see you."

My feet feel like lead as I follow behind him, my mom holding my hand the entire time. But all my senses are off. Like I'm under water, unable to hear, unable to breathe. I want to scream, like I do in the river behind my old house. But people can hear me now. People will know.

I place my palm flat against her door. And I try to breathe. A warm hand grasps my shoulder. I turn to Lucas, so much like his dad. "Be strong," he says. "She needs your strength."

She cries when she sees me, but she won't look at me.

"Baby." I sit on the chair next to her bed and take her hand. "What happened?"

She looks up at the ceiling, her eyes filled with tears. She doesn't speak. She doesn't move. She doesn't grasp my hand. She just cries.

I stand up just so I can look down at her, and I run my hand across her forehead and into her hair. "Babe."

She cries harder when she hears my voice—when she sees my tears.

"I'm sorry, Cameron." Then she pulls her hand out of my hold and slowly flips to her side, away from me. I want to climb into the bed. I want to hold her. I want to know what the hell is happening. There are too many machines, too many wires. There's too much pressure on my chest from the weight of everything.

The door opens and a doctor walks in. She smiles at me, but it's sad. And I'm starting to get pissed again. There's too much sadness and nobody's telling me why.

"You must be Cameron," she says. It's not a question, but I nod anyway.

Lucy tries to move, but she moans like she's in pain. "What happened?" I ask the doctor.

She looks up from the charts at the end of the bed, first to me, then to Lucy.

"I'm sorry," Lucy says again.

I kick off my shoes, make sure I'm not disturbing any equipment, and lie next to her.

"Can you turn to me?" I whisper.

I watch as she grimaces, but she slowly moves, the wires and cables connected shift with her.

Her eyes keep drifting closed, as if she's fighting a losing battle with sleep. "Tell him," she says, moving her head to my chest. I hold her there, like we've done so many times before.

"Are you sure, Lucy? You're still a little out of it. Maybe we should wait."

"He needs to know."

My heart picks up. "I need to know what?" I say to Lucy, but my words are meant for the doctor.

"I'm Dr. Scott, Cameron." I nod, because I can't speak. "Lucy asked that I speak to you about her condition. Is that okay?"

I nod again.

"Lucy was brought in this afternoon with severe vaginal hemorrhaging."

Lucy lets out a sob into my chest.

Dr. Scott continues, "We were able to stop the bleeding after we found the source." She sits on the end of the bed, as if getting comfortable.

I'm so fucking afraid to ask, but I do it anyway. "And?"

Dr. Scott's eyes move from Lucy to me. "Lucy was six weeks pregnant."

I gasp and hold Lucy closer.

"But she has the IUD…" I dip my head so my mouth is to her ear. "You're pregnant?"

She pulls back and looks up at me. Then shakes her head slowly.

"The IUD moved from its position, Cameron. It became ineffective. And Lucy *was* pregnant," Dr. Scott answers for her. "She had a miscarriage, Cameron. I'm sorry."

"What?"

"There's more," Lucy whispers into my chest.

I try to swallow, but the lump in my throat prevents it.

"By the time the ambulance got her here, Lucy had lost a lot of blood. We had to take her to surgery and find the cause so we could stop it. It's not normal to lose the amount of blood she did, not in a standard miscarriage, especially so early on."

"Can you please just tell me what happened?" I beg. I can't take it. The waiting. The not knowing. "Just tell me."

"Okay," she nods slowly.

Lucy cries harder.

"What's going on?" I say to no one in particular.

Dr. Scott clears her throat. "Lucy had what's called an ectopic pregnancy. Do you know what that is?"

I shake my head. "No."

"It's when the egg gets implanted into the fallopian tube instead of the uterus."

I try to think back to all the sex-ed classes, but nothing makes sense. "I don't understand. I'm sorry," I tell her. "Please just get to the point. Is Lucy going to be okay?"

She smiles, that sad same smile. "Lucy, herself, will be okay. What happens when the fetus attaches to the fallopian tube is that there's no room in there for it to grow. It can cause further damage to an already damaged tube. Lucy's tube ruptured, that's what caused the heavy bleeding. Normally, we'd be able to do a non intrusive keyhole surgery, but because of the amount of blood loss, we had to perform an open abdominal surgery."

Lucy weeps and I do my best to do what Lucas asked, to be her strength. But I'm not sure that I can.

Dr. Scott continues, "We had to remove the fetus, and one of her fallopian tubes. They also found scar tissue due to endometriosis on her other one... it's not in good shape either."

I try to let her words sink in, but I can't. I can't fucking understand what she's saying. Maybe I'm dumb, or maybe the pounding in my head is outweighing my brain's functionality. Maybe her voice is being muffled by me drowning above water.

Lucy keeps crying. She keeps saying she's sorry and I don't know why.

"Cameron," Dr. Scott says. "I don't want to weigh you down with too many medical terms so I'm just going to tell you, okay?"

Oh my God. Tell me what? I thought we were done. "Okay."

"The likelihood of Lucy being able to conceive *naturally* is quite low. Even if she does fall pregnant, the chances of her being able to carry that baby to full term are slim."

"I'm sorry," Lucy cries.

And I break.

But I don't show it.

Because I need to be her strength.

Even when I have none.

✧　✧　✧

SHE CRIES UNTIL she falls asleep. I don't speak, because I know that no words exist which can take away the hurt.

I wait until she's completely out before I leave her. If Mom and Mark felt half of what I felt, then they deserve for the wait to be over.

The second my back is turned and my feet hit the floor, it starts to hit.

By the time I open her door, I'm done. Broken. Shattered.

I lean against the wall, not even bothering to acknowledge that Jake and Micky are here. I drop my head in my hands, and I cry. I let it all out. Mom cries too, even though she has no clue why.

Mark's hand on my shoulder and his voice seem to calm me, just enough so that I can look up and face him. "Cameron."

His eyes scan mine, searching for answers. He won't ask. He'll wait until I'm ready. "It's okay, son," he says. And I break all over again.

I fall because I have no strength, but he's there to catch me. His arms are around me and I'm crying. I'm crying so fucking loud, but I can't control it. I can't keep it in. Not anymore. Mom's next to me now, holding my hand.

Micky's sobbing.

"You'll both be okay," Tom says, sitting on the other side of me.

Then a familiar voice gets louder and louder as he walks toward us. Mark moves away. I stand up and turn to my dad. "Dad," I cry, because I've never needed him more in my entire life.

He holds up his finger for me to wait, and only now do I realize he's on the phone. It feels like minutes, no—hours, while we stand there.

"He needs another ten thousand," he says to whoever is on the other end.

We all stay silent, watching, waiting.

His eyes move, and I think they're for me, but they're not. He sees Jake. "I'll call you back," he says, then hangs up.

He walks past me, his hand out ready for Jake. Jake's eyes narrow as he stands up, looking over my dad's shoulder to me. "Dad," I say in shock.

He turns now, finally looking at me. He doesn't even notice my appearance. Doesn't realize I've fallen apart. "Cameron, what's going on? You look fine. Your mother's been calling my assistant panicked, saying you're in the hospital. What's wrong with you?"

"It's Lucy," I stammer.

His eyebrows bunch in confusion. "Who the hell is Lucy?"

And all the hurt, all the pain, all the suffering, it's replaced by something else. *Hate.*

"I hate you," I seethe.

"What?"

"You heard me. You dead-beat asshole!"

"Cameron," he says, his hands up in surrender.

I step forward, my fists balled at my sides.

Tom places a firm hand on my chest, stopping me from moving in.

"I don't know what your problem is, but I had to leave a very important client to come here—"

"FUCK YOU! My girlfriend just had surgery from a fucking miscarriage. We lost a baby! We can't have kids! And all you can think about is your goddamn work! FUCK YOU!"

Tom's hand on my chest pushes harder, or maybe I'm stepping forward. "You need to leave," Tom says to him.

He turns around and walks away, mumbling something about thanking God he didn't stick around.

There's a vice squeezing my heart. It hurts so damn much I can't fucking breathe. Then Mom's in my vision, her hands on my cheeks. "I'm sorry," she says, crying as she does.

"Cameron?" Lucy stands at her doorway looking weak. Probably from the effort of moving.

Instantly, I'm in front of her, helping her to stand.

She looks up at me, tears in her heavy lidded eyes. "You said *we.*"

"What?"

"Bed," she croaks.

I help her back into bed, and pull the covers to her chin. "Tell them to leave, please," she whispers. "But I need you to stay."

✧   ✧   ✧

SHE'S LYING ON her side, her head to my chest, just like always. "You said *we*," she says again, her eyes struggling to stay open.

"What do you mean?"

"You've always said *we*, Cam. Like, *we* can get through anything. But it's different this time. This time, it's not *we*. It's just *me*. You can still have children. *I* can't."

Thirty-Four
Cameron

LUCY STAYS AT the hospital for another three days. The nurses won't allow me to stay overnight, but I'm there from beginning to end of visiting hours. Each day, she physically gets better, but emotionally, she's getting worse. On the last day, it's as if she's completely checked out. I try talking to her, but she either ignores me or gets upset. And I don't know what to say or do to make it better.

To make it stop.

To make it right.

Her dad's booked a hotel suite in New Jersey for another two weeks. He doesn't want to risk anything. He wants to be close to the hospital, to the right doctors, if anything should happen.

I zip up her bag and turn to her. "You ready to get out of here, babe?"

She stares out the window and off into the distance.

Her dad picks us up in a rental and takes us to the suite.

"It's time for you to go home, Cameron," she deadpans.

"What do you mean?" I ask, distracted with putting her clothes away.

She takes my hand and sits me on the bed next to her. "I need you to go back home. I need some time alone, away from everything. Away from you."

"Away from me?" I croak.

Her eyes are red and filling with tears as they penetrate mine. She nods. "You need to go home. You need to work. You can't put your life on hold for me. I'll be there in two weeks."

I blow out a heavy breath, as heavy as my heart. "But I want to be with you. I don't understand. Did I do something wrong?"

"No, baby," she whispers. "You didn't do anything. Neither of us did anything. I just need some time to think. I'm just... I just need time to wrap my head around everything. It doesn't mean I don't love you, because I do. I love you more than you could ever know. I promise it's not about you."

She reaches up and wipes the wetness off my cheeks.

"I'm sorry," she says.

I try to kiss her, but she pulls away.

She *always* pulls away.

I want to stay. I want to fight her on this, but I know it won't do any good. If anything, it would only cause bad.

✧   ✧   ✧

I STARE OUT the window of the car while Tom drives me to the airport. He'd already paid for my ticket, which meant he already knew she wanted me gone but never told me.

"I know you're mad at me," he says.

I'm not.

He adds, "But I had no choice. It's what Lucy wanted, and I think we both agree that what Lucy wants is most important now."

He's right, but what I want should be important too. What happened doesn't just affect her, it affects both of us. I stay quiet, because clearly what I have to say doesn't matter.

✧   ✧   ✧

WE SPEAK ON the phone every day.

The first day, we spoke for an hour. I don't know what we spoke about, but that wasn't the point. The point was she was talking to me. But just like at the hospital, each day she became more distant. So distant that she never even told me she was home. She said she'd be two weeks. It's only been one.

"Why didn't you tell me you were home?"

"I don't know," she says quietly.

"Can I come by?"

"I don't think that's a good idea, Cam. I'll call you tomorrow."

Then she hangs up.

I pick up my keys, get in my car, and start driving to her house. Because I can't *not*. She's my *heart*. And I can't survive without my heart.

✧   ✧   ✧

I KNOCK, BUT there's no answer. The lights are on, so I know she's in there.

"Lucy!" I knock again.

And wait.

Nothing.

I use the key she gave me before she left. Shit, it feels like a lifetime ago.

She's sitting on the couch covered in a blanket with balled up tissues all around her. She's crying so hard that her shoulders heave with every sob.

I get to her faster than I thought possible. "Baby, what are you doing?"

She doesn't look up. She doesn't even acknowledge my presence. She just keeps crying, her hands gripping the edge of a picture frame to her chest.

I sit on the couch next to her and wrap my arms around her.

"I told you not to come here," she shouts through her tears.

I swallow the hurt, because I know she's feeling it too. "Lucy, come on. You need me here."

"No!" She pushes me away. "That's the problem, Cam! I need you. I've always needed you! And you can't always be there. Not anymore."

"What are you talking about?" I try to keep my voice even, but I'm struggling. "Baby—"

"Stop!" She sits up higher, gripping the frame tighter. "I can't deal with this. I can't be with you anymore!"

I suck in a shaky breath and let it out in a whoosh. Along with any sense of calm I've tried to hold on to. "Why the fuck are you pushing me away? I've done nothing but want to be close to you and you keep doing it!"

She cries harder.

I shake my head—my gaze catching sight of the picture in the frame. "Lucy," I whisper, trying to pry it from her fingers.

"No," she sobs. "It's mine."

I pull the frame harder, knowing that whatever it is is causing her this type of hurt—the type that shouldn't exist. She finally releases it, giving up the will to keep it to herself.

I see the picture.

And my world goes black.

"You see?" she says, pointing at it.

I stand up, just so I know that I'm still alive, that I'm still able to breathe through the pain. I look down at the frame. A sketch. The one I made her after our first time. The one with her room in our future house. The one with her huge armchair, and all the little ones in front of it. The ones for all the children we wanted to have.

"You see?" she says again, quieter this time.

But I can't. I can't see through my tears.

She sucks in a breath, trying to hold it in so her cries aren't so loud.

"That's what you wanted, Cameron."

For once in my life, I want her to be quiet. I don't want to hear what she has to say. I can't take it.

"That's what you pictured our lives to be and I can't give you that. How can we be together? How can I stay with you knowing that I can't give you what you've always wanted? How?" Her voice is strained by the power of her cries.

She can barely speak.

I can barely hear.

"I have to live with that, Cam. I have to live with the fact that I'm the reason you don't get your dream. And I can't do it. I'm sorry, but I can't."

I wipe my eyes with my sleeve and look at her. And that's all I do. Because I don't have the words. I don't have the strength.

"I'm right, Cam."

I shake my head.

"It's okay," she says. "You're allowed to be mad at me."

"Shut up," I clip.

She cries harder.

"None of this shit means anything without you. You think those dreams make sense without you, Lucy? You're making up lies in your head because you're a *coward*. I've tried to be with you every day since the miscarriage. I would've been right there, right next to you. *You* pushed away. *You* didn't want me there. Don't use this as an excuse. If you don't want me—if you don't love me anymore—if it's too hard for you, say it!"

"It is! It's too hard! You deserve to have that! You deserve to be with someone who can give you that. Maybe you should go be with Roxy!"

And at her words, I lose it. Completely lose it. A rush of anger washes through me. And before I can stop myself, I've lifted the frame in my hand and thrown it against the wall.

She screams, a scream so loud it makes my ears ring. "NOOOO!"

She's kneeling on the floor now, with the shattered frame in front of her. "I HATE YOU!"

"Fuck." I try to get to her, to kneel next to her but she pushes me away. "Lucy, I'm sorry."

"Fuck you!" she bawls. "This is all I had, Cameron. This was everything to me. This was our forever and you ruined it."

"Baby."

I'm a mess.

I fucked up.

My head whips to the sound of the door opening. Lucas walks in with the rest of her brothers. "What the f—" he cuts himself off. "Jesus Christ, Lucy, you're bleeding."

I turn back to Lucy, who's frantically trying to pick out the sketch from the frame and cutting her fingers on the glass. I don't think she even feels it.

"Lucy, stop," I whisper, grasping her wrists.

She looks up at me. Her eyes narrowed. But I see it clearly. There is no calm. Just the storm. "GET OUT!" She pushes my shoulders until I fall back. "GET OUT!" she yells again. She pounds against my chest with her closed fists. "I HATE YOU! GET OUT!"

I do nothing. I sit on my heels and let her hit me. Let her yell. Let her get angry.

Lucas's arms wrap around her chest and lift her off the ground. "Just go, Cam."

"What's happening?" a tiny voice says. Lachlan's crying in Leo's arms.

"Cameron, you need to leave," Lucas says again.

I wipe my face on my forearm, and take one more look at her. "Forever, Luce."

And then I do what everyone wants.

I leave.

Lucy

LUCAS SETS ME on the floor of my bathroom and squats in front of me. "You okay, Goosey?"

I nod, even though it's a lie and he knows it.

"I know it's not fair, but Lachlan's out there. He's freaking out."

I squeeze my eyes shut and take slow breaths, trying to settle my emotions. "I'm fine," I tell him.

He opens the cupboard under the sink and pulls out a box of Band-Aids. He takes my hand in his and examines the cuts I didn't know were there. "You wanna talk about what happened?" he asks, applying the first Band-Aid.

"I can't do it, Lucas. I don't think I can be with him—not when I know how badly he wants kids."

His eyes move to the sketch, now stained with my blood.

"You think maybe that's his choice, not yours?"

"You know Cameron," I mutter. "You know he's always going to stand by me, even when he shouldn't. He won't leave. I have to make him. I have to make him hate me so he gets what he deserves. It's wrong. But it's *right.*"

He shakes his head, applying the third and final Band-Aid. "I don't agree with you, Luce. But it's your life." His eyes move to the living room. "You should shower, get cleaned up and changed. Come out when you're ready. The boys are here to see you. They're worried."

"Did you tell them?"

"No. You asked me not to and I haven't. But one day you'll have to. You can't hide forever."

✧ ✧ ✧

I GET OUT of the shower and stand naked in front of the full-length mirror, focusing on the fresh scar that runs under my belly button. The eternal, ugly reminder of what my forever can't be.

I close my eyes, remembering all the times Cam stood behind me, right here, with his arms around my now damaged waist. My eyes prick with bitter tears. *You're so beautiful,* he'd say in my ear. *I'm so damn lucky, Luce. And I'll never forget it.*

I push back the sob threatening to escape. He's not lucky. Not at all. Not anymore.

Running a hand down my pajamas, I fake a smile into the mirror, and carry it all the way to the living room.

And then I let out a loud gasp.

I cry.

And I laugh.

"Story time, Goose," Lucas says.

Somehow, they've created a makeshift tent using the dining table and the couches as walls, and used bed sheets to cover it.

"It's not as easy as it used to be. I think we've all grown since we did this last. Well, everyone but you," he jokes.

Lachlan's laugh warms my heart. So innocent. So clueless to what's happening. "You're short," he announces. "I'm calling you shaaawty!"

Leo laughs with him. "That means she's your girl, Lachy. You don't want your sister to be your girl."

He makes a disgusted face as we all try to squeeze into the tiny space. "I got a girl," he shouts. "I spit in her hair and asked her to kiss me."

Little Logan roars with laughter. "If that worked, *you* are my hero."

Lachlan's eyes go huge while he nods enthusiastically. "Totally worked," he says. "The next day I did it to Michele! Now I got two girls... and all they do is bug me!"

Thirty-Five
Lucy

I T'S BEEN WEEKS since I last saw Cameron. He hasn't called. I haven't called him. But I miss him. So much.

I moved back to the main house after the tent party—that's what we called it. Lucas and I waited for the others to fall asleep in there before sitting out on the porch steps and having a beer. Well, he did. I can't drink because of the painkillers.

We promised each other to try to do it once a month. He's only home another year before he goes to college, *if* he goes to college. He says he still doesn't know. He's considering staying home, working with Dad. He said that Dad's face lit up when he told him and that Dad had a meeting with his business manager to see if he could get the company name changed to Preston and Sons. Lucas didn't say it, but I knew that made him happy.

Living in the house helps. There's always something to do, someone to talk to, something to smile or laugh about.

But unfortunately, or maybe fortunately, none of those things are Cameron.

The boys spend a lot of the days by the lake. I haven't been there yet; too many memories. Lachlan and I have gotten to know each other better. It's a little sad that I've missed out on him growing up over the last two years. He's such an amazing kid, so full of life, not a care in the world. He's tried to get me to play in Filmore with him, but I can't bring myself to go near it. I don't think my heart could take it. It's always going to be the reminder of the first time Cameron told me he loved me, even though I think we both knew it well before then.

"You ready?" Dad asks with Lachlan latched on his back.

I fake another smile. "Yeah."

✧   ✧   ✧

WE GO TO lunch at an indoor play center for Lachlan's sixth birthday. Even though it's not really a party, we hired out a party room to accommodate everyone. "This is my favorite place in the whole wide world," Lachlan shouts. "Apart from Filmore. I love Filmore the bestest. Dad's going to build a teleporter in there for me so I can build ice cream machines and teleport them to all the houses everywhere."

"That sounds amazing," I tell him.

His head whips to the door. "CAM!"

My eyes follow his. "Hey, buddy," Cam says, but his gaze is focused on me. I don't blink. I don't move. I don't even breathe. I can't. Because if I do, I know I'll end up in his arms, giving him a hope which doesn't exist. It's wrong for me to want that, but it feels even more wrong for me to miss him.

"You came!" Lachlan yells, then looks to Dad. "Thank you!"

And my heart tightens.

Cam smiles, and then bends over so he's eye to eye with Lachlan. "Happy birthday!" He scruffs Lachlan's hair. "You're getting old. I think I see some grays in there."

Lachlan laughs and swats his hand away.

"Lucy?" Leo asks from opposite me. "Is it okay if I say hi to Cam?"

My eyes drift shut, letting the ache of my broken heart consume me. I swallow the knot in my throat and try not to make my feelings evident when I open my eyes to see him watching me, unsure of my reaction. "Of course you can." I look at the rest of the boys. They're on the edge of their seats, just as excited to see him as Lachlan is, but they're hesitant, like they think it's wrong to want him here. "You guys," my voice breaks. "It's okay to be excited to see him. Go."

So they do.

One by one they high-five, fist bump, shake hands, whatever it is boys do. And Cam—he takes his time with each of them, knowing the right questions to ask. He always did. He always knew what was going on in their lives. What each of them was into. He always paid special attention, always made them feel like individuals.

"Don't be mad, baby girl," Dad says. "I asked Lachlan what he wanted for his birthday and he said Cameron."

"I'm not mad," I tell him honestly.

Lachlan sits next to me, pulling on Cameron's hand until he's seated on the other side.

Our eyes lock for what feels like forever.

"Hey," he finally says.

I try to smile. "Hey."

The waitress comes to take orders. Apparently she knows Lucas, because her eyes go wide and she freezes mid-stride when she sees him. She takes the orders, and as soon as she's gone the room erupts with "oooooooohhs." Lucas just shakes his head, his cheeks burning red with embarrassment.

"Hey," Little Logan says to Lachlan. "You should go spit in her hair and ask her to kiss you. Make her your shaaaawty."

We laugh.

Lachlan shrugs. "Okay!" And then he's out of his seat and walking toward the door.

"No!" Lucas shouts after him.

Cam's on his feet. "I got it." He throws Lachlan over his shoulder and turns to Dad. "Is it okay if we play for a bit?"

Dad nods. "Of course. I'm sure he'd love that."

They leave.

And so do I—outside for some fresh air—because I can't breathe when Cam's this close.

I don't know how long I'm out there before Lucas's head pops out from behind the door. "There you are. Are you okay?"

"Yeah," I answer with feigned peppiness.

"The food's here."

The only two spots left on the table are next to Cameron. Lucas, being the asshole he is, takes the one furthest from him.

"Hey, Cam!" Lachlan shouts. I've noticed since being home that shouting is his standard volume. I guess when you live in a house with five other boys, shouting is the only way to get attention.

"Yeah, bud?" Cam asks, loading Lachlan's plate with a bit of every-thing on the table. Nuggets, fries, spaghetti, you name it, we got it.

"I got pupsended from school for eleventy-three days!"

"Pupsended?" Cam muses.

The twins roll their eyes simultaneously. "He means suspended," Liam tells him.

"You got suspended?" Cam laughs. "Why?"

"Because I did this," Lachlan yells.

A synced round of "NOOOs" fill the room, just us Lachlan picks up a handful of spaghetti and throws it across the table, toward Little Logan, yelling, "YOLO!"

Cam's head throws back in laughter.

Little Logan curses and leaves the room.

"At least it wasn't dog shit," Dad shouts after him.

That brings on another round of laughter, even from me.

When I finally settle, I see Cam watching me.

"What?" I ask him.

"You still make my world stop, Luce."

I eat my food in silence, finding it impossible to swallow, almost as impossible as continuously blinking back my tears.

He nudges me lightly with his elbow. "I gotta get going," he says quietly, leaning down so only I can hear him. "Can we talk?"

I inhale deeply and nod, my eyes never leaving my plate.

"Hey, Lachy," he says, louder this time. "Thanks so much for inviting me to your birthday party, but I have to go."

He stands up and pushes his chair back.

"No," Lachlan cries. "Not yet."

My eyes snap to him. He's looking at Dad, his eyes pleading. "Make him stay, Daddy! It's still my birthday and he's my present!"

My heart doesn't just break this time; it disintegrates into a thousand pieces.

Cam sniffs once. "I have to work, bud. I'm sorry."

"No!" Lachlan's standing on his seat, looking around the table, begging for one of us to make Cam stay. "Why?" He's bawling now. "It's summer, Lucy's home now and you're not there and I don't know why. You've always been there when Lucy's there and now you're not. Did she not like it when you spit in her hair?"

Cam laughs, but it's sad. He looks at me, and I look away—because I can't stand to see the hurt clear in his eyes. "I'm sorry, Lachy, but I have to work."

"But Daddy goes to work! And he comes home when he's finished and plays. Will you come back when you finish work?"

Lucas stands from next to me. "Hey Lachy, did you hear that? Pretty sure that was the giant red slide calling your name."

Dad stands now. "Pretty sure I just heard it call for all the Preston men. Did you hear that, Leo?"

Leo nods, his eyes wide. "It's shouting at us, Lachy! We better go."

Lachlan laughs and jumps on Lucas's back.

A second later, we're alone.

Just him and me.

And a shitload of unsettled emotions.

He wipes his cheeks with the back of his hand before facing me. Jerking his head to the door, he asks, "Outside?"

❖   ❖   ❖

WE SIT AT the outdoor tables just outside the play center. "How are you?" he asks, his voice strained.

"Okay."

He shakes his head slowly. "This isn't awkward at all."

"Yeah."

It's silent as he stares straight ahead.

"You wanted to talk?" I ask him.

He drops his head and turns to me. "Yeah, but it just seems stupid now."

"Oh."

"Not—I don't mean talking to you is stupid, I just mean—" his sigh cuts him off. Then he shoves his hand in his pocket and pulls out a piece of paper.

I gasp.

"No, it's not—" he shakes his head quickly. "It's not a sketch. I still haven't been able to pick up a pen."

A frown pulls at my lips.

He unfolds the paper and sets it on the table in front of me. I peel my eyes away from him and look down. It's a newspaper article with a picture of him and a man shaking hands in front of the ballpark near campus. The headline; UNC STUDENT WOWS CITY COUNCIL JUDGES. "What is this?" I ask, my eyes scanning the words.

"You know how you used to always tell me to enter competitions—to show people what I can do?"

"You entered a design?"

He nods. "Yeah, the city council ran this competition to design a playground in that empty lot near the ballpark. And I won, Luce."

An overwhelming sense of pride consumes me. I cry—but it's so different to the thousand tears I've shed recently.

"I'm sorry," he sympathizes, "I didn't mean to make you cry."

I shake my head, my tears in full force. And then I look up at him. He licks his lips, his eyes searching mine. "They're good tears, Cameron. I'm just so proud of you."

He laughs once. "Thanks. Honestly, I'm proud of myself. I didn't think I had a chance."

"But your work is so good. And I'm so glad that you put yourself out there, because now you know—maybe now you can believe in yourself."

"Like you did?"

I wipe my eyes and nod.

"I just wanted you to know, Lucy—because I wouldn't be here if it weren't for you and your dad, steering me in the right direction—encouraging me, believing in me." He sniffs back the tears I know he's hiding. "I just wanted to say thank you."

I look back down at the article. "Can I keep this?"

"Of course," he laughs. "Mom kind of went crazy and ordered dozens of copies of that newspaper. She's mailed it out to almost everyone she knows."

I laugh at his words. "She's just proud of you, Cameron. I can't wait to show my dad. He'll be so excited for you. When did you enter?"

"A couple weeks before you left for New Jersey."

"Oh." I fold up the article and pocket it.

"So," he starts, and then cuts himself off.

"So?"

He inhales deeply, like he's building the courage to say what he says next. "There was a prize for the winner—it's kind of the reason why I entered. It was five thousand dollars cash."

I'm smiling. Genuine. For the first time in so damn long. "That's amazing!"

"Yeah…"

"What are you gonna do with the money?"

"That's the thing, Luce. I entered hoping to win because… fuck. This is so hard."

"What's hard?"

"All of it. Everything. Talking to you. Being this close and not being able to touch you. Trying to speak to you... but it's like... I second-guess everything I'm saying because—"

"Cam," I interrupt. "What did you have planned if you won?"

He pinches the bridge of his nose and then lets out a little groan. "I looked into housing on campus. For us, Luce. I thought maybe we could get an apartment together. If I take that money and the money I saved over summer we can get one, just for a semester, but it's a start. And we wouldn't have to even room together. I looked at the two bed, two bath ones. You can have your own room. I just thought..."

I stare down at the table, crying harder with every single word he speaks. Nothing's changed. My feelings about him are still the same. So are my feelings *for* him. I love him. Which is why I say quietly, "I can't, Cameron."

"Yeah," he breathes out. He turns away, his shoulders heaving with each breath. "I didn't think so. I had to ask anyway."

The ache in my chest is suffocating. "Cameron." He flinches when I touch his arm.

I stand up, not wanting to say goodbye, because I won't be able to live through it. "Will you do something for me?"

"Anything," he whispers, not looking at me.

"Pick up a pen. Believe in yourself. Believe in your *heart*."

He laughs a bitter laugh. "You are my heart, Luce. And now you're gone."

Cameron

I CALL WORK when I get in the car to tell them I'm going to be late. Chris answers. He tells me that it's dead and they really don't need two people on. He'll clock me in and out, so I still get paid, but not to bother coming in. I thank him profusely, and pull into Mom and Mark's driveway.

Mark grins from ear to ear when he opens the door.

"Don't be too happy to see me," I tell him. "Soon you'll get sick of me asking for your help... and your money."

"Finally," he shouts, waving his hands in the air. He steps aside for me to walk in and pats my back when I do. "Pretty sure you have fifteen years of asking for my help to make up for."

We spend the afternoon searching online and making phone calls, trying to find the perfect space. There's a reason Mark's dealership is so successful. It's because his negotiation skills are amazing. He reads out his credit card number to the person on the phone and tells them I'll pick up the keys first thing tomorrow. When he hangs up, he puts his credit card away, but pulls out another one and hands it to me. "For supplies and what not," he says.

I look down at the card in my hand—it's got my name on it. I suck in a breath and try to give it back. "I can't accept that."

He scoffs. "Fifteen years, remember?"

✧   ✧   ✧

THE NEXT DAY I pick up the keys, use Mark's card to buy supplies, and go to the space he leased for the next year. And then I do something that I haven't done since the day Lucy left.

I pick up a pen.

Thirty-Six
Cameron

I SMILE WHEN I read the text from Jake. All it says is the name of a building, a room number and a time to meet there. I don't need to ask what it means.

I make Minge come with me to pick up what I need, and meet Jake outside Lucy's future room. We moved into ours yesterday. Micky told Jake that Lucy was coming the day before classes started. That gave me just under a week to get it perfect.

"I can't even thank you enough," I tell him.

"It's no worries," he responds. "Just don't tell Kayla I had to flirt with the RA. She'd be pissed."

Minge scoffs. "You're all assholes."

Jake pulls a key out of his pocket and opens the door.

And we all get to work.

Lucy

"I'M NERVOUS," I tell Heidi on the phone.

"Are you nervous for classes, or nervous for Cameron?"

"Cameron."

"When was the last time you saw him?"

I drive into campus and try to find a parking spot near enough to my dorm. "Two weeks ago at Lachlan's party."

"How was it?"

"Hard."

She sighs loudly. "I'm sorry, Luce." Her voice quiets and drips with sympathy when she adds, "For all of it. The baby thing. I guess some people don't realize how lucky they are to get pregnant in the first place, right?"

I'm taken aback by her words but try not to choke up. "Are you okay?"

"Yeah. Call me when you're settled, okay?"

"Okay." I hang up and pull into a spot.

Rose is already waiting by the doors. "Bitch!" she screams. "I missed your perfect little ass!" I laugh when she hugs me tight and lifts me off the ground. I haven't told her what happened. I don't think everyone needs to know. I still see the way Dad and Lucas are around me, like they're walking on eggshells, and I don't need that. I don't want that.

"Have you been to the room yet?" I ask her.

She shakes her head. "I'm waiting for some guy I met online to come by and unload my shit and carry it up there. I don't do manual labor, Luce." I take a box from my trunk and hand her a suitcase. "Did I not just say that—"

I exaggerate a pout.

Her eyes narrow. "You're lucky you're so cute."

We're laughing as we walk to our room.

She opens the door.

My heart drops.

And so does the box in my hands.

"Whoa," she whispers.

We walk to the center of the room and turn a slow, full, circle. I hadn't realized I'd stopped breathing until I gasp on needed air.

"Are you okay?" She takes my elbow and leads me to the bed. "It's like the blood just drained from your face."

I want to reply, but I can't. I can't speak. My gaze moves frantically around the room, trying to take everything in, but it's too much. There's too much. And before I know it, I'm sitting on the bed and crying into my hands.

"Luce," she sits next to me and curls an arm around my neck, bringing me closer to her. "Do you know who did this?"

I wipe my eyes on my forearm and nod.

"Who?"

"Cameron."

She lets out a low whistle. "Cameron's an artist?"

I take my time and settle my emotions, then stand back up and take in the room. A full-size mural on opposite walls takes up the entire space. The other two walls are filled with single page sketches. I move closer, wanting to take them in. "He picked up a pen," I whisper to myself. There are so many sheets of paper, so many sketches. So many memories of *us*. The river behind his house, our dock by the lake, the front porch of my house, Filmore, a close up of the pegs of his bike, my brothers—each on separate pages, my cabin—everything. He took everything that ever mattered to us and he made his *art*. "What's this one?" Rose asks, pointing to one I missed. It's bigger than the others, and framed behind glass. I walk to her so I can see it clearer. "Oh my God," I sob. I lift the frame off the wall and grip it to my chest. Then I sit on the bed and run my fingers over the glass. It's my room, the one he envisioned for me. The walls are filled with books, the fireplace is burning, the armchair is still there, but the little ones are gone. They've been replaced with a draft table. And underneath the sketch are the words that tear my heart in two. *None of this matters without my forever.*

"What's with the sunrise?" Rose asks, pulling me from my thoughts. She's standing in front of the mural with her back to me.

She looks over her shoulder while I wipe my never-ending tears. "It's the sunrise and sunset," I tell her. "He says it reminds him of our love." I struggle to speak, but I push it down and continue, "Because it's eternal—the rise and fall of the sun. It's *forever.* Just like us."

✧　✧　✧

I LEAVE CAMPUS and drive back home. I end up at the one place that I know will help. And I speak to the one person who I know can fix me.

"Mom," I whisper. "I need you."

I lay the flowers in front of her headstone and sit in front of it. "I'm scared," I tell her. "And I'm broken."

I sit for an hour, shedding more tears, wondering how it's possible that tears can keep flowing when your heart is left dry. Then I reach into my bag, pull out pen and notebook, and do something I haven't done since before she passed away.

Untitled

By Lucy Lovesalot.

...

Cameron

SHE WAS SUPPOSED to be on campus yesterday, but I haven't heard a word. She hasn't contacted me, or Micky—so Jake tells me. If she's seen her room, surely someone would know. I've left Rose as a last resort because I don't know if she knows anything that happened to us this summer, and I don't want to be the one to tell her.

"Dude," Minge says, walking into our room. He lifts a package in his hands to show me. "Have you seen this?"

I narrow my eyes before getting off my desk chair and taking it from his hands. Sitting on the bed, I look at the newspaper wrapped package with my name scribbled on it in Lucy's handwriting.

"So... I'm gonna go... and uh... do... something else," Minge mutters.

I glance back up at him. "Thanks man."

He nods before leaving the room and shutting the door after him.

I wipe my hands on the bedspread, waiting for my heart to stop thumping. On the first breath which doesn't feel like a thousand hammers to my chest, I slowly rip it open. It's the *Back to the Future* hoodie she had in that picture she texted from New Jersey, a model Delorean, and a folded note. The thumping of my heart starts again, but I don't wait for it to settle. I unfold it and read the first line.

Untitled – by Lucy Lovesalot.

I laugh once, and then stop myself, because I have no fucking clue what her next words will do to me.

This is a story of a boy, and a girl, falling in love.

Or at least it should be. But it's more than that. It's a story of a boy and a girl who fell so hard in love that love was the only thing they knew. And for so long, that love was enough. That love was their everything.

They shared their dreams, their hopes, their plans for their future. They shared it all, and in doing so, they gave themselves each other. Not just in the physical sense, but in all the other senses possible. Then one night, after sharing their most intimate possession, the girl got scared. She worried that maybe someday the boy would not be there, and this broke the girl's heart.

"You're wrong," the boy told her. And then he proceeded to tell her his thoughts, his dreams, and what he envisioned for their future. Kids. He wanted a perfect little house, with his perfect little wife, and their perfect little kids.

And the girl—her heart swelled at the thought of it. Not just of their future, but of their now. And the eternal love the boy showed for her.

And then one day... it was over.

Just like that.

They shed a thousand tears, over and over. And when it was done, they shed a thousand more.

Now, the boy is still there. Still watching her. Still waiting.

With their dreams of the future broken, he waits.

But the girl is scared. The girl can't let her heartbreak belong to both of them forever. Because one day, she believes, this boy will build a time machine.

He'll go back to the past, to where it began, to where their love was all they needed. Where they could imagine their future, and a house full of their children. He'll want to go back to the boy, falling in love with the girl. And to the girl who could give him his dreams.

He'll want to stay there forever, in a life that was simple, and where the only thing that mattered was love.

But here they are, stuck in the present, wondering how to move forward.

The girl thinks, and feels, and thinks some more, no matter how much it hurts her. But she doesn't have the answers. So one day the girl builds a time machine, but she doesn't join him in the past, she goes to the future. To where she sees the boy she fell in love with many, many years ago. And she sees his sadness. She sees him look into the room he designed just for her. She sees the frown that pulls on his lips when he glances at a single armchair. She sees him watching his friends' kids at little league, and wondering to himself what he did in life which was so wrong that he couldn't have that. Then she sees the way he looks at her, with so much held in regret, and sadness, and anger, because he couldn't have any of it. And one day, that regret and sadness and anger—they turn into hate. And the love they once had, the love that made their world spin, has turned into hate.

So there they are; the boy in the past, falling in love with the girl. And the girl in the future, with the boy that can no longer love her.

Thirty-Seven
Cameron

M
Y BODY SHAKES as I march to her dorm, her note scrunched roughly in my hands. I bang on her door harder than I should. People stare, call me crazy, but I don't care. "LUCY!" I bang again. Harder, louder. "LUCY!"

The door opens, but it's not her. "Where is she?"

"Whoa," Rose says, her hands up in surrender. "Are you okay?"

"No, I'm not fucking okay! Where is she?" I shove the door further open and step inside, my eyes frantically scanning for her. I push open the bathroom door, but she's not there either.

"Where is she, Rose?"

"I don't know, Cameron. You need to calm down." She settles her hand on my shoulder. "Breathe," she says.

And I do.

Once the adrenaline settles and my muscles relax, I look her in the eyes. "Rose, if you know where she is… please tell me," I beg. "I need to see her."

✧   ✧   ✧

TEN MINUTES LATER I'm parked behind Lucy's car at the front of Jake and Micky's house. I try to stay calm as I knock on their door. Jake answers but I shove him out of the way and I walk to Lucy sitting on their couch. "What the hell is this?" I yell, raising her note in my hand.

She flinches and brings her knees up to her chin.

"I'm fucking serious, Lucy. What the hell?" I tried to stay level, I really did, but I'm pissed. Beyond pissed.

"Cameron," Micky says, standing up and pushing me away.

Lucy starts crying, or maybe she already was. I don't know.

"Lucy! Look at me!"

She doesn't. She just continues to sob with her arms shielding her head, hiding herself.

Hiding from *me*.

My fists ball. "How the fuck can you feel any of this? At what point have I ever done anything, ANYTHING," I shout, "to make you feel like this! To make you feel like I didn't love you or would ever stop loving you! This is bullshit! I've done nothing but fucking love you every day since the day I knew your goddamn name and you think you can walk away! I'm not letting you go!"

"CAM!" Jake's at my side now, pulling my arm and leading me to the door. "I'm not letting you go, Lucy!" I shout, just as Jake shoves me out the door, closing it behind both of us.

"You need to calm the fuck down," he says. But there's a sadness in his voice and I want to punch him. I need for people to stop feeling sorry for me. I just need people to understand.

"You don't fucking get it!" I tell him, sitting down on the porch steps. "You don't fucking understand!"

He sits next to me, silent, for what feels like hours.

And I cry. Again.

He rubs the back of his neck before speaking, "You think I don't know what it feels like to want to be there for a girl who you love? When she's so broken and hurt that she doesn't see you standing there, with your arms open..." His voice breaks, before he clears his throat. "Trust me, dude. I know. It's the fucking hardest thing to do—to be around the person you love, every day, and not be able to love them. I've been there. I've lived it. But she needs time—"

"Time? She's had all fucking summer and she's done nothing but push me away! Nobody gives a fuck about the way I feel. She needs time? I need her. And no one fucking cares!"

"It's hard, Cam. She's here because Kayla understands. She's helping her deal with her grief."

I turn to him now, eyes narrowed. "What grief? What the hell are you talking about?"

His eyes widen slightly, as if surprised. "She has to mourn, Cameron. You guys made a baby, and that baby..."

I don't hear what he says next. I can't hear him through the sound of the blood rushing in my ears. But over that sound, I hear her voice. "Cameron?" she says, taking a seat next to me.

I turn to her, my eyes searching her face for an answer. Or a question. "I didn't know," I whisper.

She places her hand on the side of my face.

"I didn't know you were mourning." With eyes closed, I continue, "I was so focused on us and what you thought was our future that I didn't think about the past. I didn't think about what we lost. I didn't even think about losing a baby." I sniff back my sob. "I'm so fucking sorry, Lucy. I should've known. I was always able to read you, and I failed when you needed it the most."

She cries now, bringing my face to her neck. "It's okay," she soothes. "I'm hurting, Cam. And I don't know how to deal with it."

She pulls her face back but I hold onto her tighter. "Why won't you talk to me about it?"

She shakes her head. "I don't know what to say. I don't know how to explain it. I mean, with Mom I knew it was coming, and when it did, I was relieved. But this—I didn't expect this. I didn't know until it was over. And we never even got to say hello, or goodbye. There was no goodbye. No closure."

Lucy

HE TELLS ME to meet him at the river behind his old house. He doesn't tell me why, but he makes me promise to show up right before sunset. And to bring Lucas and my dad.

He must call them beforehand, because when I show up Saturday afternoon, they're ready, dressed in suits, the way they only ever do when we visit Mom on the anniversary of her passing.

I look down at my clothes, wondering if I'm underdressed. "You look beautiful, sweetheart," Dad tells me.

We get in Dad's truck with me in the middle. Lucas holds my hand the entire time. And I still don't know what's happening.

The instant my eyes see the river, and Cameron standing at the edge dressed in a suit, and Heather and Mark dressed in black, *I know.*

I try to turn around, but Lucas holds me in place. "It's time," he says.

There are six folding chairs, three on each side. One side for his family, and one for mine.

Cam won't look at me. Not directly. When he sees us arrive, he sits on the chair next to his mom, and we take the other three.

Then we sit there, facing the water, waiting for I don't know what.

"I'm sorry," a woman's voice breaks the silence. She stands in front of us, her genuine smile in place. She looks at Lucas and me with recognition. "My, you two have grown. What beautiful children," she says. I recognize her as the pastor from Mom's funeral.

I cover my mouth, to stop the cry from escaping. She clears her throat and looks at everyone individually. "I dislike these ones the most," she sighs. She opens her book, slips on her reading glasses, and starts. "There is no footprint too small, that it cannot leave an imprint on this world..."

Cam's cry has me turning to him. He grips his forearm with one hand, using it to cover his eyes. He's bent over in his seat, sobbing quietly.

His mom cries too, but her tears are silent. She rubs slow circles in his back, the way he's done with me so many times. Leaning forward, she whispers words meant only for him. He doesn't stop crying, and neither do I.

Finally, I stand up and take the few steps to get to him. I settle my hand on his shoulder, causing him to look up.

If heartbreak had a face, his would be it.

He sits up straighter, his hand on my waist. He cries into my stomach, unashamed. I cry with him, so hard I can barely stand. So I sit on his lap with our arms around each other. And we cry into each other necks, holding on tight.

We grieve.

We mourn.

And we *love.*

We take our broken hearts and we piece them back together, in the place where it all began. Where a boy who barely knew me took me to break. Taught me to let it go. And helped me to *heal.*

As the sun sets, and the sky turns orange, we each place a flower in paper boats and release them down the river. "Did you have a feeling?" the pastor asks. "If it was a boy or girl?"

"Girl," we say at the same time.

She smiles at us. "Did you want to name her?"

I look up at Cameron standing next to me with his hand on my waist. "Hope," I whisper to him. "You gave me *Hope*."

✧   ✧   ✧

CAMERON STANDS IN front of us with a piece of paper in his hands. He looks first to his mom, and then to me sitting next to her.

He tries to smile, and then he clears his throat as his eyes wander to what's in his hands.

Seconds pass before he speaks.

"More Than Forever," he says, and then glances up at me. "By Cameron Lovesyoumore."

And in a moment of complete sadness, I didn't think it was possible—but he makes me laugh.

Once upon a time there was a little boy whose mother made him watch Aladdin—*more times than what should be legally allowed for boys. Yet each time, he'd sit with her, under her magic carpet blanket and watch intently, because he knew it made her happy.*

It was a story about a boy named Aladdin—a poor boy—who found love in the strangest of places. He fell in love with a girl, a princess, living in a giant castle, filled with many, many people. Mainly boys. This girl had no mother—or at least one that he could tell. And even though people surrounded her, she was lonely. She was sad. The only thing that he found she had comfort in was her pet tiger which she took everywhere. In my story, her tiger is an e-reader.

One day, the boy found the nerve to speak to this beautiful princess, all alone in her giant house. He said to her, "Do you trust me?" She smiled, and said yes. And off they went, on an epic adventure. They went on a magic carpet ride. He promised to show her the world, shining, shimmering, splendid...

And he did.

Or at least he tried.

After a few hundred times of watching this movie, the little boy turned to his mother and asked, "Why wouldn't the genie just give him more wishes?"

His mom smiled down at him. "Because," she said. "It's selfish to want more than you already have."

The little boy spent night after night thinking about his mother's words. And he promised then, to always appreciate what he had. What was given to him. And to never want more.

But then this boy, a little older now, and definitely more hand-some and rugged, fell in love with his own princess, who was sad and lonely in her huge mansion. And even though his mom's words played in his head, he couldn't help but want more. He wanted more of her, tiny versions of her, in the form of their daughters.

Now, that boy is a man—again, even more handsome. And he sees the selfishness of his ways; his want to have more of something he already had. Something he was blessed to be given in the first place.

So for days and days, this man searches for the genie, trying to find a way to make his wishes come true. And he promises himself that if he finds that genie, and the genie offers him three wishes, he'll say what he should have said a long time ago. "You can keep your two wishes, I'll just take the one. I want my girl. My Lucy. My forever. And not just for our forever, but for eternity, and for al-ways."

Thirty-Eight
Cameron

I T'S BEEN A few days since Hope's funeral, and I haven't heard from her. I don't know if she wants more time, but I'm giving it to her anyway. Jake says she'll come to me when she's ready, so I wait. Or at least I did. But now, seeing her reading under a tree just like she used to when we were fifteen, I can't help but go to her.

I release my backpack and sit next to her.

She drops her chin to her chest, trying to hide her smile. *God, I miss her smile.*

"What are you reading?" I ask.

"Nothing."

"You can't be reading nothing. What is it?"

"It's just about a boy and girl... falling in love."

"Yeah?" I joke, repeating my words from so long ago. "Is the guy a stud? Is his name Cameron?"

She laughs, the sound so powerful it drowns out all other sounds. "Yes, actually."

"Really?" I ask in disbelief.

She nods, her smile full force. But her eyes stay down, focused on the words. "But he's a sexy, broody, drug lord."

"No shit?"

"Shit," she says.

I beat my chest like a caveman. "I could be a sexy, broody, drug lord."

She laughs again.

"Read me some," I ask her.

"No."

"Fine."

She doesn't respond, and I think we're done. But the warmth of her

297

hand skims down my arm. I watch anxiously as her hand reaches mine.

My heart picks up pace.

Then she links our fingers and curls hers.

I let out a breath I didn't know I was holding.

She doesn't speak. She just sits there, reading her book, loosely holding my hand.

After a few minutes she lifts my arm by my hand and ducks under it, so my arm is around her, our fingers locked at the side of her waist. She leans in close, so close I can smell her shampoo. I sniff once. I've missed that smell.

"Did you just sniff me?"

"No."

She scoots until we're as close as possible, and that's how we stay, in silence, until the sun starts to set. I watch as the sky turns orange, then red, then purple. And I know we've been sitting here for hours, but it feels like minutes because time doesn't exist when I'm with her.

She shivers in my arms.

"Are you cold?" She turns her e-reader off and looks up at me for the first time since I've sat down. My eyes can't take her in fast enough.

"Yeah," she says. "I should probably get back to my room."

I try to think if I have sweatshirt I can offer, something that will make her stay longer, but I have nothing. "Oh, okay."

She stands up and shrugs her backpack on. "It's late," she says, as I get to my feet.

"Yeah," I respond.

"It's like... dinner time, right?"

I nod. And just stand there.

"Do you—" she starts, and then cuts herself off.

And then it hits me. "Did you want to get something to eat?"

"Oh, no. I mean—do you?"

I nod frantically, and then try to calm the fuck down. "Y-yeah... if you do?"

She lets out a laugh. "Why is this so hard?"

"I'm nervous," I tell her truthfully. "It's like I'm fifteen and I'm asking you out on a date."

She smiles. "I don't think you ever really asked me out on a date... like... ever..."

"I didn't?" I try to think back to that time in our lives. "Holy shit. I didn't, did I?"

She shakes her head, biting her lip as she does.

"Well, would you like to go out with me?" I ask, feeling stupid and embarrassed, but most of all, hopeful.

A low giggle escapes her. "How about we get take-out and bring it back to my room... we could watch a movie or something?"

I want to crack a joke about her inviting me to her room on our first date... and if watching a movie is code for getting laid... but I don't think it's suitable. "That sounds great."

✧   ✧   ✧

WE BRING PIZZA back to her room, and I'm thankful that Rose isn't there. "It's so cold," she says. "It was so warm today and now it's freezing."

I set the pizza on her desk and watch her walk to her dresser. "You want a hoodie? I think I have a few of yours here."

I smile at the thought of her keeping my clothes. "Yeah, please."

She throws a hoodie at my head, making her laugh.

"Good arm," I joke.

She shrugs. "Jake's been teaching me to pitch."

"Huh." I force down the jealousy. First the gym, now the pitching lessons.

She pulls out pajamas from her drawer and points to the bathroom. "I'm just gonna change real quick."

It's been a long time since she's left a room to undress. I look away and nod.

I wait to hear the bathroom door close before I sit on the bed. I drop my head in my hands, and I think. I think about how long it's going to take, and how hard it's going to be to try to get back to where we were. The bed dips when she sits next to me. "Cameron," she says, and I tilt my head to face her. She must be able to tell what's on my mind because she adds, "Slow, okay?"

I nod, my heart heavy with uncertainty. She stands and picks up the box of pizza and her laptop. "Lucas loaded Netflix on my computer so we can watch whatever."

She sits on her bed with her back against the wall and pats the spot next to her.

A movie plays, but I don't watch it. I watch her.

When we're done eating and she trashes the box, she sets her laptop on her desk chair on the side of the bed. "It's cold," she says. "I think I'm going to get under the covers. You can leave, if you need to get back for an early class or something…"

"Or?" I ask her.

"Or you can stay, lie with me until the movie finishes."

My smile is instant.

Lucy

HOLY CRUD BUCKET.

I'm so nervous. More nervous than when I showered him with my virgin kisses. I want him to stay. I want to be in his arms where I know I'm safe. I want to go slow, but it's hard. Especially since I know what's waiting at the end. *Him.*

I lie under the covers at the edge of the bed and wait for him to climb in behind me, but he doesn't touch me and I don't know why.

"Are you still cold?" he asks.

"A little."

The bed moves and I feel his warmth behind me. "Come closer," he says.

So I do.

And all of a sudden I'm in his arms, exactly where I want to be.

The movie plays on and on and I cry silent tears. He doesn't speak. He doesn't move. He doesn't try to touch me inappropriately. He just holds me. And it's perfect. He's perfect. Just like he's always been.

✧   ✧   ✧

HE'S OUT, LIKE a light. I can tell because the movie's done and he hasn't moved. I feel his chest on my back, rising and falling peacefully with every breath. I turn in his arms so I can face him. He has the hood over his head and his mouth is partially open. His bottom lip quivers slightly with each exhale.

The door opens and Rose is there. I lift my finger to my mouth, telling her to be quiet. Her eyebrows narrow in confusion before she looks past me and to Cameron. She pouts, mouthing, "So cute."

"I know," I mouth back, my smile in full force.

"I'll come back in the morning," she whispers. I thank her before she leaves the room silently.

I look back down at him and my heart aches. But it's the good kind. The *love* kind. I scoot down in the bed, so we're face to face and bring the covers up to my chin. And I smile. I smile so hard my cheeks hurt. And then I do something I've wanted to do for so damn long. I kiss him.

Softly at first. Just his bottom lip. Then I move to the top one. I giggle like I did when I was a kid, after the first time he kissed me. I place my fingers on my lips, remembering the touch. And then I kiss him again. And again.

Finally, he gasps and jerks awake. "Was I dreaming?"

I clamp my mouth shut.

His voice is hoarse from sleep when he says, "Were you kissing me just now?"

I don't answer.

He pulls me closer to him. "You totally were," he whispers. "I'm kind of pissed I wasn't awake to know it."

"I'm sorry," I tell him, even though I'm not. "You just looked so cute and peaceful… and your lips were just there… waiting…"

He nuzzles his face into my neck. "You should have woken me."

"I don't like waking you."

He leans on his elbow and rests his head in his hand, looking down at me. And then he smiles. God, I missed his smile. His head drops to the crook of my neck. "I've missed you so much, Lucy," he whispers, bringing me closer again.

His lips brush my neck, up to my jaw, and I can feel him everywhere. My body vibrates in his arms, like a million butterflies trying to escape. He kisses my cheek. Just once, so softly I barely feel it. I squirm in his arms, not wanting to get away, but wanting him. "Nah uh," he mutters, squeezing me tighter. "You got to kiss me, now it's my turn."

I bite down on my lip to stop the squeal from escaping. His nose brushes against mine. And then his lips are on mine. But he doesn't move them. Actually, he pulls back.

"Lucy," he says, his voice breaking. "I know you wanted to take it slow, and that's fine. I can do that to an extent. I can do it physically, but emotionally, I need to know that you're all in. I know I should be patient. I know I should wait. But it's so hard, especially because I want all of you. I need to know that you want it too."

I nod. "I do."

A smile takes over his face. "I'm going to kiss you now," he says.

And then he kisses me.

Holy shit, does he kiss me.

Thirty-Nine
Lucy

"**T**WO MONTHS!" I tell Rose. "Two damn months! He takes me on dates, we spend every spare second together, we sleep in the same bed every damn night and he won't touch me. Doesn't even try to cop a feel! Nothing!"

"Well," she laughs from her bed. "You did ask him to take it slow, right?"

I throw a pillow at her head. "Yeah, I meant slow, not like... glacial. I'm so wound up, I take every opportunity during the day when you're not in here to flick my bean!"

Her head throws back in laughter. "Flick your what?"

"Shut up!" I growl into a pillow. "He leaves every morning and he kisses me. The type of kisses that should be goddamn illegal, Rose. And he's getting hotter. How is that possible? He's started hitting the gym again and there are muscles and his stomach and his hair's like... I don't even... and the *kisses*."

"Dude." She eyes me sideways. "Are you about to come right now? Because you—"

"YES!" I shout. "I am. I need him to... just..." I whimper in defeat. "My clitorusaurus-rex is not happy."

"Your what!" She's laughing so hard snot comes out. She runs to the bathroom... I guess to clean up her face, maybe pee, I don't know.

She comes back out as if nothing happened. "Why don't you go to him? He's probably afraid, doesn't know how far to take it, you know? If you make the move, show the initiative, I'm sure he'll be happy to oblige."

I stand up. "Yes!" I shout triumphantly. "That's exactly what I'm going to do!"

"Fuck, yeah, girl. Go get it!" She slaps my ass.

I moan with pleasure.

She looks at me disgusted. "Holy shit, Luce, you're horny as fuck."

My phone sounds with a message. I reach for it and smash my finger against the screen. Maybe I'm more pissed off than I thought. "Great," I say sarcastically, "He just said he has class all day but wants to take me out tonight—somewhere special. Do you know what that means, Rose? Do you? It means that I have to wait all day to see him and then tonight—he still won't touch me!"

✧　✧　✧

HE KNOCKS ON my door at seven on the dot, just like he said he would. He's wearing dark jeans and a light blue long-sleeved shirt with the sleeves pushed up to his elbows and his muscles on show. I want to lick him. Everywhere. Or hump his leg. Something.

He hands me a bunch of flowers and kisses me on the cheek.

I take them, thank him, and mumble under my breath that I'd rather have his dick than the flowers.

"Are you okay, babe?" he asks.

"Yup. Just give me two minutes to finish getting ready."

He sits on the bed while I go to the bathroom. I smile as I finish getting dressed. "Game on, Cam."

His eyes go wide when he sees me. Tank top, short frilly skirt, so short you can see the top of my stockings, and the bottom of the suspenders.

"Holy fucking shit," he whispers, covering his junk with my pillow.

I grab a knee length jacket and cover myself. "Ready, baby?"

He swallows loudly and nods. "Y-y-yeah."

✧　✧　✧

I TAKE HIS hand while he drives to wherever we're going, and I set it on the inside of my bare thigh. He makes a noise from deep in his throat and wipes his mouth with his shoulder. Slowly, and attempted casually, I start to scoot lower in my seat, letting his hand drift higher.

He pulls the car over into a parking lot. "Fuck."

Score one for me.

"What the hell are you doing?" he clips.

I bat my eyelashes. "What do you mean?"

He shakes his head, his darkened eyes burning with lust. "You're gonna get me in trouble, Luce."

I try to hide my smile.

He looks around the lot. "Two minutes," he says to himself, before hitting the accelerator. His tires spin as he drives away. He squirms in his seat, continuously adjusting himself.

Score two for me.

✧   ✧   ✧

HE TAKES US to a storage warehouse. "This is... um..."

He laughs once, taking my hand and helping me out of his car. "What? Like that time I took you to see Filmore?"

"A little, yeah."

We walk past five rows of storage units before he stops. "This is me," he informs, pulling keys from his pocket.

I start to shrug out of my jacket, but he stops me. "You might want to leave that on for a little longer."

"Okay?"

He smiles down at me, before holding my face in his hands and kissing me. "I love you, Lucy." He unlocks the door and slides it up.

And my eyes are everywhere, all at once, taking everything in. "What is this?"

"Mom," he says.

"This is your mom? What?"

Heather's laugh kicks sense back into me. "Bye kids," she says. And then she's gone.

"What the hell?"

He slides the door back down and walks over to me.

"I needed Mom's help. That's why she was here. It's also why I told you to keep your jacket on, but now that you're here..." He un-buttons my jacket and slides it off my shoulders, exposing me to him. But my eyes are too busy looking around at the paintings on the wall, the sketches all over the place. There are light boxes and draft tables and a..."Candlelit dinner?"

He laughs. "This is my studio. Mark helped me find it. He leased it out for a year. This is where I came to make your murals and the sketches in your room. I come here to work, study, whatever." He leans against a light box and watches as I take everything in.

"You're starting to paint a lot with colors." I glance at him quickly. "This is amazing, baby."

He doesn't speak. Just continues to watch.

"Are you thinking of changing majors? Change to art?"

He stands next to me now, taking my hand in his. "No. I've realized my passion is in design. The art stuff, that's just for us."

I turn and look up at him. "I'm kind of speechless right now. I'm… I don't know… it just seems wrong for me to say I'm proud of you, because I didn't really do anything to help you but I feel—"

"Of course you did, Luce," he cuts in. "You believed in me. That meant everything."

I blink back the tears and inhale deeply. "So candlelit dinner?"

He nods and then points to the floor.

I drop my gaze. "Rose petals?" I squeal. I hadn't even noticed.

"And," he says, walking over to a fire pit. He spends a few seconds lighting it before he says, "Open fireplace."

I pout. "Like you wanted for our first time?"

He nods again. "This is the first of many first times for us. It doesn't matter that we've experienced it all. It's different this time; there are no questions, no uncertainties. You and me, babe, forever."

Score one million for Cameron.

But I don't mind, because it's score *infinity* for me.

✧   ✧   ✧

WE EAT DINNER and talk, and laugh, and get to know each other like it's the first time. And we fall even more in love. Afterwards, he asks me to sit for him on the pullout sofa bed he has in there. So I do. He takes his time sketching me. And every time he looks up from his sketch with a slight smile on his face, he makes me feel beautiful. And I know I could be wearing what I'm wearing, or I could be wearing my frumpy pajamas, and he'd still look at me that way. Because he always has, and he always will.

He doesn't show me his work when he's finished. He says it's just for him so I leave it alone. "Now a nude one," he says.

I laugh.

"You think I'm kidding?" He flops on the sofa bed next to me and pulls me to him. "I'll make a deal. You pose nude and I'll get you off. I know you're going crazy."

My jaw drops. "I am not—I can—you don't—it's not—"

His head throws back in laughter. "Luce, you don't think I know what you're doing? I know you. I know your body. I know it's driving you insane that I haven't touched you."

I pounce on him, and sit on his waist with my knees on either side. "Why haven't you?"

His head lifts off the cushion, just so he can watch his hands roam up my thighs, softly pushing my skirt higher. "I just didn't want to do anything before you were ready. Are you?" he asks sincerely. "I mean emotionally."

I think about his words, and I think about him, and everything he means to me. "Yes."

He licks his lips before sitting up and pulling me closer to him. He kisses me slowly, deeply, for minutes that feel like seconds. And I can't get enough of him. Physically. Emotionally. All of it. His warm hands grip my waist, under my tank.

And then I panic. I push his hands away, and pull back from his kiss.

"What's wrong?"

I swallow the knot in my throat and look away, but his hand on my chin turning me to him doesn't let me stay there for long.

"Babe?"

I try not to cry. I try not to ruin the moment. I really do. But I can't hold it in.

"Hey," he soothes, wrapping me in his arms and rubbing circles in my back. "What's wrong? Talk to me."

"I have a scar," I whisper. "And it's ugly."

Gently, he grasps my shoulders so he can push me away and look in my eyes. "Are you kidding me?"

I shake my head, feeling small and insecure.

He looks away and releases a breath. "I don't know what to say," he admits. "I don't know how to make you feel better about that. All I can say is that I think you're beautiful, every single inch of you—scar or not. And if there's a way that I could prove it, I would. If you feel self-conscious about it, you don't have to show me, but I'd like to see it. It kind of belongs to both of us, don't you think?"

I inhale a confident breath and slowly take my top off. His eyes stay on mine. Then slowly, he flips us over until I'm on my back, and he kisses me. First my mouth, and then down my neck. His tongue darts out, leaving a trail between my breasts. He unhooks my bra, and slowly pulls the straps down each arm. His eyes focus on my breasts. "Beautiful," he murmurs, before paying them individual attention with his mouth. His tongue. His teeth. I close my eyes and let him take me in. His hands tug at my skirt until it's over my hips and down my legs. He kisses my stomach, down to my belly button. Tears fall from my closed eyes when I anticipate his next move—when he sees the ugly scar that mars my so-called-beautiful body. My breath catches when I feel his lips there, an inch above my pubic bone. He places open mouth kisses along the length of it; all four inches. He takes his time, letting my body shake with the sobs I can't contain. "You're beautiful, Lucy," he croaks. And I cry harder. But he doesn't stop with the kisses, he moves further down my body, removing my panties, my suspenders and my stockings all in one move. He stands at the end of the sofa, his eyes burning with lust. He licks his lips, before dipping his head between my legs.

It doesn't take long for me to come. Not once. Not twice. But three times—just from his mouth alone. "You gotta be quiet," he chuckles. "This is public space."

"Shut up," I tell him. "Get naked."

He laughs, but he does what I ask. Then he climbs on top of me and positions himself. "I'm gonna make love to you now," he says into my neck. "And I'm going to do it right this time."

"Okay," I moan, running a hand down his back. "And after we make love, can you screw me?"

He stifles his laugh with my neck.

"And then after you screw me, can you fuck me?"

He slams inside me without warning. And then his body tenses and he looks up. "Shit, Luce, I didn't even ask. Are you… I mean… can we?"

"I'm on the pill." I kiss him passionately, tasting myself on his tongue… feeling him get even bigger inside of me. "Now make love to me so we can get to the kinky shit."

Forty
Cameron

I DON'T LIKE to think that Lucy and I broke up last summer. I say that we just restarted—created a new round of firsts. Everything else is the same as it has always been. I have more spare time now that I'm not working at the firm, and I can take it a little easier because there isn't the pressure of a scholarship weighing on me.

A few weeks ago, Logan came back. He still won't really talk about what happened, but he's happy. And I know the main reason is because of Amanda.

Lucy's happy too, she got two of her best friends back. And me—I'm just happy because she's happy.

She called me crying once after the girls had book club. She asked that I come over right away. Of course, I did. She said that she told Amanda about us—about not being able to have any children. She said it was the first time she's really told anybody straight out. She hasn't told Rose, and Micky and Jake knew because they were at the hospital. But Micky didn't really understand how, or why, but she never asked. She said that she explained it in detail to them, and they all sat there and cried. It was emotionally exhausting for all of them. Amanda asked if Logan knew, she told her that he didn't, but that she could tell him. So, we were both expecting the knock that came on her door a couple hours later. He stood with his hands in his pockets and his head lowered. She said his name and he looked up at her, eyes red from his own tears. He didn't speak; he just wrapped his arms around her. It could've been minutes; it could've been hours. He looked past her and to me, sitting on her bed feeling everything she did. He told me he was sorry and that things would be okay, and that he'd be there for me if I ever needed anything—and he said all of that without ever speaking a word. Lucy hugged him back. I don't know if it was for her or for him.

When he was ready he pulled away, nodded once at her, and then shoved his hands back in his pockets and left. She closed the door after him, laid down in bed with me, and then she said something I'd been thinking about since the day we found out about the miscarriage. "What do you think she would have looked like?"

We spent the rest of the night talking about her. Talking about our *Hope*. It was a moment of clarity, and a moment of *healing*. And like every other night, we declared our love for each other and we fell asleep in each other's arms. And the next morning, we woke up, and we moved on.

✧　　✧　　✧

"LUCAS IS ON campus," she says, looking down at her phone.

I pull up to the curb in front of Jake and Micky's house. "What's he doing here?"

"He just said he was looking around."

I get out and wait for her at the front of the car. "Is he still undecided about coming here?"

"I guess."

We walk through their side gate and into the yard where everyone's already sitting. I sit on a chair and she sits next to me, typing out a text on her phone. "He said he went to my room, and then to yours. Minge was there, he somehow convinced him to drive him to some party. He's there now. He says he's only staying a little while and then he'll come here." She reaches into the cooler next to her and pulls out a drink.

"Hey Luce," Logan says. "You remember when you were scared of your vagina?"

Amanda's head throws back in laughter.

"I don't even want to ask," Ethan, her brother, speaks up.

"Remember when we sat around naming it?" Jake chimes in.

I laugh with them.

"Not funny," she says, but she's laughing too.

"Dylan had the best ones!" Logan adds. "Fuck, I miss that kid."

"I know! And every time we speak his name it's like we all have to have a moment of silence for our lost brother…" I say.

"Lost to the Marines?" Micky asks.

"We should do that," Jake says, ignoring her. "Every time we say his name we have to be quiet and pay our respect."

We all laugh, but agree to do it.

An hour later, Lucy's buzzed. Half an hour after that, she's borderline wasted. "I'm gonna call Lucas, see what's up." She dials his number and brings the phone to her ear. "Where are you?" she asks. Seconds of quiet pass, then a look of disgust takes over her face. "Dude, are you having sex?"

The guys cheer.

She hangs up and mocks a shiver. "Gross."

Ten minutes later he shows up. I have to make the introductions because Lucy's too busy making exaggerated gagging sounds.

"Bathroom, bedroom or car?" Logan asks him.

Lucy gets louder.

Amanda turns to Logan. "What? You're so yuck."

He just shrugs. "Past life, baby. Before you."

Amanda starts matching Lucy's sounds.

Lucas spins in a circle in the middle looking for a seat. I pull on Lucy's arm until she's up and on my lap, and tell him to take her seat.

Once Lucy's settled and her sounds have died down, Lucas answers, "Car."

And the gagging starts again. Lucas laughs at her. Then for some reason he thinks it's a good idea to bug her some more. "She was a screamer, too," he says.

"Shut up!"

"I didn't even have to do anything. She rode me in her backseat. Her hands gripped her open sunroof and she just went hard. *Really hard.* I had to keep looking out the window to see if we were gonna get caught. She had a filthy mouth, too."

"I swear it, Lucas, shut up!"

His low chuckle turns to a guffaw.

"I bet you didn't even know her name!"

"Yeah, I did," he says, almost looking offended. "It was... Robby? No! Roxy."

I tense. Blood whooshes loudly in my ears, but everywhere else... Dead. Fucking. Silence.

"Did someone say Dylan?" Ethan pipes up.

"Roxy!" Lucy roars.

Lucas's eyebrows bunch. "Yeah, why?" Then his eyes widen and focus on me.

I duck behind Lucy's shoulder.

"I'll murder her!" she shouts, her glare fixed on Lucas.

"Fuck," he spits.

"What the fuck is wrong with that whore! First my boyfriend, now my brother!"

His hands go up in surrender. "I swear I didn't know." He looks so fucking scared that I'd laugh if I didn't actually think he had a reason to be. He tries to back away from her but he falls back in his seat and crashes to the ground.

I must have unconsciously suspected what was about to happen because my arms are tight around her stomach. "Let me go, Cam! Let me go!"

I grip her tighter.

"Holy shit," Ethan chuckles.

"LET ME GO!"

I sigh, defeated, and then jerk my head at Lucas. "You got five seconds."

I wait until he's on his feet before releasing her. He runs. Fast. So he should. He laughs as she chases him around the yard until he's cornered. "I hope your dick gets whore poisoning and shrivels to its death! And then I hope all the girls see it and laugh at you! And then I hope it falls off! You can stare down at it and cry like a little bitch, just like you did when your pet hamster died!"

His laughter stops instantly. He straightens up, eyes narrowed, body rigid. "Don't talk about Princess Leia like that."

"Yeah?" she says, crossing her arms and cocking her hip. "Well, when your dick falls off we can bury it next to her." And then she pounces. She doesn't do much damage. He's six-two, built like their dad. She's tiny, and twenty pounds soaking wet. She's also weak as shit.

"Are you fucking biting me?" he shouts.

That gets laughs.

We all sit in silence and watch it play out. Her, somehow attached to his back, her arm around his neck and his forearm in her mouth.

"Fuck," he screams. "Cameron! A little help!"

I take my time getting up and lazily walk over to them. She tries to take me out, too, but I'm too fast and duck her hits. Awkwardly, I peel her off him. "Come on little stealth ninja, time to settle down."

By the time we sit back down, she's calm enough that I don't have to be on alert for any impromptu attacks. She's still upset, though. I can tell because her arms are crossed and she's pouting. "I hope she chokes on cock," she mumbles.

That gets more laughs.

"Whore," Amanda chimes.

Logan shakes his head at her. "Don't encourage it, baby."

Then Micky adds, "Dumbass."

"Yeah!" Lucy agrees. "I bet she's dumb. Really dumb! I bet the smartest thing that's ever come out of her mouth is cock. The fucking whore."

More laughs, even from me.

"Don't laugh," she clips.

I stop.

She growls. "I wish I could punch her in her ham wallet."

"Or…" Micky starts, her face lighting up with a smile.

"Or what?" Lucy asks her.

"Remember prom night… and James's truck?"

"Holy shit," Logan mutters. "Operation Mayhem?"

"What?" Ethan almost shouts. "You guys did that to James's truck?"

Micky covers her mouth to stop from laughing.

"He bitched about that shit for a month. I can't believe it was you guys."

"He kind of deserved it," Amanda says.

Logan sits up, resting his knees on his elbows. "It's not the same without Dylan."

And on cue, we silently bow our heads.

Lucas looks around before asking, "Why is—"

"Shut your whore loving mouth, Lucas," Lucy interrupts.

Then Jake leans forward. "We need a plan."

"We need supplies," Logan responds.

"We need a car," Micky adds.

Lucas clears his throat. "I have the minivan."

❖ ❖ ❖

OPERATION MAYHEM, WHICH Lucy has not so subtly renamed Hoperation Whore-hem, somehow consists of the following:

A tube of superglue.

8 rolls of aluminum foil.

A can of spray paint.

A roll of Duct tape.

16 cans of tuna.

A kiddy pool.

36 tubs of Jell-O.

12 tubs of chocolate pudding.

A concrete statue of the ugliest gargoyle Lucy could find.

6 bike locks.

And…

A mannequin.

That last one was the hardest. It took some heavy flirting on Logan's behalf. Luckily, Amanda was fine with it. She even encouraged it.

Lucas drives us to where he just got laid. Thankfully, it's a side street so no one will see, and even if they do, we hope they're drunk enough to find it as funny as we do.

He doesn't seem upset about what we're doing. If anything, he kind of seems giddy. I guess Lucy's excitement has worn off on all of us.

I lift her by her ass until she's on top of the car and able to climb in through the open sunroof. She unlocks the doors as Lucas opens the back of the minivan.

With everyone working, it only takes ten minutes.

We stick the open cans of tuna under the seats and hide them in the air vents. Lucas sits the mannequin in the driver's seat and superglues the seatbelt in place while Ethan blows up the kiddy pool and sets it on the roof, the statue being the centerpiece. The girls fill it with Jell-O and pudding, and whatever's left of the pudding is smeared into the car seats. I think Lucy enjoys that part the most. When we've completed the inside, Jake and Logan lock the statue and kiddy pool in place with the bike locks. And when they're done with that, Lucas and I cover the entire car, statue and all, with the aluminum foil.

We all struggle not to cackle with laughter, but it's so damn hard.

Standing back, we all take in the masterpiece. "This is our best one yet," Jake announces.

"Dylan would be proud," Logan muses.

We bow our heads for a moment of silence. And then we erupt with laughter.

"Why—" Lucas starts, but Lucy cuts in, "Shut it, slutslave."

"Fuck this is good times," Logan says. "I miss this shit!"

Jake pats Lucas on the back. "Leave your car here." He hands him a beer. "Crash at our place and get it in the morning. It's too late to drive home."

We take one more look at what *was* Roxy's car, laugh some more, and then start the walk back to Jake and Micky's.

Lucy holds my hand. "I love you, baby." She reaches up and kisses my cheek. "Thank you."

"For what?"

"For letting me have this—closure."

❖   ❖   ❖

I WALK WITH my hands in my pockets, watching Lucas and Lucy in front of me with her hand on the crook of his elbow.

"Lachy got suspended from school today," he tells her.

"Again?"

"Yeah. You know that song from Frozen, *Let it Go*?"

"Yeah?"

"He kept singing it to his teacher."

"Well that's cute, right?"

"Yeah, only he changed the words. He keeps singing, 'Let it gooo, filthy hoooo,'" he sings.

Her head throws back in laughter. "That's all Little Logan."

"I know," he agrees. "Sometimes I wonder what Mom would think if she knew."

She shrugs. "She'd probably tell him to stop, but laugh about it when she was alone. She didn't care much for punishment."

"That's true," he says. "We're lucky to have you around to remind us of her. You're getting more and more like her."

"No." She shakes her head. "Mom was beautiful."

I want to cut in—tell her she's beautiful, too, but Lucas says it for me.

She leans up and kisses his cheek. "She had fire too. Remember that time Dad got the new kitchen and he measured it wrong? Everything was higher than it was supposed to be. She had to use a step ladder to open the top cupboards."

I smile.

Lucas laughs. "She was so mad. She'd always mumble curses whenever she was in there."

"I know." Lucy giggles. "But she never really cursed. She'd just put two random words together, but it was her tone that made it sound like that."

"That's right," he says, like it's a lost memory. "What was that one she'd say every time she opened the cupboards?"

Lucy's head tilts back, as if asking the skies for an answer. "Oh yeah. Balah chicken."

Lucas chuckles. "What the hell is a balah chicken?"

"I don't know," Lucy replies through her laugh. "Dad kept telling her he'd fix it but he never did."

"Yeah, I think Dad liked to feel needed, you know? Like he had a purpose with her... every time she asked him to reach something... I'd catch them smiling at each other when they were in there. Like it was their own private joke."

Lucy sighs. "They loved each other a lot. And they showed it, too. I don't remember a time they were ever apart when he wasn't at work. They always needed to be together, you know? Even if they weren't doing the same things, they were always in the same room... just... loving each other."

He laughs once. "Reminds me of you and Cam."

She turns and glances at me quickly, a slight smile on her lips. "Yeah, like me and Cam."

Logan comes up next to me and nudges my elbow with his. "It's kind of perfect isn't it?"

"What is?" I ask him, my eyes still on Lucy.

I watch as her head throws back in laughter. The sound still so powerful it drowns out all other sounds.

"The universe," he says.

I smile and turn to him, but he's watching Amanda laughing with Micky. "Yeah, man. It really is."

✧   ✧   ✧

WE GET BACK to Jake and Micky's, with everyone on a high from Operation Mayhem. Everyone but Lucas. "Seriously, Luce. You broke skin when you bit me. It better not scar. I've gone eighteen years without a single mark on me."

She scoffs. "Seriously, Luke? You have a birthmark on your skull the size of Cam's balls!"

I roar with laughter. I think we all do.

"I do not," he says defensively.

"Yeah you do. You're lucky your hair's so thick it covers it. Did you seriously not know?"

He runs a hand through his hair. "Are you fucking kidding right now?"

She shakes her head slowly. "Don't ever shave head. Unless you want *birthballs* to be your nickname for life."

That gets another round of laughs.

"Wait," Jake says. "You don't have any scars? No falling off shit... smashing your head on a table... nothing?"

"Nope," Lucas replies, popping the *P*. He runs both hands down his chest. "I'm *flawless*."

"I have small ones, but no broken bones or anything," Micky adds.

For the next ten minutes, we share and show each other's stories.

"I win," Ethan shouts. "I have pins in my leg and a huge fucking scar from when I broke my leg."

Amanda pouts. "I'm so sorry, E, you shou—"

He raises his finger to shush her. "Dylan," he deadpans.

And we bow our heads, chuckling as we do.

"I have a scar," Lucy says quietly. "From the lapra—latra—"

"Laparotomy," I tell her. But my eyes widen when I hear others say it too.

Her face falls. "What?" she breathes out, looking at everyone. "How do you guys know?"

Micky shrugs. "Jake and I researched it after you told me about it."

She looks to Logan for an answer. "I already knew what it was, but I kind of looked up how it affected you," he says.

She turns to me. I try to smile, but I don't know if it shows. Then one by one, she looks at each of our friends. And then she sniffs, and I know she's on the verge of tears. "You guys," she cries. She inhales a shaky breath before attempting to speak. "You—" Her sob cuts her off. She covers her face with her hands and raises a finger, asking us to wait.

I put my hand under her tank and rub her back. And when she's ready, she starts again, "You guys are amazing. You're the bestest friends I could have ever asked for." She struggles to speak through her cries. "I mean, after my mom died, and Claudia left, I had no one. I hated the thought of going to school every day with no one there. And then—" She pauses for a moment to try to level her breathing.

"Babe," I say. "It's okay."

She shakes her head. "I need to say this." She turns to the group. "And then Cameron came along, and he made..." She presses a hand to her heart. "He made it hurt less, and then you guys, you became my friends, and you took me in without any question. You made me feel like part of the group and there was no reason behind it... you just did it."

Micky holds Jake's hand and sniffs into his arm.

"You guys, all of you, you became my family. And you've always been there for me no matter what."

I don't really know if it's the alcohol talking, but I let her speak. I let her say what she needs to say.

"And after what happened with me and Cam... you helped us get through it. I can't even..." She drops her head in her hands and cries, harder than I've seen her cry in a long time.

The other girls are crying now, and so am I, but I try to hide my tears and lower my cap.

"Are you okay, baby?" I whisper.

She nods. "I'm okay," she says, her voice level. "I'm okay, Cameron." She turns and looks around the group again. "It's been almost a year and I'm *healed*. You all helped me heal. And it's not so bad." She shrugs. "I mean the doctors—they said that we couldn't conceive *naturally*. It doesn't mean anything. We still have options."

I bring her closer, not for her, but for me.

She sniffs a few times and wipes her tears. "We can always do IVF treatment, or even surrogacy. But I don't know, I think..." She glances at me quickly. "I think I'd really like to look into adoption, too."

"Fuck yeah, adoption!" Logan shouts.

It brings on a mix of cries and laughter.

He leans forward, his fist out ready for a bump. She laughs as their fists make contact.

I bring her even closer, pull my cap off and use it to hide our faces. "I'm so proud of you. I love you, Lucy," I tell her, because I've never felt it more than I do right now.

"Forever, Cameron."

Forty-One
Cameron

I LEAVE LUCY in bed, quietly snoring. She had a lot to drink last night and we got home pretty late. I tell her that I'll be back in a few hours and that I want to get some work done at the studio. She mumbles an I love you and pulls the covers above her head.

I get in my car, drive past my studio, and with each passing minute I let the nerves build.

✧   ✧   ✧

I RUB MY palms down my shorts and inhale deeply. I close my eyes and count to five in my head, then I open them and knock on the door before I wuss out.

Tom answers with a smile when he sees me, but then his brows furrow. "Everything okay?" he asks, looking over my shoulder.

I can understand why he'd be concerned. It's rare that I show up without Lucy, or that I even knock these days.

His gaze comes back to me as he looks me up and down, and whatever he sees in my face has him smiling again.

"Come in," he says, jerking his head inside the house.

It's quiet, quieter than I've ever heard it. I look around, but I can't see any of the boys. He must read my mind, because he informs, "Virginia took the boys to the lake for the afternoon."

I nod, even though he can't see me.

He leads me to his office where he motions for me to take a seat. He sits on the other side of the desk I designed for him. He's still smiling and I don't know why. I haven't said a word. I've tried. When he opened the door, I tried. I tried again as he was leading me down the hallway into this room. I even opened my mouth, but nothing came out.

I squirm in the seat, trying to adjust my position. I want to look tough, like I'm in control. I square my shoulders and lift my chin. Then I open my mouth… nothing.

His smile gets wider. He unlocks his desk drawer and pulls out a little black box.

"I was wondering when you'd come around," he says.

I still can't speak.

"This is her mom's."

And my heart beats out of my chest.

"When do you plan on doing it?"

I swallow down my nerves and man up.

"I was hoping to do it September twenty-fifth, sir."

His eyes go wide.

"I thought it would be nice if you and the boys, and your wife were there to witness it."

His eyes glaze over as he nods once. "It sounds perfect, *son*."

September Twenty-Fifth

I'M SO FUCKING nervous my eye begins to twitch. Twitchy, that's probably what the boys would nickname me for a year.

I squeeze my eyes shut, trying to get it to stop. Surely I must look crazy right now—suited up, standing under a random tree, yards away from a huge family paying respect to their lost mother and wife.

I blow out a breath. I need to calm down.

Pressing my palm against my chest, I close my eyes and start counting in my head. It doesn't seem to get better.

Then I feel a tiny hand brush against my leg and fingers wrap around mine.

I open one eye and look down at Lachlan. He beams up at me, with crooked teeth on display. He's just started getting his adult teeth through. "Daddy says it's time," he whispers. The kid's cute. He won't be much longer. His older brothers have already started talking him into doing and saying some stupid shit, but I'd virtually watched him grow from a tiny baby into this boy, and soon enough, he'd be a teenager. I bet he'll be like Little Logan. That kid's a punk; his name suits him.

We walk hand in hand over to his mother's headstone.

I wanted to give them all time to pay their respects as a family. She waits at the front of the others with that same sad smile I'd gotten used to over the last six years. *Six years*. Holy shit.

"It'll be okay," Lachlan whispers. Then he takes off, running toward his dad. And it starts again. The nerves. The sweaty palms. The racing heart. The fucking eye twitch.

I stand in front of her, my ribs aching from the pounding of my heart against it. It feels like it could break bone and skin and rip through me at any second. I place my hand in my pocket and feel around for what I need.

"Are you okay, Cam?" Her voice drips with concern. "You look kind of pale."

I gaze up at her dad. He just nods and tries to smile. He fails, but I get it. I can't even imagine what this must feel like for him. Maybe he feels like he's about to lose the only woman left in his life, but he knows me better than that. He knows I'd never take her away.

I eye all her brothers one by one, almost as if asking for permission. No one gives me an out. I finish on Lachlan, whose smile's unchanged. He nods his head with as much enthusiasm as his seven-year-old body can muster.

Then I give all my attention to the girl in front of me.

Lucy.

She must've been following my gaze because her head slowly turns from her brothers behind her to me.

Eyes narrowed, she asks, "What's going on?"

Her gaze searches me from head to toe, and then back up again. But she doesn't get all the way up—her eyes fixate on what I'm holding. They widen. As if in slow motion, her hand comes up to cover her mouth.

I suck in a breath.

Let it out in a whoosh.

And then it happens.

I drop down on one knee. "Lucy…"

She squeals something similar to a yes before I even get a chance to ask. Lunging forward, she throws her arms around my neck—the power of her push so strong that I have to catch myself with my outstretched arm.

She's crying, and laughing.

And so am I.

"Did he even ask her?" Lachlan says.

Tom shakes his head. "I don't think there was ever really a question."

✧ ✧ ✧

"I CAN'T BELIEVE I'm wearing my mom's ring. It's so surreal."

I glance at her quickly while I drive us to Mark and Mom's house. "So I need you to do something for me."

"Anything," she says, distracted by the giant rock on her finger.

"I didn't tell them what I was planning. I was hoping for it to be a surprise."

"Okay?"

I smile. "So let's mess with Mom a little."

✧ ✧ ✧

MOM OPENS THE door and grins from ear to ear. "An unexpected visit from the prodigal son," she muses. "Come in."

"Do you have any aspirin?" Lucy asks, before stepping inside. She rubs her forehead with her left hand. "I have this giant headache that won't go away."

"Sure." Mom looks at her like moms are supposed to; concerned. But she doesn't notice the ring on her finger.

"Yeah," Lucy feigns, "and there's this ache in my chest, too." She rubs her chest with her hand.

"Oh, sweetheart," Mom coos. "Is Cameron taking care of you?"

"Uh huh." She nods and over exaggerates a yawn, covering her mouth. "I'm just tired all the time."

Still… nothing.

A frown pulls on Mom's lips as she leads us to the kitchen. We sit at the island counter while Mom busies herself with the unneeded aspirin. Lucy takes it anyway, along with the glass of water Mom set down in front of her. She turns to her side while she drinks, just so Mom has a better view of the ring.

"You look a little pale, sweetie."

Lucy's chokes on her laugh.

I shake my head at both of them. "So Mom, I tried calling Mark before we got here but his phone was *engaged*."

"He should be on his way home now. He had to go into the dealership real quick. I've been trying to get him to take weekends off but he won't listen." She pauses for a beat. "What's that noise?" she asks.

Lucy's clanking the ring against her glass.

"I must have a coin in the dryer, I'll be back."

We wait until she leaves the room before bursting out laughing. "How does she not see it?" Lucy asks in disbelief.

"I have no idea."

"Hey," she says, serious all of a sudden. "You didn't tell your mom?" She raises her hand and cups the side of my face. "What if she doesn't like me? Or likes me but doesn't want you to marry me?" She pouts. "What if she wants grandchil—"

"Dylan!" I snap.

She clamps her mouth shut and drops her gaze.

"Don't ever bring that up again, Luce." I pull on her legs until she swivels in her seat and her entire body is facing me. "Don't ever question the way my mom feels for you. She loves you as much as I do."

Her eyes lift to mine, before she leans up and kisses me. Soft at first, but it quickly turns to something more. Her head tilts to the side as her tongue skims my lips. She opens her mouth, giving me access. I almost forget where we are and why we're here. Almost—until Mom's scream reminds me. We both turn to her, Lucy's hand still cupping my face.

Mom's on her knees, her hands covering her face. Her shoulders lift with each silent sob.

"Are you okay, Ma?" I laugh out. "What happened?"

Lucy swats my chest and gets off her stool. "Heather?"

Mom looks up now, her eyes red and filled with tears.

Mark walks in through the door which leads to the garage. "I heard a scream! What happened?"

Mom cries heavier, waving her hand at us.

Mark sees us for the first time. Then his eyes trail back to Mom. "What happened?" he asks again.

"She—he—they—prop—wed—"

His gaze moves back to us, his brows bunched in confusion. Standing over her, he asks, "Honey, have you been drinking with the girls again?"

She shakes her head frantically. "They—ring—and—" She's gasping for breath, unable to speak.

"Mark," I say, getting his attention.

Lucy wiggles her fingers in front of her face.

His eyes narrow at first, and then they go huge. He mocks a cry, before dropping to his knees next to Mom. He covers his face with both hands and mimics Mom's voice. "They—he—she—ohmuhguuuuhd!"

Lucy and I laugh and help them both to stand. "I just need a minute," Mom says.

We wait patiently for her to calm down. Mark brings her in his arms and holds her while she cries. He smiles at us, the power of it so infectious that I find myself smiling with him.

When Mom's settled, she removes herself from Mark and kisses my cheek. Then she goes to Lucy, her face already contorting with another cry. She lifts up Lucy's hand and looks at the ring. Then she lets out a gasp and covers her mouth. "Is this?"

Lucy nods. "Yes."

"Your mom's?"

She nods again.

"How did you know?" I ask Mom.

She ignores me and speaks only to Lucy. "It's exactly the way you've described it."

Lucy's eyes well with tears.

"It's beautiful," Mom tells her. She reaches up and cups Lucy's face with both hands. Her thumbs skim Lucy's cheeks, wiping the tears that must have fallen. "Just like you."

Lucy

I RUN A finger down his chest and over the ridges of his abs. "I can't believe I'm going to be your wife," I tell him.

He smiles and moves me so I'm on top of him.

We decided to stay at the cabin overnight instead of heading back to campus. He asked if I wanted to go back so we could tell our friends. I told him I just wanted the night to be with him.

His fingers move my hair to behind my ear. "And I'm going to be your husband," he says, a hint of a smile forming on his face.

"It's surreal." I sit up so I'm straddling him.

He chews his lip, his eyes drifting shut when I move, pressing myself into him. Two more strokes and he'll be hard.

He links our fingers and kisses the palms of each of my hands. "Now will you look at the apartments on campus?"

I pull his hands until they're flat on my back and take off my shirt. He smiles, that perfect smile with those perfect lips I've always loved. I lean down and kiss his neck, slowly licking and sucking and making my way down. "I think that would be an amazing idea."

He shifts underneath me, his hard-on now prominent. His hand runs up my back, unhooking my bra and freeing my breasts. He pulls the straps off my arms and then links his fingers behind his head, his eyes roaming my body. His gaze drops to where my scar is, but he doesn't flinch, his face doesn't change, he doesn't look away. He never does. He sits up, his outstretched arms holding him in place. His mouth finds my neck, kissing me gently and moving his way up to my jaw, across my chin, and finally up to my mouth. He sighs when his tongue brushes against mine. "Do you have an idea of when you want to do it? The wedding, I mean."

I push further into him, wanting to feel him on me. "Not really. You?"

"Tomorrow?"

I laugh into his mouth.

"I can't organize a wedding in a day."

"Fine." He sits up and grabs my ass, lifting his hips at the same time. I let out a moan, my back arching in pleasure. He kisses my neck again, down my chest, and the top of each breast. "A week?"

I snake my arms around his neck, holding on. "Babe," I whisper, my hips slowly thrusting, my center rubbing against him. "I can't do a week."

He pulls away and throws his body back against the mattress. "A month, Luce. That's as long as I can wait."

I chuckle lightly, but then cut myself off when I see the seriousness on his face. "One month?" I ask.

"One month, baby. I don't even want to wait that long to make you my wife."

A slow smile builds on my lips. "One month?" I say again. "I can do that."

Forty-Two
Cameron

"I'M FUCKING BOSS at this game," Logan shouts, his hands up in victory. We're at Jake and Micky's house having a few beers. Heidi told Luce she was going to be late, something about her sorority. The girls have been spending a lot of time together since Luce announced that she had a month to plan a wedding. The girls cried when we told them. The guys congratulated me, then took me out the next night to get fucked up. It was good times. Up until I stumbled into Lucy's room blind drunk and tried to have sex with her desk. She still laughs about it. Every now and then she sees me doing something stupid and calls me Deskfucker.

Jake kicks the Monopoly board in mock anger. "I don't know why we always play this when Princess Asshole always wins."

"Don't be a brat," Micky reprimands.

Logan laughs. "Because I'm a motherfuckin' gangsta and I make it rain on the bitches!" He throws his paper money at Amanda.

She shakes her head and glares at him. "Don't ever do that again."

"Here," he says, handing her a note. "Buy yourself something pretty, you deserve it."

Lucy's head throws back in laughter.

"Yo," I speak up. "Logan and I joined a casual baseball league. We play on weekends for shits and giggles."

"What!" Jake exclaims. "I wanna play with you guys!"

"Shut your MLB face," Logan tells him. "You're not good enough to play with the cool kids."

He feigns a pout.

"Wait," Lucy says. "You guys are playing baseball again?"

"Yeah," I answer.

"Do you wear uniforms?"

"Uh huh."

She turns to Amanda, whose eyes are wide. They share an unspoken message, just as a smirk pulls on both their lips.

"What?" Logan and I ask at the same time.

Amanda giggles.

Lucy shrugs. "Nothing. It's just that baseball uniforms... we kind of miss the way you guys look in them. It's hot."

"Hey!" Jake shouts. "I still wear the uniform!"

Lucy and Amanda's heads slowly turn to him.

Micky pounces on Jake, covering his body with hers. "Back the fuck off, bitches, he's mine!"

We all burst out laughing.

When Lucy's done, she says, "You can keep him, I have a *fiancé.* And he's perfect."

I pinch my shirt, then release it. "Yup," I say, my nose in the air in true Logan cockiness. "I'm a broody, tortured artist."

That gets more laughs.

Luce pats my cheek. "Yeah you are, baby."

"What about me?" Logan asks Amanda, his eyes narrowed. He's dead serious. "Say something nice about me."

"Like what?" she giggles.

"I don't know. Like how I'm going to be a fucking doctor or some shit."

She chuckles again. "Or how about the fact that you're ridiculously hot and you have the best abs known to mankind."

"Yeah, I do!" he shouts, his head nodding slowly.

"You should take your shirt off!" Micky yells.

Jake turns to her, his full glare in place. "What the fuck, Kayla?"

She laughs harder.

"Do it!" Lucy laughs.

I cover her mouth with my hand and bring her into me. "Don't encourage that shit."

Logan makes a show of stretching his arms in the air. Then slowly, he takes off his shirt. "Yeah, baby!" Amanda shouts.

Okay, so maybe we've had more than a few beers. A lot more.

Lucy mumbles something into my hand.

"Fuck this!" Jake spits. "I'm putting on my uniform." He starts to get up but Micky pulls him back down.

Lucy's completely lost it, her body convulsing against mine while she drools on my hand.

"Fuck you both," I tell them. "I win. I'll sketch all you bitches."

Silence.

Lucy pulls my hand away and slowly turns to me, her eyes narrowed and her lips pursed.

And now I'm scared.

I swallow loudly.

"Did you just call us bitches?"

"Yeah!" Amanda adds.

"Did you?" Micky says, her arms crossed.

I look at all of them, knowing I'm two seconds away from copping an earful of crazy.

"Did you?" Lucy asks, her eyebrow quirked.

I panic.

The front door opens and Heidi walks in. "I brought bridal magazines."

If you ever want to hear four girls squeal so loud it makes your ears ring, just mention the words 'bridal magazines.'

Also, if you want to be kicked out of a room full of squealing girls and be told to do 'manly asshole shit.' do the same thing.

Jake brings out another six-pack of beer into the yard. He scratches the back of his head as he takes a seat around the fire pit Logan just started. "Why the fuck do I always get kicked out of my own house?"

Logan chuckles, then kicks my foot with his. "Two weeks and you'll be a married man."

"I know."

"Nervous?"

"Nope. Anxious, though. I just want it to be done, you know? I just want her to be my wife already."

Jake passes me an uncapped beer. "When do you move into the apartment?"

"Tomorrow."

Logan sighs loudly.

"What's with you?" I ask him.

"I'm just… I don't know. I'm all nostalgic and shit." He looks from me to Jake. "It's just strange. All the shit we've been through. Who would've thought three punks in high school would turn out to be where we are… doing what we're doing…"

I don't know that we mean to, but we all look into the house, to the girls who have changed our lives.

"I always knew Lucy was it. There was never a doubt. Not even for a second."

"Was there a moment?" Logan asks. "Like a distinct moment when you knew she was it for you."

A smile pulls on my lips. "Not really. I mean I could lie, I could tell you it was the first time we had sex, or the first time she laughed. But I don't know… maybe there wasn't a moment, or maybe it was all of them."

I see Lucy sit up straighter, her eyes wide. I lean forward, trying to get a better look. Her hand moves to cover her mouth. I start to get up so I can get to her. She says something to Amanda, and Amanda gets up and opens the glass sliding door. "Cam!" she shouts. "Lucy wants to show you something."

"Look," she says excitedly when I get into the house.

I squat down next to her. "What's up?"

She lifts the magazine to show me a picture of a dress—a wedding dress. "Look," she says again.

And it hits me—why she's showing me—and why she's so damn excited. "It looks like your mom's."

She nods frantically. "Can we go to look at it tomorrow?"

"NO!" Heidi shouts. "He can't see the dress before the wedding."

Her shoulders drop, so do the corners of her mouth. "I forgot about that."

"Babe, why would you want a dress that looks like your mom's? Why can't you just wear hers?"

And if you ever want to hear four girls gasp at the exact same time, say something like that.

✧   ✧   ✧

SINCE HEIDI MENTIONED the "no seeing dress before wedding" rule, she won't let me in on much of the wedding planning, which is fine, because I have my own planning to do.

I pull into Mark's dealership and walk into his office like I own the place. He's not there, so I pick up the phone and press the few buttons until I can hear my heavy, creeper breathing over the PA system. I start beat boxing into the phone, making sure I spit more than necessary. "Yo, Marky Mark. Please come to your office immediately, there's a funky bunch of manly stud waiting for you."

I hang up and sit in his chair. Then I kick my feet up on his desk, lean back, and link my fingers behind my head.

He shakes his head when he walks in, trying to hide his smile. He takes the seat on the other side of the desk and jerks his head at my feet. "Feet off the desk, this shit's mahogany."

I scoff, but do it anyway. Leaning forward on my elbows I tell him, "The desk is shit, I'll design you a new one."

He raises his eyebrows. "About time. You did it for your future father-in-law years ago. I've been waiting for mine."

I steeple my fingers under my chin. "All good things come to those who wait."

He chuckles. "What do you want, punk?"

I lean back and cut the cocky attitude. "So you know how I'm getting married in a week?"

"YOU ARE? When did this happen?" he jokes with feigned excitement.

I throw a pen at his head.

"Yeah, what about it?" he asks through a smile.

I laugh, a mixture of humor and nerves—because that's what I am all of a sudden—nervous.

"So I was wondering—" My chuckle cuts me off. I shake my head to clear my thoughts, and try again. "I was hoping—" I do it again.

"Are you okay?" He's no longer amused, more concerned.

"Yeah." I rub my palms down my shirt.

"You're nervous? Why are you nervous?"

"I'm not nervous," I say in defence. "Who says I'm nervous?"

"Cam, you always do that… you get sweaty palms and wipe them on your clothes when you're nervous. What's up? Did something happen? You guys need money or something because—"

"No," I cut in, shaking my head. "It's not—" I sigh, and then wipe my palms again. Then I blow out a forceful breath, mustering the courage

I need. "I came to ask if you'd be my best man."

His eyes widen, but he doesn't speak. He looks away from me, his body slumping with what looks like exhaustion. He scratches his head, while I sit here and wait for the moment of rejection. "If you don't want to—"

"No."

"Oh." My stomach drops to the floor. "Okay, I'll just ask—"

"No."

"Yeah, you said that. This is fucking embarass—"

"No."

"You can stop saying it now."

"No," he says, chuckling as he does. "I mean no, it's not that I don't want to. I'd be so—" He exhales a loud breath, and then finally looks at me. "I'd be so damn honored, Cameron. I'm just surprised is all. I didn't think that—I mean, there's absolutely nothing I'd want more in the world... but I have to be honest, I'm concerned about what your dad would say to you, I don't want him—"

"Stop," I cut in. "A, that asshole doesn't even know I'm getting married. I haven't spoken to him since he showed up at the hospital. B, even if he did know, and had something to say about it, I wouldn't care. And C..." I wait a moment for the sweaty palms to kick back in. For the nerves to start. For my heart rate to increase. But there's none of it. Just that sense of genuine calm. "C," I continue. "You *are* my dad."

Forty-Three
Lucy

"I CAN'T BELIEVE this is the last night before you're someone's wife," Micky says.

"I know. I can't believe it either."

"I can't believe you didn't want a bachelorette party," Heidi adds.

Amanda scoffs. "Have you met Cam and Lucy? They're inseparable."

I smile at her words.

"True," Heidi agrees. "Where are the boys anyway?"

Micky scoffs now. "At the cages having man time. They're probably pounding their chests and cursing profanities at people."

"Logan's probably humping the bat," Amanda laughs.

We all do.

"Why are you telling them about our bedroom antics?" Logan shouts, halfway through the front door of the cabin. He gets shoved forward by Jake, and then by Cameron as they barge through the doors.

Heidi pours seven shots of tequila. We stand around the tiny dining room table and take one each. Cam's hand goes to my waist.

Jake clears his throat. "To falling in love, even when you don't know it."

Micky leans into him. Then her eyes begin to well up. "To finding friends who become family, no questions asked," she chokes out.

Logan speaks up. "To claiming your girls, owning them and making them yours."

Cam laughs and they nod at each other. I don't know what he means, but I don't ask.

Amanda wipes her eyes. "To not dwelling on why horrible stuff happens to good people. To letting *love* win, and to moving on." Logan kisses her temple while we all take a moment to think about her words.

Heidi sniffs once, bringing our attention to her. "To finding your forever and being able to keep them." I rub a soothing hand down her back. She inhales deeply before raising the shot glass to her lips. We all follow, and cheer as we do. They all take the shot, but before I can, my eyes catch the front door opening. "Dylan," I whisper. And they silently bow their heads. "No! You guys!" I laugh, pointing to the door. "Dylan!"

Their heads whip to the door.

Dylan drops his bags. "I couldn't miss my best friend's wedding."

Cameron

I DON'T KNOW which of us get to him first, but we all end up in a pile on the floor with him at the bottom. After several jokes of *Is that a gun in your pocket or are you just happy to see me?* we finally let him go.

Turns out he's on leave for two weeks. He came back yesterday but was staying with a friend in LA. Dylan, not being that technical, or social, never had a Facebook account so he didn't really keep in touch with many people. He saw his friend logged on last night and decided to check up on all of us. When he saw that we were getting married tomorrow, he took the first flight out.

I'm not too sure what happened with him and Heidi, but she's been quiet, a little standoffish. They sit together, but they don't touch, they barely speak—not that that's strange for Dylan.

We ask him questions about being deployed, and he says he'll answer them all—after the wedding.

The girls only hang around for a little while before they head off back to the main house. They'll be staying there overnight and we'll be here.

At around midnight, I get a text from Lucy asking to meet her at the dock. I tell the guys I have to help Tom with something. I'm sure they know exactly what I'm doing, but they don't question it.

She's sitting at the end with her shoes off and her feet dipped in the water. "What are you doing, fiancée?"

She turns quickly, almost shocked by my presence. "Nothing. I just miss you," she says, looking back out at the lake.

I kick off my flip-flops and sit next to her, my arm outstretched behind her. "You all good?"

"Yeah," she lies.

And my heart begins to race. "You having cold feet or something?"

She laughs quietly. "No. Nothing like that. I'm just… I don't know. It just doesn't seem real. Tomorrow we'll be married, and I'll be your wife."

"Yeah, that's kind of what I was going for with the whole proposal thing."

She shoves my shoulder with hers. "You know what I mean."

I wrap an arm around her waist.

She sighs and leans in closer. "I don't like not being with you. Even for one night. I know we shouldn't be seeing each other, but I had to see you."

"I'm glad you did, I was going a little crazy."

She leans up and kisses me quickly. "Let's stay until the sun rises," she says. "It'll be the perfect start to our new lives."

So that's what we do.

We talk all night about anything and everything. And even though we spend every spare second together, we never run out of things to say. She cries a few times, mainly about missing her mom, and remembering everything we've been through. I sit, and I listen, and every second that passes, it's like a reminder of why it was so easy to fall for her so many years ago—why when Logan asked if there was a defining moment, I didn't have an answer. Because I think I've always loved her.

Always.

And *forever.*

✧   ✧   ✧

I TAKE ONE more look in the mirror, and chew my lip.

"You nervous?" Mark asks.

I release a breath. "Yeah. I'm kind of shitting myself, actually."

"Why? Doubts? Second thoughts?"

I shake my head. "Not for a second."

"Then what is it?"

"You know that feeling you get? That sense of calm, right before something bad happens? I feel like that. I feel calm. Almost too calm, and that's what's making me nervous."

He rubs my shoulders. "Maybe you're calm because you're just *that* sure."

"Maybe."

"Or maybe you need a shot of whiskey to get you through the calm."

✦   ✦   ✦

WE DIDN'T WANT a big wedding. Just something with our closest friends near the dock by her lake. She wanted it in the afternoon so we could say our vows and then party as the sun sets. I told her it was perfect, because it was. It was everything I didn't know I wanted.

"You're making us all look bad," I whisper loudly to Dylan as I stand at the altar that I designed and Tom built. Everyone else is wearing matching tuxedos, but Dylan's wearing his Marine dress blues. He said he didn't have much of a choice considering he had a day to prep.

"Hey, you think I can borrow it later?" Little Logan asks him. "I think the girls would love it, you know?"

Dylan ignores him.

I look down the line to where my groomsmen stand next to me. All of Lucy's brothers, Dylan, Jake, Logan, and by my side, my *dad.* "You good?" Mark asks.

I nod.

"Still calm?"

I nod again, wiping my hands down my pants.

He smiles, but stays quiet.

Turning around, I eye the bridesmaids one by one. Claudia, Micky, Amanda, and Heidi.

Amanda lets out a sob as she wipes her cheeks. The girls console her, but she tells them she's fine. She's just so happy for us.

"Keep it together, Marquez," Logan whisper yells. He shakes his head, but he's smiling. "I can't take you anywhere."

She sobs again. "Shut up, asshole. I love you."

That gets laughs, even from the pastor standing between us—the same one who helped us with our Hope.

The guests gasp and I know it means they can see Lucy.

I stand there, and I wait.

Wait for my forever.

"Breathe," Marks says. I turn to him now, my eyes stinging with tears. And there's that same feeling I had from when I was in the hospital waiting to see her. All my senses are off. As if I'm under water, unable to hear, unable to breathe. The pounding in my chest gets faster, harder.

The music starts.

Mom lets out a cry.

And then I see her.

I see everything—clearer than I've ever seen before. It's the opposite of the calm I always thought. It's the calm *after* the storm. Like after the rain suddenly stops, and the sun shines through. It's perfect.

She's perfect.

She walks toward me, her hand on the crook of her father's elbow. She smiles, and I know it's just for me.

I sniff once, pushing back the tears.

The music plays on, and it finally hits me—why Mom cried when she heard it. It's not the song we all expected. It's my mom's favorite song, the one from *Aladdin*. The one right after the boy asks the girl if she trusts him, and she says *yes*. And off they went, on an epic adventure. On a magic carpet ride, where he promises to show her the world, shining, shimmering, splendid…

✧   ✧   ✧

OUR VOWS DON'T take long. We wanted it that way. We didn't want to have to wait to become man and wife. We worked on something together, something small and personal for the pastor to read right before we say *I do*.

'There is a love so fierce it cannot be measured.
A heart so strong it will never slow.
There is a promise so sure it can never lie.
And we promise that love forever.
Forever and always.'

We write our own notes, neither reading each other's, and we release them in paper lanterns. We hold hands and watch the sun set as they rise to the sky. In those notes, we write a message for her mother, so she knows she wasn't forgotten.

I didn't say much in mine, only that I'm sad I never got to know her and that I'm thankful to her for making Lucy, the strong, witty, and beautiful girl who she is. I promise to take care of her, and to love her, through good times and bad, for richer or for poorer, in sickness and in health, until death do us part—just like her and her husband.

We cut the cake, and all sit down.

We opted for no speeches; Luce said she always thought it was strange that people talk about the love of others. She said no one could ever say anything true enough, especially when it was so personal. And the day itself—the vow of marriage—should say it all.

So when Lucas stands up on the makeshift stage and taps the mic twice to get attention, we start to worry.

"I know that the lovely couple didn't want speeches, but I have something I want to say, and I'll fight anyone who tries to stop me."

"Oh no," Lucy says, the same time I laugh.

We glance at each other quickly before turning back to him.

He continues, "A lot of you know about my mom... about her passing and leaving behind seven children. You know about the life she lived and the person she was, so I'm not going to harp on about that. The only thing I will say is that when she left, someone in my life replaced her presence. Not just my life, but my brothers, and definitely Lucy Goosey's. Now, I'm not saying that Cameron's a girl, or that he's feminine in any way, regardless of the stories you may have heard." He pauses to let the guests' laughter fill his ears. "I remember when I was twelve, before I grew into this manly, flawless body—" More laughs. "I was out in the yard, where Cameron had helped us boys make a baseball diamond... we were playing, and Lucy was out there reading, holding Lachlan in her arms... and I kept seeing him look over at her. It wasn't like he was staring or being creepy in any way; he was just watching her. Anyway, months passed and those two finally got their sh—stuff together and started dating. One day I wanted to go for a swim out on the lake, but I stopped when I saw them sitting on the dock. They were opposite each other, legs crossed, schoolbooks in front of them. And then I saw it, him—glancing up and looking at her. He didn't do it for long, maybe he thought she would catch him and think he was a creeper or something. But as soon as his head was down, I'd see her do the same thing. And I sat there watching them, for over an hour... he'd look up, watch her for a bit, then look back down at his books. Then she'd do it... then he'd do it... and I just wanted to yell at them, '*Just look at each other already!*' Months later,

I'd still see him doing it. Whenever she wasn't looking, he'd watch her. So one day, I got the balls to actually ask him why. He laughed at first and said that I wouldn't understand. Honestly, I got a little pissed, because the thing is—Cameron always treated me like a friend, like his equal. Even though I was three years younger, he never spoke down to me. He never treated me like a kid. Which in a way was odd now that I look back on it—because even though he thought of me as an equal, I kind of always thought of him as a hero." Lucy sniffs and holds my hand tighter. I clear the lump in my throat. So does Lucas. "Anyway, I asked him why he did it…"

He looks right at me and laughs once. "You said you were *reading* her. You said you liked to know what it was that made her smile, or made her laugh, or got under her skin. I asked you why you didn't just ask her—that it would be so much easier. Do you remember what you said?"

I shake my head.

"You said it wasn't the same. You said you could ask her what made her happy, and she could say books—but the answer wouldn't be enough. You told me you wanted to know what *type* of books, and you wanted to be the one to give them to her. And even then, you said, it *still* wasn't enough for you. You said you wanted to be *her reason* for loving books. You said you wanted to be her *reason* for everything."

Lucy wipes her tear-stained cheek on my arm.

Lucas clears his throat again and glances around, like he forgot he was speaking to an audience. "It took me years to work out what you meant, but I finally got it. I finally understood. Yesterday, I saw Lucy watching you when you weren't looking. Six years on and she still had that look in her eyes. The same look you've always had in yours. The kind of look that can't be described in words—only in *heart*. So, Cameron, all those years of watching her—*reading her*—it worked. You're her reason for everything."

Forty-Four
Lucy

L UCAS GETS OFF the stage, walks toward us, shakes hands with Cam, they nod at each other, and then he sits in his seat. And that's all they do.

We sit in mostly silence, my tears still flowing. Amanda sobs. Logan rolls his eyes. "Why are you crying, pretty girl?" Lachlan asks from next to her.

"Dude," Logan says, leaning forward and looking past Amanda to him. "You're *always* stealing my game."

Lachlan clicks his tongue. "Fine, you can have her." His gaze moves around the table and lands on Heather. "I'll take that one." He gets out of his seat and taps Mark's shoulder. "Move please."

Mark's eyes narrow.

Little Logan speaks up. "You can't just go from one girl to another," he drawls.

Lachlan lets out a tiny growl as a snarl pulls on his lips. Then slowly, but too fast for any of us to react—he picks up a piece of cake and throws it at him.

We watch as it flies in the air, his shout of "YOLOOOOOOOO!" filling our ears.

And then... smack.

Right on Little Logan's face.

I choke on my held in laughter.

Little Logan wipes just enough off so that his eyes aren't covered. "You little punk, you better run." He picks up his cake, gets off the chair, and starts for Lachlan. "Run, Lachlan!" Lincoln shouts.

So he does.

And so does Little Logan.

"Hey, babe," Cam says from next to me.

I turn to him, just as he smears cake all over my face.

My shoulders stiffen.

I use the napkin to wipe it off.

His lips are clamped shut, but his face is red with held in laughter. I hear Jake laugh, so I turn to him, exactly the same time Micky smashes cake on his face.

And this is how the biggest food-fight in town history starts. Even the pastor gets in on it.

✧   ✧   ✧

CAM AND I sit back down on the table after hitting the dance floor, which basically means watching Logan make an ass of himself while doing an impromptu strip tease just for Amanda. He knows he's being an idiot, but Amanda laughs with him, and if there's one thing I know about Logan— it's that he'd do pretty much anything to make her smile.

Jake and Micky watch with their arms wrapped around each other. Heidi and Dylan have been gone since Luke's speech. I'm sure we all know what they're doing.

Heather sits with us with cake in her hair, on her face, and on her chest. Mark—he's pretty much untouched. Although, he did go a little crazy with the food war. He paid my brothers to join his team. Their target: Her.

"Well, this has been an amazing wedding, kids," she says dreamily.

Mark scoffs. "You could have had one like this if you'd actually said yes any of the thirty-six times I'd asked you to marry me." He wipes a finger across her face and tastes the cake.

Her eyes search his for something. Or maybe she's just reading him, like Cameron does with me. "Ask me again," she says.

I grip Cam's hand, a squeal threatening to escape. "What the hell," Cam says, clueless to what's about to happen.

Mark's face drops and then his eyes roll. "Heather, will you marry me?" he asks, almost sounding bored.

I'm on the edge of my seat while Cam tries to pry my fingers from their death grip on his arm.

"Yes," she says, a smile forming on her lips.

I wait for Mark's reaction before revealing my own.

His eyes widen. "What did you just say?"

"Yes," she repeats.

He looks first to Cameron, and then to me, and then back to his new fiancée. He kisses her once, quickly, and then he's off.

I finally let out a squeal.

A minute later, he returns with the pastor. "Let's go," he orders Heather.

"NOW?"

He clicks his fingers at us. "Best man, maid of honor. Let's go."

"We can't do it now," Heather whines.

"I'm sorry, Heather, but I can't wait."

I laugh as Cam and I follow behind them toward the altar. "Like father like son," I muse.

They stand hand in hand, eyes locked, smiles wide, while the pastor does her second round of vows. Not everyone watches them, but I don't think it matters. Just like it doesn't matter that it's not official. They'll still need to get a license, go to the courthouse, and make it legal. The point is they did it, and they did it for themselves, and maybe a little for Cameron and me.

Cam kicks the back of Mark's knee just as he's about to say "I do." That gets a mixed reaction of laughs and gasps from the guests. Heather... she laughs. So do Cam and I.

Cameron

"IT'S BEEN SOME night," I say awkwardly as I walk up to Tom.

He turns around from his standing position at the end of the dock. He's been here a good ten minutes, alone, with his head lowered and his hands in his pockets. He hasn't spoken much throughout the night, but I've caught him watching Luce and I with an array of mixed emotions. Sometimes he smiles, but most of the time it's forced, or at least it seems that way.

"Thank you for putting it on," I continue, stopping next to him and matching his stance.

He doesn't respond right away, but I don't expect him to.

After a few silent moments, he sighs loudly. "You're welcome, son.

You don't ever have to thank me for giving my little girl what she wants."

I quickly glance back at the party, to the dance floor where Lucy looks like she's in some kind of robot dance-off with Logan. "What are you doing out here on your own, everything okay?"

His smile's tight when he nods once. His eyes wander past me, probably to Lucy. "She's been through a lot," he says. "I mean, you both have, but her especially... with her mom and everything after, and then with the pregnancy." His gaze moves back to me. "I'm proud of her, Cam. I've never been more proud of her in my life. She chose well, marrying you."

I open my mouth to speak but he does it first.

"I don't think it was ever really a choice, though. I think in your case, fate had a big hand. It's the same with Kathy and I. At least that's what she used to say. *Fate, it's all about fate, Tommy.*" His brows bunch before he looks away, his gaze now focused on the water. "Do you believe in fate, Cameron?"

I think long and hard about his question before finally answering, "I try to, sir, but sometimes it's hard. It's hard to understand the reason why certain things happen, especially to those who least deserve it."

"Are you talking about having children?"

"Yes, sir."

"Yeah," he sighs. "That's a tough one. I could sneeze in Kathy's direction and she'd be knocked up the next day. It doesn't seem to make much sense. But I believe there's a reason for everything—even when it's not clear to us." He clears his throat before adding, "Like when she passed away... you saw what I became. You were there at my lowest point, and I think that maybe you were supposed to be. Maybe that's what Kathy meant about *fate.* Maybe she was taken so that you would enter our lives. So that Lucy..." He stops and blows out a heavy breath, the struggle in his speech more than apparent. "Maybe it happened so that Lucy could find her *strength.* Her *reason.* And so my boys could find their *hero.*"

I use the back of my hand to wipe my tears.

"Not a day goes by that I don't thank her for bringing you to us, Cameron."

"I didn't do anything, sir. All I did was fall in love with your daughter."

"That's the thing. You didn't even know what you were doing for *us* while you were falling for *her.* She wouldn't be the same person if it weren't for you. You changed her life, Cam. And *fate*—it changed all of us."

✧   ✧   ✧

AMANDA CATCHES THE bouquet, but she tries to hand it off to someone else. Jake keeps telling Micky to take it, but her face goes red with embarrassment and she shakes her head. "Nope," she keeps saying. She tries to hide behind him, and I swear it—I see him mouth, "You're next."

We get in the stretch Hummer which Tom rented, along with our friends. When we know we're far enough that the guests can't hear us, we scream, and cheer, and cry.

We ask the driver to park on the side of the road and wait. Ten minutes later, Lucas pulls up behind us. "I told Dad I was going to visit Jason for a few days."

Logan hands him the fake I.D. he organized for him.

"I can't believe I'm allowing this," Lucy says.

His smile widens. "It's fine, Goosey. What happens in Vegas…"

Forty-Five
Lucy

B ECAUSE OUR WEDDING was so small and we didn't want to go on a "real" honeymoon, Dad went all out on a four-day trip to Vegas. Not just for us, but for our friends too.

"Holy shit," Lucas says when we open the door to the suite. Dad wanted it to be a surprise, so we had no idea he was renting out the Kingpin Suite at the Palms. "I'm gonna get married ten times over if this is what Dad provides," he jokes.

Cam grabs my bag out of my hands and links our fingers. "See you guys in two days," he rushes, and then he drags me away.

I WATCH AS he drops our bags just inside the master suite and takes a seat on the edge of the bed. "Hello, wife."

I try to suppress my grin as I walk over to him. His hands on my waist are soft when he pulls me between his legs.

"Say it again," I ask him, settling my arms on his shoulders.

"What?"

"Call me your wife."

His smile matches mine. "You looked beautiful today, wife."

I take a seat on his lap with my legs wrapped around him.

"Did you have a good day?" he asks, his mouth on my shoulder.

"It was everything I dreamed it would be and more. It was perfect, babe."

He raises his head, his eyes searching mine. "You deserve it."

"What about you? Was it your dream wedding?"

He nods slowly. "You were my bride, so yeah. It went exactly the way I've always imagined. But... I miss you. I had to share you with everyone today and you know I don't like sharing."

I chuckle against his neck as his arms grip me tighter. "I'm going to shower and wash the crap out of my hair, and then we can lie in bed and you can have me all to yourself."

Cameron

I UNPACK OUR bags while she's in the shower. There's a box in hers, still wrapped, and a card from Micky and Amanda telling her to open it when we get to our room. I have no idea what it is, but I'm too scared to attempt to find out. I love Lucy, don't get me wrong, but when those three get together, shit happens. I don't want to be the cause of shit on our honeymoon.

At the bottom of her bag is an envelope. This time, I don't think twice about snooping, because it's addressed to *Our Future Hope, from Mom and Dad.*

I sit on the edge of the bed and flip it over in my hands. The first page is a copy of my sketch; the one I made of her future room in our future house—the first one... with the huge armchair and all the little ones around it. There are stained splotches marring the otherwise perfect scene, most likely her blood from when the frame shattered.

I swallow the lump in my throat and take a deep breath, preparing myself for what's to come.

Dear Mom,

I know it's been a while since I've written to you. Six years and one month, almost to the day. The thing is, I haven't found a need to write because I found someone else to share my secrets with.

Remember when I wrote last? About a boy I'd fallen in love with—and he had no idea I noticed him? Well... tomorrow, I'll stand before him, in front of all our loved ones, and we'll become husband and wife.

Did you know?

When you passed away, did you know he would be there? I think you did, Mom. I think you put two people in front of each other and you let fate play it's magic.

I hope one day, I can do that for my daughters. I hope I can keep them safe, protect them from all the bad, and help them see all the right in the world.

I hope one day they'll find someone just like Cameron. Someone to be their strength, their calm, their HOPE.

I love you,
Lucy Gordon.

Lucy

"YOU JUST WANNA lie in bed for the rest of the night?"

We're in bed, lying on our sides, our faces almost touching. He nods once before kissing my chin. "Yup. I just want to hold you and love you."

"Good," I tell him, my fingers twisting his hair. "This is my favorite thing in the entire world."

"Me too," he mumbles. "And blow jobs."

My head throws back in laughter.

"And your laugh," he says, his eyes on mine. He pushes my shoulder until I'm on my back. Leaning on his elbow and resting his head in his hand, he adds, "Your laugh makes my world stop, Luce. I remember the first time I heard it, when you were at school, and you were reading. It was two days after our first kiss. I remember thinking I'd give up all other senses if it meant I could hear you laugh again."

I raise my hand to move his hair away from his eyes.

"It was like a reward for me," he continues. "Like all those physically exhausting days of being with you and the boys and trying to be your calm, it was all worth it. Just for that one sound. That one emotion *I* pulled out of you. And all of it lead to this—to you being my wife."

I can't help the smile that forms. I love hearing it—the way he calls me his wife. "Say it again."

"Wife." He shifts so he's sitting on my waist and our hands are linked. "You know what that means, babe?" he says with a slight grimace. "It means you're going to have to learn to cook, maybe even clean."

I scrunch my nose and shake my head. "Nope."

"Yeah," he jokes, nodding as he does. "I'm sorry, it kind of comes with the title."

"Nooooo," I whisper yell. "But all that stuff takes away from valuable reading time!"

"Fine!" He rolls his eyes. "I'll learn how to do it. But you have to promise to read at least two smutty books a week."

"Deal."

"Deal," he responds, a smirk forming. "Shall we blow job on it?"

✧   ✧   ✧

WE DON'T BLOW job on it, in fact, we don't even have sex. We do what we wanted, we hold each other, and we talk, and we fall even more in love.

Forty-Six
Lucy

"**H**EIDI LEFT," DYLAN deadpans from his seat next to me at the dining table.

"What?" I load up Cameron's plate with the room service breakfast we all ordered and look at Dylan. "What do you mean she left?"

He shrugs. "Ask her about it," is all he says, but his tone says what his words don't.

I pick up my phone and check for any messages or missed calls. There are none. "When did she leave?"

"Last night," Lucas answers.

My eyebrows bunch as I watch Dylan. The muscles in his jaw work back and forth while he pretends to read the paper. I look to everyone else, but they're not paying attention. "I'm glad you're here, Dylan," I tell him. "There's no way it would have been the same without you. I missed you a lot while you were gone."

He looks up, his features relaxing as he does. "You guys are my best friends, I should have kept in contact. I'm sorry I missed out on so much of it, Luce." He holds my hand resting on the table. "I should've been a better friend to you while you were going through so much."

I can't help but laugh. "Dylan, you were fighting a war."

He shrugs and looks away, releasing my hand. "I think maybe we all were."

And that's the cue that he's done talking.

"LUCY," Micky shouts. "DID YOU OPEN YOUR PRESENT?"

"Babe," Jake says. "You're shouting again."

"Oh." She looks down at the table.

Jake adds, "Kayla thought it'd be good times to jump in the pool last night, both her ears are water-logged and she can't fix it."

"OH MY GOD!" she shouts again. "I LOVE THAT BOOK!"

"What!" Cam matches her volume. "What the hell did you just hear?"

Her brows bunch and she looks to Jake and then down to her plate. "IT'S JUST BACON AND PANCAKES, CAM."

That gets a round of laughs.

"Seriously, Luce," Amanda pipes up. "Have you opened it?"

"Not yet, I didn't know if I should open it in front of Cameron or not."

"Oh." Her eyes go huge. "It's for both of you," she laughs. "Actually, it's more for Cam."

Then Micky shouts, "CAM, I AM. I DO NOT LIKE GREEN EGGS AND HAM!"

✧ ✧ ✧

"WHAT IS IT?" Cam asks, bouncing on his feet.

I slowly rip open the wrapping paper from Micky and Amanda's present. And then my eyes bug out of my head. "Wait here," I tell him, holding it behind my back.

"What is it?"

"Wait here!" I repeat. "I'm going to shower, and then I'll show you." I start to go to the bathroom but then spin on my heels to face him. "Tell the guys we'll see them tonight and lock the door."

His grin is instant. "YO! Nobody bother us for the next two days!"

Everyone laughs, everyone but Lucas and Micky.

"That's my sister," Lucas shouts.

"THERE'S NO SUCH THING AS GREEN EGGS!" Micky yells.

✧ ✧ ✧

CAM OPENS HIS mouth. Closes it. Opens it again. Nothing.

"What are you thinking, husband?"

I twirl the white fluffy handcuffs with my finger. It matches the lingerie set Micky and Amanda gave me. And the whip which came with it.

He chews his lip, his eyes scanning me from head to toe. "What are they—do—where..." He shakes his head to clear his thoughts. "Huh." He stands up and takes the steps to get to me, his hard-on already tenting his pants. "What did you have in mind?" he asks, his mouth on my neck and his hand in my panties.

"Whatever you want."

✧   ✧   ✧

I'M BLINDFOLDED, HANDCUFFED to the bedpost while his mouth works down my chest and his fingers work inside me.

"Anything?" he asks, causing a vibration against my stiff nipple.

"Anything," I breathe.

Body: I want him to eat her pussy.

Brain: You have a filthy mouth.

Body: You made me that way.

He kisses, licks, sucks, past my breasts, onto my stomach, paying special attention to *our* scar.

Brain: I love it when he does this.

Body: I'd rather he do it to her pussy.

Brain: If she weren't blindfolded, she'd be rolling her eyes at you.

He moves lower, past the scar and between my legs. The warmth of his breath heats my already moist center.

Body: Moist? Really?

Brain: Shit word. I agree.

My hips jerk up when I feel his silky tongue slide between the petals of my inner folds.

Body: She reads too much.

Brain: Yeah, she does!

"Baby…"

Body: Whoa, where is his finger right now?

Brain: Not in her whispering eye! Why did she tell him he could do anything?

"Babe?"

"You said anything," he responds.

Body: Oh no. I don't know that I like this.

Brain: WHY DID SHE SAY ANYTHING?

Body: WHY IS HIS FINGER THERE?

"Cam?"

"If you don't like it, tell me to stop."

Brain: Maybe she should just try it. She's read about it. It turns her on.

Body: I know it turns her on. I'M the one getting turned on.

His finger penetrates deeper. The handcuffs dig into my wrists when I begin to squirm. I don't know if I want him to stop or if I want more. His tongue slides up, his mouth circling my hooded nub.

Brain: Hooded nub? Really?

Body: Fuck this feels good.

"Fuck, baby, that feels so good."

I start to move, my mind picturing him naked, his veiny, throbbing member in his hand, watching me touch my silky folds.

Body: What the hell did she just say?

Brain: It's from those books...

Body: I can't focus on the pleasure if she keeps thinking like that. You control her, make it stop.

Brain: Thinking like what?

"Fuck baby, please don't stop." I feel it building, the dull ache at the pit of my stomach. His finger starts moving slowly, the muscles of my rear clenching around it. My pink walls lather in my juices as I begin to tighten. The image of his silky, pulsating rod bringing me closer to the edge.

Body: THAT! Thinking like that! Pink walls? Pulsating rod? I'm surprised I can even...

"Oh my God, Cam!"

Brain: You have no problem getting off, shut your whore mouth.

Body: Did you just call my mouth a whore?

Brain: Look at you, you're writhing under his touch. You love it. Let Lucy think whatever—

Body: You try not getting turned on when Cam does this shit. Get it, girl. Get that *O*.

Brain: At least we agree on that! Get that O, girl. Pleasure that clitorusaurus-rex.

"Stop it!" I laugh aloud.

"What?" Cam says, pulling away.

"Not you!" I lift my hips so he can keep going. I *need* him to keep going.

"But you just said—"

"Shut up!"

Brain: You're mean.

Body: Shut up, Brain. He loves it. I love it. Look at him go.
"Ahhh!"
Body: Oh shit, she's so close.
Brain: Leave her alone now, let her have it.
"Ahhh!"
Body: Fuck. Oh my God. This is—there are no words.
I thrust my hips, my fiery furnace now fucking his face.
Body: Stop with that shit.
"Fuck, Cam! I'm gonna…"
Body: GO! GO! GO!
"I'm gonna…"
Body: FUCK YEAH!
"I'm gonna…"
Body: Holy shit. I've never felt like this… this could be… is it?
"HOLY SHIT. I'm gonna come so hard all over you face."
Body: Shit. This is the biggest orgasm she's ever had.
"I'm gonna…"
Brain: Come. She's gonna come!
"COOOOME!"
My body vibrates while he holds me in place, his mouth never leaving, his finger never stopping, not until the last wave hits and I flop on the bed.

"Fuck me…" I moan in pleasure.

"I plan to," he murmurs.

I smile, even though I can't see him. "You, Cameron Aladdin Gordon, are a goddamn stud."

Epilogue
One Year Later
Cameron

I T WAS HARD, but I did it. I graduated.

Luce got her degree in journalism and joked that she'd probably never use it. It was funny until we had moved back home into the cabin for a few weeks and she realized just how limited journalism jobs were, especially close to home.

I applied at about ten architecture firms, all of which contacted me for an interview. I even got offered a few of them, but it meant moving, or travelling, and none of them offered enough money to do either.

I helped Tom out with a few of his projects for the first couple months. He paid me more than he should, which meant that it was more than enough to float Lucy and I, especially considering we were living rent free.

After weeks of staying home, Lucy started to lose her mind. And then she found a project. The only bookstore in town—the one her and her mom used to spend hours at on the first Sunday of every month—was sinking. It wasn't making enough money to survive and it was going to close down. Lucy, being Lucy, got emotional and used those emotions to fight for it. She spent every day there helping when she could to keep it open. When nothing worked, she started a campaign. She organized an event where some of her favorite authors showed up, signed their books, and spoke to the attendees. She even convinced them to donate their books so that all the money went back into the store. The owner, a tiny old lady who only went by Ma'am, and was way beyond her retirement years was so thankful for Luce's efforts. But it still wasn't enough. She cried when she found out. "It's not about the store," she said that night. I held her to my chest while she sobbed silent tears. "It's about the memories, Cameron."

The next day I worked on site with Tom and told him about the store closing and how upset Lucy was about it. I told him she spent most of the night telling me stories about her and her mom going there, and how she remembers her mom buying her her own copy of *Little Women*. She said it was one of the greatest days of her life.

A week later, Tom asked us to meet him there. We had no clue what it was about. So when we walked in after hours and saw him sitting next to Ma'am at the tiny reading corner she had set up, we were confused to say the least.

We sat down opposite them and waited.

Ma'am had tears in her eyes, but Tom didn't speak. He just pushed a bunch of papers our direction.

They were ownership papers to the business and the building with our names already printed on them. "All you have to do is sign," Tom said.

Lucy cried.

I had no idea what was happening.

"You bought me a book store?" she wept.

My eyes narrowed before realization set in.

"No," Tom answered. "I *invested* in a book store." He leaned back in his chair and eyed us both for a moment, gathering his next words. "Actually, I have my own reasons for doing this, but yes, the bookstore is yours, Lucy."

She cried as she signed the papers. I don't even remember signing my name, but I'm sure I did.

After Ma'am said her thanks, she asked me to walk her to her car. "She doesn't know does she?" she asked while I held her door open.

"Know what?"

"That her mom named her after me. My name's Lucille, but no one has called me that since her mother passed."

"No, Ma'am," I replied. "She has no idea."

"Good." She smiled. "You can be the one to tell her."

When I went back into the store, Lucy was on her feet. She was still crying, but it was the good kind. "We can do so much with this space," she announced excitedly. She went behind the counter, found a pencil and notepad and handed them to me. Then she proceeded to walk us through her ideas. Tom and I followed, our smiles almost identical.

"Please draw my vision," she asked me, and so I did.

For two hours we walked around the space while she went through, in detail, what she wanted. I sketched what she described while she looked over my shoulder, telling me what to change and what was perfect. Not much needed changing—seems our visions were similar. Tom walked around with a measuring tape and his own notepad, writing down things that needed to be fixed or built. She wanted to include a little café, one where shoppers could sit down and read for hours and hours. She walked around animated, so lost in her excitement and ideas that I found myself right there with her... just as excited as she was. "I want a reading corner, baby," she whispered when her dad was out of earshot. "One where I can do story time for the kids. I want a huge armchair and they can all sit in front of me while I read to them. Can you design me a sign for above the chair, one that says 'Kathy's Corner?'"

I smiled down at her, watching her eyes fill with tears again. "That sounds like an amazing idea, babe."

WHEN SHE WAS done, she stood in the middle of the store and turned a full circle. "I can't believe it," she said. "This is all mine."

Tom rubbed his hand across his beard. "Well, not all of it," he mumbled. "Follow me."

Luce held my hand as we followed him up the creaky stairs in the back office of the store. It led to an empty, open room. In the middle were a table, three chairs, and a lamp.

"Are we being interrogated?" she joked. I'm glad she found it funny, because even though I've known Tom seven years, he still scares the shit out of me.

"What do you think?" he asked, ignoring her question.

"Think of what?" she said.

He nodded his head at the two chairs opposite where he was now seated. "I figure this can be the new office space for Preston and Sons."

"So you'll be working here, too?" she asked.

I pulled out her chair before sitting down next to her.

Tom smiled and waited until I was seated. "I tried to think of some names," he started, ignoring her again. "Preston and Sons and Gordon, or

Preston, Gordon and Sons, but that seemed—"

"What?" I finally managed to ask. "Gordon? Me?"

"Us!" Lucy snapped. "I'm a Gordon too!"

"I know, babe." I cleared my thoughts and looked back at Tom. "I don't understand."

He didn't reply. He just pushed over more papers until they were under my nose. It was a partnership agreement to his business. "What?"

"If you want to change the name we can speak—"

I shook my head. "The name's fine, I guess, I'm just confused."

"I'd like to make you partner," he deadpanned. "You take the design part, I'll take the construction. We can work together. Though, this will be your office space, I'll be on site most of the time. Plus, I love you like a son, don't get me wrong, but you and my daughter can't keep your hands off each other; I don't want to be surrounded by that all day."

Lucy laughed.

I couldn't find it in me to do anything but stare at him.

"So?" he asked, waiting for my response.

"No."

"What?" Lucy whined.

I turned to her. "I haven't earned it, Luce."

She scoffed and rolled her eyes.

Tom chuckled. "I'll give you a minute."

Lucy watched him walk down the stairs and when we were alone, she turned to me. "Cameron…" she started. Her shoulders dropped with her sigh. "I hate bringing this up, but this attitude of yours, this pride thing you have going, it almost ruined us once. I know that you feel like you haven't earned it, but you have, and my dad wouldn't be doing this if he didn't trust you. If he didn't believe in you like he has from day one. And this way… it means we get to be together every day, we'll never have to be apart. Isn't that what we've always wanted?"

Tom and I shook hands when I handed him back the signed papers.

The next day, we got to work.

That was a few months ago.

Yesterday, we finally completed it exactly the way she wanted.

✧   ✧   ✧

"YOUR GIRLFRIEND'S HERE," I tell Logan, who's sitting next to me in the dugout.

He nudges me with his elbow. "Your wife's here."

We watch as they both get out of Lucy's car and sit on the hood, watching our baseball game.

"We suck," I say, picking up my gear bag and walking out. Someone shouts at us about the game not being over, but we don't care.

"We can't all be Jake Andrews," he muses.

"That punk deleted me on Facebook."

"That punk deleted his *entire* Facebook. He's too famous now. He was getting all these random requests and posts on his wall. Amanda said that Micky made him delete it after the fifth nude selfie he got."

I laugh. "Poor bastard."

Lucy's squeal gets my attention, and then I watch as her head throws back, her laughter loud and carefree. Amanda snorts next to her, making Lucy laugh even harder.

"What the hell are you two up to?" Logan says as we stop in front of them.

I wait until Lucy settles before pulling on her legs so I'm standing between them.

Amanda shoves my shoulder. "Waddup, Deskfucker?"

Lucy

CAMERON STOPS IN his tracks, shirtless, with the towel half lifted to his hair. He drops his hands and eyes me curiously. "You're cooking?"

I nod, trying to hide my smile. "How was your shower, husband?"

He ignores my question and stands next to me, sniffing the bowl of salad I just made. "Are you okay?"

"Yup! I made a pasta bake. It's all I can really do for now, but I'm learning."

He opens the oven and sniffs again. "I don't expect you to cook, babe."

"I know." I shrug. "But I wanted to."

"Huh." He stands on the opposite side of the counter and leans on his elbows. "Did you cheat on me?"

"WHAT!"

He doesn't flinch. "I don't know, Luce. It just seems weird. You're cooking, and the bathroom's all clean, and you've packed away the pile of books at the foot of the bed. I figure you've done something wrong and you think cleaning and cooking might make it easier for me to forgive you. That, or your e-reader's broken. You want me to go out and buy you a new one?"

I scoff. "I sell e-readers at my store, and no I didn't cheat, or do anything wrong." I shrug. "I just wanted to be wifey today."

He laughs. "You were wifey enough last night when you let me blow—"

"CAM!"

"Seriously, Luce, what's going on?"

I pull out plates from the cupboard and start loading on the salad. "Put a shirt on, let's eat out on the dock."

✧　✧　✧

"IS IT NICE?" I ask, trying to suppress my laugh.

He finishes chewing, eyeing me sideways the way he has been since he got out of the shower. He nods slowly, and then sniffs his plate.

"I'm not trying to poison you!" I chuckle.

"You're confusing me, Luce! I don't know what's happening."

I don't respond.

"And you're being evasive!"

"The sun's about to set."

He grunts in frustration, but doesn't respond. I pull out a beer from the cooler and hand it to him.

He throws it in the lake.

I laugh.

"Who is he?" he asks.

"Who's who?"

"This guy you're cheating with?"

I laugh so hard my sides hurt. He starts to stand but I pull on his arm to sit him back down. "You're being an idiot."

He crosses his arms and looks away. "I don't care."

"Babe," I get on my hands and knees and kiss him softly. After a minute, he begins to relax. "I heard from the doctor today," I say against his lips.

He pulls back, the color of his normally dark eyes matching the orange of the sunset. "And?"

"And they said we could start the IVF treatment as soon as possible. They want us to come in on Monday, so they can go through the steps with us."

He looks away and blows out a shaky breath.

"Cam?"

He sniffs once, his eyes glazed when they focus back on me. "So we're really going to do it? Are you sure, Luce, because I don't want you to do this for me. I want to make sure you want it, too."

"Of course I want it." My words are strained but I continue, "I could live a thousand years with just you and me, and it wouldn't be enough. But what we have, the love we share, it's more than enough to go around. If IVF doesn't work, we can adopt, we have options." I sit across his lap and look out to the lake.

He leans his head on my shoulder.

My fingers reach up and twist his hair.

"Are you sure?" he whispers.

"It's not fair to the world to limit your love to me alone. Your heart's too big, Cameron."

He looks past me, and to the sun, now half hidden by the water.

"I love you, Luce," he whispers. And it doesn't matter how many times he says it, the words have never lost their meaning. And they never will. Because it's more than just words spoken, it's his arms around me when I feel like I'm falling. It's his lips on mine, kissing away the pain. It's our hands holding as he leads me into the water to let me break. It's us—chest to chest—helping each other heal. It's us—giving each other *Hope*.

I turn to him now, letting the sun set behind me. "Forever, Cameron. I love you, forever."

Coming Mid 2015
MORE *than* ENOUGH

If I told you to jump, would you ask how high? Or would you just jump? If there were no reason behind it, would you still take the leap? What if I told you that at the end, there would be nothing? What if you made a splash on the world and lived in an eternal state of floating? Would you make waves? What if you couldn't float? What if air lost the battle, and you lost the war? Would you want to know what was on the other side? Would you care? Or would you just jump... because I was the one who asked you?

Coming January 2015
Where the Road Takes Me

You know how sometimes you can tell that something is about to happen, even though there are no physical signs? Like when the hair on the back of your neck stands up, or your palms begin to sweat, or butterflies form in your stomach? Like the beating of your heart thumps faster, harder—and even though you're looking down at the floor of the familiar hallways of high school—you know that when you lift your gaze, something's going to *change*. And then you look up—and the beating of your heart stops for a split second. The boy with the messy dark hair and the piercing blue eyes is watching you—a hint of a smile on his beautiful face that's enough to kick your heart back into gear. But then he turns around and walks away—not for him—but for you. Because he knows that is what you want, and you know that he only wants you to be happy.

Blake Hunter—he was my *change*.

Coming Soon
Combative

I flex my fingers, watching the dried blood shift around my knuckles. Right now, I should be at home icing the shit out of them. But I'm not. Instead, I'm in a tiny room with nothing but a table and two chairs. I don't know how the fuck I got into this mess. Actually, I do, but the asshole was talking shit and I had no choice.

That's a lie.

There was a choice.

I made mine, and I ended up here.

I should have destroyed him.

The door swings open and a suit walks in. His back is turned, talking heatedly with someone on the other side of the door. "I'll handle it," he says, before shutting the door and then... nothing. He just stands there staring at the closed door. His shoulders heave once, his head moving from side to side. And then slowly, he turns.

The corner of my lips lift, but they drop when I see him jerk his head. The action's so slight that if I weren't focused on him, I would've missed it. His gaze shifts to the security camera in the corner of the room. It's a split second movement, but one I understand. He rolls up the sleeves on his crisp, white shirt and takes the only seat available on the opposite side of the table. Resting on his forearms, he leans forward. "Parker."

I smirk. "Detective."

His features falter for a moment, but only a moment before his mask is back in place. He looks down at the open folder in front of him, his eyes scanning the page from side to side, then he lifts his gaze. "Ky Parker?" It comes out a question, but he already knows who I am.

About the Author

Jay McLean is the author of the More Series, including *More Than This, More Than Her, More Than Him* and soon to be released, *More Than Forever.* She also has two standalones coming soon titled *The Road,* and *Combative.*

Jay is an avid reader, writer, and most of all, procrastinator. When she's not doing any of those things, she can be found running after her two little boys, or devouring some tacky reality TV show.

She writes what she loves to read, which are books that can make her laugh, make her smile, make her hurt, and make her feel.

You can follow Jay on **Instagram** and **twitter** @jaymcleanauthor. You can also find her on her **blog** at www.jaymcleanauthor.com where you can subscribe to her **newsletter** and get teasers and updates first hand, her **Facebook** page at facebook.com/jaymcleanauthor or her **fan group on Facebook** at facebook.com/groups/moserieslovers, or you can **contact Jay directly** at jay@jaymcleanauthor.com

All her other social media links can be found below.
Pinterest: www.pinterest.com/jaymcleanauthor
Google Plus: http://bit.ly/1uY8DJY
Google Plus Jaybirds group: http://bit.ly/1n66EhR
Goodreads: goodreads.com/author/show/4724550.Jay_McLean

✧   ✧   ✧

For publishing rights (Foreign & Domestic) Film, or television, please contact her agent, Erica Spellman-Silverman, at Trident Media Group.

Made in the USA
Coppell, TX
23 April 2020